To Jon —
You're gonna get this one!

AN UNREMEMBERED GRAVE

ABIGAIL PADGETT

Abigail Padgett

An Unremembered Grave is a work of fiction. People, events and situations within the work are entirely products of the author's imagination. Any resemblance to actual persons, living or dead, is purely coincidental.

In Memory:

Douglas "Swede" Dennis
Writer, *The Angolite*
1935-2009

PROLOGUE

Angola Plantation, West Feliciana Parish, Louisiana, 1863

The old man stood motionless, a shadow among shadows in the steamy darkness at the edge of the cane field. With each breath he whispered his real name. The name his mother had given him. Adjoa. Even Neecie, his wife, didn't know that name. It was his strength, his secret song. He sang it and waited to kill a thing already dead for centuries.

At his bare feet a cat moved like grey silk in the hazy moonlight. Then it stopped to regard the old man with glowing yellow eyes. The cat had come to witness the killing.

From the ground Adjoa felt approaching footsteps. As a child he learned to call the monster "loogaroo," but now he understood that it wore many names. The bloodsucker was called *loup-garou* by the French slavers who took his mother from African Dahomey with Adjoa in her belly. The same beast was dismissed as primitive nonsense by the American slavers who later took Adjoa from Martinique in the West Indies to the steaming hell of Louisiana and a plantation called Angola. The slavers laughed and drank rum and never saw the telltale marks on dark bodies already pocked by a thousand scars.

Adjoa had planted and cut sugar cane for forty years under the lash. He was old now, and his body was broken with an illness called "the shaking palsy." It made his hands quiver uselessly at times, made him lose his balance and fall. The disease had been with him for a long time, and now he felt the nearness of death. His wife Neecie tried to scare death away with candles and turtle-shell rattles she'd shake in the night, chanting a sound like wind in a cave. He never told her that death was already inside him, held back only a time by her care. And he never told her what he'd decided to do.

Soon death would take him, as it takes everything. But with the last of his strength he would kill a thing more awful than death. It would be his final deed as a living man. In his belt was the sharpened stake, in his right hand a mallet. And slung across his back was the machete, sharpened for hours against a stone. When the loogaroo was pinned by the stake, Adjoa would cut off its head and burn it. One stroke of the long blade would be enough. The footsteps grew closer.

And then it was there, the creature called Grimaud. Adjoa had learned three languages in his life, the second of them French. He could pronounce the monster's name, Stéphane Grimaud, flawlessly. But the name was only a sound left over from a time when the thing had been a man. It was no longer a man, but a monstrosity.

"Grimaud!" he roared as he uncoiled from shadows and wrapped the beast in muscle made iron by a lifetime of labor. The thing was sluggish from feeding, its teeth seamed wine-dark with clotting blood. The blood of Africa. Stéphane Grimaud came only to the slave quarters at night, an orb of blue light slipping through cracks in the doors, the walls. He didn't feed on the white prisoners leased to the plantation owner. Everyone knew the South would win the war, and there would never be a shortage of dark skin to puncture, dark blood to drain. The monster had found an endless feast. Until now.

The task was surprisingly easy, like wrestling a bag of wet moss. The creature fell under Adjoa's weight near the shallow hole he'd dug days earlier and covered with branches. The stake went in like a tooth in boiled meat, only the crack of the breastbone beneath a blue silk waistcoat registering resistance as the thing watched, a peculiar sadness swimming in its eyes.

But the weakness was on the old man now, the shaking sickness moving in his fingers like leaves before a storm. Adjoa's hands fluttered and could not grip the machete. Frantically he kicked the branches aside, kicked the monster with a stake in its heart into the hole, kicked and kicked dirt over it. Now his hands were like fireflies, and a luminous fluttering traveled up his arms and slowed his heart as he staggered away. He hadn't cut off the monster's head, hadn't burned it. The thing wouldn't move as long as the stake pierced its heart. It couldn't. But it wasn't vanquished.

"Tomorrow," Adjoa said aloud. Tomorrow he would return, after the spell of sickness had passed. He would come back and slice off the head. One stroke of his machete…

But the cool fire racing through his body didn't slow, and he fell, and the flickering chill in his bones was like the old songs Neecie sang to frighten death. But death was not frightened, and it calmed the beating of his heart to stillness. The grey cat leaped onto Adjoa's fallen body, hissing and clawing at the rats who soon crept close to gnaw at the old man's eyes, his face, his motionless fingers. The grey cat kept guard all night, only vanishing into dew-laden grass when the dawn brought voices.

Louisiana State Penitentiary, Angola,
West Feliciana Parish, the Present

There was a sound like the roaring of a metal animal, and Stéphane Grimaud felt an acid wash of faint light. The light was diffuse, filtered by wet clay soil and the thick leaves of trees, but its discomfort was familiar. The light woke him from a long sleep in which at first he remembered nothing. But the light was only a mist, a vague annoyance. What he felt like a volcano spewing fire in his bones was hunger. A hunger so desperate it shrieked through him, obscuring the words of the men above.

"Three-thirty, wrap it up, the van here," a deep voice shouted. "Tarp the backhoe and we gone. Fuckin' rain again tonight. Be a mercy if it rain all day tomorrow, too. Warden won't get his golf course built this century, it keep rainin'!"

There was laughter, the sound of men moving away. Humming metal, and then silence. Grimaud fought the shriek of hunger as history swirled and fell into place inside him. A rotting stake protruded from his collapsed chest, and he pulled it loose with the yellowed bones of one hand. He could smell himself now, a faint stench of decay filling his throat. How long had he slept in the hot, wet soil? He didn't know. He only remembered a slave called Old Joe, pounding the stake. The crack of breastbone as the sharpened point drove in, puncturing a heart born under the rule of Charlemagne. And he remembered a cat, watching.

Grimaud felt the remaining shreds of his face stretch in a smile. Old Joe was a good man, full of courage but like most mortals, locked in ignorance. They all were, with their stakes and crosses. As if their pitiful little remedies could kill a race of creatures as old as time.

The thought was lost in another aching wave of hunger. He had never experienced hunger so agonizing that it occupied his every sense like an invading horde. He would have chewed open his own arteries to feed on himself if his blood had not long ago turned to moldy black dust.

There was movement above. The men had dug away all the soil covering the grave of Stéphane Grimaud but a slick, paper-thin layer, and he could feel the movement. Something narrow and sinuous, moving tentatively. Grimaud forced the bones of his left hand through the muddy film, followed by his head and shoulders. He grabbed at the sinuous movement, his carpal bones sinking into cool flesh as his hunger roared and he brought the thing toward his teeth.

It was a snake, a cottonmouth water moccasin, and Grimaud saw the yawning white mouth with fangs so like his own as the creature struck and struck again. Its venom, dripping straw-colored on bone and wasted flesh, smelled vaguely fishy as Grimaud bit through brown scales and found the three-chambered heart.

The blood was sickening, primitive and devoid of stories, and he fought the urge to vomit as he drained the last ounce and cast the empty, reptilian tube aside. Already the remaining shreds of his skin were turning pink, inching over bone, but the shriek of hunger had not diminished. He stood in his grave and shook dirt and pale, writhing worms from his hair.

Nearby was a yellow metal machine with "Caterpillar" written on it, partially covered by a shiny blanket. He could see that the machine was used for digging. It had uncovered his grave. But he'd never seen such a machine, and only then wondered how long his sleep had been. And to what world he had wakened.

CHAPTER ONE

The flight from Charlotte to Baton Rouge was turbulent, and a particularly drastic bump woke Danni Telfer from an exhausted half-sleep in which she saw the church again. The church where twenty-four years ago she'd awakened alone. She'd never been in a church and didn't know what it was when a man came in and turned on the lights. She was on a hard bench and her arm felt funny from sleeping on it, she had to pee and the bandage on her shoulder hurt. The man was putting a white tablecloth over a big stone box up some steps at the front of the room. He was whistling.

"Where's the bathroom?" Danni asked, sleepily standing and hugging her purple Fluppy Dog.

The man looked scared. "Dear God, where did *you* come from?" he said. But then he changed and said, "Gosh, I'm sorry, you just surprised me. Come on and I'll show you where the ladies room is, okay? After that, how about you tell me your name. And your dog's too, of course!"

"Danni," she told him, following him and holding the stuffed dog above her head so it could see everything in the strange room. "And Telfer."

"Teffer's a great name for a purple dog," the man said, opening a bathroom door that was down some stairs. He turned on the light and said he'd wait for her outside. She didn't know why the man said her name wrong and thought it was a dog's name, but she was glad to use the bathroom even though she couldn't reach to wash her hands.

Only when she came out of the silent little bathroom did she realize that something was terribly wrong, her heart suddenly beating so hard it made her cry. "Where's the lady that drived the car? Where did she go? Where am I?" she asked, her fists knotted in her Fluppy's yarn mane.

"Well, this is St. Mark's in Malone, New York," he said, but she didn't know what those words meant and buried her face in the toy dog, sobbing. A lady had taken her on a trip that took a long time; she remembered that. When it got dark she fell asleep to the sounds of the car. But she wasn't in a car any more and felt like she was falling and falling and couldn't stop.

Danni flexed her feet under the seat in front and stared out the plane window where water trembled in horizontal sheets. Stress always took her back to that church and the worst moment of her life, when she thought she'd dropped through a hole and there was no one to catch her. She was pretty sure nothing could ever be that bad again, certainly not the professional scrape from which she was fleeing.

The whole thing had been a B movie plot with the requisite dashing seducer and innocent ingénue. Except she had been neither innocent nor, at twenty-seven, even close to ingénue. It was an academic affair so ordinary that its lack of originality embarrassed her. He was her department chair, she fresh from defending her dissertation at Boston University and happy to have landed a tenure-track position at one of the State University of New York's campuses. And as usual, she'd thought he needed rescuing.

When his wife, from whom he said a long-awaited divorce lacked only the final signatures, flew in from California with two children he'd failed to mention at all, Danni was taken to lunch by the dean. A research grant taking her away for a semester would be approved, the dean said. And of course glowing recommendations for her first year's work would be forthcoming should she seek a position at another university. All Danni had to do was find this unexpected grant, get out of town and sidestep a minor scandal that could "negatively impact your professional future."

Her first reaction was to dig in and fight to keep her position, but secretly she welcomed the opportunity to escape. She'd done everything possible to interest students in the "Introduction to European History" and "Political and Social Origins of Western Culture" classes she taught to amphitheaters of freshmen, but in truth she was as bored as they were. She'd eventually be allowed to teach the more interesting upper-division classes, but the testing and grading, the endless faculty meetings, senates and conferences loomed before her like a road to nowhere. Her passion was research, finding lost bits of history and fitting them together like pieces of a puzzle. But years would go by before she'd have time for research. And now a silly affair had kicked open a door and shown her a way out.

"Of course this would be a paid leave of absence," she said and then watched as the dean scowled into the gleaming maple surface of his desk.

"I think we can offer a stipend equivalent to ten per cent of your salary," he said.

"Thirty per cent will barely cover travel and living expenses," she countered.

"Agreed," the dean said. "A generous stipend will enable you to apply for more modest grants. Surely you'll be able to find one."

She'd barely been able to control the exuberant grin that erupted the second she exited his office.

Scrambling through reams of material, she'd found a peculiar little grant from the estate of a long-dead Louisiana cotton baron. "…to fund academic research into the multifarious uses of cotton thread and fabric in the great state of Louisiana…" the grant description said. Why not? She'd had a thing about fabric since a childhood in which her adopted mother made quilts, all the way to a doctoral dissertation on medieval tapestries. It wasn't hard to patch together an academic-sounding proposal about research into the history, text and subtext of cotton needlework and quilting in Louisiana's river towns prior to the Civil War. Something about influences of contact with riverboats on local quilting and embroidery patterns.

Her Ph.D. dissertation on the fifteenth century Unicorn tapestries housed at the Cloisters in New York City was arguably about fabric, wasn't it? Her research included brief discussion of medieval thread-making and weaving technique, but not a word about cotton since it wasn't known in Europe until the seventeenth century. Amazingly, she got the grant anyway.

The check came in the middle of August and within a week she was given a fall-semester research leave. Now she was flying into a place she'd never been, and despite her heady sense of freedom it was feeling a lot like that Sunday morning in Malone, New York, when she'd awakened on a church pew with nothing to hold onto but a floppy stuffed dog covered in snarled purple yarn. The toy had eventually fallen apart, but she hadn't. She'd been lucky.

Assuming the child had been left by someone local, members of the little church decided to care for her until the return of a distraught mother. A couple who had a farm took her home with their three children, and members of St. Mark's distributed fliers across Malone, four adjacent communities and across the border into Canada.

Danni still had one of those fliers with a photo of her toddler self in a green Teenage Mutant Ninja Turtles sweatshirt that was way too big, holding the Fluppy, her big eyes blank with fear. The text said, "Lost Little Girl named Danni, says she's three years old, has small, fresh tattoo of a rose on her left shoulder. Anyone with knowledge of Danni please contact St. Mark's Episcopal Church, Malone."

The tattoo had hurt and she didn't know why a man she didn't know held her, screaming, while another man with a ring in his nose stuck her shoulder with needles. And then they gave her to the lady who drove a long way and left her in a church. There had been another man and a lady and a house where she lived with them, but they weren't there for

the needles or the long car trip. Had they been her
parents? She didn't know.

There was really nothing left of her past but the tattoo.
It stretched as she grew but was still no bigger than a
quarter, faded now, its edges blurring. Just the outline of a
rose in black ink. She'd studied it in a mirror with a
magnifying glass as a child, searching for a message
hidden in the black leaves or the thorned black stem. She'd
looked for letters, initials, a name, but they weren't there.
Only a rose, white against inked edges. She still had no
idea what it meant, who had left a permanent,
indecipherable message on her body, or why. Quite
possibly it meant nothing at all.

When two weeks after she was found in the church no
one claimed her, the priest at St. Mark's phoned the
diocesan offices in Albany for advice. They couldn't just
keep the child; there were laws. But neither were the
church members willing to turn her over to the regional
social services agency. Everyone had heard stories about
children lost in the overworked rural system, assigned to
careless foster parents who only wanted the money for
drugs or to understaffed group homes that were worse than
prisons. The congregation of St. Mark's would only release
the toddler mysteriously left in their care to the Episcopal
Diocese of New York, and so it was done.

The bishop's secretary drove three and a half hours to
Malone, gathered the child and drove back to Albany under
cloudy autumn skies. Danni never forgot her first sight of
the yellow colonial with black shutters and a wonderful red
door, the house that would shelter her for twenty years. And
the people who would help a strange and troubled child
survive. Ron and Wendy Bradtke, already grandparents,
opened their red door that evening to a child they thought
would stay for weeks. Twenty years later Danni would close
that door, hand the keys to a realtor and walk away, alone.

Of course the diocesan office contacted New York Family and Children's Services, but in keeping with the wishes of the little upstate congregation, the diocese retained legal care and custody of the child. Family and Children's Services would perform the necessary diligent search for relatives and then file the requisite legal forms that would free Danni for adoption. The process was streamlined; no one expected it to take long. In the meantime the Bradtkes, long members of the Cathedral of All Saints and friends of the bishop, agreed to shelter the foundling until adoptive parents could be found.

The little girl was healthy, showed no signs of abuse and tested surprisingly high on the Wechsler Intelligence Scale for Children administered by a psychologist. But there was something odd about the child that unnerved prospective parents. A peculiar stare in which she seemed fascinated by events no one else could see. A lack of interest in normal childhood activities with the exception of fairy tales and puzzles, which she would fit together over and over again until she was exhausted. One set of prospective parents reported that during a visit to their home Danni refused to speak at all, seemingly mesmerized by the pattern in their reproduction William Morris wallpaper.

Two years went by and no one wanted Danni. Except Wendy and Ron Bradtke, who were not entirely unaware that Danni was deftly sabotaging every effort to settle her in an adoptive home. Wendy was fifty-one and Ron fifty-five on that evening when the little girl in a baggy Ninja Turtles sweatshirt stumbled through their red door. They were too old; Family and Children's Services could not permit them to adopt the child. But Ron, a civil engineer who designed highways, helped Danni draw a map of the house on that first night. And Wendy, a tour guide at the New York State Museum, showed her a picture book about animals that once lived right there, maybe right in the yard outside! Danni remembered falling asleep cuddled close to Wendy on a couch, admiring a picture of a wooly mammoth. And she remembered a bone-deep understanding that the yellow house was supposed to be her home now. Nothing hiding in its walls waited to frighten her. The yellow house was safe. Wendy and Ron Bradtke, their two sons already grown and gone, had simply fallen in love with the foundling at their door.

She was five when Family and Children's Services finally gave up on finding appropriately-aged adoptive parents, and the Bradtkes went to court to secure the legal birth certificate saying Danni was theirs. They picked the night she arrived as her birthday – September 29.

Danni frowned at a cloud beyond the plane's window that looked vaguely like a front-loading washer, and wondered for the thousandth time when her birthday really was. And *who* she really was. The name on her birth certificate said, "Danielle Telfer Bradtke," and at eighteen she'd legally changed it to "Danielle Bradtke Telfer," choosing the surname she'd known at three. But lacking a story to go with it, the name meant nothing.

Well, she'd meant to *make* it mean something. Dr. Danielle Telfer had intended to become a serious historical scholar, a professor on track to tenure and a lifetime of academic achievement. The banging of the prop jet as it descended through a low-lying rainstorm forced her head to nod as if she were agreeing with this view of herself even though the image had already died. She still wanted to immerse herself in history, she just didn't want to teach it.

"Somethin' strange goin' on," muttered the man in the aisle seat beside her, a thin, elderly African American in a brown gabardine suit and a yellow shirt printed all over in tiny palm trees. It was the first time he'd spoken.

"We'll be under the clouds soon," Danni said. "And I'm sure the pilots are used to this."

"Wasn't talkin' about the weather or the pilots," the man said, his eyes searching the air under a thoughtful scowl. "You visiting in Baton Rouge?"

"No, I'm here to do some research in St. Francisville," Danni answered. "History.

The man smiled, revealing dentures and a faint concern in his dark eyes. "Best be careful, then," he said as the plane broke through the clouds and fell toward lush trees, then the runway dark and shiny with rain.

"Careful with history?" Danni asked, more of herself than of her seatmate as the wheels hit tarmac. The only history she needed to be careful of was her own.

"History in a way," the man said, now looking pointedly out the window as if searching for something in the distance. "History a big problem sometime, when it don't stay buried, 'specially where you goin'."

Danni couldn't think of a response. Her entire career involved the digging up of buried things. "Well, I'll be careful," she told the man, who turned to study her closely.

"Somethin' strange out there," he said again. "And I think you walkin' right into it."

Danni laughed. "It can't be any worse than what I'm walking away from," she told him. "But I'll keep my eyes open."

"Won't help much if you don' know what you seein'," he said as he stood to pull his bag from the overhead. "Be best if you jus' turn and go on back home."

"Not an option," Danni said brightly, hoping for a courteous end to this odd conversation. "I've enjoyed talking with you." The remark brought a shrug of brown gabardine shoulders, and then he was lost in the line of passengers exiting the little plane.

The Baton Rouge airport consisted of one terminal that emptied quickly as the passengers from her flight dispersed to waiting cars outside. In the ladies room she freshened her lipstick and raked cropped, curly auburn hair away from the back of her neck. Humidity wafting from the airport's exterior doors was already making her hair curl despite the terminal's air conditioning. Once outside, she was going to look like Ronald McDonald. Not that it mattered. There was no one to notice.

At the rental car desk a young woman wearing an immense cubic zirconium on the ring finger of her left hand smiled and handed Danni a key and a folder containing a map of Baton Rouge and a selection of discount flyers for local attractions. "You here for the rodeo?" she asked.

"Um, no, I'll be doing some research in St. Francisville," she answered. "Quilts, needlework, that sort of thing."

"Oh, but you hafta see the rodeo since you'll be right there!" The girl fanned both hands atop the desk, glancing at the stone sparkling on her ring finger. "My fiancé and me, we're going," she said, nodding with domestic content. "I've never been, but he goes every year. He says the prisoners put on a terrific show, and you can buy things they make."

Danni was only half listening, but responded to be polite. "Prisoners?"

"Yeah, at Angola. You know. The big state prison out there past St. Francisville? It's maximum security!"

"Prison?" Danni heard herself mouthing variants of the same word and wished she'd just said, "Yes, the rodeo." That way maybe she'd be in the car by now, driving away from this surfeit of information in which she had absolutely no interest.

The girl smiled. "Of course you aren't from here," she acknowledged. "There's a flyer there in your packet about the rodeo. It's famous all over! Take a look, okay?"

"Yes, thank you," Danni said, forcing herself to smile all the way to the baggage carousel where her wheeled duffle circled alone. The few airport staff standing around all smiled back. Everyone smiled and watched her progress with a sort of warm detachment that was pleasant, she thought. Nice but not intrusive. She'd be able to move comfortably among these courteous Southerners, do her research and write the article that might help pave her way to a job.

Just outside the terminal doors she rethought her original assumption of "comfort." The air was so humid she found herself gasping as a hot, wet breeze rippled an illuminated American flag over the parking lot. A clock above the terminal door showed eight-twenty p.m. Beside it a temperature gauge read ninety-two degrees. Danni wondered if a perfectly healthy woman could have a heart attack at twenty-eight, then dived into the rental car and turned up the air conditioning. Her plans were to stay for two months, through October, and then to hole up with a college friend in Binghamton while she wrote her article and decided what to do next. There were no other options. She'd just have to get used to the heat.

Determined, she launched the car through patchy fog across steaming pavement, following signs that said "Natchez" until navigating a turn onto Hwy 61. She passed a smelly refinery and then drove out into country that looked a little like country in New York, only different. More roadkill and a lot of honky-tonk bars, pickup trucks with gun racks and Confederate flag stickers. Colorful.

On a long stretch of empty road she turned on the radio. Good thing she liked Country and Western! Maybe there'd be dance classes somewhere. Maybe she'd learn to two-step. Little thrills of confidence made her sit up straight. This was going to work out. And then a sort of gospel show came on the radio, a sonorous male voice warning listeners to "walk in the light, for there ain't no map in the shadows," a statement Danni found oddly resonant. Her whole life could be described as a walk in shadows, couldn't it? The man then cut to a song called "Wayfaring Stranger" that made her grip the wheel to keep from running off the road.

It was just an old folk song by a small group, maybe two women and two men accompanied by violin and dulcimer, but every note seemed to peel away the layers Danni had spent decades building. Beneath the layers was a little girl in a baggy sweatshirt who saw scary things and had no idea who she was.

"I'm only goin' over Jordan," the voices sang in wistful harmony, "I'm only goin' over home," as Danni pulled off the road onto the puddle-strewn gravel of an abandoned gas station. The song was killing her, but she wouldn't turn off the radio. The song felt like a message, except this place couldn't be any kind of "home," could it?

When the last line faded she stilled the radio and stepped out in the wet dark. Beer cans and shotgun shells lay half buried in the mud. Nudging a shell with her toe, she picked it up and held it to a half moon barely visible behind moving clouds. The plastic cylinder was flattened and full of grit but the brass was still shiny. She dropped it, mud and all, into her jacket pocket so she'd remember the moment. She was different from other people in some way she'd never understood. She'd always been alone, really, despite Ron and Wendy and her own heroic efforts to fit in. It was time to get used to it.

Fifteen minutes later she coasted through the little town of St. Francisville and thought she could smell the Mississippi River nearby. The river whose history she would study in stitches and fabric left on its shores. It was going to be fun.

The old plantation B&B where she'd arranged to stay rented a number of charming cottages to guests, and she found a key and a note in an envelope on the porch of the main house. "Dr. Danielle Telfer, extended stay, The Old Kitchen. Welcome." A map of the grounds indicated that "The Old Kitchen" was a brick cottage close behind the main house, and Danni dragged her duffle toward it, happy to have arrived, to be somewhere.

A few of the other cottages were just dark shadows at the edge of a wide duck pond, but two in the distance shed soft yellow light on gravel paths and the thick, leaflike grass that seemed to grow everywhere. Thick, leaflike grass that appeared to be moving. It *was* moving, Danni observed, right in front of her cottage. And it was making a scratching sound, like rats in the walls of an old house. From the movement of the grass, it was one damn big rat!

"I'm really tired," she yelled over the pounding of her heart. "Basically I was never what you'd call a rat person to begin with. So will you leave or do I have to spend the night in my car? Because really, I'm not up for this."

The thing was shuffling around beneath the thick-leaved grass, moving toward the parking area where Danni stood. Maybe it wasn't a rat but a snake. Did snakes make scratching noises? The grass continued to move. Grabbing the shotgun shell from her pocket, Danni threw it at the swaying green shadows and then yelped when something that looked like a small gray pig in medieval jousting armor leaped two feet straight up, then fell back. The swaying leaves marked the creature's rapid retreat.

"Armadillo," Danni pronounced aloud. The word hung in the steamy air, its meaning obscure as the name of a distant star. The thing was sort of cute with its big eyes and perky ears, but its unfamiliarity was disorienting. It occurred to Danni that the world she'd just entered might be stranger than she'd anticipated.

"I'll keep my eyes open," she said to the image of the old guy on the plane.

"Won't help much if you don' know what you seein'," echoed his reply.

CHAPTER TWO

On an iron cot in the prison infirmary, Eugene LeBlanc struggled to lift himself on his elbows. His blue eyes, suddenly as fierce and clear as they'd been forty years earlier when he waited in the stifling woods of Bayou Nezpique to kill the man who raped his daughter, scanned the room. "Get Monk," he rasped. Need to see Monk right away."

The effort had been great, and he fell back amid the rough sheets with a groan. In the two years Eugene LeBlanc had lived in the infirmary, it was the first time he'd asked anybody for anything. He was one of the vanishing old-time convicts, men who scrupulously obeyed a code of honor more typical of ancient Sparta than the 21st century. Watchful and courteous, the old cons rarely spoke with prison employees and for that reason were often mistakenly perceived as shy. But when necessary, any one of them would calmly kill or die before breaking his word or betraying a friend.

The nurse who came to his bedside knew nothing of this. What she noticed was the fire in his sunken eyes. It happened, she knew from long experience, sometimes shortly before death, that sudden burst of clarity, or of need.

"Eugene, what is it?" she asked while feeling the rapid, thready pulse beneath one flaking ear. "Do you want the chaplain?"

"No, ma'am," he said, wrapping bony lavender fingers around her wrist with a strength that surprised her. "Have to tell Monk something. Need you to get 'im."

"Do you mean right now?" At fifty-four, she'd worked at the prison for two years. The daily drive out from Baton Rouge was a hassle, but the money was good and she'd been glad to find work. The prisoners, for the most part, were surprisingly cooperative patients.

"Have to tell Monk about Jacques," the old man whispered, then suddenly stared across the room as if something interesting were happening there.

The nurse followed his gaze and saw nothing but a long wall broken by three doors – the isolation rooms used for highly contagious or dangerous patients. All were empty, the wire-webbed windows dark. Eugene LeBlanc was observing something she couldn't see. In the last days and hours before death, the dying often appeared to be watching activities invisible to everyone else. Sometimes they smiled or called out, but mostly they watched intently, as if they were being given instructions.

"Jacques, have to tell Monk," he said again before closing his eyes.

Whatever he meant, this was a deathbed request. Born and raised among Cajuns, the nurse knew such a request could not be denied.

"Okay, Eugene, you just rest," she said. "I'll go get Monk."

The Walk, an elevated cyclone-fenced concrete sidewalk that connected all parts of the main prison, was crowded. Prisoners in jeans and plain white or gray t-shirts were going to various classes in the education building, self-help meetings in the visiting room, religious services in one of many chapels scattered across the prison grounds, or any of numerous activities from band practice to toy making that kept the prison's six thousand inmates occupied in the evenings. Most were strangers to the free woman now pushing her way through the crowd. Of Angola's large population she rarely had contact with any but those who worked in the infirmary or came there for treatment. Among those, one was dying and had asked a favor. That request was a command.

It was a hot but breezy September evening, stitched with the spicy scent of carnations, alyssum and snapdragons that bordered all the buildings. That and a damp, rich, river smell rolling off the Mississippi. Neither trees nor bushes, which could afford cover to an escaping inmate, grew near the living and working quarters on the vast plantation prison, but the odor of green things was a permanent presence. On this night the green air seemed to whisper a disturbing story, something nearby but hidden, something watching. The nurse shrugged off the feeling and hurried toward the law library, where she knew Antoine Dupre would be, having worked through the dinner hour as was his custom.

Antoine didn't remember how he'd been given the nickname "Monk," but then he didn't remember much of anything from those first two years in prison when he'd been a dead man. Then Annabeth came and told him it was stupid and a waste of time, acting dead when you weren't, an issue on which she as an actual dead person claimed expertise. He knew it had to be a dream because he knew his wife, his beloved Annabeth, was dead, and at the same time he knew perfectly well it wasn't a dream. Somehow Annabeth had crossed enormous distances to push him back among the living, and he woke to a world in which men named "Moose" and "Drano" called him "Monk." He never questioned her presence but accepted it as a last gift of her love. And after a while the name seemed to fit.

Now, eight years later, Antoine was the Inmate Counsel of choice among prisoners charged with rule infractions who needed representation before the Disciplinary Board, or men hoping for help in putting together a *habeas corpus* petition to plead with the court for a new trial. He headed the law library under the supervision of the Director of Legal Programs, and personally took only those cases that had been screened and deemed viable by the library's staff of eighteen trained jailhouse lawyers. Too many men needed help. He wouldn't waste time on nonsense.

He looked up when a free woman he recognized as a nurse from the infirmary barreled through the door to the law library. It was a large cinderblock room with a dozen wooden conference tables fabricated in the prison carpentry shop, arranged in rows as workspace for inmates who wanted to research law that might apply to their cases in the books that lined one of the walls. Carrels along two other walls served as open offices for the prisoner inmate counsels who staffed the library. The fourth wall had a bank of casement windows that could be opened to let in fresh air in mild weather and were open now. Several inmates turned to look as the nurse whisked past them through the library to the storeroom that Antoine had converted to a private office.

He smiled slowly and broadly when he saw her. It was a practiced, neutral smile that had taken him a long way in the ten years he'd spent behind bars and razor wire. The smile, however, was no more for the woman at his door than it would have been for a guard, another prisoner, or thin air. Antoine Dupre kept himself apart from the invariably disastrous love affairs into which both male and female staff were sometimes drawn with their lonely, caged charges.

He sat in the castoff tan Naugahyde chair with a loose arm that he'd fished from the trash. One of his long legs was extended and the other crossed at the knee, but he quickly unfolded himself to stand politely. His hand rested on a sitting cat, carved of cypress, that adorned his desk.

"May I help you?" he asked, his gray eyes fixed on a point just behind her forehead.

She nodded. "Monk, Eugene LeBlanc is asking for you. He says he needs to see you immediately."

"All right," he agreed, then thought it best to say something, to define his relationship with the man. "I know Eugene's been failing. He must want me to finish the article I was reading to him last night, though I don't know why this is so urgent. It's a *National Geographic* article about fishing for White Marlin in Venezuela. I'll have to go to my dorm to get it."

The nurse glanced at her watch. "This isn't about fishing. I'm not sure what he wants, but you need to come with me to the infirmary now. I'm afraid there may not be much time."

"I don't really know Eugene, just read to him on nights when I volunteer at the infirmary. What can he want with me?"

Antoine knew Eugene LeBlanc might be dying. It was necessary to establish distance from the old man and any possibility of confidences that even now might be of interest to police or other prisoners.

"I don't know, but we shouldn't linger," the nurse said, hurrying him across the polished gray cement floor of the library, past the Control Center, and down the Walk. At the infirmary Antoine was searched, or "shook down" in prison parlance, by the guard at the door, then took a seat beside Eugene LeBlanc's bed.

He touched the old man's hand, trying to wake him. The big hand was cold. Too cold. Antoine felt beneath the covers, the flat of his hand pressed to the man's chest. There was no heartbeat.

He looked at the nurse. "I think you'd better come, ma'am."

Retreating to a position against the wall beside the nurse's station, he watched as several of the staff inspected the form on the bed, nodding somberly but performing no actions that might revive the still body. There was no crash cart in the infirmary; no extraordinary measures would be taken. When death claimed a prisoner at Angola, the claim was not contested. Most believed it to be a final, longed-for freedom.

Antoine remained motionless, leaning against the wall and watching. Calls were placed to the doctor, who maintained a house on the prison's 18,000 acres, and within minutes he arrived. A man of fifty, he'd once quarterbacked for LSU and later had run a successful practice in Baton Rouge. But a desire to prosper by too freely writing prescriptions for Oxycodone and Vicodin drove him from the ranks of respectable society and into this hidden gulag.

Prison had been good to him. He earned a handsome living with the full benefits of a ranking government employee and wrote a popular book about what criminals were "really like," based on his years of treating them. The book led to invitations to speak at clubs and gatherings all over the state, if not to attend high society affairs, and he was content.

Antoine watched as the doctor stripped the blankets and hospital gown from LeBlanc's chest, pressed a stethoscope to arteries and shined a penlight into one and then the other lifeless periwinkle blue eye. When he gently pulled the sheet to cover the man's face, the nurse handed him a clipboard.

"Time of death?" the doctor asked.

"Say eight-thirty," she said. "I checked him around eight-ten and he asked to see Monk Dupre. He died while I was gone to get Monk. He was dead when I returned."

The doctor signed the death certificate and laid the clipboard on the nurse's station counter. "Any family?"

"I don't think so, at least nobody's been to see him since he's been in the infirmary, and that's two years, but there may be names in his file," she answered. "Monk, did he say anything to you about family when you talked to him?"

"No," Antoine said. "He mostly talked about fishing, if he talked at all. I read fishing articles to him. He didn't say much."

An inmate orderly named Perry Bordelon had been trying to catch Antoine's attention, and now went to stand beside him, causing an inadvertent shift in Antoine's shoulders. He didn't like Bordelon, whose bunk was on the less desirable end of their shared trusty dormitory, away from the fan that stirred the fetid air in summer and gave off enough noise year round to muffle the sounds of sixty men trying to sleep. Bordelon, a short, muscular man whose mottled complexion and bad teeth marked years of drug abuse, had few friends in the dorm and didn't socialize much in the various club activities that made doing time bearable. He had other interests of which everybody was aware. There are no secrets in prison. Bordelon was one of prison underworld ringleader Hoyt Planchard's cadre of misfits. He was trouble.

"Gene talked some before you got here," he whispered. "Kept calling for you, man. Said he had to tell you something about 'Jacques.' You know what he was talking about?"

"No," Antoine answered. "I have no idea."

"I snuck a look at his chart when the nurse went to get you," Bordelon went on. "Only thing I saw is orders from way back sayin' he's not supposed to be housed with anybody from St. Landry Parish. That's where his crime went down, y'know? He killed some dude over near Opelousas. Maybe this Jacques is Gene's brother or somethin'. Maybe Gene wanted a message sent."

Antoine nodded as the nursing supervisor asked him to help the orderly move Eugene's body off the ward and into a refrigerated container maintained in the infirmary for that purpose. The dead were stored there until families could claim the bodies, or they could be buried in the prison graveyard. Most of the elderly dead, long forgotten by the outside world, would be buried on prison grounds in carefully marked graves no one would ever visit. Antoine crossed Eugene's cooling arms across his chest and hoped Perry Bordelon hadn't observed his reaction to the information Bordelon had culled from Eugene LeBlanc's medical chart.

LeBlanc was from Opelousas. And it was in Opelousas that Antoine Dupre had been found guilty of a murder he did not commit. The dead man was an old con, one of the few who still lived and died by a code that would demand, at the hour of death, any long-hidden revelation that might help another convict. Antoine pushed Perry Bordelon aside and bathed LeBlanc's body alone. Then he carefully wrapped the body in clean sheets, lifted it in his arms and carried it to the refrigerator.

The other prisoners in the infirmary had turned off the television and the room was respectfully quiet. Some crossed themselves; one of the Cajuns called, "Adieu, Eugene," as Antoine gently closed the top of the refrigerator and headed back to the law library.

On the Walk he breathed deeply, trying to relax a throat tight with unaccustomed emotion. Eugene LeBlanc had in his last moments bestowed a great honor.   The dying man had tried to observe a custom reserved only for his kind – convicts. Not "prisoners," not "inmates," but convicts. A bygone identity, nearly forgotten by the current crop of self-absorbed murderers, child molesters and rapists who wouldn't have survived long in the old days.

Eugene LeBlanc had regarded Antoine as an equal, a knight in service to a creed unknown except in the dark history of all prisons. Antoine felt the honor like a glowing cloak as he walked beneath moonlit razor wire and shadowy guard towers. He had committed no crime, but amid criminals Eugene LeBlanc had named him a convict. Now all he had to do was figure out whatever in hell the old con had been trying to tell him.

CHAPTER THREE

Stéphane Grimaud knew where he was – the plantation called Angola – but it wasn't the same. Unfamiliar scents moved in the air and far above he saw metallic birds with tiny wings that didn't move. They were machines, he realized. Flying machines. Such things had been dreamt of for ages as men envied the flight of birds, but when had the dream become real? He had no idea how long he'd slept and experienced a rush of fear.

The men who'd uncovered him spoke to each other in English, so that hadn't changed. He'd be able to communicate with mortals, but without help he'd be defenseless, at the mercy of predators he wouldn't recognize. In whatever age this was, there would be those who hated, hunted and tried to destroy everything inconsistent with their view of reality. He was such a thing.

The stake Old Joe had hammered through his sternum was nothing but wet wooden shreds, and the little flesh that clung to his yellowed bones was like rotting parchment. It fell in clumps from the faint pink edges of new arteries, muscle, sinew and skin trying to blossom in patches he could feel both in and outside his body. His heart quivered and jerked with every beat, a dry, ruined thing too weak to support him for long. His heart must be fed, and soon.

Over Grimaud's grave a cherrybark oak stood as tall as the mainmast of a sailing ship, squirrels skittering on its branches. One stopped to watch with rodent eyes as a blue light spun up through the leaves. The light became a hand of bones. A skeleton stood in the tree and pulled the squirrel to its teeth, then another and another. When seven furred, empty bodies lay on the ground, Grimaud whispered a spell learned when he died in an ancient brothel and became a thing that can never die. Only rodent eyes saw the clumsy, tattered bones of a man become spinning blue light and fall lightly to earth.

He was still ravenous, but watched a moment as translucent pink skin crawled fitfully over his ribs and the twin bones of his lower arms. The new skin was like gossamer, insubstantial and transitory. It wouldn't last. He needed real food. He needed human blood. And he could smell it, not far away.

Marshalling a discipline learned over centuries, he dragged himself beneath the yellow machine called "Caterpillar" and waited until the sky turned from coral to violet, then black. In darkness he stood and heard the pitiful rasp of naked bones as he staggered toward the scent. Within his ruined body a thousand budding systems demanded nourishment. The blood of reptiles and rodents could sustain a vampire briefly, but could not resurrect a vampire from the ruin of long sleep. He had to feed properly soon or become the nightmare of his kind – paralyzed and dead, but not asleep. A mind imprisoned forever in nothingness.

His tarsal bones made a clacking sound on a hard surface suddenly beneath him. It was black and smelled of coal. Shiny metallic huts on soft black wheels sat in rows, each with benches inside, like coaches. They *were* coaches, he realized. And with the realization came another wave of disorientation. He was in a future unimagined when the old slave tried but failed to destroy him.

Staggering toward a rectangular, one-story building, he drew air through the fissure that had once been his nose, and sensed the presence of many men inside. His papery heart fluttered like a bird in his chest as he made himself a ball of blue light and slipped through the crack between a door and its frame.

A man in a dark blue uniform sat at a desk watching figures move inside a small box. Beyond the man was a doorway covered in bars. Grimaud smelled rivers of blood waiting beyond the bars. But the man in the blue suit, whom he assumed to be a Union soldier, was large and healthy. The soldier dressed in blue must mean that the North had won the war, and long ago. Grimaud found that such things made no difference whatever. There were always wars. He materialized in the glaring light that smelled like lightning, and sank his teeth into the man's neck.

The blood was ambrosia, a silken river of warm images in his throat. The man was white, his blood laced with the taste of Gaulish words and Druid fires, salt-water journeys and beautiful, knotted drawings. For a fragile second Grimaud thought he smelled milk and felt the softness of his mother's skin, but the vision vanished in the coppery rush of blood through his teeth. His mother had been dead for centuries, but her son Stéphane still held the stories of time.

The man was massive, and Grimaud could hear the heart still beating faintly when he pulled away, sated. He hadn't fed for so long that he felt like a pig's bladder stretched with wine. He would have to rest now, hide himself in the dark where he could watch the new flesh creep over his bones like a pink tide. One more feed and by the next nightfall, he would be whole.

Argi, argi, he whispered in the Basque tongue of the woman who'd taught him to make love as a man rather than an animal, taught him to eat from a plate, and then made him a vampire. "Light, light." The Basques worshipped light, and that dark soul taught Grimaud how, for a moment, to become it. Blue light, always blue, the color that cannot, like the vampire, exist in nature unless tempered by red. *Urdin*, he said. "Blue." As he became a disc of dim azure at a crack in the door, he sensed eyes watching from beyond the bars. Two eyes, wide with terror. And a voice. "Jesus fucking Christ!" it said, and then Grimaud was gone.

He knew where to go; he'd lived in this place beneath which ancient channels of the Mississippi River lay dry and empty until filled at flood time. Only when the river flooded could they be mapped by eruptions of "sand boils" through weak points at the surface. The channels were everywhere, stretching like fingers beneath the ground. He could rest in one of these, reinforced with oak beams and then abandoned by the Tunica Indians long before Grimaud crawled from the Mississippi River.

Stumbling into the dense undergrowth of the Tunica Hills, he spent hours searching, but at last he located the entrance to a tunnel in a paw paw thicket. The smell of rotting fruit was everywhere; the ground littered with blackened paw paws considered a delicacy by the slaves.

As Grimaud crept into a musty, earthen cave beneath a wilderness untouched since he'd last seen it, he wondered what happened to the slaves. And how he would make his way in a future about which he knew nothing.

CHAPTER FOUR

Danni woke groggily at 2:00 a.m. and pulled a pillow close to her chest. As a child she'd slept with a beloved Jack Russell terrier named Daisy. Warm beneath the covers, the terrier would wake and growl at a little girl's frightening dreams, scaring them away. Now Danni slept banked in pillows and invariably reached for that old security when awakened in the dark. And was invariably saddened. There was no Daisy. The guardian of her childhood had died when Danni was twelve, leaving her to confront her dreams alone.

Often they weren't really dreams but curious paintings or movies, burdened with feelings that made no sense. At a diner a man in suspenders eating mashed potatoes was really an ogre, secretive and menacing. An ordinary tree in a city park sheltered sparkly things that giggled amid its leaves. It was as if the images were trying to communicate in a language she'd never heard.

She'd been a strange child more interested in fairy tales than Sesame Street, and the things she saw when nobody else did sometimes frightened her. But her mom Wendy always said you got to choose what you paid attention to, and taught her how to ignore the scary things. It had been years since she'd thought of those terrors, but her isolation in a steamy, unfamiliar dark brought them back.

There was a fabric store in Schenectady where Wendy liked to shop, that felt so airless and suffocating inside that it made five-year-old Danni cry. She couldn't *breathe* inside the store! Wendy eventually bought a little folding beach chair so Danni could sit on the sidewalk outside the shop while her mom selected fabric for the quilts she was always making. A nice cat lived in the store and would come outside to be petted while Danni waited.

She remembered the place when years later it burned to the ground, exposing the skeleton of a young woman inside a wall. Authorities determined that the woman had still been alive at the time she was bricked into the wall when the building was constructed in 1908. She could not be identified, but Danni knew how it felt to gasp for the last molecule of oxygen inside a crushing dark. As a small child, she had felt it.

And then there was the time when she went with Wendy and Ron to a big Ford dealer to buy a new car. At six, Danni had frozen at the edge of the parking lot, terrified of a seething anger she felt careening across the pavement and bouncing off the gleaming cars like an invisible pinball. Wendy took her to an ice cream shop across the street and sang "You Are the Wind Beneath My Wings" while Ron picked out a silver car Wendy always said should have been metallic blue. In high school Danni learned that the Ford dealership had been built over the site of an ancient Mohican village, and for a while she made up stories for her friends about Indian ghosts haunting Fords and causing wrecks on winter roads. The Ford stories were a way of explaining things that scared her, things nobody else seemed to experience.

As a teenager she read books about dreams and even waded through Jung's *Man and His Symbols*, but quickly realized that the images flashing through her mind fit no classic model. Long before that she'd learned never to talk about them.

When she was in first grade the other kids told stories about scary crazy people and pointed in fear at a disheveled man who sometimes rummaged through the school trash cans after lunch. The man talked and laughed even though there was nobody there, and the janitor always made him go away. Danni sensed that he might be telling about stories no one else could see, and that frightened her. Because she sometimes saw pieces of stories, too. She didn't want the janitor to make her go away, so she never talked about her dreams and after a long time they didn't happen much any more.

But it was no surprise that a dream had disturbed her now. After all, she was stressed and disoriented in a strange place. Still, this dream was strange – a man made of bones leaning against a tangle of tree roots in an earthen tunnel. When he held a skeletal hand barely covered in translucent, infant skin before his eyes as if admiring it, she gasped and wakened abruptly.

Rising, she turned on a bedside light and then wandered in to the cottage's comfortable living area. There was no sound but the hum of an air-conditioner, and rivulets of condensation on the windows obscured the landscape outside. She felt adrift inside a bubble. Not good, but she knew what to do – connect to something!

A quick email to somebody, a plan to meet for breakfast, a link to some terrific cellist in Venezuela or conceptual artist in the basement of her own building, just threads securing her to the world of people with normal dreams. But where those connections had been was an emptiness she knew predated all of them. She'd been casting threads across that abyss for a very long time, clinging to them like a web across which, spiderlike, she navigated. And it worked. Except now there was no one to catch the thrown link.

Opening her tablet, she scanned her emails. Nineteen new, eighteen of which were group notices urging her to sign petitions and one was a reminder that the car she'd left with her friend in Binghamton was due for an oil change. The three social media sites in which she rarely participated provided weighty political commentary, cat videos and photos of trendy food eaten hours ago by people she barely knew.

Out of long habit she clicked on the bookmarked page for the Unicorn Tapestries that had inspired her dissertation. Wendy had taken her to New York City the first time when she was five. They'd visited The Cloisters and Danni had burst into tears at the scene in which ugly, long-nosed men in strange clothes stabbed the unicorn with spears. When she saw the next tapestry with the dead unicorn slung over a horse, her stricken wails brought museum guards and Wendy had to take her away. She'd loved the unicorn at first sight. She still did.

In the intervening years she'd had unicorn coloring books and stickers, unicorn stuffed animals and ceramic figures. She begged to be taken to The Cloisters at every chance, and when she was old enough she saved money to pay for day trips into the city to study the tapestries. The unicorn's magic never abated, and as her understanding of its imagery matured, her commitment to it deepened.

The creature was beautiful, magical, untamable, and so was hunted down and killed by people who wore their ignorance as if it were finery. Danni devoted every word of a 350 page dissertation to an analysis of the unicorn as it was before the spears of arrogant stupidity dimmed the story in its eyes. But her work, bound, labeled and unread in the stacks of a university library, was only a beginning. It made no sense, but somehow she still had to save the unicorn. She'd known it since she was five. She also knew she'd been looking for the magical creature in all the wrong places – "boyfriends" who invariably fell short of magic.

Sighing, she touched the woven image on the screen, then closed the program. She might have nothing else, no connection to the world, but her connection to a magical creature that never existed was enough. Smiling ruefully, she curled again beneath thick sheets, the odd dream forgotten.

CHAPTER FIVE

It was late before Antoine reached his office in the law library the following morning. The Mississippi fog that rolled in the night before had caused a lockdown until it lifted mid-morning, when the Walk was again open to foot traffic. In his office he found a breakfast stick-out tray on his desk that had been sitting there since 6:00 a.m. The meal was delivered in a standard Styrofoam box as a courtesy to men who were working during mealtime and couldn't get to the dining hall. Because of his irregular work schedule, Antoine had permission to eat all his meals in the law library. While this didn't improve the taste or quality of the food, his cubbyhole office was a more peaceful place than the chow hall, which was always noisy with barracks humor, friendly vulgarities and rancorous disputes.

Antoine lifted the lid of the white foam box to find the common fare – a mottled yellow lump of unseasoned scrambled eggs hugging a leaden biscuit covered in pasty white "country gravy" that blended seamlessly with a congealed puddle of that Southern staple, cornmeal grits. In the corner of the tray of tasteless and odorless food was a medallion of fried sausage. He broke off a chunk and offered it to Bastet, his illegal pet cat, who was not hungry enough this morning to eat what she apparently did not recognize as food.

Antoine had rescued the whimpering kitten from under the Walk after Bastet's mother and litter-mates were slaughtered by Shorty, the inmate whose job it was to keep the stray cat population on the prison's eighteen thousand acres in check. Antoine found it interesting that among the murderers, rapists, and armed thieves who would call this prison home for life, Shorty was one of the most reviled men in residence.

The official word put out by the administration was that the cats captured in traps were released into the wild Tunica Hills that ran along the Eastern border of the prison grounds. But prisons keep no secrets, and although Shorty worked only by moonlight, even the darkness could not cloak his loathsome trade. The shrieks of cats being clubbed to death sometimes rode the pitch black air for hours, and more than one guard with levee duty told stories of Shorty dumping gunnysacks of dead cats into the Mississippi River.

It was a dangerous job. Shorty's predecessor had been knifed to death on the Big Yard less than a year after he took the job. He'd been found in the end zone of the football field, his hazel eyes wide open and a look of surprise frozen forever on his face. That no ordinary prison feud lay behind the murder was evident from the smiling cat's face that had been carved to the bone in the skin of his forehead.

Even so, there was no shortage of men who would take Shorty's place in an instant if they got the chance – the reward for five years of this service was a highly unusual recommendation for parole. Apart from that unlikely scenario, the prisoners related to the cats' plight. Some had also had grown up as outcasts, often homeless, scuffling to survive in inhospitable landscapes where everyone was either predator or prey. The prisoners instinctively sided with the cats against Shorty. And they sided with Antoine, who risked serious time in the Hole, should someone care to bust him for rescuing and keeping Bastet.

"Monk, what the hell kind of cat name is that?" one of the inmate counsels asked when Antoine fished the little fur ball from the pocket of his denim jacket the day he rescued the kitten. "Why don't you call her Smoky or Gray Lady, to go with her color?"

"Give the little girl a handle that means something," another said, reaching out the index finger of a hand tattooed with the word "sinner" to gently scratch the tiny forehead.

"It was the name of a goddess in ancient Egypt who in the form of a cat was the protector of Ra, the Sun God," Antoine explained. "That's why cats were sacred in that culture and killing one, even accidently, could get you the death penalty – whether by a judge or by a mob. People back then used to buy little cat amulets for protection, and even for fertility because the cat, as we all know around here, is a world-class baby maker."

"Witches, they always have cats," somebody joked. "You a witch, Monk?"

He laughed. "No, but let's say I wouldn't object if one turned up and handed me a magical broom. Not very likely, though."

Antoine's co-workers in the law library never failed to be amazed at the things he knew, and pronounced Bastet a great name for the kitten. They adopted her as their mascot and fed her scraps from their own plates or shared tidbits with her when they scored fried chicken or catfish on the prison's lively black market in stolen food. When scraps were scarce, somebody would spring for a can of tuna or sardines from the commissary. Their running joke was that maybe in return for looking out for her, she would use whatever ancient powers had passed to her to protect them against the routine evils of life in a cage.

Antoine had made a bed and safe haven for her in a file drawer, but Bastet loved all the laps in the library and would go from one to another like a therapy cat, a bit of mewing fur among life-hardened men. She learned to dart to Antoine's cubbyhole and jump out the window when unfamiliar steps entered the library and to jump back in when Antoine whistled for her. She had been the office mascot for nearly three years, and even though she was technically "contraband," most of the security officers who worked the Main Prison detail knew about her. They left her alone, largely on the strength of their respect for Antoine, whom many believed did not belong in prison.

Antoine was just settling into his old Naugahyde chair, Bastet curling into his lap beneath the wooden gaze of the carved cat on the desk, when one of the inmate counsels walked in. The man seemed restless.

"You were over at the hospital last night," he said. It was more a question than a statement.

"Yeah."

"Anything unusual going on over there?"

"You mean besides Eugene LeBlanc dying?"

"Word down the Walk is that there was some kind of emergency," the man said. "Some guard brought in near death. Any truth to that?"

"I don't know. What time was that?"

"'Bout time the news comes on, I guess. Dude in Camp J said the guard was watchin' the news on that little ole TV they have on their desks."

"News comes on at ten," Antoine said. "I left the infirmary by eight-thirty. I wasn't there." He had work to do and hoped his response would serve as a dismissal, but the man continued to stand there, thick fingers drumming Antoine's desk. "Is there something else?"

"Well, this thing was *unusual*," the man said.

Antoine sighed with impatience. In a place where nothing changed from day to day or year to year, boredom was more painful than any injury. Rumors flared in reaction to anything of possible interest.

"We have a ton of work that's been sitting all morning," he said pointedly. ""Unusual" is not our problem."

The inmate counsel scuffed his feet and laughed. "Word is some dude down there swears he saw a skeleton with rotting skin hanging off its bones bite the guard in the neck. Says it was a *vampire* skeleton. Crazy, I guess."

"And it's not even Halloween," Antoine said, tapping a pen on the pile of papers stacked on his desk at the feet of the carved cat. "Get to work. We've already lost most of the morning."

"Just sayin'," the man replied. "Hell of a story."

Minutes later Perry Bordelon interrupted the quiet of the law library.

"Need your signature on this," he told Antoine, shoving a typewritten form on the desk. "It's about Eugene, says you were there and confirm he died normal, nobody messed with him. We all had to sign, everybody who was there."

The muscle-bound little orderly seemed edgy and checked his watch as a guard on rounds outside stopped to light a cigarette.

"Got a lot of work here," Antoine said, sensing that Bordelon, as usual, was dying to say something.

"They brought in a guard half dead after you left last night," he whispered loudly enough to be heard by most of the inmate counsels and prisoners seated at the library tables. "From Camp J. The doctor was still there and checked him out right away, said he'd lost a lotta blood. But here's the thing, Monk. The guy wasn't in no fight or nothin'. Alls he had was these two little marks on his neck smeared with blood, like a snake bit him."

"Then a snake probably bit him," Antoine said, causing chuckles among those listening.

"Snakes don't suck the blood out of you," Bordelon replied, scowling. "This wasn't no snake. The doc took him on in to the hospital in Baton Rouge, drove the ambulance himself in the fog. Pretty strange, huh?"

"Yes, strange," Antoine said with finality as he signed the document. "But not our concern. That will be all, Perry."

"There was a funny smell comin' off him, too, like meat that's gone bad. Like something dead."

"That will be *all*," Antoine said again, gesturing to the guard at the door.

"Mr. Bordelon is finished here, officer. Thank you."

The exchange had not gone well and he immediately regretted having involved the guard. It was a mistake, a breach of the complex web of protocol that governed interactions between inmates. Perry Bordelon was an annoying sycophant blatantly out to make a name for himself with Hoyt Planchard, one of the criminal element who ran the prison underworld. Everybody knew it and merely watched to see how it would all shake down.

A small-town football star in high school and smart enough to graduate without doing any work, Hoyt Planchard thought highly of himself. Eleven years after high school, a failure at everything he tried, he'd drunkenly butchered his wife with forty-three knife wounds so he could move in with his latest love interest, a single mother of two. Ironically, his girlfriend turned on him as soon as the police questioned her. He vowed to take revenge if he ever got out of prison. That revenge, he said, would involve killing her children as she watched.

Planchard was a bottom-feeder who hung around with the prison thugs who ran protection rackets and dealt dope with help from corrupt employees. He was scum but used his veneer of intelligence and his freelance work as a jailhouse lawyer to present himself as an educated and reformed prisoner. In reality he was a sadistic loser just smart enough to get by. Antoine saw straight through Hoyt Planchard and avoided him. And now Bordelon would run to Planchard with a legitimate complaint against Monk Dupre, who'd called a guard to throw him out of the law library.

It wasn't done, and Antoine cursed himself for a moment of bad judgment. He was so tired of it all, the endless backbiting and status-mongering among men who in reality had no status at all. Pariahs, the world was unaware of their existence except to wish them dead. Including the good among them, who'd long ago regretted whatever crime had brought them there and quietly did their time. And including Antoine Dupre, unless he could find a way to prove his innocence and escape to freedom.

Bastet leaped from her file cabinet drawer to purr loudly against Antoine's chest. In the cat's yellow eyes Antoine imagined an ancient strength at his service, if only he knew how to access it. Then he turned to his work, aware that Bordelon would make his way to Hoyt Planchard at lunch in the chow hall, eager to relate the vampire saga. And eager to mention that Monk had called a guard on a prisoner.

There were a hundred like him, but something about Hoyt Planchard felt more "off" than the others. Something diseased but carefully masked. Antoine shifted in his seat and looked down the row of tables.

"Say, who around here knew Eugene LeBlanc?"

Ten pairs of eyes looked up.

"I never knew him to be a part of any of the clubs or hang much with anyone," someone said. "He was too old for sports. Course, he was over in the hospital for a couple of years, too sick to do anything anyway. Why?"

Antoine measured the possible danger in whatever he said being broadcast outside the law library, then replied. "Oh, something he said on his deathbed about somebody named Jacques."

"Lotta coonass dudes around here named Jacques," another said. "Old Gene, he coulda meant anything, or nothing. Hard to say what dying people have on their mind, y'know?"

"Old Gene?" a third man said. "I heard he killed the bastard that raped his daughter. Heard he stood up in court and told the judge he'd dig the son of a bitch up and kill him again if he could!"

The men laughed appreciatively, but Antoine was unwilling to let it go. He stroked Bastet and thought about LeBlanc's message. Who was Jacques and what did he have to do with Antoine? The Convict Code demanded that the dying man divulge any information that might help another convict. LeBlanc believed that something about "Jacques" would help Antoine. And the only "help" of any interest was information that might set him free.

"My grandma knew Gene's mama back when they were kids," another of the inmate counsels mentioned. "Every year at Christmas grandma tells me, 'You go see Loretta Boutte's boy Eugene and tell him his mama's friend is ninety-two and still prayin' for him every day.' Loretta Boutte, that was Gene's mama."

Antoine leaned to rifle through a desk drawer to mask his reaction to the story. Eugene LeBlanc's mother was Loretta Boutte before she married Eugene's father and became Loretta LeBlanc. The name, Boutte, ricocheted in his head like a pinball.

A man named Jacques Boutte was one of five witnesses who testified at Antoine's trial for murder.

Boutte was the cook at the Palace Café, where Antoine had been involved in what he remembered as a minor quarrel with a man named John Thierry, the records clerk at the St. Landry Parish courthouse across the street from the café. At trial Boutte contradicted testimony given by two patrons of the restaurant, who heard and saw nothing but a mild administrative dispute between the stranger, Antoine Dupre, and John Thierry. But Jacques Boutte recalled that the stranger was angry, shouting at Thierry. When Thierry wound up dead from a blow to the head in the narrow passageway beside the café with Antoine standing over him, Antoine was booked for murder. His life had ended in that passageway as well.

He tried to imagine what Eugene wanted to tell him. Was Jacques Boutte the "Jacques" Eugene wanted to discuss in his dying moments? LeBlanc's mother's name had been Boutte when she was a child, which could mean that she, and thus her son, might have some familial connection to Jacques Boutte. Was Boutte a cousin, a nephew to the corpse now lying cold in the infirmary? If so, if this Jacques and the witness at Antoine's trial were the same man, then Eugene's message might have been important.

Had this Jacques divulged something to Eugene that Antoine needed to know? What? That he killed Thierry and allowed an innocent man to take the fall? Or that he was through playing along with whomever he was protecting? To Antoine, the only thing that made any sense was that Jacques Boutte either killed Thierry or knew who the real killer was and had fingered Antoine, a stranger passing through town, to protect that person. But why? Why would he have killed the court clerk or whom was he protecting?

Antoine couldn't even guess. He knew no one in Opelousas, where the crime occurred. At the time he was so crushed by grief over his wife's death that he couldn't think, couldn't begin to grasp what had happened to him. He had no idea who the people were who testified either for or against him at trial, or how they were related to one another or to the victim.

Later, only when they learned of his plight after his conviction, a few of his friends and Annabeth's brother back in Chicago had retained a lawyer to organize an appeal. But the critical thirty days had elapsed since his trial, making an appeal legally impossible. The lawyer had no recourse but to begin the arduous process of applications for post-conviction relief through the district court. With no new evidence the process failed, and his supporters quietly stopped sending checks to an attorney who couldn't help.

Antoine had gone to Opelousas to finish the research Annabeth found so fascinating, in the courthouse records. Endless questions for which he had no answers caromed in his head. Last but not least was why Eugene hadn't given him this information even one day sooner. Why did he wait until he was seconds from death to say something?

Whatever Eugene knew, Antoine wanted to believe it held the key to his freedom. He had to find out if there were really any connection between the old man to whom he'd read magazine articles and one of the witnesses who'd lied at his trial. It might all be sheer coincidence.

"Going to the infirmary to check on something," he said. "Be right back."

The Walk was quiet, everybody at work, and he was glad for the time to think. If LeBlanc's family had made arrangements for his burial outside the prison, the infirmary staff might have talked to them and would know their names. But if no one claimed the body, then Eugene would be buried in the prison graveyard and

Antoine would never know what connection, if any, existed between Jacques Boutte and the dead man.

He wasn't familiar with the duty nurse on the morning shift since he volunteered at the infirmary in the evenings, and approached her carefully.

"I sat with Eugene LeBlanc nearly every night for over a year," he said through the window of the nurse's station. "I'm Monk Dupre, Head Inmate Counsel. I come here most evenings to help with the patients, just thought I'd like to get a sympathy card and leave it for Jacques, if that's okay." He pronounced the name casually, as if he knew there was a relative named "Jacques."

"I don't see why not," the woman said. "You go get your card and bring it back here. I'll see it goes to Mr. Boutte with the undertaker when he comes for the body. That nephew, Jacques Boutte, said they're going to have a nice funeral over in Opelousas. Said he's going to cater the wake himself, since he's a cook. Your card would be real nice for the family, since you knew Eugene."

"Thank you," Antoine said, hiding his elation. The cook who lied at his trial was Eugene LeBlanc's nephew! And that meant Eugene had tried to hand Antoine a piece of information that might make a difference.

"I'll just run over to the commissary and get the card right now," he told the nurse.

"Sure," she said.

There were no sympathy cards among the sparse collection of old greeting cards available at the commissary, so Antoine chose one that just said, "Thinking of You" over a watercolor of kittens in a basket.

"Gene was brave to the end and didn't suffer," he wrote. "He was respected and will be missed."

He signed it, "Monk D., Infirmary Volunteer," so that the man who'd sent him to prison wouldn't recognize his name.

Not that it mattered. If Boutte was the gift Eugene had hoped to give Antoine, it was an empty gesture. Antoine had no money, no attorney, no way to reach the man. Nonetheless, it was more than he'd ever had before. It was something, where before there had been nothing.

The others had gone to lunch when he returned to the law library. As he sat in the solitude of his office staring out the window at the gun tower in the distance, he fought an eruption of feeling. It had been ten years since he'd allowed himself to feel anything. Now, on the strength of one word pronounced by a dead man, he was drawn to that most seductive of all traps - hope.

CHAPTER SIX

Grimaud didn't sleep during the night, but merely rested as his body manufactured itself again in the darkness of a subterranean passage created by the Mississippi River. He could feel organs stretching inside his chest and belly – heart, lungs, stomach, intestines and a host of others he couldn't name – all vibrating with life as they linked in a pattern begun when he was a skinless, tailed embryo with gills and paddle-like hands growing from his shoulders. The pattern was a song, and with new vocal chords he tried to replicate it, but the sound he made was only his name – Stéphane.

The sound was hollow and reminded him that he was alone in a place both the same and entirely different than it had been on the night Old Joe pounded a stake through his heart and kicked him into a shallow hole. Time had passed, but how much time? What were the metal coaches on soft, black wheels, and where did the bright, whining light come from inside buildings? He had seen fields of sugar cane and assumed that Angola was still a plantation, but the slaves were both black and white now, and kept behind bars.

Grimaud knew the Tower of London, France's infamous Chateau d'If immortalized in *The Count of Monte Cristo* and had himself flown from countless gaols over the centuries. The bars. There were always bars, metal grilles, heavy locks behind which misery snarled and whimpered and eventually died. He'd smelled the misery and realized that his old home was now a place of incarceration, a vast cage where once handsome mansions stood. Angola was a prison.

He felt the stretch and pull of muscles in his legs and back. Mud and twigs made shapes he could read with the soles of his feet, and with his hands he touched the familiar contours of his face. He hadn't changed, but the world had. He would have to be careful. He would have to learn much before he could leave this place and make his way in a realm he barely recognized.

Crawling from the tunnel, Grimaud stood in hazy moonlight and listened to the sounds of the dark, the scratches and paddings of soft feet, the muffled shrieks, the liquid slip of snakes. The sounds were familiar; they hadn't changed, and he knew his place as a shadow among them. His kind was safe there, amid owls, coyotes and bobcats, alligators, rattlers and bats. A family of raccoons scuttled over his bare feet, unaware of his existence.

No animal in the wild possessed the ability to perceive the nature of a vampire. Only animals who lived in close contact with human beings – dogs, cats, the occasional parrot or guinea pig – had absorbed a sensitivity to the nearness of the undead. Grimaud remembered the gray cat with yellow eyes who'd watched an old slave drive a stake through his heart. The cat had known what he was. But, he laughed, baring his teeth to the moon, that cat would have died long ago and the slave as well. Nothing now alive had the slightest awareness of the Vampire Grimaud. The realization was deeply satisfying. It meant he was free to become whatever he wanted.

Walking softly at the edge of the forest surrounding the huge plantation, Grimaud disciplined his mind. He'd learned to think carefully in the 17th century from a hawk-nosed Frenchman whose wide, dark eyes missed nothing. It was in the Dutch town of Utrecht that the man, Descartes, had discovered Grimaud feeding on a barmaid.

Bloedzuiger!, the man pronounced with a combination of fascination and horror. Bloodsucker! Then he merely stood in the darkened street, staring, as the girl fled and Grimaud returned his gaze.

"You are cursed most curiously," the man said. "Not for the drinking of blood, for we all eat the bloody flesh of animals. No, your curse is to bear throughout time the burden of thought that sets us apart from all other creatures.

We exist only because we think we exist. For you that
thought cannot end, an unspeakable fate! I pity you,
monster, and urge you to bear your curse wisely."

At that he threw down a card bearing his name and
position at a school in the town. Grimaud picked it up and
for three years sat in the classes of the man named
Descartes. He learned much. He learned to think, and he
thought now. There had been few books when he died and
became a thing that cannot die. But there was a library in
Utrecht, and he devoured it. Then there were endless
libraries. There would be one in the village he remembered
lay downstream from the plantation, where he could learn
what had happened while he slept. Where he could learn
how to live.

Built on a narrow ridge above the Mississippi River, the
village of St. Francisville slept in a river-scented darkness
unchanged for centuries. The Houma, then the Tunica
People had watched the river from its bluffs, followed by
squabbling Spanish, French and English. Now the village
lay in silence as autumn mists drifted across gas stations,
Victorian plantation manors, a moss-choked cemetery. No
one saw the blue light, teacup-sized and flitting in the dark
from street to street until it slipped through one of six brick
arches comprising the façade of a single-story building half-
buried in trees. The blue light slid like mercury over the
deadbolt lock on the building's door, and vanished amid
shelves of books.

Just before dawn a local trucker speeding through
dense fog toward Mississippi with a load of fertilizer lacking
both the required quality analysis tags and shipping ticket,
saw a blue flash moving in the fog over St. Francisville. The
trucker figured it was the transformer on an electric pole
shorting out, except it was moving. Something going on
with the ground wire, then? Whatever it was, he figured it
was dangerous, but he couldn't call the cops to check it out

because they'd be sure to ask for the paperwork he didn't have. Better to just keep driving.

Grimaud, still hungry but anxious to get back to his cave before the fog burned off, briefly considered a taste of the trucker, then rejected the idea as dangerous. He was tired from reading all night. He needed to rest.

*

Hours later a librarian would find on a table the complete 1992 *World Book Encyclopedia* that somebody had donated and then nobody ever used because 1992 was ancient history and the Internet was so much faster. Instead of reshelving the books, she decided to pack them in boxes to be sent to the prison that few in St. Francisville had ever seen, but of which none was unaware.

Angola was close but invisible, the last home of over six thousand men who had raped and robbed and murdered and, hopefully, would never appear at Mandy's Candies or the Femme Fatale Boutique, their hands gripping knives and their eyes burning. Everybody sent old books to the prison library, and at Christmas church groups filled plastic baggies with soap, facecloths and peanut brittle for the prisoners. No one admitted that the gifts were bits of magic, sent to reinforce the invisibility of a barred city so close to their own that on steamy summer nights they could smell its despair.

At nine o'clock that morning Danni Telfer saw the librarian loading a set of encyclopedias into a box, but paid no attention. So far the day had been surprisingly productive, with contacts established at both the historical society and the Bayou Sarah Quilting League, named for a thriving community just below St. Francisville long since obliterated by the river. The League president had given Danni the names of several local people who possessed collections of ancestral linens, needlework and quilts, although she warned that none dated as far back as the Civil War. Danni hoped the woman was wrong, since without antebellum artifacts, her grant to study them was doomed. She'd already made an appointment to see a collection at a farm called Acklen's Ditch the next day, and hoped to begin her historical research at the library.

"Wow. I'm afraid we can't help you," the librarian told her. "What you're looking for, you'll be better off at the state library in Baton Rouge or on over to Jackson. Or LSU, of course. You can see we just don't have room for a historical section. We're pretty bare bones here, although we do keep up with everything the kids need for school, and we get all the best-sellers. Have you read the *Crypt Mistress* series? She's a vampire. I hear it's going to be a movie."

"Um, no," Danni answered. "But thanks for the tip. Maybe when I have time. Do you have local maps? I need to visit a farm tomorrow. It's called Acklen's Ditch and I'm not sure..."

The librarian's smile was pleasant. "The Ditch? Can't imagine why you'd go out there when we've got so many beautiful plantations, all restored."

"My work," Danni said. "So if you have a map of the area..."

"Oh, no need for a map. It's out near Angola, the prison, y'know, just off the Angola Road right before the post office. I think there's an old sign on the road, or at least there used to be. Says, 'A.D.' with an arrow."

Danni grinned, trying for friendly. "Anno Domini?"

The librarian returned the grin. "Always Damp is more like it, out there in the swamp. I sure hope you'll visit some of our other historical sites while you're here."

"I'll hit them all," Danni agreed, backing toward the door and nearly overturning an easel on which a hand-lettered poster announced an art exhibit called "Hard Time Paint." It featured an eagle in acrylics, struggling to fly while its feet were weighted with chains. "What's this?" she asked.

"Oh, we try to help when we can," the woman said. "We advertise the art and craft show. All the merchants, city hall, the library, everybody displays the posters for their art and craft."

"Whose art and craft?" Danni asked.

"Well, you know, the prisoners. Angola has a big rodeo twice a year, the prisoners ride bulls and that sort of thing. People come from all over! But they let the prisoners sell things they've made, too. My sister went one year and got a beautiful rocker made of cypress. The rodeo's going on right now. You should go!"

Danni had never been to a rodeo or given rodeos the slightest thought, but this one seemed to be a major local attraction. "It sounds interesting," she said.

The woman had resumed the task of packing encyclopedias before Danni opened the door to a wall of heat.

"Oh, why not?" she said to her car's steering wheel, which was so hot she wrapped it in a couple of tissues from her purse before exiting the library parking lot. There were people on the street, tourists in Bermudas and sandals, all perfect strangers. The place itself felt strange, like the stage set for a musical. *Music Man*. At any minute a chorus in straw boaters might coalesce in the street, singing. The feeling was eerie, like a ghost of the secret things she saw as a child. She was going to be there for *months*, and the air-conditioned car felt like a cage.

Okay, she'd done it to herself, she admitted. Yet again. Ignored her friends, slighted her students, stopped going to yoga, dropped out of the early music group just when that great crumhornist joined and they started getting a lot of hits on YouTube. She wanted to rescue a man she thought needed her. And the fact that he was attractive didn't hurt.

Who *wouldn't* put aside a recorder to lie beside the devilishly handsome and much published professor whose latest novel was rumored to have been shortlisted for the Mann Booker? He had charmed her with brilliant discourse in a faint British accent she knew was fake; he'd grown up in

Iowa. Even that affectation had endeared him to her, hinting at a vulnerability beneath his brash exterior. A vulnerability shared with her alone, making her want to protect him. Of course she'd help with his research, fact-check his data and edit his professional articles. He was fifty years old and his position threatened by ambitious younger scholars. She wanted to rescue him.

But now it was over and she was alone and transparent on the stage for a play in which she had no part. It made her feel dizzy and weird, like something was about to happen. Or else it was the heat. Either way, she might as well locate Acklen's Ditch so she wouldn't get lost the next day. And she might as well drop by a prison to look at art at a rodeo.

The Angola Road joined St. Francisville's main thoroughfare, Highway 66, a few miles past the plantation B&B where Danni was staying, then wandered for twenty-five miles through dense greenery, creeks and sandy marshes where the tracks of deer, raccoons and bobcats left glyph-like tracings visible from the road. Occasionally there was a house with a tin roof and wide porch from which piebald dogs with dark hound ears watched her car pass. Danni saw a leaning township sign announcing "Solitude," and stopped to photograph it.

The sign was at the edge of a dirt road that vanished behind a kudzu-covered mound that might once have been a shed. She'd print the photo, poster-sized, at Kinko's in Baton Rouge and tape it on the wall across from her bed, she decided. Just a little reminder of her current social status. As if she needed a reminder.

The "A.D." marker was where the librarian had said it would be, creating a satisfying confidence that it would still be there tomorrow. Rounding a curve further on, Danni saw an ordinary gas station/convenience store, bustling with people as if it weren't in the middle of nowhere. Cars, pickup trucks and vans lined the parking lot, most embellished with a circular emblem showing a pelican in a nest feeding three chicks, surrounded by the words, "Union, Justice, Confidence." The emblem was inside an outline of the state with the words, "Louisiana Department of Corrections." Men and women in dark blue uniforms with red stripes down the pants legs chatted near the door, gesturing with cans of Mountain Dew and Dr. Pepper. A few wore sidearms, and the rifle racks in the trucks were not empty.

Danni felt an unaccountable chill. She had no reason to fear police and had actually dated a cop during her freshman year at college. He'd taken her skiing and given her a white cashmere sweater for Christmas. These prison guards would be no different. What was different was the incongruous isolation of the place, a normal hangout seeming to float in a sea of green so silent that the air hummed. Something was strange. Something expansive and heavy hanging in the sky. She could feel it as she pulled into the parking lot.

"I thought I'd come and see the art and craft show at the prison," she told a beefy, uniformed man who was fishing in a cooler full of ice for something in particular.

"Root beer," he said. "Damned if they're not always outta root beer!"

"It's supposed to be good for digestion," she offered, grabbing a Coke. "So where do I go for the art and craft show?"

"Jus' keep on a ways," he said, jerking his bald head toward the road. "Angola's about a mile. You'll see where to park."

The man hadn't really noticed her, had merely spoken into a vat of ice and cans churned by his searching arms. If asked, he wouldn't remember her question or his response. She was invisible even in this intensely remote place where her clothes and accent instantly marked her as odd. She wondered how long it would last, then bit her lower lip so hard she tasted blood. It was coming back, the weird feeling she'd had as a child. She felt as if she were walking into weighted skies, alone.

When she neared the prison, cars were backed up along the road for a quarter-mile. She took her place and eventually advanced to the toll booth where she bought a ticket and was directed through the gates. She was stunned to see a huge sign saying, "God is my rock, in whom I take my refuge! II Samuel 22:3." The sign was impossible to miss. Was this a rodeo or a revival? She followed the line of drivers along a precisely landscaped and manicured road to a grassy field where hundreds of cars were already baking in the autumn sun. Feeling like a sheep, Danni joined the herd of rodeo-goers as they made their way to the cyclone-fence enclosed arena.

She handed her ticket to one of the attendants, who stamped her hand as if she were at a bar or a museum. "I came to see the arts and crafts," she said.

"Head off to your left once you get in. Rodeo's starting right now, though. Don't wanna miss that."

Danni found herself on a path lined with food booths and games of chance that resembled nothing so much as a carnival midway. Scents of barbecue and cotton candy drifted on the sultry air, mixed with the acrid odors of frightened animals. On her left she saw loops of razor wire atop two-story-high chain link fencing. In a guard tower a man holding a rifle stood motionless. He didn't see her. Nobody did.

Many of the concessions at the rodeo were run by men in jeans and white tee-shirts stamped "INMATE" in black. Apparently the prisoners had clubs, because many of the booths run by prisoners bore large identifying signs. The Jaycees sold catfish po-boys and hot links drenched in chili. The Drama Club offered Cheese Nachos, Frito Pies, and funnel cakes dusted with powdered sugar. The Toastmasters Club peddled fiery barbeque and curly Cajun fries as Danni wondered exactly where inmates at a maximum security prison would be invited to make toasts.

The Human Relations Club sold tee-shirts that said, "Angola: A Gated Community," and "Angola: Three Hots and a Cot." Convict humor, Danni surmised, sanctioned by the institution. Like the stand where visitors could get a digital photo of themselves inside a cell with Styrofoam bars, or with their faces in a cardboard cutout of an old-fashioned black-and-white striped convict uniform. Though she'd never actually thought about prisons or prisoners one way or the other – they were simply not part of her world – she was vaguely disturbed by the idea of turning a prison into entertainment.

She found her assigned seat in the rodeo arena and was shocked when the warden, a short, floridly heavy man in a rhinestone bedecked cowboy shirt whose pale blue eyes broadcast both intelligence and a peculiar churlishness, opened the ceremonies by riding around the arena in an open Roman chariot drawn by Clydesdales. This figure was flanked by female riders sporting white angels' wings, the vignette so bizarre it might have been a surrealist painting. Deciding to escape whatever came next, Danni left the arena and headed for the arts and crafts displays.

There were tooled leather belts, wallets and handbags. Beaded earrings, bracelets and necklaces. Sturdy wooden toys seen nowhere for a century – rocking horses, trucks, a wheeled duck on a string. There were wooden cradles, clocks, chairs, knickknack shelves, small tables and gun racks. And there was art.

Danni paid for a catfish po-boy and wolfed it while glancing at day-glo paintings on velvet of the Last Supper, naïve acrylics of violins and spilt rose petals lacking in perspective, pen and ink drawings of Indian princesses. An orange acrylic leopard with bared teeth and only one eye regarded her with a rancor she thought was probably deserved. The leopard saw her and knew she didn't belong there. She should go back to her cottage and do some work. Maybe a swim in the pool, a glass of wine and a good book.

Turning to leave, she noticed a series of smooth shapes among a string of stalls selling all manner of wood crafts – cypress rocking chairs, desks and tables, dressers with mermaids woodburned on the drawers. The smooth shapes were cats, each exquisitely carved and polished, more stylized than realistic. Many were made of pine, varnished in shades of honey, slate, weathered white and coal black, but others were inlaid with cypress, mahogany and other woods. A few lay prone and curled as if beside a fire, but most were seated on haunches, watching from carved eyes like waiting guardians. They ranged in size from five feet to a lifelike eighteen inches and for some reason reminded her of unicorns.

"These are beautiful," Danni told a wizened man whose white tee shirt hung in folds from his skeletal shoulders. His blue eyes beneath flyaway white hair were clouded with cataracts and the hand he held out to her was frail and spotted.

"Name's Timer," he said. "Because I make clocks. You got a name?"

Danni took his hand, then looked away from something in his eyes. Something muffled by time and hopelessness. The man would die in this place for a crime committed long ago. He was as alone as she was, and she wondered how much anyone should have to pay for bad judgment.

"Danni. My name's Danni," she said. "How long have you been here, Timer?"

"Thirty-four years, three months and one week," he answered. "But you ain't 'sposed to ask."

"I'm sorry," she said. "I just... it was rude."

"Yeah."

She took one of the life-sized cats, carved from cypress, from the collection and inspected it closely. In her hands it seemed to breathe, and its smooth wooden flanks felt warm. She stroked it, almost against her will.

"Do you make the cats, Timer?" she asked.

"Nah, I already said, I make clocks. The cats, that's my buddy Monk. Monk makes them cats. Got one of his own, a real one name of Bastard. Hell of a name, Bastard. 'Course I've heard worse."

A coppery hand fell softly on the old man's shoulder. "You know perfectly well it's Bastet, Timer," a lean prisoner with ragged, curly dark hair pronounced, smiling. "Not Bastard."

The two men were clearly friends, and Danni turned her attention to the one called Monk. His tawny, racially-mixed coloring and slate-gray eyes set against jet-black brows and lashes made him seem another artwork. A Diego Rivera portrait, like *The Mathematician.* That sense of deep, perhaps ponderous, thought, captured in the shadows of a secluded carnival. She would later wonder who he was and why he was there, but in the moment she merely felt light-headed, as if the air had suddenly become silver and cool.

"Are you all right?" he asked, reaching to touch her shoulder before Timer deftly deflected the move.

"Bastet?" she said. "Egyptian. How do you...? I mean, your cats aren't like..." She gestured at the midway. "... anything else."

"It was my field, Egyptology," he said, nodding at the largest of the sculptures. "At least for a while. I find that remembering it... helps. I'm Monk," he said, "and you are holding another Bastet."

His gray eyes sparkled with enjoyment of the moment, but Danni sensed in him a sorrow like the old man's. They were prisoners. They must all live with the dual sorrow of some terrible crime and also of its punishment. Or else she was merely projecting some half-baked idea learned from TV shows and they didn't look sad at all, merely uncomfortable in the steamy heat.

"So all these cats have names?" she asked, grateful that the man could see her, could acknowledge her presence. The sleek wooden cat in her arms regarded her with a curious intensity.

"They are all representations of Bastet," he said. "You could say she's my muse."

"I want her," Danni said impulsively, holding the creature close to her heart. She felt tears filming her eyes and blinked them away. The need to *rescue* the wooden cat was overwhelming. What was the matter with her?

"She's yours," Monk answered, wrapping the cat in newspaper and a plastic bag while Danni fumbled for her wallet. "We're not allowed to handle money. I'll write you a receipt, and you can pay at the booth over there."

"Oh," said Danni, nonplussed. "I didn't realize ...."

"A card with my name and email address is taped to the base of the carving, in case you should want a companion for her in the future."

"Thank you," Danni said, moving away from the two men into sunlight that roared in her eyes.

In the car she sat for several minutes as the landscape fell in place around her like pieces of a jigsaw puzzle. Something was different, breathy and frightening and fierce. She felt the way she had as a child when she saw storms lurking behind bright blue skies. Nobody believed her when she told them, but later somebody would scowl into a downpour and say, "Guess the little girl felt it coming." She touched the wooden cat inside its wrapping and smiled as she tore the paper and plastic film from its head.

"At least *you* can see me, Bastet," she whispered. "That's a start."

CHAPTER SEVEN

After his shift with Timer at the rodeo Antoine walked with a guard to his office in the law library, where a letter had been left on his desk. He recognized the logo printed on the envelope – "Innocence Project" against a black background above a row of vertical white lines like a fence. Eleven of the white lines were missing. These, he assumed, were meant to symbolize prisoners set free after being exonerated of their crimes by DNA testing. His heart was pounding.

"You get the name of that lady bought one a yer cats?" the guard asked. The question was friendly, even concerned. The rodeo offered a rare opportunity for prisoners to interact with free people other than prison employees, and the men hungrily watched the crowd for possible connections, especially connections with women. A pen pal, someone who might visit now and then, maybe a romance might evolve from a chance encounter at the rodeo.

"Um, no," Antoine answered, his attention riveted to the letter. "Didn't think of it."

"You *shoulda* thought of it," the guard insisted. "Way she was huggin' that cat? You had a chance there, man!"

Antoine tried to remember the woman. Short auburn curls, pale skin and an East Coast accent. She'd felt familiar for some reason, but why hadn't he even tried to talk to her? She'd seemed a little skittish, but then it might have been the first time she'd been anywhere near a prison. And she was alone. Why hadn't he reassured her that she was safe, that the only convicts allowed to participate in the rodeo were trusties, men who had earned the privilege through years of good behavior? He stared at the letter on his desk. Would she have believed him if he'd said, "And by the way, I didn't commit the crime for which I'm imprisoned"?

"You blew it, Monk," the guard noted as he turned to leave. "You know nobody gets outta here without help on the outside. Damn good-lookin' lady, too."

Antoine fingered the letter, remembering another woman named Annabeth who'd been his wife until a sudden, deadly cancer took her from him. They'd met in graduate school, both Anthropology majors until he realized how difficult finding steady work as an Egyptologist might be. He'd switched to Business Administration, causing their only serious breakup. Annabeth wanted a life of fascinating research; she'd live on peanut butter to get it. Antoine graduated, got a job in a bank and courted her ferociously with his willingness to underwrite her research, her doctorate, whatever she wanted. They lived in an apartment near Northwestern and were so happy together that by now his memories felt fictional, impossible.

It was Annabeth who wanted to write her dissertation on his family, the mulatto descendants of a French plantation owner named Antoine Dupre and a West Indian slave named Ansi, who had been his mistress. When Dupre died, he freed Ansi and their children and deeded the plantation to her. Ansi Dupre, Annabeth discovered, had then successfully run a thousand-acre plantation until she died. That his great-great-grandmother had also bought and sold slaves shocked Antoine, but Annabeth just said, "Face it, honey; she wasn't the only black slaveowner. It's not pretty, but it's history. *Your* history."

After Annabeth died, Antoine quit his job and drove to Louisiana. He didn't sleep, didn't eat, barely knew where he was. He had to finish her research, her project. As long as he did her work, he imagined that he kept her alive somehow. Now he thought he might have spent the rest of his life writing a ten-volume history of a single antebellum plantation owned by a man whose name he wore, if fate hadn't intervened. Fate, in the form of a man named John Thierry, dead in a passageway beside an Opelousas café with Antoine Dupre standing over him like a scarecrow holding a sign saying, "Murderer."

He opened the letter and then carefully controlled the cataract of disappointment that in other circumstances would have made him gasp, yell, smash something against a wall. The Innocence Project did not have the manpower to look into his case just now, the polite and regret-filled document informed him in 12-point Courier. He was assigned a number that reminded him of the Chicago delicatessens where he and Annabeth ordered soup and Reuben sandwiches on cold Sunday evenings. Number thirty-eight. The Project would look into his case, but there were thirty-seven cases ahead of his in the New Orleans office.

Although he would have advised any of the prisoners he worked with that being accepted by the Innocence Project at all was a huge step toward eventual vindication and release, it was for him a crushing blow. Innocence Project investigations could take as long as a decade before retrial based on new evidence. He was already thirty-six; his life was half over.

Stifling his distress, he made his way to the infirmary, a random book he'd grabbed from the library tucked in the white plastic grocery sack he carried, along with the chili cheese nachos he'd picked up at the rodeo. Today he would talk to a newly-arrived inmate, a young "fresh fish" who'd fought off a sexual attack. It didn't happen so much any more, but there were occasional incidents. The youngster had a concussion, a broken nose and three cracked ribs, but he'd made his point. The predators would leave him alone.

Antoine remembered his own first days, back before the prison was largely cleaned up of violence, when he hadn't really cared if he killed the man who was trying to rape him or died in the fight. Back then you had to fight, but once you did, they left you alone. Occasionally it was still that way. Some who didn't fight, or simply chose to exchange sexual favors for the friendship and protection of a stronger prisoner, became "whores" whose duties mimicked those of a housemaid. Some embraced their new identity and became "gal-boys" with mincing steps and garish makeup fashioned from hobbycraft paint. Others withdrew into shock and depression, and of those, some never recovered. Antoine had realized then that all women in the free world were vulnerable to precisely this sexual violence, all the time, and wondered why so few carried weapons. He hoped the chili-cheese nachos, a rare treat not on the normal prison menu, would cheer the wounded survivor.

"Hey, Monk," said Perry Bordelon, the blabbermouth orderly who had spread word up and down The Walk about the Camp J officer who'd been sent to a hospital in Baton Rouge for loss of blood. "Heard the latest?"

"What's that?" asked Antoine, more out of a wary courtesy than any interest in what Bordelon had to say.

"They rolled another one in on a stretcher early this morning, a guy from Camp C. He'd lost about half his blood. No knife wounds or nothing," he said. "I overheard the guard saying the dude wasn't even in a fight. They found him splayed face down on the TV room floor. Don't have a bloody clue what happened to him."

Antoine smiled at Perry's use of the word "bloody." Ever since the Christian fundamentalist Dwight Tilly had taken over as Warden of Angola, cursing was punishable by a loss of privileges. For those prisoners who had no privileges, it was punishable by two days in the Hole – Solitary Confinement. Most prisoners still cursed liberally among themselves but had adopted strange locutions while at work or in the presence of free people. Perry favored "bloody."

"Is that right?" Antoine asked. He walked to the coffee pot and poured himself a cup of Community Coffee. The infirmary was one of the few places outside the visiting room where Louisiana's signature brew could be found in Angola. In the mess hall, prisoners were served something like brown water with a hint of chicory flavor. The coffee was one of the reasons he volunteered. That, and the quarterly reports filed in his record, indicating his "rehabilitation."

Perry trailed behind Antoine like an annoying puppy, adding, "The doctor sent him straight out to the hospital in Baton Rouge, just like he did the guard from Camp J."

"Curious," Antoine said to him, turning away. "Perry, if you'll excuse me, I need to see about my new assignment."

The nurse who'd brought him too late to Eugene LeBlanc's death bed was in the windowed nurse's station. Antoine rapped softly on the glass. She waved him in. "Monk, come, have a seat," she said, reaching for a file from the table behind her desk. She turned to look at him. "What does Hoyt Planchard have against you?" she asked without preamble.

"I'm not sure," he said, meeting her gaze directly. "He wanted a position as a paralegal in the law library earlier this year but didn't get it."

"Do you know why he didn't get the job?" she asked. "He has a reputation as a hotshot jailhouse lawyer, doesn't he?"

"He does, but his reputation's a joke. He knows how to write and file briefs and how to blow his own horn, but he doesn't win in court. He doesn't do the necessary research and he wastes time on unwinnable cases, mainly because desperate men are willing to pay him," he said.

Antoine waited for a response. There was none. He briefly weighed whether he should trust the free woman he was talking to. He decided he had to take the gamble.

"To be completely honest, I blocked Hoyt's appointment as a paralegal based on his poor track record and on what I knew about whom he associates with and how he spends his free time. If he knows I did that – and there are no secrets in here – he's going to be angry." He didn't mention his gaffe of the previous day, when he'd called a guard on Bordelon, but tried to read her reaction. Again, there was none. He forged ahead, "But why do you ask?"

She shifted in her seat. "Apparently there are some rumors flying around about you and me, the usual "They're having an affair' garbage. It seems Hoyt Planchard's behind it."

Antoine bristled inside but his gray eyes revealed nothing. He'd learned long ago the prime directive of prison life – say nothing, reveal nothing.

He lowered his eyes. "I'm sorry to hear that. I hope it hasn't caused you any trouble."

"No," she said. "Gossip circulates around here all the time. It just doesn't usually circulate about me. I'm just trying to get the backstory on this. Hoyt's behind it. He's dangerous. You'd do well to keep an eye on that."

"I brought nachos for the new patient," he said. "Better get 'em over there before they're stone cold."

"You go on, then," she said, dismissing him.

The youngster on the iron cot had a black eye bruised and swollen shut. The white splint bandaged to his nose stood in sharp contrast to his dark-chocolate skin, but he smiled at the bag Antoine swung onto the bed.

"Name's Monk. Brought you some goodies," Antoine said.

The boy surveyed Antoine with his one good eye, suspicious. "You a brother or what?" he asked.

"Breed," Antoine replied, using the common term for "half-breed." It applied to mixed-race Mexicans and Indians as well as blacks, but they all knew if there were trouble you stuck with your own kind, not with whites. In a riot, Antoine would be this boy's ally whether he chose to be or not.

"Muthafuckin' sumbitch faggot after my ass a white dude," the boy said. "Name of Hoyt. Know who I'm talkin' about? Whupped his ass good, him and his boys. Think they'll come back after me?"

Antoine saw fear jittering in the boy's good eye beneath long, curly lashes women must have admired before some last, serious crime landed him in a walled city inhabited exclusively by men. He wasn't surprised that Hoyt Planchard had ordered the beating and then attacked the boy only when he was bloody and broken. Antoine hoped the kid had enough left by then to hurt Planchard, not that it would take much. The man was notoriously squeamish.

"No," he said. "In here it's called 'manhood,'" and you have to fight for it. Once you fight, it's over. What you need to know right now is *don't* go bragging and throwing names around. Everybody knows what happened. Just keep your mouth shut. And watch your language. Warden doesn't like cursing."

"I heard that," the bandaged form replied as he wolfed the nachos. "Seem stupid. This ain't no church meetin'; this a hardass ole prison. I talk anyhow I please."

"Fine. I'm just telling you the way it is. Spend a few days in the Hole for cursing and you'll understand. Want me to read to you?"

"*Read?*" The open eye grew wide in disbelief. "What you gonna *read*?"

Antoine glanced at the book he'd grabbed on his way from the library. "*David Copperfield.* It's a classic. Dickens."

"You got to be kiddin' me!"

"No. Beats lying around in here watching church tv, but it's up to you."

"Fuck," the boy sighed, crumpling the now-empty Styrofoam plate in his hand. "Go on. Read."

"'Whether I shall turn out to be the hero of my own life, or whether that station will be held by anybody else, these pages must show,'" Antoine began, but his mind was fifty miles away in an Opelousas courtroom ten years in the past.

"Hey, man, you drifting," the young man said. "You gonna read or jus' fall asleep here?"

Antoine looked up. "You like the story?"

"Don' understand a fuckin' word, but it kill the time."

"Good idea to get into books," Antoine said. "Killing time is what we do here."

"Yeah," the prisoner replied, stroking his broken nose. "You got that right."

CHAPTER EIGHT

At dawn the next day Grimaud stood on the wide porch of a mansion he remembered from his last sojourn in the area. He now understood that he'd slept where the old slave buried him for a century and a half. He knew that the North had won the war but Lincoln had been slain by a Southerner named John Wilkes Booth. He'd read about electricity, automobiles and the fourteen states that had joined the Union since his time. He'd come to the plantation house called The Willows because he needed to ground his spinning mind in a familiar context. He'd attended soirees at the elegant mansion during the Civil War, pretending to be a visiting French count, his top hat and cravat of imported silk and his frock coat of the softest cashmere.

Now he stood on rotting, moonlit boards in ill-fitting clothes stolen from a clothesline, and experienced an odd sorrow. No stranger to the passage of time, he was still fresh to its recent reality. The Willows had been beautiful and was now fallen to ruin, its columns cracked and broken, its rooms gutted and home only to animals. A wild goat stepped gingerly through the leaf-strewn entryway and bounded into the surrounding woods as clouds of bats swarmed to hang from blackened, exposed rafters. It was nearly dawn, and Grimaud joined them in the moldering darkness inside, lightly touching a shred of flowered wallpaper peeling from a damp wall. The paper vanished like smoke.

He was still weak even though he'd fed again during the night, this time choosing a prisoner who'd gone for a three a.m. smoke to the TV room adjacent to his dormitory. Nonetheless, he felt strong enough to risk exposure to daylight if necessary. He'd searched for "vampire" in the encyclopedia at the library and laughed to see himself again defined as, "a corpse held by European folklore to roam at night, sucking the blood of the living. A vampire is said to be burned by the sun and to fear garlic, mirrors and artifacts

of Roman Catholicism such as holy water and crucifixes."
The fools clung to their nonsense, understanding nothing.

The blood hunger, yes. No words could describe the ecstasy, the salty-sweet annals of time filling his throat like music. Every feed was an orgasmic symphony in which the river of time was derailed, diverted, *possessed* by a thing that could preserve it, forever. The vampire was a codex, a book, a record roused into being by the forces of change. Only the vampire could hold the past, its teeth dripping blood like the ink of a thousand histories. But the time-enslaved fools saw only a monster, and cowered.

The sun was their god, its glaring rationality daily burning away the ancient voices murmuring in every brain, the stories inherited in all the earth by a single species – the human. The vampire drank the stories, preserved and honored them by shunning the censoring light. But any vampire could walk in its discomfort when necessary. The rest of it, the garlic, mirrors and churchly toys, were just bits of chaff left by individual vampires with quirky tastes. Grimaud himself disliked the scent of garlic, but wouldn't hesitate to swim in vats of the little herb if he had to.

Some people had come to the old mansion during the night, unwashed youngsters smelling of beer and futility. Irritated by the intrusion, Grimaud thought idly of killing them but stopped himself, choosing instead merely to snarl. Lost and vulnerable in this new world, he couldn't risk exposure. They fled, and amid the soft cheeping of bats he curled near a mossy stone fireplace where Jefferson Davis once toasted the Confederacy, and allowed his eyes to close.

*

Fifteen miles away, Danni Telfer woke from a dream in which an indistinct figure moved from room to room at a large, candlelit party. She followed it but could never get close, until at last she opened a strange, narrow door behind which the figure seemed to be asleep although it stood upright. A little girl sat in a corner playing with a pair of glasses. When the child held the glasses over her eyes, they sparkled with candlelight although the room was dark.

Danni woke to a sense of discomfort like a translucent film on her skin. She knew the little girl was herself but also someone else. Someone able to *see*, and yet Danni stood outside, able to discern only a meaningless reflection in the lenses over the child's eyes. Her eyes.

In the shower she decided that the dream meant it was time to watch closely and see everything, not just what she wanted to see. Well, she could do that! The decision made her feel dressed, as if a sturdy, invisible cloak had been draped over her body. She savored a cup of Community Coffee and a fresh croissant in the kitchen of her cottage, and felt robust and tough. She was singing "The Battle Hymn of the Republic" at top volume as she washed her cup in the sink, when she heard a knock at the door.

"One of my favorites," said an older woman with well cut champagne-blonde hair. She was holding a carton of orange juice. "I especially like that line that goes, "He is sifting out the hearts of men before his judgment seat." Can't you just see God with a big old sifter and a bowl, throwing *thousands* of bad-man hearts into a garbage can?"

Danni grinned. "I think I know a few of those bad hearts," she said.

"We all do," the woman answered cheerfully. "Listen, we ran out of OJ when the maids were making up the cottages yesterday, so I brought you some. I'm Victoria Stewart, Vicki to my friends; I'm your hostess. So what brings you to St. Francisville? I noticed that you're paid for two months."

There was something open and engaging about the woman, plus an aura of confidence Danni liked. "Truth or fiction?" she asked.

Vicki Stewart slid into a chair at the little kitchen table after pouring orange juice into two white hobnail glasses from a cupboard. "Both," she answered.

Danni provided a thumbnail sketch of her professional melodrama and devoted more time to describing her study of antebellum cotton. Her hostess was more interested in the latter topic.

"You won't find quilts with secessionist or Confederate themes," she said, "although of course they were made. But after the war men were arrested for wearing even a stitch of their gray uniforms! So women burned their patriotic quilts to avoid trouble with Yankee carpetbaggers. There are probably more old Confederate flags hidden out in the swamps than there are alligators! I know a bit about the period before the war, though. What are you looking for?"

"Cotton, anything about cotton," Danni said. House linens, clothes but especially decorated items like quilts. I want to trace the patterns used, the motifs, everything."

"Come on over later. I'll show you a whitework quilt my great-great aunt made in 1850, right here!"

"I'd love that," Danni said. "This morning I'm going to a farm called Acklen's Ditch…

"Ah," Vicki interrupted, "you'll drive by The Willows. It's a ruin now, but at one time it was the most beautiful plantation home on the Mississippi." Her blue eyes sparkled. "Check for vampires when you go by."

"What?"

"News travels fast in little towns like this, and it's all over that some kids looking for a place to smoke dope and get pregnant last night wound up at The Willows. They swear a vampire with fangs and leaves in his hair swooped out of the fireplace and chased them."

"The vampire as deterrent to drug abuse and teen pregnancy," Danni said. "I approve. What do you think they really saw?

"Old Acklen, most likely," Vicki said. "Acklen Pate's been living in those woods by his granddaddy's place since he got out of Angola twenty years ago. Something happened to him in prison, broke his mind." She looked away for a second as if avoiding a disgusting image. "People look out for him, leave food and clothes on the veranda at The Willows. We see him around here some nights, stealing figs off the trees. Acklen's harmless, poor soul. Looks more like a corpse than a vampire, though."

"I think vampires *are* corpses," Danni offered, realizing that she didn't think anything of the kind. About vampires she thought nothing at all. There was no such thing.

"I'd love to see your whitework quilt when I get back," she told Vicki as the older woman stood to leave.

"I live on salads to leave room for dessert," Vicki said. "Bet y'all don't have Blue Bell ice cream up there in New York. It is the *best*, absolutely addictive. Come by for dinner tonight and I'll introduce you to Dutch Chocolate, Homemade Vanilla and Strawberry."

"Deal," Danni agreed.

Forty-five minutes later she turned off the Angola Road at the "A.D." sign and found herself in a canopy of tall pines with an undergrowth of pecan and other trees she didn't recognize. The winding road was shady and only occasionally dappled by sunlight piercing the dense foliage. On the right she saw a muddy area littered with trash beside a dilapidated wooden gate. The gate was chained and padlocked to a sagging barbed wire fence that showed evidence of frequent break-ins. The fence was cut in several places, leaving gaps big enough to crawl through. Beyond the gate an avenue of oaks hung with Spanish moss shrouded what must have once been a road. At its end she could barely see pillars and a veranda oddly tilted in the gloom, as if viewed through wavy glass.

"The Willows," she said aloud, drawn to the place. It seemed to murmur in the silence, to be telling a story it expected no one to hear. The feeling was familiar, an awareness she'd always had of hidden things, things people didn't want to talk about. Something extraordinary was there, and she wanted to crawl through the fence and go to the crooked, murmuring house. Glancing at her watch, she thought maybe she'd stop on her way back and take a few photos. At the moment she had an appointment.

Acklen's Ditch turned out to be a large organic farm with fields labeled "Eggplant, Broccoli, Cauliflower, Cantaloupe," and "Cukes." The fields were bounded by apple trees, the latter being picked by workers who carefully loaded large flats onto a truck. A single green tractor pulled a plow in straight rows across an empty field labeled, "Chard."

Danni parked in an oyster shell driveway beside a new, ranch-style house with a tin roof. An attractive African American woman in jeans and a workshirt was waiting on the screened porch.

"I'm Sarah Reeves," she greeted Danni. "Sorry I don't have much time, but there's a ton of apples and I've got a driver out sick. Afraid I'll have to leave soon, drive a load in to Baton Rouge. But I've laid out everything I've collected so far. Like some ice tea?"

"Love some," Danni said. "This place is amazing! How long have you been involved in organic farming?"

The woman laughed while pouring tea over ice in tall metal tumblers. "Would you believe six months? Before which I was a buyer for Dillard's in Cincinnati. Linens. Then I fall for this sweet-talking Southern dude and the next thing I know I'm up to my double-D's in cucumbers! Go figure."

"So your husband's a farmer," Danni said.

"He is *now*, she explained. "My husband's brother Clifford is National Guard. His unit got called up, he had to go and we had to come down here and hold the fort. This is Cliff's place, but to tell you the truth, I'm kind of enjoying it. I grew up on a farm, so I guess it's like coming home. We may just stay on when Cliff gets back. But you didn't drive out here to hear my life story. Let me show you this stuff Cliff found in the old house, the one he tore down before he built this one. I knew it was something special when I saw it, joined a historical group in St. Francisville just to find out what we had. Pretty interesting."

"Do you mind if I take photographs?" Danni asked.

"No problem. Now *this*, I learned from the ladies at the historical society, is what's left of a hand-embroidered petticoat. It's cotton for summer and embroidered in redwork, which would have been rather daring in the 1860's. Every year on a particular day, the plantation owner's wife would give the family's outworn clothes to her house slaves, who would keep some and distribute the rest to the field hands. The only other clothes the slaves had they made themselves from rough blue 'Negro cloth' specially woven in mills back east, so the hand-me-downs would have been cherished and cared for. The old house that stood here was built up from the slave quarters, and this petticoat and the other stuff I found in an old trunk almost certainly belonged to slaves. But wait 'til you see…"

Danni was busily photographing the petticoat, a badly stained plaid skirt and a threadbare half-blouse called a "chemisette". "The embroidery patterns," she began, "are any of them local?"

"Oh no," Sarah Reeves answered knowledgeably, "nothing was, really. The country was young; American women, Northerners and Southerners alike, looked to Europe for fashion advice. *Godey's Ladies' Book* provided monthly plates and patterns, mostly French, that were slavishly followed."

Danni looked up. "But surely there were local fabrics, regional patterns of design?"

"Afraid not, "Sarah said. "God knows they grew the cotton here, but then it was shipped in bales to mills back east. That's where it was cleaned and spun into thread and woven into cloth. Southerners had to buy their cotton muslin from bolts shipped *back.* There were no mills down here, not much industry at all. Pretty much doomed the Confederacy and, as they say, set my people free! If you're looking for fabrics and designs originating here before the war, I'm afraid you're barking up an empty tree, hound dog. Except maybe..."

"I'm doomed," Danni said bleakly, polishing off her iced tea as if it were a shot of Jamesons. "If you're right, I have a grant to document something that doesn't exist, on which I obviously can't write the research paper I need to get another job. Vicki Stewart already explained that women burned their Confederate-themed quilts to avoid being hassled by Carpetbaggers, and..."

"By 'women' you probably mean *white* women, right?" Sarah Reeves interrupted, her brown eyes sparkling. "Didn't mention nuthin' 'bout us po' black folk down heah singin' *Old Man River* all day in the hot sun. Shame!"

"I'll bet they loved it when you burst into song at Dillard's," Danni laughed.

"Yeah, except I did *Let's Hear It for the Boy* with three gay guys from the designer salon doing do-wop accompaniment in Janet Jackson drag. It was the hit of the Christmas party! But hey, there's one more thing you haven't seen. It's a quilt. Take a look."

Danni watched as Sarah Reeves carefully unfolded what looked like a collection of rags stitched to a moth-eaten horse blanket. The fabrics were stained and disintegrating, but on close inspection bore traces of embroidery. There were stylized leaves and flowers, a three-legged horse, pigs, cows and chickens. Near the center medallion of appliquéd roses in an appliquéd urn was the outline of a house and a man holding a stick. The man stood beside what remained of a golden cross. Another man lay sideways on the other side of the medallion, a bit of red silk thread hanging from his chin. In thick, black chain stitch at the bottom was the name, "Neecie," and the date – "1863."

"Who's Neecie?" Danni asked while photographing the quilt from every angle. She thought the little figure with red silk on its chin *moved* once, its threaded arm reaching toward her. Just a glitch in the camera angle, she told herself. A distortion in the lens.

"A slave," Sarah said. "No last name, just 'Neecie'. But there's a story around here about an old man named Joe, who was her husband. Neecie's husband, so he was a slave, too, until after the war. Except he was dead by then, poor dude. Supposedly he killed a vampire just before he died. Right here! How about *that*?"

"Wow," Danni agreed, oddly shaken. The little figure reaching to her was a Civil War vampire, and both the figure's movement and the existence of vampires were impossible, silly. "You know, this is the third time today I've heard the word 'vampire'," she said, forcing a laugh.

"I think, well, the whole historical society thinks, maybe Neecie's quilt tells about it. That's her husband Joe with the gold cross, meaning he's in heaven, and there's the vampire lying dead with no cross and blood dripping from his mouth. He's damned."

"Lovely," Danni said, nodding thoughtfully as a new idea took form.

"We're trying to raise the money to have it professionally restored. Maybe hire somebody from LSU to research the story, except of course we haven't raised any money yet. Hey, maybe you might be interested? You know, while you're here?"

"Let me give it some thought," Danni said, mentally recalibrating a plan that was dissolving by the minute. She was going to have to think of something, some way to justify the grant that had rescued her from a bad movie. So far, a vampire quilt was looking good.

"Speaking of restoration," she said, "I saw The Willows from the road on my way here. Vicki said it was once a real landmark, the house beautiful of its day. You'd think somebody would buy it and fix it up like the other plantation manors around here, make it a tourist attraction."

"You and everybody else, including a guy who owns half of Texas and two separate movie stars," Sarah answered. "That is, people with huge money have had the same idea, but the place is in some kind of legal snarl. It was owned by a family named Acklen back in the day, and this place was part of it, called Acklen's Ditch for a creek that runs through it. I guess an Acklen daughter married somebody named Pate, because the last person to live in the place was old Curry Pate, but he died sixty years ago. The Willows has been empty since then, gone to rack and ruin and nothing anybody can do because the estate's all tied up."

"Vicky said something about a man named Acklen Pate who lives in the woods?"

"Sad," Sarah agreed, nodding. "The story is, Curry Pate was Acklen's grandfather. Apparently Acklen's mother was bad news; Curry disinherited her and nobody knows what happened to her. Acklen didn't fall far from the tree, as they say, and got in trouble with the law, wound up in Angola. When he got out there wasn't much left of his mind."

Sarah, Danni noticed, looked away in distaste just as Vicky had.

"You've only been here for six months and you know all this history?"

Sarah grinned and shrugged. "It took me a while to get used to it, too, but the South is like that," she said. "Once people know who you are, they tell you everything. And they expect you to tell *them* everything."

"Oh, God," Danni laughed. "I don't think so!"

"Yeah, girl. Better get your story together. Hey, the truck's here. Gotta run."

After thanking Sarah Reeves and promising to do lunch as soon as the apples were finished, Danni drove slowly toward the Angola Road, stopping at the gated entrance to The Willows. It wouldn't hurt to explore a little, she told herself, even though the venture was pointless and sure to involve mosquitoes. Ducking to crawl through the barbed wire fence, she felt her blouse snag and tear. Pulling it off, she tied it around her waist and headed into the gloom in the skimpy white tank top she'd worn underneath. Her sandals squished as she jumped over puddles in the overgrown track leading to the house, but she didn't care. The sensation was curiously rewarding, as if it proved her merit as a commando or a secret agent on a mission requiring complete indifference to barbed wire and mud.

She was humming "The Hall of the Mountain King" when she saw a man watching her from the shadowed doorway of the mansion only twenty feet away. He was barefoot under the pooling cuffs of khakis tied at the waist with a vine, stocky with filthy, tangled dark hair and skin so pale it seemed faintly blue beneath extensive patches of dirt. He was also wearing a woman's flowered blouse that strained at his shoulders. Danni thought of Bo Peep, or shepherds anyway. The figure, she thought, must be Acklen Pate, the local recluse, who for some reason made her think of shepherds. His gaze was fixed not on her face but on her left shoulder, where the faded tattoo was visible. The woods and ruined mansion felt suddenly dangerous.

Peer Gynt, the man pronounced in a voice that reminded her of lake ice cracking in the night. A voice long frozen, making a sharp rumble in the still morning air. His comment was so incongruous that she answered automatically. Academic cocktail party chatter without the cocktail party.

"You know Grieg?" she replied. Acklen Pate apparently liked classical music, knew the opera from which the tune she'd been humming was taken, but so what? She was alone with him in a dense woods far from anything and could feel her body turning instinctively, the need to run.

"I had the honor of meeting him once in London," the man said with a slight foreign accent, revealing white teeth in an assassin's smile that also seemed eager, even childlike.

When she noticed his eyes, she did run.

CHAPTER NINE

Antoine stared at the paper on his desk and carefully read the instruction aloud to the man sitting before him. "'State concisely and clearly every ground on which you claim that you are being held unlawfully.' Remember? We talked about this, Lamar, the three irregularities in your trial."

"I didn't do it," the man said. "That what wrong." He jabbed a stubby brown finger against a copy of the same form on his side of the desk, glaring at the title – "Application for Writ of Habeas Corpus - The United States District Court for the Western District of Louisiana." "Why do it say 'corpse'? I didn't kill nobody. Didn't even drive no car like they say. I wadn't even *there*, Monk! And Delane said so."

The last statement was pronounced in wide-eyed awe, as if disbelief in statements made by Delane were impossible.

"I believe you," Antoine said, nodding. "And I know this is hard to understand, but it doesn't matter now that you weren't there and didn't do it. What matters, what might get you released, are mistakes that were made during your trial. That's what we write down on this form, okay? And it doesn't say 'corpse,' it says *corpus*. It's Latin for 'body'."

"Mean the same thing, don't it? Dead body?"

"No. It means we're asking a court to get *your* body out of this prison because your trial had mistakes in it."

Lamar Sellers, a muscular twenty-eight-year-old whose reading skills would never surpass those of a second-grader, could not be expected to understand Louisiana's ancient European legal system. Carbon monoxide from a faulty heater had killed his mother and sister while an infant Lamar lay sleeping in a dresser drawer on the floor beside his mother's bed. Carbon monoxide is slightly lighter than air. Had he been in the bed with his mother and sister, he, too, would have died. But near the floor enough oxygen remained to save the life of an unconscious baby until a five-year-old brother named Delane wandered into the room. Antoine tried not to think that it might have been better if Lamar had been in that bed. Because the toxic gas robbed his developing brain of any hope for even low-normal cognitive skills. And the brother who rescued him, later cruelly betrayed him.

Before his execution for murder three years in the past, Delane "Eight Ball" Sellers confessed to driving the car from which two pounds of cocaine cut with a veterinary drug called Levamisole were delivered to a Shreveport brothel. Used to de-worm large farm animals, Levamisole in humans is a flesh-eater, causing patches of skin on the ears, nose and face to turn black and die. When the son of a state senator lost his left nostril and half his face after snorting a month's worth of lines at the brothel, a high-powered investigation snared Delane. At the time he gallantly fingered his "retard" little brother, Lamar, who would do anything Delane told him to do.

Always eager to please the hero who saved his life, Lamar said yes, he drove the car and delivered the drug, even though he didn't know how to drive. Nobody noticed that, and he got twenty-five years. Delane then killed another drug dealer in Mississippi, and on his way to the death chamber at Parchman tried to undo the damage by telling the truth. Lamar hadn't driven the car full of flesh-eating blow; Delane had. He might as well have saved his breath. Nobody believed him. Nobody even listened.

Lamar Sellers had been in Angola for seven years when another prisoner who knew his story brought him to Antoine in the law library.

"See what you can do, Monk," the man said after providing the history. "Lamar ain't done nothin'. Jelly-ass brother set him up, walked away clean. Now the brother dead and this man stuck out in here."

When Lamar began to cry at the mention of Delane's death, Antoine felt a headachy weight of responsibility.

Lamar Sellers was a child, would always be a child. The other prisoners looked after him, but only the most skilled inmate counsel might be able to get the new trial that could set him free. Antoine had worked on the case for months, searching for and finding in the trial transcript several legal irregularities that might get Lamar a new trial in which Delane's confession could be introduced.

"Why don't I just go ahead and fill out this form, answer the questions for you?" he suggested. Bastet was prowling the floor and finally jumped onto Lamar's lap, her eyes watching Antoine intently.

"Yeah, okay," the man answered, clumsily petting the feline back. "Nice kitty," he said. "Nice kitty you got here." Leaning over Bastet, he painstakingly printed his name on the lines Antoine indicated.

"I'll send this out in legal mail now," Antoine said. "I have to see the warden about something, so you can go. Good luck with this, Lamar."

"Luck," he said as he walked away. "Don' know about that."

The Walk was crowded at noon with prisoners surging toward the chow hall, but Antoine scarcely heard the frequent salutations – "Monk! Hey, man. Keep workin', Monk." He held up a hand in general greeting, the other gripping an envelope that held the single, hair-fine hope of a man who still loved the brother who sacrificed him. A man so cognitively compromised that without help he might perish in the free world. There would be help, wouldn't there? A halfway house or group home where Lamar could live free, catch a movie or a ball game, maybe, with a little help. Antoine slid the envelope through the Legal Mail slot at the prison post office with a sigh.

The warden's office in the Main Prison Building was only slightly less utilitarian than everyplace else, with institutional carpeting and several framed photographs of Dwight Tilly grinning beside sequential governors and state officials. There was also the mounted head of a bobcat with a plastic cross hanging around its neck on a choke chain.

Antoine sat beneath the bobcat, waiting to see Tilly about arrangements for an Inmate Counsel training Program. He'd called ahead and had permission to be there, but he could hear voices behind the closed office door. The warden was still in a meeting. When the door opened, three men in polyester suits filed through the waiting area, two carrying Bibles. The receptionist smiled and said, "Bye now, Reverend Brandt, Reverend Guidry, Reverend Hines. Y'all come back!"

From the office Dwight Tilly yelled, "Monk, come on in. Haven't got but a minute. Hear you're helpin' Lamar Sellers. Poor s.o.b. don't belong in here."

"Just mailed off a writ for him," Antoine replied, watching the warden scratch his signature on a requisition with a pink, corpulent hand. His thick, graying hair needed a cut and his neck bulged over the tight collar of a striped dress shirt from which he pulled a shiny tie. Antoine's contact with the man had always been limited to brief encounters like this one, dry administrative matters. He neither liked nor disliked Tilly, finding him difficult to understand. A redneck, come-to-Jesus good ole boy on the surface, the cornflower blue eyes nearly buried in his fleshy face were not stupid. He was unquestionably crooked; his muscular political connections guaranteed a history of traditional Louisiana corruption. It was nothing unusual.

But Tilly's penology was unique. The suffocating cloak of religiosity he'd spread over the prison, familiar to most of the prisoners as the memory of their mamas' fried chicken after church on Sundays, enjoyed a measure of success. Antoine didn't try to imagine a real Dwight Tilly beneath the corny religious façade. Tilly's method, which would have both penologists and prisoners north of the Mason-Dixon Line doubled over laughing, was effective in the Deep

South. Quite possibly, Tilly actually *was* his own façade, an idea Antoine found disturbing and sad. But not frightening.

"I think maybe we got us a problem here," Tilly said, staring out a window at the Big Yard. "You been hearin' anything funny, Monk?"

"I'm not sure what you mean by 'funny,'" Antoine answered, sensing that now was not the time to ask for more Inmate Counsels. Tilly wanted to talk about something else.

"Funny like monsters, Monk, creepin' around in the dark. Like *vampires*." He snapped a pencil in half and scowled at a wavy heat mirage rising from the Walk beyond his window.

"Oh," Monk said. "Something about a guard. He was bitten by a snake and somebody started talking about vampires."

"It wasn't no snake and I got another one down with the same thing. One corrections officer and one inmate in the hospital in Baton Rouge gettin' blood from the blood bank because somethin' *here* drained off what they had."

"I heard that, too," Antoine said. "About the prisoner. But surely you don't..."

"You make them cats, right? Egyptian things?"

"I do, but what...?"

"Somethin' about Egyptian gods, all that?" The cornflower blue eyes were curious and cold. "I hear you got a real cat, too, down there in the law library. Think maybe all this cats and Egyptian mess might be stirrin' up trouble, Monk? Gettin' people to think strange?"

"No, sir, I don't think that," Antoine said, showing no reaction although his throat was suddenly dry.

"You some kind of pagan heathen, Monk? You worshipin' Egyptian cats down there? You know the Bible says, 'Thou shalt not suffer a witch to live.'"

Deep in the blue eyes a spark smoldered. Maybe humor, maybe the fanaticism of the true believer. Antoine couldn't tell which.

"I studied anthropology in college, really liked Ancient Egypt," he said conversationally, as if he were talking with a buddy over a beer. "I carve the cats because they remind me of those days. I made the first one back then, for my wife."

"It's in your file; she died," Tilly said, genuine sympathy in his voice. "Look, Monk, just make somethin' else in the hobby shop, got it? Plenty of things you can make besides cats."

"Yes, sir," Antoine said. "Maybe ducks."

"Decoys might be good," Tilly pronounced thoughtfully. Prob'ly sell a whole slew of decoys in the visitin' room."

He wasn't really talking about decoys and wasn't really talking to Antoine now, but seemed deep in thought. Antoine chose the moment to leave.

"I'll just make an appointment to discuss Inmate Counsel training with you later," he said.

"Do that," the warden answered and waved him away with a pink hand.

As Antoine left, he heard Tilly bellowing to the secretary. "Call security to radio the driver and get them preachers back here before they hit the main gate. I got a idea!"

Antoine stretched as he jogged back down the Walk, enjoying the warm breeze and quiet, now that everybody was at lunch. A guard nodded to him, then seemed to remember something.

"Hey Monk, you're tight with Timer down at the hobby shop, right?"

Antoine knew the guard. He could be trusted. "Sure," he answered, still jogging in place. "Friends for years."

"Well, I just heard he's in the infirmary. Don't know why. Heard he just collapsed somehow."

"Damn," Antoine said, stopping to grab the chain link fence in one hand. "Could be his heart. Thanks for letting me know."

"I didn't hear that 'damn' and no problem, Monk. Hope it's nothing serious."

It might be serious, Antoine knew. Timer had high blood pressure and permission to carry a little green shrink-pac of pills he tossed in the air and swallowed whole. He might have had a stroke. Timer, whose real name was Stanislaus Barrow, had supposedly been a hit man for the New Orleans-based Louisiana Mafia back in the day. Stories of bravado and connections to powerful crime syndicates were common among prisoners and usually devoid of truth, but Antoine suspected Timer's link to organized crime was legitimate.

With no family or outside connection that anybody knew about, the wiry oldster had plenty of money and clothes from Lands' End, the prison equivalent of Armani. A new watch every year and subscriptions to any magazine he wanted. Timer was being taken care of. But, Antoine knew, that care stopped at the door of the infirmary. Even the Mafia couldn't stall death.

He understood that Timer was a criminal, unlike Lamar, himself and a few others who'd gone down for crimes they didn't commit. But he'd come to trust the old man in the years they spent together in the woodworking shop. Timer became the mentor who drew for Antoine the intricate map to survival in prison. His death would mean the loss of the one person Antoine could actually call a friend. Squaring his shoulders against the thought, he headed into the law library and the distraction of work.

CHAPTER TEN

Twenty miles away, Danni Telfer toweled her chlorine-scented hair and dropped into a chaise lounge beside the pool. She still didn't know what to make of the man on the veranda at The Willows. His eyes... She shaded her own and watched a crow stalking aggressively up and down on the tiles at the edge of the pool.

Dark and so deep-set that he almost seemed blind, the man's eyes were swirling spirals, helixes of shining mahogany, umber and cinnamon flecked with a greenish gold like new moss. Van Gogh eyes in a pugilist's face, regarding her curiously, as if through a microscope. The man said something after his comment about meeting a Norwegian composer who died in 1907, but Danni didn't hear. She was already hurrying away, not sprinting but almost, unnerved by those preternatural eyes she thought she might have seen in dreams. Like the waking dreams she had as a child. Dreams in which she saw things nobody else knew about. A young woman sealed alive inside a wall, a Mohican village buried beneath a Ford dealership. The man with the strange eyes was like that.

An hour later, over chardonnay and a huge spinach and fig salad on Victoria Stewart's screened back porch, she mentioned seeing the man at The Willows.

"That wasn't Acklen Pate," Vicki stated definitively. "Acklen's short, bald on top with long, stringy gray hair. Always wears an old purple LSU sweatshirt with the sleeves cut off, says 'GEAUX TIGERS,' spelled 'g-e-a-u-x," on the front. Whoever you saw, it wasn't Acklen."

"G-e-a-u-x?" Danni repeated, laughing.

"You're in Cajun country," Vicki explained. "You know, *Evangeline*? French Canadians driven out of Canada in 1750, called Arcadians. Many traveled down the Mississippi and settled in Louisiana. They're still here, big tourist attraction now."

Danni watched several ducks flap out of their pond onto a floating wooden structure that looked like a duck-sized dollhouse made of Lincoln Logs. "Okay, I get 'geaux,' but if that wasn't Acklen Pate I saw, who was it?"

"Good question," Vicki said. "St. Francisville is *small* and we all know everybody. Well, not the tourists, but tourists don't hang out at The Willows. It's too far out, too isolated. Tourists wouldn't be able to find it and there's nothing there, anyway, just a ruin."

"But it's close to the prison," Danni noted uneasily, causing the other woman to grin and shake her head.

"You're thinking Escaped Convict!" she said, laughing and pouring more wine. "Only in movies. Oh, occasionally, like once every fifteen or twenty years, somebody manages to break out of Angola, but they never get far. And we'd know about it right away. I mean, the prison authorities inform the local radio and TV stations immediately, there are regular announcements and everybody keeps an eye out. All prisons, at least maximum-security prisons like Angola, do a count every few hours, keep track of where every prisoner is, 24/7. If somebody's missing at the count, the prison's locked down and trained search teams fan out. Bloodhounds, the whole thing. The guy you saw at The Willows wasn't an escaped convict."

Danni imagined the prisoner named Monk, the curly-haired carver of Egyptian cats, thrashing desperately through an alligator-infested swamp while bloodhounds bayed under a full moon. The thought was upsetting.

"You mean *nobody* ever escapes from that place?" she asked.

"Nope," Vicki replied. "Angola Road's the only way in or out and easy to patrol. The other options are the river, where the currents are deadly, or the Tunica Hills. Uncharted even to this day, impassably rugged and full of snakes. Wolverines and wildcats, too. The Tunica Hills are so wild that some people say an extinct species of woodpecker still lives in there, the Ivorybill."

"Wow, have you ever seen one?" Danni asked.

Vicki looked thoughtful. "No, but I believe it." She turned to regard Danni. "You may have noticed by now that things are a little, well, *different* around here."

Danni nodded. "Southern, I guess you'd say. Humidity, armadillos…"

"Not just that," Vicki said. "Not just plantations and the Civil War, Cajuns and alligators and drawls. There's something else…"

"What?" Danni asked, inhaling the fresh, green scent that seemed to descend with dusk and the sudden chorus of cicadas and frogs.

"I don't quite know," Vicki answered quietly, her gaze somewhere beyond the duck pond. "I grew up here, couldn't wait to get away. Went to college in California, got married, got divorced, brought the kids back and raised them here. Nothing else works for me, no place else has the atmosphere, the sense of history and things just out of sight and waiting…"

"And the stories!" Danni interjected. "Acklen Pate, The Willows, a prison the size of a small town buried in the middle of nowhere with criminals who carve images of an Egyptian cat goddess, Sarah Reeves's vampire quilt…"

"Plenty of stories," Vicki agreed as they both finished dessert cups of ice cream. "But about that cat statue you brought back? I noticed it when I popped in this morning. My daughter-in-law's a cat fanatic. Probably wear off when they start a family, but right now she'd adore one of those. I wonder if I could contact the prisoner who made it, get one for her."

"His name's 'Monk,'" Danni said, wondering why she hadn't asked his real name. "I think he said there's a card with his email address taped to the bottom of the statue, in case I wanted to order another one."

Vicki stood. "Terrific. Let's go have a look."

Bathed in sunset, the wooden cat on the Victorian writing desk in Danni's cottage seemed to stretch languidly as they opened the door, then settle into watchful stillness. Danni held it gently as they looked at the slip of paper taped to its base.

"Antoine Dupre," Vicki read, making a note on a paper towel. "DOC 66708 – Ash One, Louisiana State Prison, Angola, LA, 70712. Hard to believe they've got so many people out there, they have their own Zip Code. Here's his email 66708@jpay.com. You have to pay thirty cents or so, and their emails are censored before they go through to a kiosk in their dorms."

"What's 'DOC'?" Danni asked.

"Department of Corrections. And 'Ash One' will be the name of his dorm."

"I thought prisoners lived in cells."

"The bad ones do; everybody else lives in dormitories." Vicki looked thoughtfully at the cat for a moment, then went on. "Louisiana's sentencing laws are harsh," she explained. "And there's almost no clemency or parole. Only a handful ever make it out of Angola. The prisoners know the only life they're going to have is whatever life they create in there, and many do fairly well at it, like this cat guy."

"He said he majored in Anthropology in college," Danni said, "loved the Egyptian stuff."

"Hard for him to find anybody to talk to about *that*," Vicki said, shaking her head. "There aren't many smart people in prison. Bet he'd love a visit if you go get me one of his cats. I'd go myself but it takes half a day to get in and out of that place and I'm running a business here, can't be gone that long."

"Visit him? You mean like go talk to him on a phone through a plastic window with armed guards lurking around? What fun!"

"Why not?" Vicki said. "You could get me a cat and I hear the oyster po-boys in the visitor's room are fantastic. Nobody talks through windows on phones except the bad guys, the 'no-contact' visits. Everybody else sits at tables, talks, eats muffalettas, drinks coffee."

"I thought they were all bad guys," Danni said. "I've had enough of bad guys, especially the ones that *aren't* in prison."

"Sometimes the best way to forget your own troubles is to hear about somebody else's," Vicki said.

"I have a habit of leaping to rescue troubled men," Danni said, shaking her head.

"Well, you can't rescue this one," Vicki replied. "He's already caught and tied, as we say. But at the very least it'll change your view of things, hearing his story. One warning - if he asks you for money or to come back with drugs, say bye-bye and leave within ten seconds. Hey, I forgot to show you the whitework quilt!"

Danni sighed. "Between what I've learned from you and from Sarah Reeves, I think I'm going to have to revise my research plan. There really wasn't any local, indigenous fabric or design or anything! Even the cotton fabric wasn't made in the South, and all the patterns and embroidery designs originated in magazines that copied European fashions. But Sarah has this fascinating quilt..."

"Ah, the vampire quilt," Vicki said as she stood to go. "Now there's a project to sink your teeth in!"

"I don't believe you said that!" Danni yelled as the other woman vanished in the steamy late afternoon shadows beyond the door of her cottage.

*

That evening at the Mall of Louisiana in Baton Rouge, people glanced uneasily at a manikin in Macy's window. The display showed two women in office attire near a conference table where a big man in a three-piece suit seemed to be opening a leather briefcase. An adjacent window featured a back-to-school vignette in which an animated dog wagged its tail at a pigtailed little girl boarding a school bus with flashing lights. But passers-by ignored the dog and lights to notice instead the manikin with the briefcase. It didn't look right.

"Guy looks like he could use some sun," a man remarked to his wife, who merely nodded. She was pushing a stroller in which a fussy baby boy suddenly grew quiet. She thought she could hear music of some kind, a man singing in a foreign language. The song was haunting and sweet, like a memory from another time.

"*Lo egi*," she whispered, mimicking the song.

"What?" her husband asked.

"Nothing, just a song," she said.

"I don't hear any song. That dummy gives me the creeps, though. "'Sposed to look like a corporate exec? Looks more like a wrestler. That suit's way too small and the eyes... I'd swear his eyes moved!"

Grimaud, absolutely motionless in the department store display, watched the couple amble slowly beyond his line of sight. He was enjoying himself, observing an endless stream of people from whom he was quickly learning a little of what he needed to know in order to fit in. Both men and women wore long denim trousers like sailors or else short trousers like those of little boys. And like sailors, many young men and even some women were tattooed! Grimaud wondered why the young were defacing their bodies, but assumed it was one of the fads that erupt and vanish like bubbles. He'd seen hundreds, from false teeth made of pearls to watch fobs woven of the hair of dead relatives. He'd never understood fads.

The suit of clothes he'd taken from a manikin before he assumed its place in the window was too small but nonetheless bore similarities to those with which he was familiar. Apparently men still wore waistcoats, but only in the same dull fabric as the matching jacket and trousers.

He would miss his brightly colored silks. Neckwear seemed the single opportunity for color, and that only in peculiar, narrow strips. He looked forward to the store's closing, when he would select a wardrobe suitable to his new identity – a traveler. It was apt, he thought. A traveler who hadn't moved in a hundred and fifty years.

The woman who'd surprised him at The Willows made clear the fact that he needed to do something about his appearance. He's seen the white rose on her shoulder and knew that she was an adept, one of those among the living who glimpse the many layers of reality that dance through time. Called "witches" by ignorant mortals, no vampire would use that term. An adept would recognize a vampire, and yet the woman had turned from him in discomfort if not outright fear. Embarrassed, Grimaud found an empty house in which to bathe and steal some shoes and a shirt.

He'd flown toward Baton Rouge then, finding a barber on a street called Airline Highway because it was near a place where the roaring metal tubes with tiny wings rose and dropped from the sky. Airplanes, they were called. The barber seemed oblivious to the noise and gave Grimaud a shave while shaking his head and laughing, "You about the *whitest* white man I ever saw! That'll be fifteen dollars unless you want a haircut."

Fifteen dollars! Grimaud fumbled in his pocket for a coin he'd retrieved from his grave.

"What's this?" the barber said, scowling at a gold disk with a funny-looking woman's head and "1854" on one side and an eagle on the other. The eagle side was embossed, "United States of America," with "21/2 D" at the bottom.

"Two and a half dollars, as it's marked," Grimaud said. "I'm sorry. I've been... away. With your permission, I'll return later with the remainder of your fee."

The barber bit the coin, his right canine incisor leaving a dent. "Man, this is *gold,*" he told Grimaud. "You outta your mind? I can't take this. You don't know what you got here!"

"A coin," Grimaud said. "US, not Confederate. The North won, the Union was preserved. Even though it's old, it's legal."

"It's legal all right," the barber said, regarding Grimaud with concern. "It's also worth a lot more than the fifteen bucks you owe me. Listen, do you have somebody I can call? 'Cause you don't know what you're doin' here. I think you need help, man. Forget the shave. Take your coin to one of those coin places and find out what it's worth. And don't be showin' it around on the street, hear what I'm sayin'?"

Grimaud smiled. "It's good to meet a true gentleman," he said. "Thank you for the fine shave." With that he walked into the street and vanished.

The barber would later be met with complete disbelief when he told his wife, his children and several friends that a white man who paid for a shave with an antique gold coin worth $350 turned into a ball of blue light that flew above the street called Airline Highway and was gone.

At nine o'clock the store closed and by ten Grimaud sensed no living thing inside except a night watchman. The man remained in an office watching the box Grimaud now understood to be a conglomeration of electronic sounds and images called television. He appreciated the word's Greek root and planned to own such a device later, once he was established. For now, he intended to garb himself appropriately and establish contact with the woman he'd frightened at The Willows. How fortuitous that there was an adept nearby! She would help him, teach him the nuances of her time. Without such tutelage he would be helpless, clumsy, and prone to mistakes that would not go unnoticed by the enemies of his kind. In return, he would help her.

After selecting a wardrobe based on the dress of the mannequins looming here and there in the store, he found a traveling case that spun on four wheels and could be pulled along by a retractable handle. It was made of a lightweight metal he'd never seen, and delighted him. From a glass case he extracted an interesting timepiece meant to be worn on the wrist, and spent twenty minutes reading its accompanying instructions. He recognized the name - Tag Heuer – because of his fascination with chronography. Time is the avocation of vampires, and Edouard Heur's 1860 invention of the complicated device in Switzerland had been much discussed among the undead in New Orleans. Grimaud fastened the gleaming band to his wrist with a satisfactory click, observing that its price was thirteen hundred dollars. The price reminded him that he would need contemporary money. A great deal of it, from the shocking cost of things!

There would be money in the store, but he feared the watchman would be blamed if he took it. A bank, then. A directory outside the department store showed the location of such an institution, and minutes later he'd slipped inside its vault. Choosing fifty thousand dollars in small denominations, he returned to a shadowy corner outside and arranged the paper bills neatly in the traveling case with his clothes, placing only six hundred in a pocket of his trousers.

Across the street from the mall was a brightly lit inn called "Hyatt," where he took a room, paying in cash after explaining that a cutpurse had stolen his wallet and identification. When the desk clerk scowled and said, "Do you mean 'pickpocket'?" Grimaud answered in French to excuse his mistake. *Oui, un pickpocket*, he said, shaking his head. "My English, it is not good." He told the desk clerk that he could not be disturbed until dusk of the following day. In his room he spent the night eagerly watching television, stepping into the hall only briefly to feed on a drunken salesman whose blood was cloyingly sweet, its inherited stories numbed by alcohol.

*

At Angola Antoine also watched television in his dorm, half asleep until the duty officer gestured toward him through the glass window of the guard station. Rising to see what the man wanted, Antoine was aware that the news wouldn't be good. The guard's eyes were somber.

"Got a call from the infirmary," he said after unlocking the door and allowing Antoine to step through. "Nurse left instructions this afternoon that you were to be told, but they just got around to sending the message on. 'Sposed to tell you, Timer died."

Practiced in the control of every reaction, Antoine merely inhaled deeply and sighed. "Was it a stroke?" he asked. "Heart attack?"

The guard looked beyond the exterior door at the empty but well-lit Big Yard, chewing the inside of his cheek thoughtfully before speaking. "Could be," he finally answered, suggesting the existence of information he couldn't divulge. "My instructions are just to tell you he's dead. Sorry, Monk. Everybody knows you and him were tight."

Back in the TV room Antoine slumped in a chair, pretending interest in a months-old copy of *Cycle World* somebody left there. When his parents died he felt the sudden absence of gatekeepers between himself and death; he felt orphaned. Now the experience was similar. Timer had been such a gatekeeper, standing between him and the tedious death-in-life of prison.

Perry Bordelon turned from a commercial for low-fat yogurt on the TV, his small eyes mocking. "Bad news, Monk? Look like your cat died or somethin'."

"Bastet's fine," Antoine answered, intent on the magazine. "Think I'll order some of this silicone tape for the fans in the library. Cords are all frayed." He tore out the ad and strode away toward his storage locker, revealing nothing.

*

When the first wash of dawn appeared on the Baton
Rouge horizon, Grimaud closed the heavy hotel drapes and
settled into a bed so expansive that even his long arms
failed to reach both sides. The sleep of vampires, weighted
with time, is like a fall through rock, intense and soundless.
Grimaud fell until another rotation of the planet brought a
refreshing dusk and he awoke, completely restored and
eager to create a life.

CHAPTER ELEVEN

Two weeks later it was already hot at 7:30 a.m. as Danni pulled into the prison parking lot and took her place in a long line snaking to a small brick building with "Reception Center" over the doors. Within, she could see several guards moving around behind a long counter.

"They open them doors at eight," noted a black woman ahead of Danni in line. The woman wore a curly blonde wig and probably weighed three hundred pounds, most of it muscle. "This yo' fuss time?" she asked.

It took Danni seconds too long to understand, resulting in a slow, hostile narrowing of the woman's eyes.

"Um, yes," Danni said, scrambling to avoid offense. "I mean no, if you count the rodeo. I bought a cat at the rodeo, and a friend wants another one, so I'm coming to get it. The other cat."

The other woman slowly rolled her eyes, shook her head and turned to stare at the closed doors of the brick building. Further ahead another woman in stiletto heels and a satin cocktail dress under a man's suit jacket was telling a short, wiry man who looked like an aging jockey that she hoped the guards would not remove the entire head of garlic tucked in her bra. The man fingered the crucifix on a rosary circling his neck and said, "*Cooo, sha! Dit mon verité!*"

Danni felt as if she were in a play again, this one Theater of the Absurd. "Excuse me, but what language is that guy speaking?" she asked the wide shoulders in front of her.

"Coonass," the woman answered without turning around.

Danni focused on the cement beneath her sandaled feet, taking comfort in the fact that cement made sense. Cement was cement; coonass, however, was not a language. "Um, is there some reason the woman in the cocktail dress would put garlic in her bra?" she asked.

The blonde wig turned with glacial sloth, its Saran fibers throwing sparks in the oily sunlight. "They say they's some vampire inside," the woman explained. "He been suckin' blood from guards and prisoners, all same. So folks bringin' garlic, crosses, holy water for they men. Me, I ain't been up heah in a while, but since the vampire come I thought to see my husband, know what I'm sayin'?"

Danni nodded, unsure of an appropriate response. "So did you bring garlic for your husband?" she asked.

The blonde wig shook ruefully. "Hell no!" the woman replied. "Come to say good-bye. Muthafucka try to kill me. I'm prayin' this vampire kill *him!*"

The doors to the guard house opened, mercifully ending a conversation Danni regarded as the strangest in her entire life. But then the last two weeks had been strange, beginning with a luncheon with Vicki, Sarah Reeves and the St. Francisville Women's Historical Society, in which she'd signed a contract agreeing to research the history of the vampire quilt. The Historical Society would publish her findings in a number of journals, under her byline, and print an expanded version both as an eBook and a paperback to be sold in local shops, ten per cent of the proceeds earmarked "to author, Danielle Telfer, Ph.D." A phone call to her grantor provided assurances that the new plan was acceptable and would not affect the terms of her grant, and her preliminary research into the quilt's time frame had already provided reams of interesting background data. Things were going too smoothly. In Danni's experience, smooth things invariably preceded the eruption of change, and she wondered uneasily what the change would be.

During her work on the quilt's context she'd emailed Antoine Dupre, the imprisoned carver of cats, about buying another "Bastet" for Vicki's daughter-in-law. "I'm a history professor and staying in St. Francisville to do some research," she'd written. "I can easily come to pick it up."

"I'm afraid 'easily' doesn't apply to maximum security prisons," he wrote back two days later. "Under normal circumstances you'd have to submit to a background check that can take months. However, since you're an academic you can probably get permission. We have academics through here all the time."

The email was cool, businesslike and devoid of grammatical errors. What had he said at the rodeo? That his field was Egyptology? What was an educated guy doing in a maximum security prison full of rapists and murderers? Danni thought educated guys committed crimes like tax fraud and insider trading, whatever that was. They went to nice federal prisons with handball courts. Danni called the number he'd provided and was given permission to visit.

"Since you'll be visiting an inmate rather than taking the media tour," she was told, "do not wear provocative attire, bring in nothing but your identification, one pack of cigarettes and under two hundred dollars in cash, which you may deposit for the prisoner at the desk."

"I haven't worn 'provocative attire' since I was fifteen, I don't smoke and I'll only need about thirty dollars to pay for the cat," Danni replied.

"Cat?"

"I'm coming to buy another cat. One of Antoine Dupre's…"

"Ahhh," the woman, presumably a secretary, said, sudden interest lending tension to her voice, "I see; you're visiting Monk."

"I think that's his nickname," Danni answered. "At the rodeo another man named Timer called him Monk."

There was a silence in which Danni sensed a muffled pattern in the woman's thoughts, unspoken but palpable as insects batting against a screen. Apparently the woman knew something about Timer, or Monk, or both, and it wasn't good.

"Thank you so much for your help," Danni said briskly and then snapped her phone shut.

Now she was moving toward the reception center, a severely air-conditioned room in which she would have to stand in a phone-booth-sized cubicle under a powerful fan. Beside the cubicle a dog sniffed professionally at an exhaust vent. Danni hoped no previous renter of her car had smoked anything funny, leaving a scent in the upholstery that might cling to her clothes.

"Step on in," the guard with the dog told her. She felt like a rabbit, wide-eyed and trembling, her fingers curled inward like tiny claws.

Antoine sat on a bench in the main prison holding cell with thirty other prisoners. He'd never had a visitor. His parents were dead, he had no siblings and few friends from his college days. Annabeth had been his best friend, his wife and lover, his life. Her death left him alone in a way that, even after a decade, made him unsure of his own existence. There was no one who would come to this dismal outpost in the middle of nowhere to see him, a fact that had held little significance until now. Now that Timer was dead and he was expected to do something about it. Now that he was expected to kill.

"Hey, Monk, lookin' sharp!" one of the prisoners called to him. "You got a lady comin' from the look of that shirt!"

When word got around that he was on call-out for the visiting room, many prisoners galvanized to optimize the experience for him. One of the barbers showed up in the law library to clip his tangled curls to Hollywood standards, and the tennis shoes left by his bunk at night were mysteriously bleached to a blinding white the following morning. A plastic bag containing a new block of deodorant, a mini bottle of mouthwash and an aftershave powder he thought smelled like dried toothpaste, appeared on his desk. But the most effort had gone into his clothes, particularly his only regulation blue chambray shirt, which had come back from the laundry so scrupulously starched and ironed that it shined and crackled when he moved.

"Remember, jus' bring the lady to Toastmaster's, Clean and Sober or Lifer's an' you don't pay nuthin', got it?" Another prisoner reminded him.

The prison clubs ran the visiting room concessions and among their members were many whom Monk Dupre had helped. They wanted to repay him, and this was a chance.

"Thanks, man," he said, watching through the white bars of the holding pen to the main prison lobby where the visitors would arrive. He was sweating and the starch in his shirt was sticking to his skin. He thought he probably smelled like a Chinese laundry. In his lap was one of the carved cats, wooden and lifeless. He fought down a bitter-tasting panic, wondering why this college professor should give a damn about whether he lived or died. Because if she didn't, if she refused his plea for help in proving his innocence, the question was moot. He would have to kill or be killed, and either would be death.

"Hey, man, sorry about Timer," another prisoner said as every head turned to nod somberly, knowingly.

"Yeah," Antoine replied, trying not to remember the funeral two weeks earlier. He'd recited Prospero's speech from *The Tempest* as Timer's body was lowered in the prison cemetery, and paraphrased the first line now. "His revels now are ended."

"Dude," one of the men said respectfully as the rest looked at the floor.

At the reception center Danni silently cursed the dog booth for its effect on her hair as she showed a guard at the desk her driver's license and was given a slip of paper that said, "Antoine Dupre, 66708, Main Prison." Then she was directed to one side of the desk where women visitors were being body-searched by two female guards. It was like an airport search in a minor key. A sign on the wall stated that any visitor might be subject to a body cavity search at the discretion of corrections personnel.

"Not in this life," she muttered behind clenched teeth, then stood barefoot on a rubber mat as a guard efficiently checked her bra and the waistband of her slacks for glassine packets the dog might have missed.

"You're good," the guard muttered and pushed her to a rear waiting room where another guard was reading names from a clipboard as she put on her shoes. When he read "Antoine Dupre," she handed him the slip of paper and exited a back door where three blue school buses emitted a film of exhaust that hung in the steamy air like a toxic grey stripe. She didn't know which bus she was supposed to take until the guard with the clipboard said, "Monk Dupre, that's Main Prison," and pointed to cardboard signs in the bus windows. She clambered aboard and sat beside the man with the rosary around his neck.

"*Cooo, sha,*" he said, smiling broadly, "you be in dis place before?"

"Never," she anwered.

"You not from 'roun here."

She shook her head, warming to his smile. "I'm from New York. State, not city. So why is everybody talking about vampires?"

"Don' aks," the man said softly, his breath scented with coffee. "Better if y'all don' aks, *sha*."

Danni took the advice and merely nodded, looking past him as the bus sped between fields where armed guards on horses watched lines of men hoeing the black dirt between row upon row of green. When the bus stopped in a large parking lot before a sprawling building, Danni got out with everyone else and followed the crowd inside, where they were herded through a lobby into what looked like a high school cafeteria. When the last visitor was inside, the guard in the lobby slammed the heavy barred door shut. They were locked in, a sudden fact Danni felt in her lungs, her jaw, even her hair.

Everyone took seats at the tables filling the room, and Danni followed suit, choosing a table near the back where a row of thick windows faced a ledge. No one seemed to notice her, and she looked around, feigning a cheerful interest in the setting. There was a telephone on the ledge in front of each window, and a chair. These would be the windows of TV shows, she realized. The windows through which bad guys in jumpsuits and chains talked to their simpering girlfriends on phones, only at the last minute pressing their palms to the glass for a simulacrum of touch. Now the windows were uninhabited, black and ominous in the brightly-lit space. She guessed the really dangerous prisoners who had to talk through glass received visitors on a different day.

The front wall held a long counter behind which three guards talked on cell phones and moved clipboards around, none of whom looked at her. To the right of the desk was the door through which she'd come, matched by an identical barred door on the left. When it opened, several men in jeans and blue chambray shirts came in and were greeted with hugs and handshakes from waiting visitors. There were smiles, high-fives and then enthusiastic movement toward the left wall where prisoners in hairnets worked a long counter offering a cornucopia of food and drinks.

Danni watched as two more groups of five or six prisoners erupted from the barred door, but Antoine Dupre was not among them. What did you do if you got stood up in a prison, she wondered. What if she were as invisible as she felt, what if everyone left and she were still sitting there? What if she just sat there forever, locked in a nightmare high school lunch room full of hardened criminals who couldn't see her? Kafka might have written the story, except Kafka had never been to Louisiana. She was getting a headache from smiling into thin air and was about to approach one of

the guards to ask if she could leave, when the door of bars
to the left of the desk clanged open again.

She wasn't looking, didn't see him, but he saw her
immediately. She was impatient, angry, glancing at her
watch and then at the guard desk. The drug-detection
blower had left her auburn hair in tangles that shined
greenish in the fluorescent lights, and she was shivering in
air-conditioning lowered to accommodate the mass of
people who would slowly fill the room. He saw her
discomfort and wanted to pull off his starch-stiff shirt to
drape over her shoulders and warm her. A move like that
would land him in the hole for a week until they transferred
him to the disciplinary unit, and the impulse unnerved him.
He hadn't talked to a woman other than prison personnel for
ten years. And he had to manipulate this one, not protect
her from air-conditioning.

"Thank you for coming," he said as he approached her,
placing the carved cat on the table. It was one of his
favorites, inlaid with diamonds of zebrawood and ebony that
gave it a harlequin feel. "Would you like some coffee?"

Danni felt a subtle jerk as something shifted very
slightly and the room came into focus. Nothing changed,
except everything did. Across the room the man with the
rosary around his neck smiled and waved to her. She was
no longer invisible!

"What does 'coonass' mean?" she asked Antoine as if
the answer might determine her decision about coffee.

He grinned. "Cajun," he said. "Around here a Cajun's
a coonass."

"Then I'd love a coffee. I'm freezing my... it's cold in
here."

His deep laugh drew attention as they walked toward
the food concessions.

"Hey, Monk, how it goes?"

"When you gonna introduce me to your lady?"

All the prisoners and many of the guests seemed to know him, some standing to slap him on a shoulder, shake his hand, offer the two of them a seat. An older man in a worn three-piece suit and cowboy boots reached out to grab Antoine's arm.

"Jus' want to thank you," he said, nodding toward a young man in blue chambray and dreadlocks sitting at his table. "You done brung this boy back from perdition in time for his grandma to see him 'fore she die."

The young man stood to grasp Antoine's hand. "This my grandpa," he said awkwardly. "Good to see you, Monk."

Over steaming Community Coffee at their table Danni asked how the dreadlocked boy had been saved from perdition.

"Just some legal maneuvering," Antoine answered.

"You're a lawyer?"

"Inmate counsel."

Her cocked eyebrow suggested interest, and he forgot that he'd meant to manipulate her into a role she'd never have taken anyway. This was no prison groupie eager for the sick but safe thrill of a prison romance, but an attractive, intelligent woman whose presence in this place was sheer happenstance. He'd never see her again and decided just to enjoy himself. What waited for him would wait.

After a lunch of muffalettas, barbecued French fries and red velvet cake washed down with 7-Up, Danni considered the likelihood that she'd gained five pounds and didn't care. They'd talked all morning, about their pasts, their work, politics, music, old movies the prisoners watched on DVD's. Curiously, as children both had memorized Shel Silverstein's poem, *Where the Sidewalk Ends*, and recited it at grade school talent shows. Both loved *Nashville* and knew the words to all the songs. He liked William Carlos Williams; she liked e.e. cummings. When he left her to stand at the guard desk to be counted for the third time, she couldn't stop laughing.

"This is ridiculous," she told him. "You're right here; the room's locked; they can *see* you! Why go stand there so they can count you?"

"It's The Count," he said, laughing with her. "You obviously haven't spent much time in prisons. It's like kneeling toward Mecca. Has to be done incessantly or the earth will tilt on its axis, gravity will fail and we'll all be thrown into space like so much dust."

"Oh," she replied. "I didn't realize it was a religion."

"I didn't either, but it meets the criteria."

"Which reminds me," she said. "What's with the vampire thing? People in the line to get in were talking. One woman had a whole garlic bulb in her bra. They were bringing things to protect prisoners from vampires. Should I have brought you some garlic?"

In his smile she could see the little boy he had once been, impish, smart, prone to taking apart toasters and blowing fuses. The brother she'd always wanted.

"This place is full of con artists," he explained. "Guys who haven't cracked a book since third grade, but will spend *years* planning Machiavellian scams, escapes, catchbacks when they think they've been 'dissed'. Somebody's playing vampire, drawing blood, leaving holes in necks. My guess is it's somebody with a grudge, setting up the sort of hysteria that can take root in an isolated place in which fifty percent of the population is functionally illiterate and ninety percent sees the world only in terms of violence."

"You sound like a sociologist," she said, grinning. "Maybe you should write a paper – *The Role of the Vampire in a Maximum-Security Prison: Elastic Cohorts of Contemporary Folklore.*"

His laugh was engaging and the warmth in his grey eyes warm. But then his smile faded. "Prisons are ugly," he said. "Ugly things happen in prisons."

She looked hard into his face, tracing its lines with her eyes. "What about the other ten percent, the ones who can see beyond violence?" she asked. "You must be one of those. Why are you in this place?"

He returned her look. "Why spoil the party? In a few minutes you'll leave. I haven't talked this much in ten years. I thought I'd forgotten how. Let me have the memory."

"Did you kill somebody?" she said in the same tone she'd employ while asking if he liked Wagner.

"I am a convicted murderer," he answered.

"That's not what I asked you."

"Then no," he sighed. "I didn't kill anybody. However, most murderers will say the same thing. Don't believe them."

Danni licked a crumb of red cake from the corner of her mouth and rattled the ice in her plastic cup. The sound was pleasant. "I believe you," she said.

His look was angry. "Then you're a fool."

"There's some evidence for that, but this isn't it," she answered. "What will happen because I believe you?"

"Nothing." He turned to look pointedly at the clock over the guard desk. "Nothing is going to happen to you. You're going to take a wooden cat to your friend, write about the history of a quilt and then go home."

She focused on the back of her own hand, pale beside his bronze one. He couldn't be her brother, but she couldn't shake a sense of connection to him. "I don't have a home," she said.

"Then *make* one!" he whispered hoarsely, not moving his hand.

She placed hers over his and felt warmth. "I'd like to be your friend," she said. "It's not complicated."

His laugh was bleak. "My friends die, Danni."

"What do you mean? Who died?"

"You remember Timer, from the rodeo?"

"It was only a few weeks ago; of course I remember. Did Timer die? I'm so sorry, Antoine! Was it cancer? A heart attack?"

His face seemed carved of wood like one of his cats, while a darkness swam in his eyes. "Timer was murdered," he said as a guard announced the end of visiting hours.

CHAPTER TWELVE

Danni opened her car doors in the prison parking lot and stood aside as churning heat escaped in invisible torrents. The steering wheel was again too hot to touch, and she went back into the reception center to get wet paper towels from the ladies room. Steam rose as she wrapped dripping brown paper over the black molded plastic. Her car reminded her of 19th century paintings depicting the plight of iron workers. Cauldrons of molten iron, billowing smoke, workers like ants in a hellish nightmare. Antoine had said there was no air-conditioning in the prison cellblocks or dorms where sixty men slept in bunk beds. At least her car had air-conditioning. She turned on the engine, pushed the blower to high and closed the doors. She was dizzy from an exhaustion she knew had little to do with the heat.

The place had drained her, and so had the man. He'd asked for nothing, had been charming, courteous and interesting in some way she couldn't quite identify. She'd felt a bond with him, as if he were a brother she didn't know existed, lost in a Southern gulag and forgotten. She wondered why no one was trying to save him.

He'd told her only a little about his wife Annabeth, her terrible death, his grief-blind move from Chicago to a Louisiana town called Opelousas so he could complete her research into his own ancestors. And then another death - a man in a space between two buildings. A death for which Antoine Dupre was convicted of murder and sentenced to life in a maximum security prison buried in a swamp. She more than half-believed him in the way she believed biographies or newspaper articles. There were facts, and then there was interpretation. The facts pointed to Antoine as the culprit; her interpretation of the man did not.

But the fact that she could leave and he could not brought tears to her eyes, a wrenching sorrow. It was, she thought, the sorrow of philosophers, an impersonal sorrow at the very nature of things. Or else she was just stressed and hot and would forget the whole thing once she could get in the pool at Vicki's B&B.

"So how did it go?" Vicki called from the back porch of the main house when Danni dragged herself from her car, cradling the wooden cat.

"I honestly don't know," she told Vicki, handing over the carving. "It was… weird."

"My God, this thing is exquisite!" Vicki said, trying various locations for the harlequin feline and finally settling on a wicker side table beside the plaid couch on the porch. "I'm gonna keep it until Christmas when the kids come. Now here, you have a big glass of ice tea and then go soak in the pool. By the way, there's a new extended stay. Nice guy, talks funny, awfully quiet. Says he's a pump systems analyst here to audit compliance with safety regs at one of the Baton Rouge refineries. A ton of paperwork and he wanted a quiet place to work. I put him in the Tree House. Hope he doesn't mind the owls."

Danni felt her friend's chatter like a balm but actually heard little of it. "Pool sounds good," she said and stumbled to her cottage to change.

Once in the pool she noticed concentric rings of awareness reestablishing themselves in her mind. She was returning to normal, but returning from what? The prisoner's story had been fascinating, but it also triggered that need to rescue men-in-peril that she was determined to crush. There would be no more affairs in which she devoted her strength, her mind and her love to saving a man from whatever mess he'd gotten himself into. Still, if ever one needed help, it was Antoine Dupre! And she didn't feel the usual romantic tug toward him, but something both deeper and more fun, like the link to a brother who could always make her laugh. Too bad there was nothing she could do for him.

After two or three lazy laps and sequential dives to cool her head, she pulled herself from the water and stretched on a well-padded chaise lounge. It was late afternoon, still hot, but a light breeze hinted at oncoming dusk. The ducks were quacking softly as she closed her eyes and didn't fight the drift toward sleep. The vampire quilt, Antoine Dupre, the rest of her life – all could wait.

She woke to a silver sickle of moon in a violet sky and the howling of Vicki's Bassett hound, Ray Bone, from the porch. Something soft and warm and smelling of sage covered her from neck to knees. It was a man's summer blazer, camel cashmere with bone buttons, silk lining. On a nearby chaise a pale, stocky man in khakis and a black polo shirt seemed deeply engrossed in a bound sheaf of photocopied charts. Even though the sun had set he wore mirrored sunglasses, and his long, dark hair was fastened with a leather thong in a ponytail.

Danni observed him through half-closed eyes while figuring out how to wrap herself in the damp towel beneath her shoulders before returning the jacket she assumed was his. Her Speedo tank, even dry, was revealing.

The man appeared to be engrossed in his charts, making occasional checks in the margins with a mechanical pencil. There was something not quite right about him, something odd. His clothes were all new and might have been chosen from a preppy menswear catalogue, but didn't go with the ponytail. In Danni's experience, men in ponytails wore jeans and boots. And his chart-checking seemed casual and too regular. He wasn't really reading, just turning pages and making checks on every other page. He was putting on a show, but for whom? She was the only other soul around.

"Thanks so much for the use of your jacket. It's lovely," she said, standing self-consciously to extend an armload of cashmere in his direction.

"It was my pleasure," he replied formally, leaping to his feet as soon as she approached. "The miasma. One must be careful of ague."

His voice was in the baritone register and bore a subtle accent. Danni struggled with a feeling that she'd heard his voice before, even though he seemed to be reciting lines from a period play.

"Ague?" she said, tucking the towel snugly around her torso and slipping her feet into sandals.

His smile was elegant and puzzled at the same time. "The miasma, the evening air. It is said to incite ague, is it not?"

It was a question that might have been asked by Jane Austen.

"Um, I've never heard anyone actually use that word," she said. "No one has gotten 'ague' since the 19th century. And please, sit."

"Only if you will join me," he replied, leaping to lift her chaise with one hand, depositing it next to his. The knit cuff of his polo shirt stretched to contain a biceps the size of a small grapefruit, yet he didn't have the physique of a bodybuilder. He looked like a man who worked outdoors, a lumberjack or shrimper working the boats along the Gulf, except for milky skin Marie Antoinette would have envied.

He inclined his head toward her in a graceful move Danni had only seen in movies set in castles. "Indeed I have not spoken since that time and I look forward to your guidance," he said, glancing at the tattoo on her shoulder.

The nocturnal chorus of frogs and cicadas was warming up, creating a background for Ray Bone's sonorous howling. Another play, Danni thought with a frisson of discomfort, only this one felt dangerous. There was something peculiar about the man, something forbidding. And his remark made no sense.

"My guidance?" she said, crossing her arms over her chest.

"I apologize," he said, again inclining his head. "I am Stéphane Grimaud, returned from a long sleep and unaccustomed to your time." Standing, he towered over her but his attitude was businesslike. "You are an adept, are you not?" he offered as if this explained everything.

"I'm afraid I must go," Danni mumbled, falling into the pattern of his speech. "Thank you again for the use of your coat."

As she turned away he seemed puzzled, but bowed again and removed his sunglasses before returning to his paperwork. In that second Danni glimpsed his eyes and controlled a gasp of recognition. The color of burnished mahogany laced with Madagascar cinnamon and flecks of old gold, his eyes shone in the falling dusk like a nocturnal animal's. History swirled there, as did a terrifying intelligence constrained by courtesy and an almost childlike longing. Danni forced herself not to run to her cottage, but was glad to close and lock the door when she got there. The man's eyes were not new to her. Stephen Grimaud was the vagrant she'd seen at the ruined plantation called The Willows!

*

"Monk!" Perry Bordelon yelled from the door of the law library, "security officer told me to tell you he'll get you at 7:30. Be ready."

Antoine was enervated from the day in the visiting room and his meeting with Danni. His head swam with feelings he'd forgotten. He was confused, couldn't think straight and wanted to do nothing but sit in his office with Bastet curled in his lap. His dinner in its Styrofoam stick-out box sat untouched on his desk, and the other inmate counsels had left early to give him space. Every prisoner knew how disturbing visitors could be, and this had been Monk's first. Visitors brought the free world with them in their easy movement, their talk and colorful clothes. And when they left they took the free world with them, leaving only darkness and the smell of iron.

"Why don't you come in, Perry?" Antoine said. "You know I have no idea what you're talking about."

The smaller man ambled toward Antoine's cubbyhole office, hands stuffed in his jeans pockets and a sneer on his face. "Didn't want you callin' security on me again," he said. "Do that again and we'll have to hurt you, Monk." His sneer broadened to a twisted smile revealing brown teeth. "Too bad about your buddy Timer. Guess it was his time to go, but I'm sure your lady gave you a little fun in the visiting room today, took your mind off it, huh?" He grabbed his crotch and made stroking motions. "A little of that under the table?"

Antoine felt his blood turning to ice as it filmed under his skin, drawing his muscles tight. Bastet leaped to the floor and then through the window as Antoine stood to glare at Perry Bordelon. He was so tired of it all – the incessant posturing, insults and petty vengeance, the obscenities, the stupidity. He wouldn't rise to Bordelon's bait although he wanted to. He wanted to pound the smarmy little jerk to a pulp.

"I didn't understand your message," he told the grinning man. "Why would a security officer come for me at 7:30?"

"Warden wants to see you, is what I hear."

Antoine didn't betray his unease at the news, but merely said, "Thank you, Perry."

Tilly had undoubtedly heard the story behind Timer's death. Everyone who lived or worked in the main prison could repeat variants the tale, some had even witnessed bits of it. But Timer had been old and sick. There would be no follow-up to the rumors, no investigation. Everyone merely waited to see what Monk Dupre was going to do about it, because Timer had been Monk's friend. And the Code demanded that Monk avenge his friend's murder.

"Warden prob'ly wants to extend his sympathies," Bordelon said in a high, nasal parody of concern, wiping his nose with his wrist. "What with your boyfriend dyin' out from under you like that." He giggled. "Hoyt be happy to send you a nice gal-boy. Ease your pain right away tonight. Just ask, Monk."

"I will ask you to leave," Antoine said through his teeth. "Now." As he moved toward Bordelon the muscular little man moved backward, knocking a stack of law books from a table. "Pick them up," Antoine ordered.

"Yeah, nigger, who's gonna make me?"

Only feet from Bordelon now, Antoine could smell the faint gasoline odor left by the extraction of cocaine from coca leaves. Bordelon was using and had a bag in one of his shirt pockets. Antoine wrapped one wire-taut hand over the back of the other man's neck and forced him to his knees among the fallen books.

"Pick them up," he repeated as watery strings ran from Bordelon's nose.

"You're next, Monk," Bordelon snarled after slamming the last book on the table. "You know your sorry half-breed ass is next." He reminded Antoine of a mouse on steroids as he stumbled through the door and into the shadows of the Big Yard.

Antoine knew Perry Bordelon had played a role in Timer's death, but he was not the killer. Hoyt Planchard was. Several of the inmate counsels had seen Perry and two of Planchard's lackeys in Ash 1, the trusty dorm where they all slept. The men had been horsing around near Timer's foot locker, throwing a Nerf ball. When Timer came back from the woodworking shop that night, his blood pressure pills were missing. Only then did Planchard show his face, mocking the old man, stepping on his feet, tripping him in the shower. It went on for days. All harmless fun, if anyone asked.

Antoine hadn't known of the abuse, and Timer didn't say anything. You were expected to handle your own problems, and Timer intended to. Antoine had found a woodworking chisel, sharpened to a razor edge but camouflaged with sawdust and splatters of paint, among the tools in the shop after the funeral. But Timer hadn't found the moment to use it before an artery in his brain exploded.

Antoine could imagine how it had happened. That day two weeks ago there would have been a smell in the shop when Timer opened the door. Glue and paint. He might have thought somebody screwed up and left materials out, but then he switched on the lights. His clocks, the work of a lifetime, all of them were splattered with paint. Permanent, oil-based enamel paint, dried in smears of red, yellow, a green he'd always hated. Prying open one clock after another, he would have found the delicate wheels and pinions, the springs and pallets, frozen in glue, ruined. Antoine was sure Timer had reached for that sharpened chisel then, seconds before his skyrocketing blood pressure blew through a fragile artery like a grenade.

Hoyt Planchard's goons were observed to have colored paint under their fingernails on the day Timer died, and men who worked in the laundry later noticed yellow, red and green stains on the shirts and jeans of the same prisoners. But Hoyt Planchard had told them what to do. Everyone knew, nobody did anything, and the razor-sharp chisel lay in its drawer. No one would touch it. It belonged to Monk now.

In the gloom of the empty library he thought about Hoyt Planchard. In the free world, in his life before prison, he hadn't met such a creature. As a boy he'd known others who tormented animals and smaller children, and he'd avoided them. Planchard was one of those, he assumed, now grown into a sadist who delighted in inflicting pain, but too cowardly do it himself. He'd sent his drug-addled minions to play the tricks of schoolyard bullies on a sick old man, and waited for the inevitable result. Hoyt Planchard killed Timer as surely as if he'd shot him, but the slow death of a sick old man by a thousand small tortures was not, legally, murder. It was only contemptible, unclean.

The warden had called him in to warn against the expected retribution, Antoine guessed as he loped beside the security officer along the Walk toward the administration building. The warden would suggest that he ignore Hoyt Planchard, that he refrain from *killing* Hoyt Planchard even though the Code demanded it. Antoine clenched his fists, imagining Planchard's face, the skull beneath it, cracking and breaking like pottery. He imagined teeth and blood and brains glistening on the Walk as he obliterated a sick monster, a creature who reveled in the pain of others.

The guard glanced at Antoine's fists. "Be a shame, you blow your job, wind up in a cell for the next ten years," he said, checking his watch. "Lotta guys, you're the only help there is, y'know?"

Antoine said nothing, merely nodded. He didn't know what he would do; there was nothing in his head but a bitter, ringing alarm warning that the man he had once been was only a memory. And the man he'd become, without really noticing the change, was capable of cold-blooded murder. He felt like two people, neither of them real or rooted anywhere. Annabeth was dead, his former life a ruin. In prison he'd apparently been transformed into a violent criminal, but he didn't recognize that man as himself. He didn't know who that man was, who wanted to, and could, deliberately kill another man.

He wished there were someone to talk to. Timer would have something to say, but Timer was gone. He thought about the woman who'd come to see him. Danni. He'd been careful not to let her see his admiration, the odd closeness he felt with her. He liked her reddish curls and wide, intelligent eyes, and they'd had so much to talk about. He'd felt like his old self with her, but that self was only a

dream now, wasn't it? The man moving inside his skin had
murdered no one, was nonetheless a convicted murderer
and was thinking of committing a murder. He wondered
what Danni would say about who he was, if he could tell her
everything. He wondered how she could possibly
understand that he had to escape this hell or it would
destroy him and leave a killer in his place.

"Monk, I hear you a college boy, that right?" the warden
said from his desk chair as the security officer closed the
office door and stood outside.

Antoine studied a framed photo on the wall of Tilly and
a tall man in a suit beside a rank of staffed flags on a stage.
Beside the other man Dwight Tilly looked like a pink balloon
in a shirt and tie, and Antoine felt a twinge of sympathy.
The warden, too, spent his days among the ignorant and
vicious and survived by erecting a barrier of flesh.

"What?" he answered.

Tilly narrowed his cornflower blue eyes to thoughtful
slits. "You heard me. Got a job for you, college boy."

"A job?"

"Yeah, a job. You gonna work for me a while, write up
some things. Creepy things, know what I'm sayin'?"

"No," Antoine said. "What are you talking about?"

The warden locked both meaty arms behind his head
and addressed the ceiling. "Talkin' about a *vampire*. Thing
been suckin' blood around here, y'know?"

"Warden," Antoine began, "I don't understand…"

Tilly unlocked his arms, stretched, then appeared to be
reading the back of his left hand. His eyes never met
Antoine's. "Well, you gonna have to," he said. "See, we
gonna have us a revival, a exorcism kind of thing. Get rid of
this here vampire."

Antoine rarely laughed but couldn't restrain the guffaw
that escaped his throat. Tilly brought in impressive revenue
every year with his two prison rodeos. Now he was taking a
couple of snake bites and copycat pranks to the bank. The

man was shrewd, an opportunist playing redneck good ole boy like Br'er Rabbit in the briar patch. A carefully worded rumor of supernatural goings-on in this isolated prison, followed by a come-to-Jesus revival subtly promoted as an exorcism, would draw bigger crowds than the rodeos.

"Smart," Antoine said, nodding. "Except what are you going to do for a vampire since they don't exist?"

"Don't need no vampire," Tilly said, finally looking at Antoine. "Jus' need the *idea*. That's where you come in." He jabbed a finger at a folder on his desk. "Got your file here, Monk. Says you got some fancy-ass college degree in an-thro-pology, which you say is why you make them Egyptian cats. Figure you can do some talkin' about all sorts of heathen nonsense, make it sound like a professor talkin'. Figure you can talk about a vampire that way, am I right?"

Antoine shrugged. "I have a degree in Anthropology, but my doctorate was in Business Administration. You want me to write press releases and promotional flyers for your revival; is that right?"

"Yep."

"You want a subtext suggesting that the revival is meant to exorcise a vampire that's stalking Angola without actually saying so because you don't want to look stupid."

"Wouldn't know a 'subtext' from a front-loadin' brassiere," Tilly said, smiling. "But you got the idea. Talk about them Egyptian gods, all kinda monsters, maybe some from the Bible. Don't hafta say 'vampire' at all. Word's already out that we got one. Everybody will make the connection."

Antoine rooted his feet to the floor to keep from swaying. Too much was happening too fast. This was crazy, he needed time, but there was none. "What's in it for me?" he said.

Tilly rolled his head on the folds of his neck. "Hoped you'd never ask, but how about my undyin' gratitude?"

"Touching," Antoine said.

"Oh, and I forgot... your buddy Planchard's on his way to an isolation cell right now. Seems he's been dealin' drugs. Save me a lot of trouble if I jus' let you kill the s.o.b., but you can still go for it after the revival if you want. I got a better use for you at the moment."

"This is going to take all my time," Antoine said.

"So? Time's all you got."

"So one more thing. Get Lamar Sellers out of here."

Tilly cocked his head. "Sellers. That the re-tard took the fall for his brother?"

Antoine nodded. "The day before his lethal injection at Parchman, Lamar's brother Delane made a full confession exonerating Lamar of the crime for which he was convicted. Lamar is mentally impaired as a result of carbon monoxide poisoning when he was a baby. Delane was five at the time and saved Lamar's life. Lamar worshipped his brother and did whatever Delane told him to do. Lamar took the fall like you said. I'm trying to get him a new trial, but that will take years. You could have him transferred to a supervised facility for non-violent offenders while he waits."

"Done," Tilly agreed. "Now get to work on this revival." With that he signaled the guard and swiveled his chair toward the window. Above the brightly lit but deserted Walk outside he saw a sphere of blue light and wondered idly how a lightning bug could get that big.

CHAPTER THIRTEEN

Several nights later, Grimaud half-heartedly fed on a woman walking alone on the Angola Road with a double-barreled shotgun broken open over her shoulder. Her blood was crisp with undertones of faint African chants and more recent stories he didn't understand. He drank little and sang to her the song of forgetfulness so that she would only remember his bite as a dream. He was strong again, could survive without feeding for weeks if necessary, and only enjoyed a nightly taste in the way mortals might savor a nightcap. He was restless, eager to construct a new existence and find adventures in which his wisdom might play a part. But without the guidance of an adept he would be clumsy and obvious. He'd make mistakes, draw attention to himself and unwittingly fall into hands that would delight in destroying him.

There had always been adepts, mortals gifted with an awareness of vampires and the countless other figures who exist outside the narrow band of routine human consciousness. And in every age some humans would become hunters, tracking and trying to kill vampires and also adepts, whom they called "witches," invariably killing only innocent scapegoats - impoverished, ignorant and often ill people too helpless to fight back. But adepts throughout time had seen value in liaisons with the undead, and had offered protection in exchange for particular gifts. That was the pact between vampire and adept human, a covenant reflected in secret rituals and in open symbols so common as to go unnoticed. Except to those who understood their meanings.

He had not been surprised to see the Eye of Horus and the capless pyramid on American dollar bills. Adepts were frequently leaders in government and commerce. Those in government had left messages in plain sight on currency in use since, he calculated, just after the Civil War. A network was there, but he was still too clumsy to access it and had always preferred to live apart from too many connections anyway. He enjoyed solitude, but after a long sleep he needed assistance. Clothes, language, the thousand cultural references that had accumulated since an old man pounded a stake through his heart – all these must be learned before he could slip safely into a new life.

An adept could guide him, and there was one nearby, the woman with the telling tattoo on her shoulder who'd seen him at The Willows and must have recognized him for what he was. But she was behaving strangely, refusing to acknowledge their bond. She seemed afraid, a quality not characteristic of adepts. They were sensitive and easily bored, but not fearful. He wondered if he'd failed to observe some new courtesy of which he was unaware, and offended her. But surely she would recognize white roses, the ancient symbol for the calm silence with which those who share secrets confront the world. He had seen the symbol on her shoulder. He knew what to do.

*

Danni awoke the following morning to Vicki at the door of her cottage, holding a bouquet of twenty-four long-stemmed white roses in a crystal vase.

"These were just delivered from a florist in Baton Rouge," she told Danni. "They're gorgeous! So what's going on? Surely your cat carver didn't..."

"Those are for me?" Danni asked, still half-asleep. "It's got to be a mistake. There's nobody who would... I mean, I don't get it."

"How about you look at the card," Vicky suggested while settling a filter in the coffee maker. "And if they're not for you, I'm keeping them!"

Danni pulled the tiny envelope from its ribbon and removed a plain white card.

Est alba flos Veneris cujus quo furta laterent was written on the card in a flowing calligraphic script.

"It's in Latin," she said. "Something about a blossom and silence, or secrecy. I haven't studied Latin since high school, but I'm sure these weren't meant for me."

"Then why did the florist's delivery guy say, 'Delivery for Danielle Telfer'? You must have made quite an impression on cat man up at the prison yesterday. It wouldn't have been easy for him to manage this, you know. So tell me everything!"

Danni shoved two croissants into the toaster oven and shook her head. "It's not that guy, not Antoine. I mean surely prisoners don't send flowers, do they?"

"Only if they've got somebody on the outside to do it for them, somebody with money. Does he speak Latin?"

The toaster oven dinged and Danni opened the glass door, inhaling a scent of warm butter. "Nobody speaks Latin," she said. "But hey, I'm going to be in Baton Rouge all day doing some research at the state library. You keep the roses today and I'll get them when I come back. They'll look great on your dining room table for the 3:00 house tour and then tonight I'll pretend to have a wealthy lover who sends passionate love notes in languages I can't read. He's royalty, of course. A count or something."

"Deal," Vicki agreed while pouring coffee and nibbling a croissant. "But since you're going to be in town anyway, why not check with the florist and see who sent them? The address is on the little envelope."

"If I have time," Danni said, admiring the profusion of creamy white blooms. "They do sort of suggest silence, don't they?"

"Well, they're not talking," Vicki replied, draining her coffee and carefully lifting the vase with both hands. "See you later!"

Danni felt isolated in the air-conditioned car as she drove toward Baton Rouge. People, dogs, flocks of birds appeared in her periphery, each seeming to pursue a sensible purpose. Not one of them, she was sure, had received mysterious roses accompanied by undecipherable messages that morning. None made a living excavating fragments of forgotten lives, and none saw dreams while they were awake. The people, dogs and birds were real; she was anomalous and inauthentic, unclear about what she was. For distraction she turned on the radio and listened to a report on agricultural commodity price indexes, idly wondering what "perique tobacco" was.

After parking near the Louisiana State Library on North 4th Street, she straightened her shoulders and assumed the mantle of her profession. She was a historian and a damn good researcher. So what if she lacked the focus of a turkey vulture? Focus was overrated.

The plan for the day was simply to identify documents she would use in reconstructing the world in which the vampire quilt was made. But as usual, the minute she opened the door to the past, she was drawn in.

A local 1850's magazine called *The Parlor* provided a glimpse into the strangely desperate intellectualism of educated women before the Civil War. They wrote of art and philosophy in language strangled by the need to conflate broad ideas with narrow religious ones and a "morality" only available to the wealthy.

In *Affleck's Southern Rural Almanac and Plantation and Garden Calendar* she read grisly descriptions of death from "diorrhea" in full-page ads for patent medicines. Yellow fever, bilious fever, a vast compendium of fevers routinely afflicted people who lived in brutal heat with poor sewage disposal, swarms of insects and no screens. The South seemed poisonous, a sort of hell, and yet a fervent romanticism accompanied even the most horrific acknowledgments of discomfort, disease and death. There was an allure, a sense of lush beauty that attracted and held the hearts of these long-dead Southerners.

Danni spent nearly an hour tracking down a song called *La Belle Louisianaise Valse,* then felt tears as she listened to a scratchy 1918 recording of it through a headset. A French composer and graduate of the Royal Academy of Music in Paris named Henri Fourrier had written it in 1859, before the Civil War. The song had been popular, played at dances and sung by traveling theatrical troupes. The French lyrics were simple, the music so evocative of place that for a moment Danni felt the devastation of the war personally. A sweet, sad song.

Had the maker of the quilt she was researching sung it while stitching a tiny vampire on cotton muslin? The woman's name was Neecie and she stitched the quilt in 1863, only four years after the song was published. Danni thought Neecie would have heard the song, sung it to herself as she documented in fabric the story of her husband's bravery minutes before his death. According to Sarah Reeves a husband named Joe, who was a slave and killed a vampire.

At the resources desk, a college kid with what appeared to be a mature salmon tattooed on his forearm took her five dollars and burned a CD of the song. She could play it in the car and later put it on her iPod. *La Belle Louisianaise Valse* would be the soundtrack for the quilt project! It made her feel grounded.

After a break for lunch in a coffee shop near the library, Danni disciplined herself to stop randomly reading period material. She needed to focus on documents specific to the plantation called Angola. Documents that might mention a slave couple named Joe and Neecie. A reference librarian suggested a collection of letters between a young woman named Mary Laura Butler and her mother-in-law, Lucinda Butler. The younger woman, the librarian recalled, had visited a nearby plantation called The Willows for a wedding during the Civil War. She had written exhaustively about the event in a letter to Lucinda.

"I don't know when I have passed a time more pleasantly," Mary Laura wrote, "as The Willows provides sufficient variety to give constant interest. Not only were the wedding festivities delightful and the many guests charming, but even the house servants provided entertainment with their quaint ways. I found one of them placing little crosses made of twigs at all the windows and doors to the room John and I shared with a prowling gray cat. When I asked the purpose of this activity, the woman whispered that a 'loogaroo' was in the vicinity. When later I enquired of our hostess what a 'loogaroo' might be, she laughed and explained that many of the servants are only a few generations away from their heathen roots in Africa. They believe in all sorts of monsters and think one of these is stalking the plantation. Apparently it bites the necks of its victims and swallows their blood. John wears his pistol at all times and swears to protect me from 'loogaroos' and anything else lurking about, but I have no fear of servants' tales. One of the guests, an elegant Frenchman named Grimaud, told us that in New Orleans the servant classes hang garlands of garlic across windows and doors to drive away these imaginary beasts. He was quite amusing!"

Danni stared at the photocopied handwriting on her computer screen. *Grimaud.* The peculiar man at the pool had said his name was Grimaud. It must be a common surname in the area. There were French names everywhere. Still, it made her uneasy.

Or maybe it was just the headache she'd developed from reading a backlit screen for hours. Stretching, she decided to call it a day and go back to St. Francisville for a swim before dinner with Sarah Reeves, who was bringing a DVD of *Nosferatu*, the 1922 German version of Bram Stoker's *Dracula*. Sarah was going to decorate their roadside produce stand for Halloween and thought the movie would provide some ideas. Plus, she said, it was good research for the quilt project.

Beyond the glass doors of the air-conditioned library Danni quickly wilted in air that felt like hot soup. She'd worn a lacy tank under a silk big shirt and pulled off the overshirt before she reached her car. In its pocket she felt a stiff paper rectangle and remembered what it was. The card from the roses. She entered the florist's address in the car's GPS and saw that it was downtown, not far from the library. It seemed silly, but Vicki would be sure to ask. She followed the teacherish voice in the GPS to a florist called Heroman's and showed the card to a woman arranging gerbera daisies at the counter.

"Oh, I heard about that one!" the woman said. "I don't come in till ten, but that guy had everybody hoppin' at eight, when we open. Had to pull extra roses from one of our other stores, and we *don't* deliver clear out to St. Francisville, but he was willin' to pay the extra, in cash. Wanted immediate delivery. Some lucky girl at a B&B out there got a nice surprise, I'd say."

"I'm that girl," Danni said. "And the roses are lovely, but I have no idea who sent them. See? The card's in Latin and there's no name. Could you please check your records and tell me who sent them?"

"No problem Miz... did you tell me your name?"

"Danni. Danielle Telfer. Here's my driver's license. Thanks so much for checking."

"Okay then, Miz Danni," the woman said, "let's see here. Ah. Two dozen long stems, white, premium vase, paid cash. Here's his signature."

Danni looked at the name in the same stylized script as the words on the card. "Louis-Jacques Daguerre."

"Probably a Cajun," the woman said. "You know who he is?"

"I do," Danni replied, smiling. "Thanks again."

Louis-Jacques Daguerre, the inventor of the daguerreotype, died in the middle of the 19th century. Danni was confident that he hadn't sent her any roses. Somebody was playing a game and it could only be Antoine Dupre, the cat-carving murderer who said he was innocent. They all probably said that, and the thought of him made her feel soiled. She should never have gone to visit him, never listened to his story. He was a killer and she'd actually sat around in a prison visiting room for hours talking with him. She'd believed him, *liked* him. And now he had an accomplice somewhere sending her expensive gifts. It made her uncomfortable, and it would end *now*.

"I think the roses are from Dupre, the prisoner," Danni told Vicki Stewart when she returned. The bill was signed 'Louis-Jacques Daguerre.' Funny, huh?"

"The guy who invented daguerreotypes," Vicki said. "But there could be somebody around here with that name. It could be legitimate. And what makes you think it's Dupre? Did the two of you talk about photography or something?"

"No," Danni answered, "but who else can it be? I really don't like this. I'm going to send him an email telling him if he pulls any more of these pranks I'll contact the prison authorities."

Vicki scowled. "Take it easy with that," she said. "You don't know for sure that he's responsible. His emails are read before he gets them and if you accuse him of harassing you he'll be subject to an investigation. He could lose his job and his trusty status, be moved to a cell, who knows what else. All because you *think* he sent you flowers. This is not making sense."

Danni glanced at the roses gleaming white on Vicki's ancestral dining room table. They broadcast nothing but silence.

"You're right," she told Vicki. "I'm overreacting. But I will send an email politely *asking* if he had anything to do with this. I'm not going to visit him again and if you don't mind, the damn roses stay with you."

"Fine with me," Vicky replied, grinning. "My ex is dropping by tonight. Those roses will drive him nuts with curiosity. Think I'll put on the *Moonlight Sonata* and glance longingly at the phone every seven minutes."

"You're good!" Danni said.

"Lots of practice," was the reply.

In her cottage Danni composed a low-key email to Antoine Dupre.

"Going to be very busy with research now, but enjoyed meeting you and wish you the best. Afraid I'm allergic to roses.

Danni Telfer"

But when she hit "send" it felt as if she'd hurt a friend. It felt wrong.

Spending another thirty cents, she sent a second email "I'm confused. What do white roses mean?

Danni"

Dinner with Sarah Reeves was fun, but they gave up on *Nosferatu* after fifteen minutes of the cadaverous actor Max Schreck muttering in German.

"I thought I ordered the one with English subtitles," Sarah said. "But at least we got an idea of what Neecie's Joe killed that night. A scrawny guy in a coat with braid toggles down the front."

"Classic German coat because it's a German movie," Danni replied over a yawn. "But a Civil War vampire probably wore clothes like Lincoln."

Sarah yawned in return. "Good point, but I like that coat for my produce stand vampire. Hey, did you hear he's back? Our historical vampire, I mean. Something's chomping necks out at the prison, or at least that's what's going around. Warden's going to have a revival up there, if you can believe that. Just in time for Halloween. Every redneck Bible-beater for a hundred miles will be at Angola driving out a vampire. Girl, you are about to learn about the real South!"

"Revival?" Danni said. "At a prison?" Wendy and Ron had raised their adopted daughter amid the elaborate rituals of the Anglican Church, and she loved the music and candles and flowing robes. She'd even been an acolyte, worn a hooded white alb, carried torches and, when she was big enough, the heavy gold crucifix down the aisle on Sunday mornings. The church was beautiful and seemed to hold something wonderful behind its stories that never changed, but at thirteen she thought she'd heard the stories enough times. Surely there were different ones, weren't there?

Ron said there were and they spent a year reading about Jains and Hindus and going to Jewish and Buddhist services. Danni was fascinated by it all and couldn't understand why people killed each other over which one was best. As an adult she was still uneasy around rabid religionists, and the word "revival" sounded like something to avoid.

"Think of it as a cultural experience," Sarah said, laughing. "And it won't be the first at Angola, but they never had a vampire before. Fifteen bucks a head to get in and all the chili dogs you can eat. You can't miss it; we'll go together just for the music. Gospel choir up from New Orleans, they'll make you cry for mama while that conniving warden pockets a bundle. Corruption is a way of life here, but everybody enjoys it. Talk to you later, okay?"

Danni managed a shower before falling into bed as the nightly frog-and-cicada chorus filled the steamy dark outside. She couldn't say what woke her much later, just a sudden, uncomfortable awareness. Moving groggily beneath starched white sheets, she glanced at the digital clock glowing green beside the bed. 3:13. And then something covered the green numbers. A hand.

Abruptly, painfully awake, Danni heard herself gasp as she looked up into gold-flecked eyes that seemed to swirl and eddy like deep water in the gloom. Her heart, instead of accelerating, seemed to have slowed to a reverberating tympanic dirge that hurt her eyes and filled her mouth with a bitter taste. She wanted to move, get out of the bed, run to the door, but her fear was like paralysis. Her leg kicked slightly and one hand clutched the edge of a sheet, but she couldn't coordinate her movements. He was going to attack her, rape her, possibly kill her and she couldn't move!

"What the hell are you doing here?" she tried to yell through a throat locked in terror. The words came out as an indecipherable croak. It was the man named Grimaud, now an impenetrable shadow with swirling eyes, standing by her bed. When he bowed toward her, his darkness a dense threat like a thundercloud, she screamed but heard only a muted hum emerge from her mouth.

"You are frightened. I offer my apologies," he said thoughtfully. "But how is it that you cannot read white roses?"

CHAPTER FOURTEEN

Chaztu, chatzu, Grimaud sang, *amets bat bakarrik ikusten duzun.* "Forget, forget, you see only a dream." He knew the song of forgetfulness could not completely erase the vision of an adept, but would give the woman time to adjust as the skin of blindness peeled away. It seemed that she had no awareness of her gift. No one had provided instruction; she was trapped inside the hair-fine reality of her time. He wondered why no parent or relative had explained the gift and how to protect it in secrecy. Adepts occurred in families. Where was hers?

Her eyelids trembled, signaling the trance-like half-sleep induced by his song. She would wake to a world at once familiar and peculiar, as an ancient legacy stretched and breathed in her mind. He considered her name, "Telfer." It had been a nickname in long ago France, *Taillefer,* that meant "cut iron." A man with strength sufficient to force his sword through an opponent's armor would be given the name. Grimaud hoped Danni Telfer had inherited an inner strength to match her name. She was going to need it.

Argi, he chanted softly, became a coin of pulsing blue light and slipped through the locked door of the cottage. A mother possum with seven babies in her pouch saw the blue light as she pursued a garter snake through the monkey grass, but the light meant nothing to her.

In his bunk Antoine awakened suddenly. The dorm was quiet except for the drone of the ceiling fans. No one was snoring, a dead giveaway that no one was sleeping. Fifty-nine men lay unnaturally still in narrow beds, waiting for something. Antoine didn't move even though his pillow was wet and stank of blood. They were waiting to see what he would do, how he would react to the symbolic message, which simply meant, "You will die."

Without opening his eyes, Antoine slowly turned away from the smell, forced his breathing to maintain the slow, even pace of sleep and allowed one arm to flop from the side of his bunk. His chest hurt and his teeth were clenched so tightly he couldn't swallow, but it was necessary to appear oblivious. He knew that before being escorted to an isolation cell, Hoyt Planchard had told his little band of misfits to begin the campaign of small tortures that was his trademark. Antoine expected it and was not surprised at the blood, but Timer had taught him well. He would show no response.

Nor was he surprised that no one had warned him, wakened him in time to catch Perry Bordelon or another of Planchard's goons slopping gore on his pillow. The prison grapevine is efficient. Within an hour of Antoine's meeting with Dwight Tilly, word was all over the Big Yard that Monk Dupre had his nose so far up the warden's ass you could see shit on his shirt collar. Monk had sold out, gone to work for the enemy. It was a gross violation of the Code, even among prisoners who had no respect for codes. Collusion with guards or wardens would result in a form of shunning even more virulent than that of extreme religious sects. A wall of indifferent silence would surround Antoine now, even if he were screaming and hemorrhaging through the eyes. He'd known that when he cut the deal with Tilly to write suggestive press releases about vampires in exchange for Lamar Sellers' transfer out of Angola.

But he didn't care about shunning or the Code or any of the million delicate and deadly rules that governed life in prison. In the sweltering dark he cared for one thing only, the thing whose blood might be drying on his pillow. Bastet! He was sure Planchard told his goons to gut the cat and put the ruined little body in Antoine's bunk. Perry Bordelon would have delighted in the task, although Antoine doubted that Bordelon had sufficient wits to catch a cat, especially Bastet.

Moving as if in sleep, he felt with his shoulders and back for the small lump that would be a dead gray cat. His skin felt nothing but rumpled sheets. Still, there was blood. Antoine felt something break inside, not just in his mind but throughout his body. He felt his heart slow as a certainty formed where before there had been confusion. The certainty was cool and solid, devoid of question.

If the blood on his pillow was Bastet's, he would kill both Hoyt Planchard and whichever among Planchard's goons had stalked and killed her. Almost certainly Perry Bordelon, but Antoine would have to know for sure. Then he would wait, and plan, lay a trap and spring it. Not right away, but later when everyone had forgotten the soft gray cat who once lived in the law library. It might take years. Antoine would wait. He had become a killer, and the knowledge was not uncomfortable. It was simply a fact.

His breathing remained deep and even as he lay awake all night, waiting.

In the morning he showed no interest in the bloody pillow. "Nosebleed," he muttered to the few who mentioned the now-dried gore. "Fuckin' heat." Nobody questioned the nonexistent relationship between heat and nosebleeds, but everyone heard. They saw that Monk was playing along with the game and obviously had an agenda. In a place where nothing ever changed, the unfolding drama was like a drug.

Antoine showered, dressed and then took his time walking to the law library. He expected to see something unspeakable when he got there, and was prepared. He would show no emotion because he felt none. There was nothing inside him now but a flat, featureless landscape across which he would move until a future time. A time at which he would efficiently kill two men. Perhaps it would feel good, although he doubted that it would. Nonetheless, it was right. It was all he had left.

The law library was empty and dark, the inmate counsels who would work there all day still at breakfast. There was no Styrofoam container, no stick-out breakfast on his desk and he knew why. No one wanted to find what everyone assumed would be there. They were lazy, illiterate, impulsive and trapped in an environment in which violence was the common language, but few prisoners were sadistic. They recoiled from seeing what Hoyt Planchard had almost certainly arranged for the eyes of Monk Dupre.

Antoine switched on the overhead lights, then approached his little office in a closet. His desk was in disarray, the lamp overturned, papers and books torn and knocked to the floor. A battle had been fought there. Righting the desk lamp and turning it on, he saw splatters of blood, smears of it, and paw prints. The bloody prints crossed his desk to the carved figure that stood with its back to the wall. His favorite among the carved cats, its wooden eyes betrayed nothing when he saw blood on the cypress paws, the cypress mouth. The scene made no sense, but the paw prints made an acid impression on the still terrain in his mind. And then he heard a sound. Mewing.

"Bastet?" he nearly sobbed, searching the floor, the bookcases and finally the closed file drawer from which a gray cat leapt into his arms. She was safe, intact, unbroken, and Antoine fell into his chair with a guttural cry that made him blind until tears slowly restored his vision. He felt weightless then, and tore one hand from warm gray fur to grasp the chair arm. He was afraid he'd float, drift up and up until he hung above the buildings, the razor wire, the guard towers. He was afraid he'd float so high that he'd vaporize, unless the guards in the towers shot him first. He thought they would, and that he'd vanish like a cloud when the rounds hit. He gripped the chair and held himself down while the flat, clear landscape of the night before shattered and fell inside him like broken glass.

Bastet was alive, unharmed. Antoine Dupre did not have to kill.

At least not yet. He stared at the wooden statue on his desk. Clotted blood hung in ropes from the carved feline mouth, and all four paws dripped red where claws would be, if he'd carved claws. Bastet pressed her face against his chest as he struggled to find himself where a man perfectly capable of murder had recently been. He was still light-headed, but able to think. Either a wooden statue of a cat had attacked an intruder and saved Bastet, or someone was playing tricks. He found either scenario both acceptable and irrelevant. What mattered was that Bastet was alive, and that he had a chance to rescue a man who didn't kill. That man was himself, and he could bring the same implacable determination to his own survival as the certainty with which he'd known he would kill two men. But he needed a plan, and there would be very little time.

With Bastet tucked inside his shirt, he headed up the Walk to the mess hall. A blanket of silence fell across the normally noisy room as a thousand eyes failed to meet his.

"Need a wet rag," he yelled at one of the hairnetted men working the steam table. "Got a little mess in the office."

Every fork, water glass and coffee cup froze at his words. The security officers who stood along the walls straightened uneasily and let their hands fall to cell phones clipped to their duty belts. Several made calls as Antoine scanned the room for Perry Bordelon, found him and walked toward the table where Hoyt Planchard's chair was obsequiously empty. Bordelon's face and neck were crosshatched with deep scratches, one eye reduced to pulp and swollen shut.

Five security officers were running toward Antoine, yelling, "Back down, Dupre! Move away!"

Antoine smiled at Bordelon and unbuttoned his shirt, pulling out a gray cat. He barely had time to say, "Cut yourself shaving, did you, Perry?" before the room erupted in the regular, deafening sound of plastic cups, glasses and plates pounding on tables. They couldn't cheer; Antoine had violated The Code and was no longer one of them. But

they could make noise, and several couldn't mask smiles as
Antoine walked the length of the room with Bastet on his
shoulder. The racket made a ground for him, a platform
from which he could do what he had to do. He had to
protect Bastet and he had to save himself. The rhythmic
crash of tableware told him he might just succeed.

But he would need help.

Back in his office he saw two emails on his desk, pulled
from the dorm kiosk and printed. They were from Danni and
they made no sense. In the first she blew him off, saying
she was busy and wished him the best, followed by
something about roses. Then she'd sent a second
message minutes later saying, "I'm confused. What do
white roses mean?" He had no idea what she was talking
about, and wondered if she'd sent the messages to the
wrong address. But twice?

He stroked Bastet and felt the responding purr. He had
to do something, to protect Bastet, immediately. Whatever
had happened during the night could not be relied upon to
happen again. Danni told him she was staying at a place in
St. Francisville called Plantation Bed and Breakfast. There
were old phone books under most of the law library
bookcases, used as shims to keep them from toppling under
the weight of heavy law books. The local directory,
containing numbers for several villages lining the river on
both sides, was just the right thickness. Antoine leaned
hard against the nearest bookcase and kicked a phone
book from under its corner. The Plantation Bed and
Breakfast had been in business long enough to be listed in
a fifteen-year-old directory. Carrying Bastet again under his
shirt, Antoine sprinted toward the dorm and its pay phone.

Deserted, the building smelled of sweat and laundry
starch, but absent the men who filled its stifling night air with
stories, it might have been a black and white photograph. It
seemed two-dimensional, uninteresting. Antoine went to the
phone on a wall of the TV room and dialed the number for

the Plantation Bed and Breakfast. The system clicked on when a woman's voice answered. "Plantation B&B, this is Vicki Stewart. How may I help you?"

"This call is from an inmate in a Louisiana correctional facility," recited a taped female voice. "The inmate's name is…"

"Antoine Dupre," he pronounced, triggering the rest of the message.

"If you wish calls from this inmate permanently blocked, push 6. If you will accept charges, push 5."

Vicki Stewart did not hesitate to push 5. "This is highly irregular," she told Antoine. "I've been around here long enough to know that. What is it you want?"

Antoine's hands were slick with sweat. He had to get this right, but he hadn't talked to a free person in so long he'd forgotten how. "Thank you for accepting the call," he said. "I'll pay for it; I'll get the money to you. Just thank you. Would you let me speak to Danni Telfer, please? She's a guest."

"I know she's a guest and I know who you are," Vicki replied. "I also know this call will be terminated automatically before I'd have time to get her to the phone. You'd better give me a message."

Antoine sensed no judgment in the woman's voice, nor any prurient interest. Just a willingness to carry a message. He took a deep breath.

"I need Danni's help," he began. "I need her to come visit me today, and I need her to take my cat."

"What?" Vicki said.

Antoine couldn't imagine the words that might convey his desperation.

"Please," he said, trying to sound calm, "they're going to kill my cat. Bastet, that's her name. They already tried, last night. I've got to get her out of here. I have no one else to ask."

Vicki had lived near Angola most of her life, attended church with a few prison officials, knew their wives. She'd heard the stories drifting like tendrils of smoke from the swamp-locked fortress where this man carved wooden cats. One of these cats, the harlequin-patterned gift she'd bought for her daughter-in-law, regarded her from a wicker table. In the hazy morning light the elegant feline head seemed to nod.

"I'll give Ms. Telfer the message," she said.

Danni was nursing her third cup of coffee when she saw Vicki in white capris and a blue silk top, walking thoughtfully toward her cottage. Still in pajamas, Danni felt remiss. She should have left for the state library an hour ago, but something was wrong. She'd awakened with a dizzy feeling she remembered from childhood, the feeling she had in the fabric shop where no one knew a young woman had been buried alive in the walls. And that Ford dealership with its invisible pinballs of outrage careening across an acre of asphalt above the remains of a Mohican village.

The dizziness was like double vision somehow, like seeing the same thing two different ways. It was as if some things were layered, and she could see both layers at the same time, or at least *feel* the hidden layer. It had been this way when she was a child and Wendy had taught her to focus her attention on songs or puzzles instead of the "other" things. When she grew older, it didn't happen so much. Now it was back. She watched Vicki's approach and saw no double image, no hidden story. It was comforting.

"You look a little peaked," Vicki said when Danni opened the door and poured her friend the last cup of coffee. "Working too hard?"

"I don't know," Danni admitted. "Maybe the heat."

"Ever find out who sent the roses?"

Danni shook her head. She knew the man named Grimaud had sent them, but she didn't know how she knew.

And while the knowledge made her uneasy, it also felt interesting, like a new book in a bookstore. A book with an unusual cover. A book that nobody was talking about, buried among remaindered cookbooks on an ill-lit table. A book you buy and read alone on a rainy afternoon in a coffee shop with your cell phone turned off.

"I don't think it was Antoine," she said. "It had to be somebody else."

"Well, Antoine just called," Vicki said, "and I'm here to give you his message. He wants you to go up to the prison today. He wants you to take his cat."

"Take his cat?" Danni said.

"He says the cat will be killed if he doesn't get it out of Angola. He said you're the only person he could ask."

Danni wrapped her arms across her chest and rocked softly. The request was bizarre but eerily familiar. At five she'd wanted to save the unicorn locked in a medieval tapestry. She'd been trying to save it in a series of men who turned out to be nothing like the unicorn. This, on the other hand, was real. For the first time, maybe she could actually save something.

"I'll go get the cat," she told Vicki.

"Could always use another mouser around here," Vicki agreed as the shadow of a cloud created the fleeting illusion of chill.

CHAPTER FIFTEEN

The odd feeling hadn't dissipated by the time Danni left for Angola. The road was the same but felt different, familiar, as if driving to a prison in the middle of nowhere to pick up a cat were routine. As if she'd traveled this isolated little scrap of Louisiana for years. As if she belonged. A skyline of trees seemed to relax as she drove, like the shoulders of a stretching dragon.

An overweight man in faded jeans walked beside the road, carrying a child's green plastic bucket covered with a plastic bag. The whites of his eyes were yellow as he watched her pass, and for a second she smelled woodsmoke and the crackling flesh of an animal. The word "possum" emerged in her mind despite the fact that she'd never had occasion to pronounce it. She wasn't sure she could identify a possum in a lineup, but somehow she was sure the man had part of one in his bucket and was going to cook it. The information was neutral, as much a feature of the landscape as kudzu. It meant nothing, and yet her awareness of it made her uneasy. The culinary habits of a stranger on a road did not involve her, were not hers to imagine. But her mind seemed to be practicing some skill it enjoyed, and continued to scan the terrain for items of interest.

At the edge of the convenience store parking lot around a curve before the prison gate, an ancient black woman wearing flip flops and a tattered blue track suit stood smoking a cigarette. She didn't look at Danni, didn't see her car or recognize the movement of air caused by its passing. There was no connection between them, but Danni sensed a delicate power in the woman's gaunt hands. A scent of vinegar tempered by garlic, lavender and other herbs moved in the air-conditioned car and then was gone, leaving Danni to wonder why the woman made her think of salad dressing. And then two words leapt out from the babble on the radio to which she'd paid no attention – "four thieves." It made no sense but had something to do with the woman in the blue track suit. Danni shook her head and focused on the long curve that straightened to end at the single gate to Angola.

Vicki had given her a tote bag for the cat, an item not on the list of things visitors were allowed to take into the prison. Danni took the tote bag back to her car and had to go through the dog booth a second time before boarding a blue bus for the visiting room.

Antoine was waiting in the holding pen adjacent to the lobby when she arrived, sitting on a bench with five other prisoners. A large sign on the bars warned, "No talking to inmates," so she merely nodded to him, afraid even to smile. He was holding a gray cat that everyone, the guards and the other prisoners, assiduously ignored. A thick, edgy pall hung in the air. She was walking into a play again, a drama cloaked in obscurity. Invisible swirls of darkness moved in the dim air of the prison lobby like slender, toothed fish. She was walking into danger, and a part of her mind turned to flee.

It was the part she had learned, the part that drew maps to acceptance, to safety. This prison and this prisoner belonged to a world with no connection to her own. A bleak world of ignorance, boredom and cruelty rightfully hidden far from good, normal people, according to every impression available to her over the twenty-eight years she'd been alive. She had no reason to be there. Her presence was some kind of mistake.

But another Danni, nascent and straining to breathe, would not turn. She didn't know why, but she allowed the guard to usher her through the two barred doors to the visiting room. When Antoine approached from his own barred door, carrying a cat, she waited for whatever would happen next.

His gray eyes betrayed nothing as he sat beside her at the same table they'd shared before, but suddenly she could see the man behind the guarded eyes, the animating decency and strength of him. It was as if his skeleton were visible and glowing. A grounded, intelligent soul unaccountably caged with the dangerously ignorant, he nonetheless exuded the sort of spirit she associated with great music. Handel, Bach, Beethoven.

It occurred to her that all the men she'd wanted to help or protect or whatever it was, had been mere rehearsals. Years of freezing on football bleachers, feigning interest in vintage cars, micro brewed beer and obscure rock groups, typing term papers, *writing* term papers, all the way to a disastrous relationship with her department chair, had been preparation for the moment in which her efforts might actually matter. This moment. The thought was crazy, baseless. She hardly knew Antoine Dupre: their situation lacked every facet of rationality. And rescuing a cat was scarcely heroic. Still, the feeling was there.

"Are you all right?" he asked, still holding the cat softly against his chest, watching her with those gray eyes.

She regarded the dark curls, the copper skin and carved lips and tried to imagine kissing him. The idea held no interest even though that had always been part of the deal, that gift of herself meant to demonstrate the strength of her presence, her intent to *save* the man from some something. The first had been a boy running from an abusive father, dulling his pain with drugs. Then an Iraq vet with PTSD followed by a miserable seminary student afraid to admit that he didn't believe a word of the doctrines he was training to represent. And finally an aging historian struggling to maintain an academic reputation that now seemed ridiculous.

"Yes, I'm all right," she said. "Tell me how I can help you."

Antoine thought he must seem an automaton, so frozen did he feel as he fought back an awareness that this woman had come out of nowhere to help him. He wanted to offer her his life in exchange for her presence. Instead, he handed her the cat.

"Thank you for saving Bastet," he began, his voice breaking at the openness in her eyes. He let his hand touch hers in the transfer of warm grey fur. She wrapped her fingers through his and pulled his hand to her side, under the cat. He could feel the two heartbeats, cat and woman, one small and one that filled the room, his mind, the sky. It wasn't erotic, but something more, an assurance that he wasn't alone.

"I... I don't know how to thank you," he said. "I need your help." The words settled in his gut, a dead weight.

Danni noticed a guard scowling at Antoine's extended arm, and pushed his hand away.

"It's no problem; I want to help," she told him. "And I don't want you to get the wrong idea, but something's happening to me. It started... it really had nothing to do with you at the beginning. I feel strange, like I keep wandering in and out of plays where I have no part. But this one, you... I have a part. I'll take your cat out of here now, at the end of the first act, but that's only the beginning. What's my part in this, Antoine?"

He stretched and arched his head back, looking at the louvered windows through which hazy yellow sunlight struggled to fill the room. "I have no right to ask you for anything," he said.

"That's true," Danni replied, "but you're not asking; I am. *I* have the right. And I may fail. That's likely. But I'm asking. What's my part?"

A single shaft of sunlight fell momentarily across the table, her hands, the cat, and Antoine felt its warmth like a breeze from a suddenly open door. She was real, she was serious.

"I have to get out of this place before I'm killed or I have to kill," he said. "A man named Hoyt Planchard is responsible for Timer's death. It was catch-back, retribution, for my refusal to let him become an inmate counsel. He's... he's the reason there must always be prisons, Danni. Smart enough to con everybody, but a sadist and a coward. He's in lockdown right now, but he has a gang of losers who obey his orders. One of them tried to kill Bastet last night, then dumped blood on my pillow as I slept."

Danni felt a hint of bile at the back of her throat. Nausea. The events being described were both childish and diseased. "You said one of them, one of these losers, tried to kill Bastet. What saved her? And where did the blood on your pillow come from?"

"Oh, I'm sure the blood came from the kitchen," he said and then cocked his head. "As to Bastet's protector, either somebody's playing jokes, or last night one of my carved cats ripped the face off a dirtbag, one of Planchard's gang named Perry Bordelon. The carving has blood on its paws and mouth, and Bordelon looks like he tried to kiss a jet turbine. I think he lost an eye. Weird, huh?"

Danni heard herself creating rational scenarios. A practical joke. Or Bastet actually attacked Bordelon while defending herself and then touched the carving with her bloody paws. Wooden carvings didn't move.

But the new Danni, bored with rationalizations, accepted the unacceptable. If it happened, then it *could* happen. It happened in some realm close to this one, but not this one. Another place, concurrent but invisible except in brief flashes. Like a wooden cat leaping to shred the face of a man trying to kill a real cat. Danni thought she'd known about that other world for a long time. It was there and it didn't frighten her.

"These things happen," she told Antoine. "There's no explanation; they just do. What's important is that Bastet is unharmed and I'll take her to a place where she can live safely. I can rescue a cat, but what about you? How can I help you?"

Antoine felt the clash of conflicting emotions as he prepared to answer her. Hope rose in him like a gust of air, but hit a wall of jagged impossibility.

"I need somebody on the outside who can find out who really killed the man I was convicted of beating to death," he said.

The weight of his words hung suspended between them. She was certain that he was innocent, but uncertain about her fitness for so crucial a task. "Okay," she replied, smiling to lighten the moment. Her head felt airy and twice its normal size. "I'm an out-of-work history professor here to write an article about a quilt. Of course I can solve a murder on the side. Are we both *crazy*?"

"You may be," Antoine said, laughing. "I think that's a strong possibility, but thanks. I need ..."

"Why did you say you have to kill or be killed?" she interrupted. "If this Planchard guy killed Timer, wouldn't there be an investigation? Surely you just can't *kill* people, even in prison."

"I don't expect you to understand," he said. "No one who hasn't lived or worked in a prison could possibly understand. It's a different world."

"I'm beginning to think I have a certain facility with 'different worlds,'" she said. "Tell me."

When he finished she merely nodded. The society he described was simply male, a rigidly hierarchical structure of status, intrigue, battles and codes of honor. Tennyson's Galahad, she thought, would be entirely comfortable in a prison. Tennyson's Galahad would also not hesitate to run his gleaming sword through Hoyt Planchard. Antoine was not a fictional knight in the service of a mythical king, but a man nonetheless trapped by the same ancient code.

"I understand," she told him. "But what about you? What happened?"

Hurriedly he told the story again. Annabeth's cancer. His grief-maddened determination to complete her dissertation on his own family, descended from a French plantation owner and his mistress, a slave from Barbados named Mansi. The original Antoine Dupre had freed his mistress and their children and left her the plantation when he died, Antoine explained with a mixture of pride and chagrin. Mansi Dupre had succeeded well enough to get her children out of the South, but she had bought and sold slaves in the process.

"You never think of black people owning slaves," Danni said.

"Well, they did," Antoine answered. "My great-great-grandmother did, and Annabeth wanted to write her dissertation and then a book about it, but then she died. I was crazy, Danni. I thought finishing her work would keep her alive somehow."

"So how does finishing Annabeth's work land you in here?" she asked.

He shook his head. "To be honest, I don't know. I don't remember. There was a man at the courthouse where I was looking for some records, a clerk named John Thierry. One of those impossible little people who enjoy wielding petty tyrannies over others. He refused to let me see the notarial books from the 1840's, claiming that the material was too fragile for public use. I explained my university credentials and said I was quite accustomed to archival research protocols. I said I'd be happy to wear gloves and a mask, that I had them in a pocket, despite the fact that I knew the records were rotting in the moldy courthouse basement because I'd already been there and seen others. He refused, adding that he couldn't imagine what I was up to, but it wasn't going to happen in *his* office."

"So you killed him," Danni said, nervously trying for a joke that wasn't funny. "I've often wanted to do the same with people like that! Justifiable, I'd say. So what happened next?"

Antoine stared into the table. "I went to lunch at a diner across from the courthouse – The Palace Café. I admit I was angry, but when Thierry came in I went to talk to him. I thought if I told him about my wife, about Annabeth, he'd loosen up, but he didn't. What he said was, "Get lost."

"Not a courteous guy," Danni said, exhaling. "So who killed him?"

"Not me," Antoine answered. "What I did was walk outside where I'm not sure what I planned to do. He'd left right before I did but I didn't see him anywhere on the street. I hadn't been in a fight since seventh grade but I wasn't thinking straight back then. It was so insufferably hot; I wasn't used to that. I hadn't been sleeping, eating right, nothing. I just wanted to do this for Annabeth, this crazy thing, and it felt like Thierry was killing her all over again."

"So?" Danni asked. "What happened next?"

Antoine took a deep, shuddering sigh. "I went outside and sat on a bench, looking for him. I don't know what I would have done, probably just tried to talk to him again, but as it turned out I did nothing. I heard a sound, a man's voice although I couldn't hear what was said, coming from a little passageway between the café and the building next to it. I guess I thought maybe it was Thierry, wanting me to fight, so I stood up and followed the sound. It was dark in there even at noon, just a narrow space between two buildings."

He looked pointedly at Danni. "I saw a man, I'm sure it was a man, come at Thierry from the back of the passageway. He hit Thierry on the head with something, hit him hard. Thierry fell and the man ran back behind the restaurant. There's a real alley there. It all happened so fast. I ran to Thierry, leaned over him. I saw a piece of pipe on the ground. There was so much blood, it just kept running out of his head. I could see his brain, bloody hair sticking to his brain, and there was bone."

Danni saw her own hands holding Bastet, the bones motionless beneath freckled skin.

Antoine continued. "Before Annabeth died she got so thin I could see her bones, see her skull under these ridiculous hats she'd wear because her hair had fallen out. Seeing Thierry's skull, that broken bone, froze me. I couldn't move. And then the people from the café came out. The waitress, screaming, then others. They saw me standing there over Thierry. After that I don't remember much, except that I didn't care what happened. I was dead, Danni. For a long time."

The part of her mind that wanted to run, now recoiled. There was too much pain in his story, too much loss. In her world such things could not occur. Criminals did these things, denizens of a netherworld she would never see. Except she was seeing it. She was *in* it, the last outpost of that world. And she had a part to play.

"I'm so sorry about your wife, about Annabeth," she said. "But right now I have to think. Why did the patrons of the restaurant come out then? Did Thierry yell when the man hit him? Did they hear and come running out?"

Antoine recreated the scene in his mind. "No," he said. "It happened so fast. Thierry didn't make a sound."

"But maybe somebody followed Thierry and then you out to see if there would be a fight. You said the waitress came out first, so maybe she saw something. How many people were in the restaurant?"

"Five," Antoine said. "I remember from the trial. They had to testify, tell what they saw. I don't remember all their names. They'll be in the trial record, though. You can get a copy of it at the Opelousas Courthouse. Ask for 'State of Louisiana vs. Antoine Philippe Dupre.' The docket number is V-20096. Ten years ago, August."

With nothing to write on, Danni repeated the information, memorizing it.

His grey eyes suddenly focused. "There's something else," he said. "A man named Eugene LeBlanc died recently in the infirmary here. He asked to see me just before his death, said he needed to tell me about 'Jacques.' The cook at the Palace Café was named Jacques Boutte. I've learned that Eugene had a nephew named Jacques Boutte. I know it's a long shot, but I think they're the same man – the cook and Eugene's nephew. I didn't get there in time to hear whatever Eugene wanted to tell me. He was dead when I arrived."

Danni rubbed the back of her neck and stared at him, wide-eyed. The story seemed thin, devoid of detail, impossible. It couldn't have happened. And yet she was sitting in a prison with the man convicted of John Thierry's murder.

"I'm sorry, it's wrong to involve you," Antoine said, sensing her disbelief.

"I'm involving myself, so stop apologizing," she told him after inhaling deeply. "It's just... it doesn't make any sense."

"No, but if you can make sense of it...," he began, then shook his head. "Let's talk about something else for a minute, give you a little distance. So tell me about this quilt before I tell you where to look for the man who should be sitting here instead of me. I thought you were going to write about 'Cotton in Louisiana' or something."

Danni was happy to discuss something, anything, that didn't make her dizzy.

"The cotton thing didn't work out," she said, "but I lucked onto this fascinating quilt from the Civil War Era, made by a slave. It's a picture quilt, a story about a vampire..."

"Vampire?" he interrupted. "Must be an epidemic. You know there's supposedly one here. You've heard about the warden's 'Exorcise the Vampire!' revival? He's got me writing the press releases and promotional material."

She made a face. "You're kidding. I heard about it from a friend, Sarah Reeves, who owns the quilt. She says the revival will be worth seeing for the gospel music, but I can't believe you'd have anything to do with it. It's nonsense."

He scowled, creating a bronze dent in his forehead. "This is a prison, Danni. Do you imagine I had a choice?"

"Sorry," she said. "It just... it's so silly."

"I made a deal," Antoine said. "An innocent man with the mind of a six-year-old will be transferred to a facility where he'll have a chance at some happiness until with luck he can get a new trial."

Danni nodded, thinking. "How many innocent men are locked up in here?"

"Very few," he said, "almost none, if you mean 'innocence' in its larger sense. Some didn't commit the crime they're in for but did so many others that they hardly qualify as innocent."

"And then there's you," she said, veering back into the story of a murder in darkness, at noon, in a southern town she'd never heard of. "What happened? What am I supposed to find out?"

His answer was cut short when a security officer, a blonde woman on whom the uniform looked like a Halloween costume, approached the table.

"Can't have animals in here," she said. "I'll take that cat."

"Warden Tilly gave permission," Antoine said abruptly, long legs pushing his chair back. "Ms. Telfer is consulting on details of the revival, but will be leaving now."

The guard rolled her eyes. "You're telling me this cat has something to do with the revival?"

"Of course," Danni said, standing to take Bastet from Antoine's arms. "Surely you know there are no cats in the Bible. Very significant."

The guard seemed to consider the information, then nodded. "Well, there's no cats in here either. I'll escort you to the door."

"Shall I email you details as they fall in place?" Danni asked Antoine. "There's so much to do before the revival!"

"Yes, I need details for the promotional material," he answered. "Send everything."

Danni walked ahead of the guard toward the barred door where another guard watched, rattling keys on a long chain attached to his belt. She glanced professionally at her watch and showed no distress at the claws piercing her arm as Bastet strained over her shoulder to see Antoine a last time.

CHAPTER SIXTEEN

Vicki's car was gone when Danni returned, demolishing any hope of advice about what to do with a cat. The other guests appeared to be out as well, nobody around but the ducks. Danni carried Bastet into her cottage and poured some milk into a bowl, which she set on the kitchen floor. Bastet lapped the milk and then carefully licked one upraised paw.

"Will you be all right here if I run to the grocery for some cat food?" Danni said, focusing on pet necessities to avoid the weight of the impossible task to which she'd just agreed. She knew nothing about police work, had no idea where to start. The cat was inspecting the cottage, dashing behind furniture and batting at drapery fringe.

"And I suppose you'll need a litter box," Danni went on, mentally shelving an image of herself in a tweed cape and deerstalker hat like Sherlock Holmes. "I've never had a cat. Did Antoine have a litter box for you? I have no idea what I'm doing." The remark encompassed more than cat care.

Bastet walked to the door and meowed.

"I guess you need to go out," Danni said. "I'm glad you told me. I'll go with you, okay? Don't run away."

But the cat, moving like gray silk through the monkey grass outside the door, vanished in the direction of the woods.

"Damn," Danni breathed, and ran after her. "Bastet," she yelled, racing along the paved path beside the pool, past a cottage that looked like a windmill and then coming to a stop at the last cottage. It was called the Tree House for its proximity to the woods, and through its white fence Danni could see a three-level deck descending into a densely wooded ravine. On the bottom deck Bastet stretched luxuriously on a bench, her extended claws batting at an insect. Hadn't Vicki Stewart said the man named Grimaud was staying in the Tree House?

Danni remembered white roses and a nightmare in which Grimaud stood over her bed. Except the nightmare lacked that surreal quality in which time and space have no boundaries, in which a childhood schoolroom is revealed to have been a Victorian train station or a birdhouse. The man had simply been there, standing in the bedroom of her cottage. She'd been terrified, but her terror only bewildered him. He'd said something about the roses, hadn't he? She couldn't remember. It was just a dream anyway. And she needed access to his deck stairs in order to retrieve Bastet. Reluctantly, she knocked on his door.

There was no answer, no sound but a woodpecker's sharp drumming on a nearby tree. Danni had seen no car parked beside the cottage and wondered how he got around. She knocked again. Silence. He must be gone. Maybe he took cabs, except she wasn't sure there *were* cabs in tiny St. Francisville. Whatever, she had to get the cat.

Moving to the side of the cottage, she climbed over the railing to the first level of the deck and started down the wooden stairs, but stopped as a shadow fell over her own.

"I apologize," murmured a baritone voice behind her. "I must have been asleep and failed to hear your knock. May I inquire as to your errand?"

Danni turned, uneasy in a shadow that felt too dense, as if it had substance. She pointed to the lower deck. "My cat. Actually somebody else's cat, Antoine's. She's down there. I'm so sorry; I didn't realize you were here."

His hair was disheveled as if he'd been asleep and only hurriedly donned dark slacks and a blinding white dress shirt with French cuffs. The cufflinks were tasteful and appeared to be gold. With his ponytail, he looked like a has-been rock star costumed for a court appearance. His eyes were hidden behind wrap-around sunglasses.

"Please, sit down," he said, gesturing to a chaise in the dappled sunlight of the middle deck as he followed her down and pulled a matching chair into shade but didn't sit. "May I offer you something to drink? I'm afraid I have only water and orange juice."

"Thank you, but no," Danni replied, moving toward the stairs. "I really have to get the cat."

"The cat is fine," he said, moving to block her way. "This is a paradise for animals where it will enjoy a long life. You need do nothing for it beyond routine care. But please. We must talk."

It was not a request, nor was it a demand. It was merely a statement. Below, Bastet yawned and curled to sleep in a patch of sun. Danni stood facing the man, so close she could smell him, a scent of old books and ozone, as if lightning had struck a library.

"All right," she said, sitting on the chaise, knees drawn to her chest as she assessed possible escape routes. There were none, short of throwing herself over the deck railing into forest undergrowth full of brambles and, no doubt, snakes. "What do you want to talk about?"

He appeared to be deep in thought, then turned both palms up as if there were some topic of which they were both perfectly aware. "White roses are the symbol for a manner of secrecy, of, shall we say, a *discretion* that is the natural state between those who share a bond. Do you know that roses were carved over the doors to confessionals in ancient cathedrals? White roses are the sign of those who may be trusted to keep secrets."

"You sent the roses," she said.

He nodded. "Of course."

"They're exquisite, but I don't understand. What 'bond' are they supposed to represent?"

He pulled the chair further into shade and sat gracefully, Danni thought, for a man of his bulk. "Please don't be frightened, but there is a bond between us," he began. "You are..."

"No," Danni interrupted, standing abruptly as conflicting reactions arose in her mind. The familiar voice of her rational self suggested that this was apparently one of those men who imagine a deep mystical attachment to some woman they saw buying potato chips at a convenience store. They stalk the woman and then kill her when she fails to recognize the mystical potato chip bond. And she was alone with one in the dense quiet at the edge of a wooded ravine.

But another voice, forgotten but equally familiar, merely said, "Listen."

Grimaud remained seated but spoke with authority. "You are an adept," he said. "What mortals call, among many names, a witch. You are unaware, untrained and ignorant of your gift." He again held both palms up. "But you perceive things that others cannot. Tell me this is not so and I will simply extend my apologies for offending you. I will not approach you again in this life."

Danni thought the "again in this life" phrase was peculiar, but his tone was professorial, detached. She felt no threat from him, but rather the promise of a story. "Everybody senses odd things once in a while," she said, standing over him. "They mean nothing. I don't think I'm a witch."

A pair of crows squawked on the roof and then flapped down to strut along the deck railing, their eyes like black beads.

"Everybody *doesn't* sense odd things," Grimaud said. "But you do."

The crows reminded Danni of ancient rabbis, nodding. She remembered the old woman in the blue track suit, the scent of vinegar and lavender and the words, "four thieves," leaping from radio garble. "Okay," she said, hands on hips, "I saw an old woman today. Something about herbs and four thieves came to mind. Are you going to tell me this means something?"

The crows stopped pacing and seemed to be waiting for an answer.

Grimaud visibly relaxed and a thoughtful smile animated his lips. "You saw a rootworker," he said. "A woman who makes medicines from the rich plant life here. Her home will be hung with leaves and roots, herbs she digs in these woods. The slaves depended on such women for medical care. She will be a descendant of rootworkers as you are a descendant of adepts."

"Why did I smell salad dressing when I saw her? And who are the 'four thieves'?"

Grimaud nodded. "That is her heritage, or an aspect of it. "During the plague years 'four thieves vinegar' was a popular, if useless, defense against the horrible death sweeping across Europe. It was made of vinegar and four herbs, the 'four thieves,' usually lavender, sage, rosemary and thyme, later with the addition of garlic. The recipe has endured over time and the rootworker you saw will almost certainly offer flagons of it for sale."

The crows seemed to smile, then flew away.

Flagons? Danni was pretty sure she'd never heard the word used in actual speech. But "sage, rosemary and thyme," in that order, were familiar. "Are you going to Scarborough fair," she sang, adding the chorus of herbs.

Grimaud's smile was curious. "How do you know this song?" he asked. "Simon and Garfunkel," she answered. "My adoptive parents were fans so I grew up with their music. Surely you've heard that song."

"Oh yes," he said. "I don't know what is meant by 'Simon and Garfunkel' but the tune is ancient and has many lyrics. The song tells of a boy stricken with plague and banished from the city to die alone. He sends a message to his love, demanding that she perform an impossible task, that she make him a shirt with no seam, before they can be reunited. The shirt with no seam is a shroud. She answers with impossible tasks that he must perform as well. He must find an acre of land between salt water and the sea strand, the beach, plant a crop from a single seed of pepper and harvest it with a leather sickle. All impossible even though the antidote to plague, the ingredients of the magical vinegar, is sung as a chorus with each demand. The boy and girl both know he will die. Their impossible demands acknowledge that."

"How do you know all this," she asked, intrigued. History was her field.

"I know because I was there," he answered.

"Because you were where?"

The question was meant to buy time; Danni knew what he meant. But the struggle occurring in her mind still raged. She was rational, educated, and intelligent, not a crackpot draped in crystals who organizes workshops on past lives and auras. For a split second she imagined herself in sparkling shawls, bent over a crystal ball or riding a broom while silhouetted against a full moon. It was ludicrous. But in the same second she felt her childhood terror at a secret inside a fabric store. A secret no one else could feel. It seemed that she was both, an intelligent, highly functional adult who at least in childhood had been able to sense hidden things to which others were impervious. She sat again on the chaise, on its edge, ready to flee.

Grimaud stared into the ravine. "There were many plagues," he said. "Do you not know that?"

"I hold a doctorate in History," Danni answered. "I know what has been recorded, or bits of what has been recorded, about plagues. But you're telling me you were 'there.' The spread of bubonic plague began in the 1340's. That would make you over six hundred years old."

"I am older than that," Grimaud said, shrugging, "but I know what I am. It is you who remain in darkness, you whom we must discuss."

Danni felt the slight dizziness that always accompanied discussions with members of the Philosophy Department back at the university, that sense of stepping onto a floor made of balloons.

"You say you know what you are," she began. "What are you?"

She could see his chest expand as he inhaled deeply, then spoke. "I am a vampire," he said.

Danni sifted the word and her reaction to it for fear, disgust, contempt, any rational response to a stranger's assertion of his identity as a silly myth. She found that she had no reaction but curiosity.

"A strange metaphor," she countered, "but scarcely informative. Unless you fly around at night as a bat until you swoop down to sink your fangs in the necks of people whose dinners didn't include garlic, you aren't a vampire. What do you mean by saying that?"

Grimaud shrugged again, then sighed as he gazed at Bastet, still stretched lazily on the lowest deck. The cat seemed to catch Grimaud's gaze in an arched paw, then leaped from the deck and vanished into the ravine.

"I have slept here for a century and a half," he said quietly. "I need your help in acclimating to a time in which I am lost, clumsy and in peril. In exchange, I will help you. My considerable resources, while they end at the time of your Civil War, are at your disposal."

Danni felt the conversation stretching toward a breaking point at which she would have no choice but to leave. Her rational mind understood that the man must be mentally ill, lost in some interior world to which she had, and wanted, no access. But she sensed not the slightest threat from him, and another part of her mind urged her to stay. He was oddly intelligent, interesting, and not completely unfamiliar. He was like a figure from a forgotten dream or a barely remembered story overheard while concentrating on something else.

"Am I to assume, then, that you guzzle blood from the necks of those unfortunate enough to attract your attention?" She involuntarily raised a hand to her own neck and felt beneath her thumb the warm cadence of her heart. The soft pulse was even and unafraid, a fact that did not escape Grimaud's notice.

He leaned back, as if launching a long story. "You already know that I will not harm you," he said. "You merely don't know how you know that. It is because you are an adept, born with a capacity of which you are unaware. The traditional relationship between vampire and adept is one of mutual honor; I hold that tradition inviolate and because of it I cannot harm you in any way. Why were you not trained? Where were your parents or others in your family who would have taught you?"

"If I had biological parents I don't remember them," she said. "I was left in a church as a very small child and adopted by an older couple in Albany, New York. They tried everything to learn where I'd come from, and so did I, when I grew up. There was nothing, no information. But you haven't answered my question."

"Will you run from me if I do?" he asked.

"I don't know," she answered, playing along. "I might. The idea, drinking blood, sickens me. It's unspeakable, hideous, a taboo."

He raised one large hand to his face and removed his dark glasses. "It is well that you feel so," he said, nodding. "But do you know why? Let me tell you. All history lies encoded in blood, all the stories of life racing red and silent through every living human being. No library could hold the histories written in the blood of a single individual, histories extending back in time to forebears who painted images on the walls of caves. Nothing human can bear the weight of history, but history cries out for preservation. *You* cannot drink history, cannot save it from darkness. I can; I do."

Danni remained focused on the sunglasses dangling from his hand, avoiding his eyes. He could be one of her grad school professors. He actually sounded like one she'd especially liked, an intense, poetic medievalist with a specialty in 12th century grammar. Stéphane Grimaud's passion for history was the passion of her field. All historians felt it. *She* felt it. Except she researched in books and manuscripts rather than in blood. Still, he seemed a colleague.

"There are no vampires," she said, continuing to focus on the sunglasses in his hand, "but if, for the sake of argument, you actually were such a thing, explain why. How did it happen? You don't look..."

"Like Dracula?" he interrupted, laughing. "I lay blind in the ground of Angola Plantation when that Irishman Stoker wrote his book, but I've since read it. Have you?"

"No," Danni admitted, "but the image is generally accepted. Dracula is the prototype..." She looked up, forgetting in her enthusiasm for the topic that she'd meant to avoid his eyes, and gasped. His look was that of a lover in the last moment before all pretense of reticence is abandoned. His eyes made her think of wet, dark wood laid on a fire, smoldering and laced with sparks, about to blaze. She felt her face grow hot and cursed the thin, freckled skin that routinely betrayed her by blushing at the slightest provocation. Then she remembered the physiology of blushing – the sudden tide of blood into a thousand minute capillaries.

His nostrils flared; she sensed that he could smell the blood throbbing in her traitorous face and for a moment she felt a sickening power. His hunger for the secret river flowing through the maps of her body was palpable in the air between them, a need so profound that she heard it in her bones. He wanted to possess her. He wanted to swallow her history in some soft, suckling ritual only she could allow. And in exchange he would give her...

"No!" she whispered, suddenly faint with terror.

His teeth, the canine incisors, were different, and his breath was ragged. But he didn't move.

"It is only the smallest pain and then an ecstasy you have never known," he replied softly, but the softness was inverted, like the breathless silence that precedes a storm.

"No," she said again. "No." The word rose in a tide from deep within her, an incontrovertible statement, an absolute. At the same time she felt crazy. Vampires were myth, amusement for people too young to drive. Grimaud was deliciously sexy, a diversion from the life and death drama of Antoine. He was playing vampire in a game she knew only too well. Seduction. Damn, he was good at it!

He merely watched and nodded, the magnetic heat in his dark eyes fading to courteous warmth.

"You said I knew you would not harm me," she tried to pronounce with outrage but managed something less. "I don't know that."

"I offer an exquisite passion," he replied as a slight breeze moved between them like an invisible wall, "but no harm."

Danni touched the breeze with an outstretched hand. Maybe there really were other worlds and she could see them. But she could also see the world in which passion is a runaway train headed straight for a collapsed bridge. She'd just come from there.

"*No harm*?" she pronounced, laughing. "You could seduce single-celled organisms with those eyes, just not me."

His smile was fond, even comradely. "You must learn to protect yourself from the swarm of history in vampiric eyes," he suggested. "The stories we bear are more seductive than love. I would not taste a single tale from your life, save you offer the gift, but others…"

"Other what?" Danni interrupted. "Other vampires? Stop! It's getting old."

He sighed. "We are brought into existence by change, by the terror it engenders. From what I have observed, this is a time of unprecedented change, an Age of Vampires if you will. There will be many, and all will hold the storm of history in their eyes. Do not be seduced. I will not force my need upon you, but others may."

He seemed stuck in his story. Best to play along until she could find a way to extricate herself from a deck in a ravine. "Do you always ask permission before... before invading the arteries of strangers?" she asked.

"No," he said.

"So you're creating an endless chain of vampires all over Louisiana?"

He seemed puzzled. "What do you mean?"

"People who are bitten by a vampire become vampires," she explained. "Everybody knows that."

He grinned and shook his head, dappled sunlight raking patterns in his dark hair. "Then 'everybody' is mistaken. Those from whom a vampire drinks have no conscious memory of the event, although they may remember its ecstasy in dreams for as long as they live. But none may be reborn as a vampire save they request the transformation. All who are vampires choose to be so."

Danni felt an urge to walk away, get in her car and drive back to New York, away from Antoine's desperation and this man's delusions, toward a safer excitement. History. The heady rush of research, the exultation at finding a single, original document that clarifies or obliterates a scene from the past. Still, this stranger was playing a game that felt like history.

"Then you made that choice," she said. "Why?"

"I am at my best after dusk," he offered. "May I extend an invitation to dine with me this evening? I will tell you my story then."

"Dinner?" Danni nearly choked. "I'm supposed to believe you're a vampire. What do you *eat*?"

"I meant the term in its social sense," he explained as Bastet leaped to the deck and sat washing a paw, watching their exchange as if observing a tennis match. "My culinary skills, while of another time, are at your service. Would you enjoy a cold pease porridge followed by battered oysters, then a blancmange? Something light for a warm evening?"

"You're inviting me to a dinner you will prepare," she said thoughtfully, "although of course you will not eat. Here, in your cottage, alone. Do I have this right?"

He smiled genially. "Yes. It will be my pleasure."

Danni couldn't restrain herself. "I think *not*," she said, laughing. "I'm only too familiar with romantic dinners; no thanks. Although the pease porridge is tempting. I do want to hear your story, though. Just not alone by candlelight. How about a restaurant?"

"But I cannot eat..."

"No problem," she said, gathering Bastet into her arms and standing, "I'll take your dinner home in a doggy bag."

He looked lost. "Doggy bag?"

"Stéphane, just how long have you been, um, back?"

"Not long, weeks only. You see that I need your help!"

"I do see that," she said. "And since there were no cars during the Civil War and you don't seem to have one, I'll drive. Meet me in the parking area by Vicki's porch at six. I think everything in St. Francisville closes at eight, so we'll go early."

He stood and bowed as she left.

Walking away, Danni quietly recited a synopsis of the moment. "I'm in the middle of freaking nowhere, Louisiana, carrying a falsely convicted prisoner's cat as I leave the cottage of a man who thinks he's a vampire." Saying it out loud did nothing to diminish her sense that she'd wandered into yet another play, this one from a children's theater. Except the actors had all grown up, and the play was by Ionesco. At least she had a part. Dinner was going to be interesting.

CHAPTER SEVENTEEN

"Hey Monk! You hear what happened? I get to go to Baton Rouge tomorrow, get to stay there instead of here until I get out!"

Antoine looked up from his desk into Lamar Sellers' childlike grin. "I heard, Lamar. You be careful and try to learn a lot so you can get a job some day, okay? It's going to be great!"

"I hear you get to go places there sometimes," Lamar went on, his eyes wide. "Like to a restaurant or a movie." Then he looked down, wide shoulders suddenly hunched in a posture of grief. "Me and Delane, we went to movies a long time ago," he whispered. "Delane take me to see *Toy Story* one time, buy me popcorn. *Shrek*, too. Me and Delane, we like *Shrek*."

Antoine stood to wrap an arm around the shoulders of a man who would remain a little boy forever. "I think your brother would be happy about you getting out of here," he said. "I'm pretty sure Delane would want you to have a Big Mac and fries, go to a few movies, get yourself some friends. I think Delane is up in heaven just whooping a big cheer right now, don't you?"

"Well, I guess so!" Lamar agreed. "Guess he'd want me to eat that Big Mac and see that movie for him, like he was right there with me. That right, Monk? That how it work with dead people?"

"Sure," Monk said. "That's how it works, Lamar. You make yourself a good life for Delane. Thanks for coming by to tell me the good news, okay?"

"Okay, Monk. You'll come see me, help with my law papers, won't you?"

"People there will do all that," Antoine said. "But I'll be in touch when I can. Good luck, Lamar. Stand tall."

"You bet," the damaged man replied, then strode away to the Walk where both guards and prisoners reached to shake his hand.

Antoine sat heavily in his old Naugahyde chair and watched a few grey cat hairs rise in the displaced air. The warden had kept his end of the deal, had arranged Lamar's transfer. In return, Antoine had to write ridiculous press releases about a prison revival to exorcise a vampire. Without mentioning the vampire.

At least it would take his mind off a rather short future in which he would either die or kill Hoyt Planchard. Unless Danni could find something, anything, to prove that he didn't kill a man named John Thierry a decade in the past, which wasn't likely. He thought it shouldn't be difficult to advertise an exorcism in Louisiana. Its governor had written publicly about performing such a rite himself while a student. Antoine grabbed a legal pad and began to make notes.

Email Danni to get copy of the governor's article about performing an exorcism. We might need to verify if we use it.

He tried to remember tales of Ouija boards and demons that circulated on the playground at his Catholic grade school. You were supposed to yell, "Get thee behind me, Satan! The Lion of Judah casts thee out," and the devil would vanish. There was a girl named Mary Margaret Mitchell who liked to chant the exorcism on the teeter-totter. He jotted a header.

Angola Invites Neighbors to Cast Out...

It sounded like an invitation to a garage sale, and to cast out what? He couldn't use "vampire," and there was something different about them anyway. Vampires weren't demons; nobody ever exorcised a vampire. He remembered boyhood stories about stakes in the heart, silver bullets and sleeping in coffins full of Transylvanian dirt, but on the subject of vampires, religions were curiously silent. Still, this was going to be a revival.

Angola Rallies to Cast Out the Unholy, he wrote. Surely vampires would qualify as "unholy" and it had a nice, suggestive ring. *Warden Dwight Tilly Announces Prison*

Revival? Boring. How about *Get Thee Behind Me! Angola Prison Targets the Unholy in Gospel Revival?* It sounded good. Now all he had to do was write the copy to go with it, a separate text from which Tilly could read when the press called for details, and then design a poster. The prison print shop needed the design immediately.

Email the warden's office ten or twenty public domain graphics of crosses, stakes and maybe a few gargoyles, he wrote in his notes to Danni. A gargoyle would be good, especially one with bat wings. *Winged gargoyle!* he added, wishing he had access to the Internet and could just do it himself. Maybe he could get permission to use one of the computers in the warden's office.

He tried to remember exactly how she looked, all the details he hadn't had time to absorb. Her hair was reddish brown and curly, but what color were her eyes? Hazel, he thought, with long lashes. Clear eyes that had not looked away when she offered to help him. She would fail. They both knew that. She was as lost and inept in this strange place as he had been ten years in the past. And she was a historian, not a trained criminal investigator. There was no way she could unearth information and witnesses, record statements and manipulate Louisiana's curious French legal system in time to save him. But she would try.

Antoine felt a curious exhilaration at the thought of her. He had trusted no one for so long that the feeling was odd, as if he'd opened a door into a forgotten room. If by some miracle he survived what lay ahead, if even more miraculously he were a free man again, he would owe her his life. He forced his thoughts again to caped creatures with needle-sharp incisors, and smiled.

*

Grimaud was waiting beside her car when Danni approached, observing it intently from various angles. She'd chosen a crisp white blouse and conservative little black jacket for this dinner with a man who wouldn't be eating because he thought he was a vampire. He didn't notice that she'd dressed as if they were going to a business meeting.

"Why are you staring at my car?" she asked. "It's your basic rental."

"I have read of these," he answered. "Henry Ford, the Model T, internal combustion of oil fuel that is drawn from far beneath the ground. It is like a steam engine except that the power derives from exploding oil." He smiled. "But I do not know how to use such a vehicle."

Danni cocked her head. "You're telling me you don't know how to drive?"

Grimaud turned slowly to face her, his dark eyes glowing gold in a lavender sunset. He spoke slowly, as if addressing a child. "In autumn of 1863 a slave called Old Joe would have killed me, but he was ill. He died before he could decapitate and burn my head. He did pound a stake through my heart and bury me. I have slept since then, Danni. Of course I have never driven an automobile. I must learn that and a thousand other skills that did not exist when I last walked among mortals. I have explained; your help is essential."

Danni rattled her car keys. "You know, this vampire thing is getting old. If you never learned to drive for some reason, it's okay. I've met New Yorkers who never bothered. They take cabs everywhere anyway. Get in; I'll explain how it works on the way to the restaurant. When we get back you can practice a little."

The light was fading, the sky layered in darkening shades backlit by flickering orange. Grimaud didn't move.

"Your ignorance is tiresome," he pronounced. "I will end it now."

Danni had bent to slide into the car when instead of a man, a teacup-sized disk of blue light moved in the shadows where he had been. She stood again, staring. The light made no sound, but from inside her head a song was barely audible. The language was unfamiliar, but the deep voice was Grimaud's.

"So you see," the voice intoned, and the blue light stretched and faded to the shape of a man.

"What the *hell*!" Danni gasped, shaken. "What did you *do*?"

"It is a compression of spirit," he said as if explaining how to change a tire. "Each vampire takes a spiritual shape in the manner natural to its mortal life. I was Basque, from an ancient people to whom light was holy."

"You *were* Basque?" she said, holding the car for support as her legs threatened to buckle.

"I am dead," Grimaud said thoughtfully. "What you see is a thing given the illusion of life only by history's hunger for preservation. When great change threatens to obliterate all that has gone before, a thousand vampires rise from the teeming pool of human awareness. Our purpose, our single reason for being, is to take into ourselves the stories of time, and to keep them. We will vanish only with the last human soul, and with us every story since the beginning. I thought I had explained this."

Danni watched the familiar battle within her mind as if from a distance. She was obviously crazy, seeing things. She should drive into Baton Rouge to a hospital with a psychiatric unit and ask for help. Except she wasn't crazy and Grimaud's words resonated in that consciousness she'd buried with her childhood. There were countless realities just out of reach, scattered at the edges of the obvious. A woman buried alive in the wall of a building might make herself known to the child who would feel her presence. A man who was blue light might be a vampire. There was a space inside her where these things were simply true. They had always been true.

"Why did no one teach you how to be what you are?" Grimaud asked softly.

"I told you, I don't know anything about my family. The only family I ever had were the people who adopted me, Wendy and Ron. I think I frightened them at times, but they loved me."

He shrugged. "Love was not enough," he said. "For you, it will never be enough. No adept can exist entirely within human attachments. You bring too much to them, and human mortals recoil. You are meant to walk carefully in many worlds, not only this one that you know. Is there no one who can help you?"

"Not really," she said, still rattled. "But if you really are a... a vampire..., I have questions."

"At dinner," Grimaud pronounced courteously. "It will be my pleasure to entertain you."

Danni thought her driving probably approximated that of a ninety-year-old as she made her way toward a restaurant no more than a mile from Vicki's B&B. It was hard to function in two worlds at once – a two-lane road in a Southern village and a car in which a vampire had to be told how to put on a seat belt. She focused on mundane explanations of automobile functions, to which Grimaud listened intently.

"Why do you need to drive a car when you can turn into a light and fly wherever you want?" she asked.

"It is necessary to appear mortal," he said. "In your time, mortals drive cars, and I cannot fly far before the effort exhausts me."

"So you don't turn into a bat," she said, oddly disappointed at the loss of the image.

"I am unaware of any human culture in which bats are so revered that a vampire would assume that form," he answered. "I think the connection has something to do with three species of bats that live on the blood of animals." His smile was disturbing. "The similarities are undeniable."

She was relieved to see the restaurant parking lot. "But what will you do now that you're… back? I mean besides… the blood thing."

He inspected the restaurant's façade. "I don't know. For the time I wish only to learn from you, and to help you. Have you a need I may fulfill?"

Danni sifted the question for innuendo and didn't find it, but his elegant speech patterns might mask anything. "I need to track down the history of a quilt made during the Civil War," she said as they exited the car. "I guess you might be able to help with that, since you were *here* during the Civil War."

He walked politely at her side, held the restaurant door for her, nodded to the hostess. His feet in polished loafers left impressions in the carpet. He was solid, a big man, breathing the same Cajun-cooking scents she was breathing. He couldn't have been alive when Abraham Lincoln wrote the Gettysburg Address, except he had been. Well, not exactly alive, but existent.

"Did you ever see Lincoln?" she whispered after they were seated at a linen-draped table in the middle of a crowded room.

"No," he laughed. "Remember where you are. Louisiana seceded from the Union in 1861, severely curtailing local dinner invitations to Abraham Lincoln. However, I had the honor to dine with President Jefferson Davis on several occasions. A fine man, but doomed."

Danni read the menu as Grimaud ordered wine. Red. "Doomed?" she said into the appetizer list. "Do you mean you…?"

"Egad," he replied, "what a wretch you think me! Of course not. I have read that President Davis lived for thirty years beyond any further possibility of my acquaintance, since I lay in the ground of Angola Plantation the while of his remaining life. I meant only to suggest that the Confederacy, and thus his presidency, were doomed. Davis was a private man, meticulous and aloof, no kidney to Lincoln, who was friend to oiler and captain alike."

"Kidney? Oiler?" she asked after ordering something that sounded deliciously fattening. "What do you mean?"

He nodded. "'Kidney' suggests similarity. I might say two gentlemen are 'of a kidney' in regard to their shared views. And an 'oiler' works below decks on a steamship, a workman, a menial laborer."

"The only steamships left from your time are a handful that operate tourist trips on lakes and rivers," she explained. "Nobody talks about oilers and captains. Or kidneys. Your speech is... archaic."

"Of course it is," he agreed while sniffing the wine in his glass. "You must tutor me in the language of this century. Meanwhile, I will order a case of palatable wine to be sent immediately. This is swill!"

"It's local," she noted after reading the label.

"Impossible. The climate in Louisiana is unsuitable for grapes."

"Apparently they're growing them anyway," she said. It was a topic on which she knew more than she wanted. Her department chair had fancied himself a connoisseur of wine and imagined a similar interest on her part. "There are wineries in all fifty states," she told Grimaud. "It's 'in,' fashionable, and not just with grapes. Northern wineries specialize in lilac wine, wines made from apples, rhubarb, various berries, honey-based wines, even pumpkin wine!"

"Anything will ferment," he remarked with disdain. "But *wine* is made of grapes."

"Welcome to the 21st century," she said and touched her glass to his.

"Pumpkin wine? I fear this time will prove barbaric," he answered her toast.

"This time would say the same of you," she replied.

Over an appetizer of fried green tomatoes topped with crab étouffée, Danni watched as Grimaud made all the gestures common to eating his plate of crab cakes while not actually eating a bite. "How is it that you can drink wine if you can't eat food?" she asked.

"Shall we merely say that the practice is all that remains of a lost mortality? And the red sparkles with such sanguinity!" He was teasing, testing her comfort with subtleties.

"Surely you'd prefer a Bloody Mary," she replied, playing along.

He looked puzzled. "Bloody Mary, the daughter of Henry the Eighth and Catharine of Aragon, Catholic Queen of England who slaughtered Protestants?"

Danni sighed. "We have work to do. A Bloody Mary is a drink, basically vodka and tomato juice, a little horseradish, Worcestershire sauce and hot pepper."

"Some still regard the tomato as poisonous," he said.

She shook her head. "No, some don't. That idea died long before you... slept, I think. Tomorrow we'll go into Baton Rouge and get you an Ipad or something. You need access to the Internet where you can look up whatever you want to know and then I'll answer questions. For the moment, push your crab cakes under your lettuce until I can ask for a doggy bag. That means a bag in which patrons take uneaten food home, ostensibly for a pet but actually for themselves. I'll order coffee and enjoy it while you tell me your story."

"Of course," he agreed, "but before I do you must understand the message of white roses. My secrets are no less solemn than yours, and my story is a gift deserving of your respect. May I trust in your protection?"

Danni glanced out the restaurant window at fog swirling in yellow globes around the sodium lights. She saw herself inside the glowing globes, each a story. A little girl who longed to save the unicorn in a 15th century tapestry. A young woman involved with an older man who was only too happy to let her rescue him. Herself in a prison visitor's room with a stranger who desperately needed her help, and now in a restaurant with aqua-blue walls where a vampire asked if she could be trusted.

"You may," she said, and he began to draw a picture.

In it a sick and dying man, no more than thirty, although he didn't know the year of his birth, staggered into a brothel in an ancient settlement called Bayonne, at that time an obscure region of a country extending from the coast of France through the Netherlands and into Belgium. The place was little more than a stable, its low ceiling lit by a single candle. On a stool a woman with shining dark hair sat cloaked in rags, but her eyes gleamed like jewels.

"I was dying of an illness that would later be called typhoid fever," Grimaud said, the shade of something bitter clouding his eyes. "Death spilled into my body. I only knew that the light inside me was faint and would soon extinguish. I couldn't read and spoke a language that is only an echo now. But my mother was Basque and taught me to worship light. It is the way of those ancient people. Dying, I moved toward the only light I could see, a candle in a wretched hovel."

Danni stirred her coffee but didn't drink. "And the woman?" she said.

"A local whore, on the surface. Her name was Hilargi, 'moon,' and I knew the meaning of silver paths in darkness that cannot lead to day. She gave me cooked meat on a wooden plate, and an iron knife with which to eat it. I was so sick, but I had never eaten from a plate, and the meat was like wine on my tongue."

He looked down. "And I had never enjoyed intimacy with a woman from the front, only as an animal performs the act. I had never seen the eyes of a woman as she draws the seed of a man to the mystery hidden inside her. But she showed me her eyes as I moved within her, faint with a single need even as I died. In her eyes was a question, and her teeth grew long and sharp in the guttering flame."

Danni watched her coffee grow cold. "This woman, Hilargi, was a vampire," she said, watching him.

He looked up. "Not that word, not then," he said. "*Betiereko* perhaps, or *deabru*. An unspeakable thing, an abomination that cannot die but feeds on the living. I understood with a mortal's horror, like yours. But I was dying. And as the last of my life spilled into the darkness of her womb, I nodded. I said yes, Danni, and felt the brief pain of her bite, then an ecstasy too vast to describe. Stars, winds, music I could hear with my eyes. When we stood, I was no longer dying. I was dead but whole and could never die again."

He sat perfectly still but his eyes were wild with the memory, full of leaping flame and dangerous need. "I offer you those winds, that music," he whispered hoarsely, "but not the terrible gift. Let me..."

"No," Danni answered, forcing herself to trace the pattern in the carpet with her eyes. She couldn't look at him, wouldn't, but his desire filled the space between them like a muted symphony.

She shook her head slowly, clicking a fingernail against her sweating water glass to muffle the responsive chord she heard in her hands, her belly, her tongue. "I do not let you," she said. "I do not want what you offer. I do not offer what you want."

Then she looked at him, feeling the danger but meeting it with a cool, irrefutable resolve that rose from the part of her he named "adept." She could see worlds hidden at the edges of shadows, but the seeing carried an ancient strength she hadn't known was there. "If I am ever willing to experience the ecstasy of your bite, I'll tell you," she told him quietly. "Until that time I demand that you withhold the invitation. Do you understand?"

He stood and bowed from the waist. "I do," he said.

Outside, the village was lost in drifting mist that wrapped spectral fingers about the moving car, and neither woman nor vampire spoke at all.

CHAPTER EIGHTEEN

After a week of intensive tutoring and a trip to Baton Rouge for an iPad, Grimaud sounded slightly less like a Victorian character actor. But it was becoming apparent to Danni that even after the salon haircut she'd forced him to endure, he'd probably never appear "normal." His eyes…

"Wear sunglasses during the day and tinted lenses at night," she told him. "Claim to have an obscure eye condition, allergies, sensitivity to industrial pollutants. Probably a good idea to carry a book in Russian or something with you everywhere and appear to be reading it with rapt interest. People avoid foreigners."

"My Russian is very bad," Grimaud said, smiling. "Vampires prefer to eschew the Slavic as well as the Balkan countries, as you may imagine."

"You don't have to read it, merely pretend. And what's wrong with Slavic countries?"

They were sitting in the shade on one of Grimaud's decks, sipping wine he'd ordered from someplace called Baigorri. Bastet was curled in her lap, watching the vampire from hooded eyes. Danni didn't like the wine, which had a funny licorice taste, and wasn't sure she could accurately name a single Slavic country.

"Poland," Grimaud said as if reading her mind. "Czechoslovakia, Croatia, Bosnia and Herzegovina. All of Russia. Should I go on?"

Danni grinned. "What about Transylvania?"

"Part of Romania now," Grimaud answered, "in the Balkans. But yes, even though Vlad Dracul was *not* a vampire, merely a sick and brutal man." He smiled broadly, stippled sunlight moving on his white teeth. "Did you know that Prince Charles, heir to the throne of England, in 2011 claimed Prince Vlad, the historic 'Dracula,' as his ancestor? This in connection with an effort to preserve the forests of Transylvania. Surely the throne of England would not claim a vampire as ancestor, do you think?"

"Probably not," Danni agreed, laughing. "But I assume vampires avoid those worlds because of Dracula anyway, even though he wasn't..."

Grimaud shook his head. "We avoid the people of certain regions, not a long-dead Balkan sadist. The spirit of those places, the remote mountain villages and untouched forests, produce a sensitivity similar to your own. Most Slavic and Balkan people are somewhat adept; most can sense a vampiric presence even if they can't name their discomfort. Even so, that discomfort is dangerous to us." He glanced at his watch. "But this information is unproductive. It cannot help you function as an adept. Is there nothing you know of your history, Danni?"

"My history is entirely the creation of the people who loved and raised me," she said. "It was such a short time. Wendy died in an automobile accident on her way to the grocery when I was fourteen. I was devastated, but Ron never left my side. He said we'd keep making the life she wanted for me, and we did. We lived in their yellow house while I finished high school and then four years of college. The college was right across the street and I could walk there. But by the time I graduated, his health was failing. We sold the house, he gave me half the proceeds and went to live in an 'assisted living' community near one of their sons while I went to graduate school in Boston. We talked on the phone almost every day until he died two years ago. And now I'm alone."

Grimaud turned to gaze with seeming carelessness at a woodpecker drumming on a nearby crab apple tree. He smiled at the bird, but Danni felt a penumbra of darkness and longing gather about him.

"The story of your past, your real parents and ancestors, is written on the river now flowing through you," he mentioned, more to the woodpecker than to Danni. "Any vampire could read your story. Any vampire could tell you who you are."

He continued to stare at the crab apple tree even though the bird had vanished into the ravine, but Danni felt the magnetism of his suggestion. It was an undertow, invisible and powerful. And it was a trick.

"You gave your word," she said evenly, not hiding her anger. "You agreed that you wouldn't ask."

"I'm not asking, merely stating a fact," he whispered into the moving shadows of trees. "You are ignorant of your own story. A vampire can read it as it is written in your blood, and tell you who you are. *Any* ... vampire."

He was offering a gift she'd longed for all her life, but at what price? Danni shook her head and polished off her wine. "There's only one vampire in the immediate vicinity," she said. "That would be the one who agreed to stop begging me for platelets. Really, Stéphane, this is beneath you."

At the word, "begging," she saw his shoulder muscles lock beneath the fabric of his shirt as a dark flush crept up his neck. The word had shamed him.

"I'm sorry," she began. "I didn't mean to..."

"You try my forbearance!" he bellowed, one hand gripping the deck railing as with the other he pointed at Danni. "Like most mortals you live in a stupor of ignorance from which I could take you at will, drain you and leave you lifeless. That I do not is a *kindness!*"

Danni gasped as an aura of pulsing indigo shuddered around him like electrified smoke. Bastet screeched as Grimaud became a filthy, feverish shepherd in reeking, bloodstained rags, then a gravestone that looked like the circle of light thrown by a candle, then a vampire in a silk waistcoat and cravat, buried in orange clay soil, a stake protruding from his chest. The buried form disintegrated; only feathery shreds of flesh still clung to bones that did not move. Except for a hand. Danni watched in terror as dusky white phalanges curled around the deck railing, watched as the railing splintered and broke. A desperate pounding in her chest reminded her to breathe as Grimaud, now just a big man in khakis and a forest green polo shirt, released his grip on the broken railing.

"I must apologize," he said without looking at her. "After too long a sleep, I blunder."

Danni felt lightheaded and somewhat sick, as if having narrowly avoided a fatal accident. But at the same time another part of her mind considered the creature before her. Stéphane Grimaud might be ancient, dead, terrifying and alien, but he was also oddly human. How could it be otherwise? He existed to preserve the human story.

"I… I understand," she managed to say while stroking Bastet as if to solidify her connection to the living. The cat stood against her now, back arched, hissing at Grimaud. She felt claws, fully extended and ready to attack. "But you must also understand. Foolish or not, my short, ignorant life is as important to me as the eternity of your task is to you. I have tasks as well, and you have offered your help, so…"

"Agreed," Grimaud interjected somberly. "I will be grateful if you allow me to begin now, this minute. My lapse in courtesy demands immediate reparation. I am your servant, Danni. Please, what are your tasks?"

Bastet relaxed but continued to watch as Grimaud flung the broken railing into the ravine. "I've told you, the quilt," Danni began. I need to research its history and write a paper. And I'm helping Antoine write press releases for an exorcism at the prison. A *vampire* exorcism. You can definitely help with that!"

Grimaud looked puzzled. "I know the prison," he said. "But a vampire is not a demon and cannot be exorcised! How could anyone think such a thing?"

"I can't explain it," Danni said, standing after Bastet leaped down to chase a cricket. "There are areas, especially in the South, where people of little education still cling to primitive ideas. Google 'religious fundamentalism' for an overview. I need to come up with some fancy biblical references, that sort of thing."

Grimaud smiled. "There are no biblical vampires," he said thoughtfully. "But do you remember what I have told you of blood? It is there, in the Bible. Leviticus, I think, warns that mortals are forbidden to drink the blood of any creature, for the blood is the life."

"That's great, I'll tell Antoine," Danni said, "The quilt research is really a problem, but it will have to wait. Right now there's something else and I don't know where to begin. A crime. I have to discover who killed a man in Opelousas ten years ago."

"Was this someone you knew?"

"No. It's about Antoine, the prisoner. He was convicted of this man's murder, but he didn't do it. Someone else did."

Grimaud scowled. "How do you know that this man, Antoine, did not commit the crime?"

"I know," Danni answered.

"Because he told you he was innocent? That claim is so common among the imprisoned as to be laughable."

Danni straightened her shoulders as the sky grew dark with the promise of rain. "No," she said slowly. "I know because I'm an adept."

Grimaud nodded. "Ah," he said. "Then I will help you."

*

Two hours later Antoine sat in a yellow plastic chair in the warden's office, a laptop balanced on his knees.

"Mr. Dupre, ah cain't hardly read all these emails comin' in all of a sudden," said the new office worker who'd been assigned to censor Danni's emails before allowing Antoine to read them. She scrolled through at least ten, all with headers saying, "For Revival."

Antoine smiled at the young woman's use of his surname, a courtesy she'd soon learn was not extended to prisoners. The afternoon was rainy and the office smelled like damp carpet. Antoine wished he were back in the law library where he could open a window. Then he realized he didn't want to be in the law library at all. He didn't want to see the sky through chainlink and razor wire, didn't want to smell another plate of grits as long as he lived and most of all, he didn't want to live every damn minute in fear. Fear of the wardens and security officers, who often had agendas a prisoner might cross without knowing. Fear of Hoyt Planchard and others like him with their gangs of slavish morons. Fear of becoming like them because there were no other options.

Antoine thought of his mother playing an upright piano in the dining room of his childhood home, his father reading comics aloud to him at the table. Sometimes they would all sing *Oh, Suzanna* or the *Marine's Hymn* because John Dupre had been a Marine and fought at the end of the Vietnam conflict. His father told Antoine sometimes you had to fight, but his father had never been in prison. There the time to fight was permanent, and in the end you'd still lose. Antoine stared at the gray sky outside the warden's office and felt lightheaded with desperation for freedom.

"Mr. Dupre? You all right?"

The young woman stood beside him holding out a sheaf of papers and a black book.

"Sorry, just thinking," he said. "What's this?"

"This here is *the Bible*," she answered, cocking her head in dismay at his failure to recognize a cultural icon. "See? It say 'Holy Bible' on the front. Your Miz Danni sent all this and something to look up in the Bible. For the revival. So I got you one out of the warden's bookcase."

"Thank you," Antoine said. "It was good of you to help."

He felt a smile tug his facial muscles at "*your* Miss Danni." Danni wasn't his. She was wonderful, smart and brave and they had connected; he was sure of that. He just wasn't sure what it meant.

"Mr. Dupre, you sure you all right?"

The room came into focus – scratched walls, cheap carpet and a stuffed bobcat head wearing a plastic cross. Antoine thought hell would probably look better. Except this *was* hell. "Yes, thank you. Guess I'm a little tired," he answered, turning to the sheaf of notes Danni had sent.

"Use the term, 'the Infernal Hunt,'" she wrote. "Hunting is big around here and locals will relate to the idea of vampires hunting. Apparently it's Greek and has to do with souls of the dead who have unfinished business among the living, not vampires, but I think it'll work okay in this context. 'Let us arm ourselves against the Infernal Hunt now raging in the night' kind of thing."

The next page listed, "the insatiable dead, the disquieting stranger and iron teeth," all in Danni's opinion appropriate for strewing throughout the promotional materials.

"You asked for some Egyptian references," she noted, "so you might try Sekhmet, the ancient lion-headed goddess always depicted wearing red for shed blood. Some scholars trace the vampire image to her. Then there's Ka, the spiritual doppelganger soul everybody has to accompany their Ba, the soul in the body. I like that one for the vampire thing, although it's probably too complicated for this gig!"

Antoine wondered where she was getting her material. "The Infernal Hunt" was good, but "iron teeth"? Whatever. He'd work it in.

The next page had the biblical reference, Leviticus 17. Antoine flipped through the King James Bible from the warden's bookshelf and read all sixteen verses, which said the same thing over and over. Drinking any blood at all was strictly forbidden because the life of every creature was in its blood, which had to be drained and buried before the flesh could be eaten or burned as an offering.

"Huh!" he said. Good stuff.

"Y'all find something interesting?" asked the young office worker, who was organizing her desk prior to leaving.

"Old Testament," Antoine answered. "They believed that life was in the blood instead of in the brain."

"Well, that's true," she said conversationally while shutting down her computer and then applying a generous coat of lipstick. "My doctor told me that."

"Your doctor?" Antoine said. "I can't believe a doctor would..."

"Oh yeah," she interrupted, smiling. "I had a miscarriage, know what I'm sayin'? Felt real bad but then my doctor, he explain my baby still in my blood. Baby DNA stay in the mama's blood forever. DNA, that what we all made up of, y'know? So my baby live on inside me even though she don't get to live *outside*, see? I think she was a girl so I call her Ellie after my grandma. Even talk to her sometimes, show her things, y'know? She there, Mr. Dupre, deep in the blood."

Antoine could think of no response and merely said, "Ah."

"You believe in them vampires?" the young woman asked, turning back from the door.

"No," Antoine said. "That's just a story."

She regarded him thoughtfully. "Everything just a story, Mr. Dupre. Y'all have a good night now."

Antoine nodded courteously as she left, then rose to watch dusk fall on the Big Yard beyond the window. A guard in the hall observed the movement but didn't come in to correct it. No one seemed to care that a prisoner was alone in the warden's office, looking out the window. The illusion of freedom, of a normal life in which you could look out of windows without punishment, felt strange. Antoine wondered how institutionalized he'd become, how awkward and frightened he might feel in the free world. He wondered how others would feel about a man who hadn't driven a car in ten years, who didn't know how to use a cell phone and was accustomed to having no control over anything beyond his thoughts. The idea embarrassed him. Just as well it would never happen.

An hour later he'd selected a particularly disturbing gargoyle for the program from the examples Danni sent, this one from a chateau in Blain, France. He'd roughed out a utilitarian press release listing the New Orleans gospel choir, the twenty-piece orchestra, the evangelical TV personality and the five local clergymen who would be on stage with Warden Dwight Tilly at the first-ever vampire exorcism to be held in a maximum-security prison.

Heavy footsteps at the end of the hall alerted the guard, who boomed, "Evenin' warden," as Tilly barreled into his office and turned on the TV.

"Look at this!" he told Antoine. "Some locals stealin' my vampire!"

A television newsman stood on the veranda of a restored plantation beside a woman in an antebellum costume and a Dolly Parton wig.

"He comes here at night," the woman said into the camera. "The vampire. Why, my son-in-law saw him just the other night, right over there under our historic oak where Robert E. Lee courted his beautiful young wife, Marian."

The newsman looked somber. "I understand that precautions have been taken to protect visitors?"

"Of course," the woman said. "Garlic and finger crosses are available in our gift shop, and there's a special daily guided tour at dusk with the Reverend Billy Delahoussaye. Reverend Billy will stand right there under that oak and cast out the evil spirit!"

Tilly flipped the TV off with the remote and slammed a pink fist against his desk.

"Robert E. Lee's wife was from Virginia, never set a damn toe in Louisiana and her name was Mary Anna, not Marian," he told Antoine. "'Maid Marion' was Robin Hood's lady, not Robert E. Lee's. Buncha local vultures tryin' to weasel in on my revival doin' nuthin' but insult history!"

"A shame," Antoine offered.

"So what we gonna do about it?"

Both men watched as bats swooped in the Big Yard lights, feasting on mosquitoes.

"I suggest that you send out these press releases tonight under a header saying something like, 'Angola Takes Leading Role in Dispelling Regional Panic.' Attach a photo of you in the Big Yard pointing at a bat."

"Hard to take a picture of a bat," Tilly replied. "They don't sit still."

"Graveyard, then. Photo of you in the prison graveyard, crosses all around. You can point at the moon."

"You're one smart college boy," Tilly said after calling a guard, to meet him in the graveyard with a camera. "Be a shame, Hoyt Planchard put your lights out."

"Yeah," Antoine agreed, the familiar chill spreading through his mind like a quiet storm. "Might not happen, though." *Because I might kill him first.*

CHAPTER NINETEEN

A day later Danni sent the last of her research to Antoine at the warden's email address. Between tutoring Grimaud and helping Antoine, she'd neglected her own work and needed to get back to it.

"You might want to include a footnote in the program warning that blood in quantities sufficient to drink is actually toxic," she wrote. "Just in case some stupid kids decide to be vampires. It's full of iron, which the human body can't eliminate fast enough. An overdose is called haemochromatosis and can cause liver and nervous system damage." She hit "Send" and wondered why she hadn't heard from him. Of course he couldn't use the warden's email, and prisoner email wasn't immediate because it had to be censored. But too much time had gone by.

"Are you still there?" she wrote to his prisoner address. "Haven't heard from you in days. Danni."

Then she pulled up the photos she'd taken of the vampire quilt and stared at them. Grimaud, who not surprisingly said he preferred to sleep during the day, would be by at dusk to look at them. In the meantime, Danni half-heartedly scrounged around the Internet, looking for detailed historical data relevant to the quilt while wondering how she was supposed to locate a killer. And even if she did, then what? After three hours she was completely lost.

Prior to 1730, two-thirds of Louisiana's slave population had been captured in Senegal. Thus, Senegalese music and folklore found its way into the region's culture. "Uncle Remus," she learned, was originally a Senegalese tale. But the slave named Joe had staked a vampire more than a hundred years after 1730 and so probably wasn't from Senegal.

A historian named Gwendolyn Midlo Hall spent fifteen years crawling through mildewed Louisiana courthouse basements, cataloguing French and Spanish records of slave sales. Her work resulted in a database of 100,000 slave names and origins, some including personal histories and characteristics. But to find Joe and his wife Neecie amid the 100,000, assuming they were even recorded, Danni would need the names of those who had bought and sold them. The task wasn't impossible, but would take more time than she could afford if she were to investigate Antoine's crime. Snapping her laptop shut, she washed a coffee cup, read the nutritional information on a box of Wheat Chex and idly stroked the carved cat she'd placed in the middle of the table.

"It will take months to research the story behind the quilt," she told the statue as Bastet slept on the couch. "And right now I really need to be in Opelousas trying to find out who really killed a man ten years ago."

The wooden cat seemed to sigh.

"And on top of that, I'm an adept and a vampire wants to consume my history."

At the word "adept" she was pretty sure the carved eyes widened approvingly. Outside, Ray Bone was chasing ducks on the grass surrounding the pond. The basset was enthusiastic but slow, the ducks merely annoyed. Danni wandered out to pet the dog and give the ducks some peace. She needed to think, organize priorities, figure out how to do, and be, the impossible.

Vicki was discussing the arrangement of a bed of dwarf iris beneath a white azalea with the gardener as Danni circled the duck pond, pausing every ten steps to ruffle Ray Bone's fur.

"You look like somebody just sent you the weight of the world with postage due!" Vicki yelled over azalea leaves. "I'm on my way into Baton Rouge, need to find an outfit for a wedding up in Jackson. My cousin's granddaughter. I met her once ten years ago at a funeral when she was eighteen. Ugly as a mud fence, bless her heart, but I hear the husband's even worse. Wanna come along?"

Danni grinned. Shopping would be fun. "Great!" she yelled back, abandoning the basset hound, who went back to barking laconically at the ducks, and letting Bastet out to join the fray.

"I love your life," she told Vicki as they drove through dinner time traffic. "Beautiful house and grounds, everything cloaked in mist. It feels safe here. I can see why you came back."

The older woman smiled. "What you see is an illusion," she replied. "It's what we do; we create it. Every Southern woman understands that, black, white, we all knock ourselves out to maintain the illusion. The overdone courtesies, gloves in 90-degree heat and absolute silence about anything that might shatter the mirage – well, it's a way of life, I guess."

"But you know reality is there; you just don't acknowledge it," Danni said.

Vicki deftly passed an 18-wheeler hauling stripped pine tree trunks that filled the air with a scent of Christmas. "Oh, we acknowledge it in our way," she answered. "For example, everybody knows poor old Acklen Pate lost his mind up at Angola twenty years ago because he was raped, turned out as a whore, forced to live on his knees 'til he got out. We don't talk about it, but we know, and we make sure he has food and clothes. One of these days a hunter will find Acklen dead out there in the woods, and we'll give him a funeral fancy enough for a senator. Flowers knee-deep and in the eulogy the minister will make subtle references to an evil that tried to break Acklen's soul, but *we* wouldn't let it happen. Here, we understand that illusion trumps evil in the end. See?"

Danni nodded. Most people understood the need to maintain illusions. Except a lot more than evil got swept under the rug. Like everything outside the slender little world deemed acceptable. Vampires, for example. And people who could see them.

"I guess that's why Dwight Tilly's revival at the prison is practically sold out already," she said. "The revival's the illusion, right?"

"Yep," Vicki answered. "And this vampire nobody's actually seen, he makes a terrific idea of evil. You got your ticket yet?"

"Um, I've been helping Antoine with the press releases, doing some research for him. I can get comp tickets for all of us – you and me and Sarah Reeves, if you want to go."

"Why, thank you, I'd love that," Vicki answered. "Now, what does the cousin of the bride's grandmother wear to a September wedding?"

"This is all part of the illusion, right?" Danni asked. "You're supposed to look familial or ancestral or something?"

"Of course!"

"Silver," Danni decided. "You can go as the ancestral silver somebody buried in the swamp during the Civil War. Shiny slub silk jacket over a blousy knit top and bias-cut skirt. Gray kid gloves, matching shoes with rosettes and a pillbox with a half-veil."

"You're good," Vicki said. "And I've already got the hat."

After a quick lunch at the shopping center food court Danni felt awash in normalcy. Vampires, prisoners and whatever mysterious gift she had for seeing things paled beside the fun of shopping with a friend.

"Sounds like you've got something going with this Antoine guy," Vicki mentioned casually from a dressing room cubicle beside the one in which Danni was trying on a coppery knit dress that brought out the highlights in her hair. The scoop neck scooped daringly low and would require a particular bra, she realized. Plus something at the neck.

"No, not really," she answered, her voice tentative over the top of the cubicle. "He's... he's different, not like anybody I've ever known. I like him, but..."

"But he's not available," Vicki said lightly, her voice muffled by fabric. "This top's perfect but I need a medium."

"I'll get it," Danni answered, pulling on her clothes. She was going to buy the knit dress. It didn't have to be *for* anybody; she just liked the way she looked in it. Vicki picked up the conversational strand the minute Danni returned.

"Antoine Dupre might be interesting, but he's in prison," she said in her tour-guide voice. "He might even be innocent, but he's still in prison. He'll be there until he dies, Danni. I hope you're not considering the life some women choose, moving down here to be near a man who will never lie beside them in bed or even sit beside them at a movie. Prisoners can have visitors twice a month. That's two days out of thirty. The other twenty-eight days, those women sit alone up here in Baton Rouge writing emails that will be read by strangers and paying hugely inflated phone charges for conversations that are taped. It's no life, Danni, no matter how you feel about him right now. Remember, you're still getting over a heartbreak and you're vulnerable. Hope you don't mind me meddling, but..."

"No, it's okay, I appreciate it," Danni said. "You're right, I'm kind of a mess right now. I'm not *involved* with him the way you mean, but I did tell him I'd do some research for him, about the crime. He didn't do it, Vicki. He really is innocent."

"And you know this how?" Vicki asked while turning to inspect the back of the dove grey top she'd pulled on.

"I just know," Danni said. "I believe him."

"We've got to get you out of here," Vicki replied, suddenly businesslike. "You're going to finish your work on the quilt and then go somewhere *else* to write the article. Where's your family?"

"What?"

"Your family, somebody I can call."

"I don't have any family," Danni said, "and I'm not going to become one of those women you were talking about. I told Antoine I'd go to Opelousas and get a copy of his trial transcript, see if I can interview the witnesses. I have to try, and I will. But that's all."

"Lord help us," Vicki whispered into the dressing room wall.

Grimaud was sitting in a wicker chair beside the door to Danni's cottage when they returned and she got out of Vicki's car, eliciting a grin from Vicki. "That one's good for a rebound fling," she whispered. "Looks like he's working on it, too!"

The comment was in response to a beautifully wrapped package Grimaud held in one large hand, moonlight reflected in a trail of tea rose-colored ribbons. Danni gathered her dress in its bag.

"What's this?" she asked as he stood to hold the door for her.

"A gift," he said earnestly. "After so long a sleep, my urgencies have been those of a scoundrel. I am lost in your time, Danni, and was filled with such joy to find an adept who might help me that I failed to honor you appropriately. Please accept this token of my gratitude. Will you?"

Danni draped the dress over a chair, then took the gift from Grimaud's outstretched hand.

"I'm afraid to open it," she told him, touching the ribbons softly. "It's quite lovely, but..."

"Please," he said, "I wish to redress the harm my desperation and fear have done. It's only a bauble, but chosen especially for you, who have shown me how to survive."

She tugged at the ribbons and removed the creamy paper, revealing a box embossed in unreadable gold lettering.

"It's Arabic," Grimaud said, smiling. "An Algerian jeweler in New Orleans..."

"You've been to New Orleans and back?" Danni said. "But that's a three-hour drive and you don't drive. Never mind; delete that. I don't think I'll believe you even if you tell me how you did it."

"Let me see how it looks," he said, taking a hammered silver and copper torque from its nest of shredded paper in the box and fastening it about her neck. "Ah, perfect!"

Danni moved to the mirror beside the door and studied her reflection. The hammered copper was overlaid in delicate silver tracings, and a froth of silver curled intermittently over the edges like sea foam. It fit her neck perfectly, resting loosely on both clavicles.

"It's lovely," she said softly, "but I can't accept..."

"I have been importunate," he answered. "I ask your forgiveness with this shining band, which only we will understand. Do you see that it cradles your throat, where the pulse of your history lies beneath a gossamer covering of skin? Should you ever deem me worthy of that gift, remove the torque in my presence and I will know. Until then my longing will lie cloaked in silence."

His dark eyes were inky with intensity and small muscles moved beneath his lips.

"I understand," she said breathlessly, turning away. "Thank you."

"Good," he replied. "You have been of inestimable service and now I will help you. Shall we begin with this quilt you mentioned? Or with the crime to be solved?"

"Quilt," she said, remembering Vicki's warning. Her historical research was her livelihood; it was reality. Without it she would have no job, no income. She'd come close to sacrificing her career to a love affair once. She couldn't afford to do it again. And her relationship with Antoine wasn't a love affair anyway. It was just the emotional collision of two lost souls in a dangerous place where both were broken and alone. She would try to help him, but her own survival came first.

Grimaud was scrolling through photos of the vampire quilt on her laptop when Danni returned from putting away her purchases.

"What is it that you need to know about this object?" he asked.

"I need to learn where Neecie got her ideas for the design. The center medallion was very popular, especially in Baltimore, and she might have seen diagrams for it in newspapers, but I need to trace the vampire story."

"Who is Neecie?"

Danni warmed to the subject, remembering how much she loved forgotten things. "The quilter," she explained. "She was a slave, and her husband Joe – That's Joe with the yellow cross. – supposedly killed a vampire – see? That's the vampire with red thread trailing from his mouth. – back when Angola was still a plantation during… the… Civil War." She felt her eyes widen with realization. "Didn't you say that that's when…?"

Grimaud stared at a close-up of the two figures on the computer screen. They had been little more than primitive drawings in thread when new, and now were faded and disintegrating. A man holding a stick beside a yellow cross, and a man lying horizontally, red thread falling from his mouth.

"He was called 'Old Joe'," Grimaud said, touching the upright figure on the screen with a finger. "The other is no stranger to you, Danni. *I* am the other, the vampire."

Outside, the frogs and cicadas began their nightly chorus in gentle fragments, like an orchestra tuning. Danni looked at the brick wall of her cottage that had once been a plantation kitchen. Each brick was stamped, "LaClede," and had been brought down the Mississippi from St. Louis on barges. She'd read about the bricks in the historical materials Vicki placed in the cottages. Everything had changed since then, or had it? The river was still there, the woods and swamps and bricks. Only the superficial, the fleeting, vanished. While the solid, the framework, remained. Stéphane Grimaud had remained; she would not.

"Danni?"

She pulled a chair close and sat beside him, her shoulder touching his arm as they regarded the photograph.

"This man, Old Joe, tried to kill you," she said quietly. "He drove a stake through your chest and buried you. A hundred and fifty years ago."

"Yes," Grimaud answered, turning toward her. "Had he succeeded in decapitating and burning my head, I would not be here. But he was ill and when the shaking fit came upon him his hands were useless. He kicked me into a hole and then kicked dirt over me. I remember a gray cat, watching. I knew the man would die within minutes, but I didn't offer him the gift. He was a brave and wise man. He did not want to live forever."

"But you did?" Danni said.

Grimaud sighed and looked back at the screen. "I was young when I made that choice," he replied. "You will learn that most vampires are young, too inexperienced and arrogant when the gift is offered to understand that it masks a curse. I appear to you as I did then, although I have existed for centuries. Had I the choice now, I would welcome a mortal's death. Only the naïve or the willfully stupid would choose otherwise. I was naïve."

Impulsively, Danni turned to embrace him, her arms stretching over his wide shoulders. "I'm sorry, Stéphane," she said, and didn't recoil when he gently wrapped his arms about her in return. For a moment he felt like a trusted comrade. But in the next moment she felt the warmth of his breath on her neck.

"How can I identify the plantation owner who bought Old Joe and Neecie?" she said, standing abruptly and moving away from him. "I've located a database of

Louisiana slaves that may include them, but transactions are listed under buyer and seller."

Grimaud smiled. "You may ask me," he told her. "Remember, I was here. A man named Isaac Franklin owned the four plantations that are now Angola Prison – they were called Panola, Belle View, Killarney and Angola. Franklin was an infamous slave trader and millionaire, renowned among slaves for his cruelty. I could show you the mass grave in a swamp where the bodies of over a hundred slaves whose deaths he ordered during an outbreak of yellow fever were discarded. Old Joe and his wife either avoided getting sick or were purchased later. If they had survived previous yellow fever infection, they would have been immune and thus valuable. Show me this database and let us see if their sales were recorded."

Grimaud was businesslike, but Danni felt slightly sick.

"I've known about slavery since grade school," she told him. "Even in graduate school it was academic, a social evil, blot on the nation's history, all that. But here... It really happened here, didn't it? Real people were slaughtered like infected livestock and dumped in a swamp?"

"Slavery has been common since the beginning of human interaction," Grimaud said impatiently. "One might say that civilization is built upon the institution of slavery. Agriculture, architecture, everything demands labor. Stop thinking like a child, Danni. Now, this database?"

"Respect for the experience of others is scarcely childlike," she answered, bristling. "If I were 'thinking like a child' I'd try to kill you. Don't say anything else. Here's the site." She leaned across his shoulder and pounded computer keys.

"I have offended you," he said thoughtfully.

"Yes," she answered. "Now let's find Joe and Neecie."

By midnight Danni could not have said with certainty that she lived in the 21st century, so real were the stories emerging from the computer screen. The names, thousands of them! "Alexis, called Azor, male, black, British Creole," had in 1825 been bought from somebody named Lafon by a free black planter named Tabuteau. Alexis was twenty-eight and at the time of his sale had tried to run away more than once. Danni wondered if his new owner, Tabuteau, had been kind, or if Alexis had again tried to run. There was no further record of Alexis.

"What happened to him?" she said, pacing around the table as Grimaud scrolled through the record and made notes in an elegant script that reminded Danni of embroidery. She heard an echo of hounds baying, smelled sweat and blood.

Grimaud looked up and watched for several seconds before answering.

"You are particularly sensitive," he said. "Any adept may travel in the past, but you must learn that to do so without protection is unwise. You are mortal; you cannot bear the burden of history as I can. This man, Alexis, is not your concern. Do not allow his story to touch you. Learn to guard your mind."

"How?" Danni said. "He was real, something happened to him. I want to know!"

Grimaud's dark eyes swarmed with gold, hypnotic and commanding.

"No," he said. "As in mortal life, you must discern. You may know the stories of but a few who share your time. Very few. It is the same with the past, which will overwhelm you in an instant, should you enter it unguarded. Your training as a historian will guide you. Choose one story; ignore all else."

Danni remembered sitting on the floor in a library with other children as a lady with white hair read a book and showed pictures before she turned the pages. It was the story of Chicken Little, but Danni already knew the story and looked around at all the books. Walls and rows of shelves holding so many books nobody could read them all. Not in a whole life. She'd felt sad for the stories that wouldn't be read, that would just stand quietly forever on their shelves and nobody would ever know what they said. She'd hugged her knees and rocked on the library floor, sobbing until Wendy gathered her up and carried her outside to the car.

"There, there, the sky can't fall," Wendy said. "It was just an acorn falling on a silly chicken."

Danni hadn't been able to say she wasn't crying about the silly chicken but about the books in the library.

"I know," she told Grimaud. "I've known for a long time. But the names... it felt like they were calling me."

"You are an adept," he replied. "Everything calls to you. Not only human history but all the thousand beings who exist just beyond mortal awareness. Elementals – elves, gnomes, faeries, trolls, countless bogeys and ghosts - that have too many names to mention. Learn to listen only to what you need. Silence the rest."

"Gnomes?" Danni said, laughing. "You can't be serious! I'll concede that you're a vampire, but I've never seen a gnome except for those creepy little statues in yards."

Grimaud sighed. "Yes, you have," he said. "You simply did not know what you were seeing. There are elemental creatures everywhere, although ephemeral, unable to sustain the illusion of human form for long. They're mischievous, but sometimes willing to help in human endeavors. Do not discount them."

Danni regarded him thoughtfully. The light from a brass chandelier over the table gleamed on his dark hair and wide hands spread over a computer keyboard. He might be a rancher or an FBI agent, the sort of man who says little and does what needs to be done. Except he wasn't a rancher or an FBI agent. He was a Basque shepherd who died in an ancient French hovel before there was France. Now he was a dictionary of folklore.

"I don't mean to dismiss the things you teach me, so thank you," she said, her shadow touching his hands as she bowed slightly.

He nodded, sharing a silence with her. Then he said, "You are overtired. With your permission I will return to my quarters and continue the search for the man who tried to kill me and the woman who captured the story in a quilt."

"Yes, all right," Danni agreed, and turned away from him. Later in her sleep she saw a dark man named Alexis running, heard dogs and harsh voices. And then her own hand fell over the scene, pushing it far away.

CHAPTER TWENTY

She awoke when the phone rang at eight.

"This is Warden Tilly's office," a young woman's voice informed her cheerfully. "Would y'all be able to come on up here today? Warden says he wants to go over all the things for the revival you and Mr. Dupre been working on."

"I suppose so," Danni answered while shuffling into the kitchen to measure coffee into its basket. "What time?"

"Soon as you can get here," the voice said. "Just tell the guard at the main gate to bring you on to the warden's office."

Only after she'd poured a cup of coffee and slathered strawberry jam on a warm croissant did she notice her tablet on the table, a sheet of paper folded beside it. Grimaud's spidery handwriting filled the entire page.

"The slave called Neecie was listed as a mulatto from St. Landry Parish when she was sold at twenty-two years of age by Etienne Gaiennie to Jean Mercier," he had written. "Her price was three hundred dollars, including an infant at breast, male, named Toussaint. Her occupation was wet nurse. She was born in Louisiana Territory and listed her mother's place of birth as Caribbean. Her father was white, unnamed.

"Toussaint Mercier was sold twelve years later with two younger brothers, Alexandre and Benedicte, born to Neecie during her tenure with Jean Mercier, to Fr. Jean-Christophe Decuir. The priest was attached to a monastery near New Orleans. We must imagine that in addition to field work the boys were educated there, as was the custom. Neecie was sold at the same time to Isaac Franklin, her skills listed as *domestique, blanchisseuse* and *cuisinière*."

Danni stood at the door of her cottage, once a plantation kitchen, and imagined Neecie there, a *cuisinière*, a cook. Had she wept as her three boys were sold, hoping they might learn to read and somehow use that skill to escape bondage? Toussaint, the eldest, would have been closest to her heart. What happened to him? And when had she met and married Joe? In the soft quacking of the ducks Danni imagined Grimaud's warning. There were too many stories, endless corridors of stories in which she would be lost forever.

For a moment she considered the fact that her own story was hidden somewhere in the past as well, a recent past that should be easily accessible, but wasn't. Surely there was a birth certificate, but where? At three she had spoken English with no noticeable accent, so she was probably American, although she'd been left in a village only ten miles south of the Canadian border. Maybe she was Canadian. Who had named her "Danni" and was "Telfer" really her surname? The questions echoed through her life, always unanswered. But now Grimaud could read the answers, volumes of them encoded in her blood. All she had to do...

"No," she said aloud, shaking her head. The danger was immeasurable, terrifying. She feared that the ecstasy he promised, an accumulation of centuries, would destroy her utterly. At the first prick of his teeth she would die or go mad. But how deeply she wanted to know who she was! If only she could just cut a finger, drip some blood into a spoon and hand it to him. Except she was pretty sure the practical approach wasn't what he had in mind.

Showering quickly, she chose to wear her new dress, fastening Grimaud's torque at her neck. Except she looked as if she were going to dinner at a restaurant with a trendy name, Danish flatware and an eighteen-page wine list.

"It's nine o'clock in the morning and you're going to a prison," she told her reflection in the mirror, "where the only other women are guards in ugly uniforms." Sandals would tone it down, she decided, scanning the few clothes she'd brought for a modest little jacket she already knew wasn't there. The only thing she could find was a tan wool cardigan she'd packed in the mistaken idea that nights in Louisiana might be chilly. It would have to do.

The morning air was still pleasant and she drove the Angola Road with the windows down, enjoying the scents of lush greenery and damp, loamy soil. From a tin-roofed shack with a goat in the yard she sensed discord. A woman hungover and violently sick, and the spirit of a dead mother weeping in anguish. She pushed her hand at the shack, shoved the awareness away. Grimaud had been right. It worked.

At the prison gate she told the guard that she'd been summoned by Warden Tilly, then stood in the sun while her car was briefly searched.

"We really shake you down on the way out," one of the guards told her, grinning. "Make sure you ain't carry no prisoners hangin' underneath on yer exhaust pipes."

"Wouldn't exhaust pipes burn?" she asked, considering how this might be done.

"Guy tried it once maybe fifteen years back, wrapped his hands and legs in newspaper under his jeans. Pipes ain't hot anyway if the car been sittin' for a while. "Cept he was up under a truck."

"What happened?" Danni asked, unable to relinquish the story.

"Well, that ole truck had a leak in one of the exhaust pipes, so the guy was breathin' carbon monoxide the whole time. Got dizzy and fell off right here at the sally port. Truck drove off and there he was on the ground, couldn't even stand up, poor dude. Attempted escape, got him three more years on a thirty year sentence. Think he died a few years back. This here officer will escort you to the warden's office. Just follow the van."

The guard waved her on and Danni smiled, wondering how she could be smiling while driving over the scene of such a loss. The man had been desperate, resourceful and brave. He might have made it. She wished he had, then reminded herself that he was a criminal and would only have committed more crimes. Unless he wouldn't have. Maybe he'd have just caught a bus to someplace far away and never been found. Did that ever happen? She guessed if it did, the escaped weren't giving interviews.

"Mornin' Miz Danni," the warden said, standing as the guard escorted her into the prison's main office. He wasn't as tall as she was. "Sure do appreciate the help you been givin' Monk. Come on in and have a seat. I got the design for the last batch of posters and such right here, just want to go over everything before it gets printed up. Coffee?"

"No, thank you," she answered, inspecting a poster in which the winged gargoyle she'd chosen seemed to cower in fear at a blazing cross held aloft by a hand of indeterminate racial heritage. Beneath the cross and gargoyle, gothic-looking text in gold announced, "Angola Casts Out the Unholy!"

"It's, uh, very nice," she said. "Probably a good idea to use white text there at the bottom for the admission fee, date and time. You want that to show up against the dark background."

He made a note and stapled it to the poster. "These'll be in every business around here by five o'clock," he told her. "St. Francisville, New Roads, on over to Zachary, get a few up in Baton Rouge, Natchez. We already got a busload comin' from Texas!"

"Texas," she repeated brightly, having no idea what one said about revivals.

"Monk, he's a college boy," Tilly mentioned, his cornflower blue eyes suddenly boring into hers. "And you a college teacher. Good thing, him havin' somebody he can talk to. Not many like you 'roun' here."

Danni returned his look. "Do you think he killed that man in Opelousas?" she said.

Tilly sat heavily in his desk chair and turned to gaze out the window at the Big Yard. Danni studied the folds of flesh bulging over his shirt collar, the florid skin and graying hair. He seemed a man long ago poisoned by a reality he now simply accepted. Dwight Tilly's world was reptilian, brutal. But he wasn't. He merely used the tools at hand – in this case his command of a hidden city – to his own advantage.

"No," he answered. "But what I think don't matter."

The door to the outer office opened and Antoine approached the receptionist's desk.

"Come on in, Monk," Tilly yelled, suddenly bon vivant. "Let's finish up this job."

Danni's smile was businesslike, Antoine's courteous. He smelled like soap and his dark curls were still wet from the shower he must have taken in preparation for this meeting. His eyes stopped at the shining torque at her neck.

"Very pretty," he said. Then, "How may we help you, warden?"

For an hour they went over the final series of press releases and the warden's speech, making minor changes. Antoine was distant, and Danni wondered why. When Tilly took a camera from his desk they both looked up.

"I got a idea!" he said, calling for a car and driver on the desk phone. "You know, a photo of the place where them boys was diggin'? People say that's where this vampire was dug up. Make somethin' for the newspapers, see? Picture of a hole in the ground. They love that."

Danni stifled a smile. "The accompanying text should actually say nothing," she offered. "Like, 'Civil War Secrets Buried in Angola Plantation Grounds.' Then a long article about broken French china and chicken bones, with an old recipe for Creole Chicken Fricassee."

Tilly beamed. "Monk, we ain't got much time. Just called a security officer to run you on over to the park where they diggin' for the golf course. Take some pictures of anything looks like a hole over there, hear me? Bring the camera back and we send the picture with the press release for tomorrow. Shouldn't take you more 'n' an hour. Go."

He walked them to the parking lot, then stood at the gate barking orders into a cell phone. Antoine was tense, silent as they sat in the back seat of a white state vehicle moving toward the interior of the vast prison grounds. At least the driver was one of the security officers he'd known for years, a friend. As they passed a body of water with a sign saying, "Lake Killarney," Danni said, "One of the four plantations that make up the prison was called 'Killarney.'" Antoine merely nodded, his eyes watching the empty road as if it were about to explode.

"Antoine," she tried again. "Talk to me. Where are we going?"

"Further on, next to the old cemetery," he said. "It's a park. Trusties could come there with their visitors, their friends and wives and families if they had any. Picnic tables under roofs for shade, barbecue grills, a playground for the children. I was there once with Timer. He set us up for a work crew. We unloaded the bags of groceries from a little store less than a mile from the main gate. When the warden closed down the park, the owner sold the place; it's a convenience store now. Timer and I helped people cook their food and then cleaned up after. We played with their kids. It was the best day of my life in this place."

The guard turned at the end of a field and pointed. "See, there it is," he said. Hillside Park, they used to call it. Then it was Butler Park. Now it's nothing, just a picnic ground for the fishermen and soon the golfers who'll pay to come in here for a day. The park is theirs now. No prisoner has been here in years. Kind of a shame."

A thin cloud cast a shadow on a grassy hillside where widely spaced cement tables with benches and shingled roofs looked like a child's drawing of a village. Near the road were an empty sandbox, basketball goal and rusting swing set. One of the swings had broken from its chain and hung limp in the grass. At the edge of the park, mounds of earth indicated a leg of the planned golf course.

The driver stopped on the gravel verge beside the park. "You take those pictures and I'll be right here havin' a smoke," he said.

Danni left her sweater in the car and looked around. The flat fields were empty, the roads bare of a single vehicle.

"So let's take some photos of dirt," she said, moving toward mounds of orange clay baking in the sun.

The day was warming but not yet hot, and a soft breeze moved visibly through the dense trees shading tables halfway up the hill. Antoine followed her toward the upturned earth, his eyes never leaving the ground. She could feel his presence in the quiet air like an electrical thrum. Something was wrong.

There was no dearth of holes where a backhoe had gutted the landscape, and Danni took scores of photos.

"Good. Better get back," Antoine said to his feet as Danni stopped dead and he bumped into her.

"What's wrong?" she said without turning around. "Why are you acting like this?"

He didn't move, but spoke against her back. She could feel his height behind her like an evasive ghost.

"It's no good, Danni," he said, following her as she wandered up a hill that bounded the park on one side. "I had no right to ask you to do something you can't possibly do. I don't know how this happened to me, this place. But it did and I can't do anything but be in it. *You* are not meant to be in it or anything connected to it. I was wrong to ask."

She turned to face him and he stepped back but didn't refuse to meet her gaze. The abandoned park rose below them, its memories swarming in the empty air. She heard faint singing, a song Wendy sometimes hummed, and she smiled. "Somebody's singing "You Are My Sunshine," she told him, and saw his eyes narrow.

She didn't know why her reference to the song had upset him, but his remarks were grim. She had promised to help him and would try, but the task was beyond her and they both knew it. Soon she would leave, find another job, make a life far away. Antoine would stay, and he would perish. The man before her would either die or become something utterly different, something brutal and cold. A murderer. But not yet.

"This is where the sidewalk ends, Antoine," she told him, referencing the poem they'd both learned as children. "But I'm going to do the best I can to help you before it does. Don't give up yet."

His smile was pensive as he recited lines from the poem. "'We shall walk with a walk that is measured and slow, And watch where the chalk-white arrows go, To the place where the sidewalk ends.'"

For a moment Danni saw him as a little boy in khaki pants and a school sweater, and beside him a little girl with auburn curls. The little girl was herself. They had learned the same poem as children and it bound them now, siblings in their early love of an elegy. Now they were adults in a park where no child had played in years.

The guard motioned for them to come back, but Antoine stood studying the empty tables and broken swings, smiling. "That song," he said. "You heard 'You are My Sunshine,' but there's nobody here, nobody singing."

"So it was the wind," she said, breathing deeply. The landscape was as uninhabited as a painting.

His grin was devilish. "No," he said. "You're hearing history. In the old days the benches had high backs providing just enough privacy for a man and a woman to, you know, make love. These tables way up here were highly prized; couples would take turns, move in and out during the day. And if one of the guards began walking up the hill, everybody would start singing that song, 'You Are My Sunshine,' as a warning."

"You're kidding," she said, laughing. "Why that song?"

"It's a Louisiana tradition," he told her. "Supposedly a governor named Jimmie Davis wrote it for his horse back in the forties." His eyes grew somber again. "Have a wonderful life, Danni. Don't let me and this place intrude, okay?"

She stared at the guard in a prison van with its pelican shield on the doors. "That sounds like good-bye," she said, not ready to accept it what was going to happen. She *wouldn't* accept it.

"It probably is good-bye, Danni," he said, his voice ragged. "The warden stuck Planchard in a cell long enough for me to write up his revival, but it won't last forever. Hoyt Planchard will order my death soon, just as he did with Timer. He won't do it himself; he's nothing but a sniveling coward. But he's smart enough to run a gang of brainless scum who do whatever he tells them in exchange for drugs and the illusion of status."

As they walked toward the van he picked up a pebble and flung it over the road toward the cemetery, rows of whitewashed cement crosses behind a low board fence. "I have no choice but to be tortured and killed by them, or to kill Hoyt Planchard. I don't want to die, Danni. I don't know what to do."

From somewhere deep inside she felt a wavering certainty. It was cold and clear and perfect, like ice, but alien. "If the only way you can survive is to kill, then you have no choice," she said, finding the words both bitter and true. "I understand, but it can never be right."

He said nothing. If he were to become that murderer, the man who had been Antoine Dupre would perish.

In the main prison parking lot a security officer was waiting when they returned. The guard was courteous, but seemed edgy. After directing Danni to leave, he turned to Antoine.

"Warden sprung Planchard an hour ago," he said. "He's out, Monk. Watch your back."

Antoine felt his life drain into the pavement. A last interlude of freedom in an abandoned park had been Dwight Tilly's parting gift to a dead man.

"I have to tell her," he begged the guard.

"Go!"

He ran to catch Danni, who'd turned up the air-conditioning and didn't hear him call her name. She'd already begun to navigate her way through the parking lot to the main road when she heard something pounding on the back of the car. Stopping, she looked back and saw Antoine, wild-eyed in yellow-white glare.

He stood tall then, fists clenched as she slid from the car, puzzled. "He's out, Danni," he said. "Planchard." His voice was soft but final. "I won't do it, Danni. I won't kill just to stay alive as a monster. We won't see each other again, but remember me, okay?"

He turned and walked back to the guard, who ushered him through a door. The lock cracked like a shot in the hot air.

CHAPTER TWENTY-ONE

Danni felt herself shut down, a glide of silence spreading from head to hands like a numbing mist. She had to get out of the prison, away from the fences and razor wire and guards, before she could analyze the words Antoine had spoken. She couldn't allow the meaning of those words to penetrate her mind. Not yet.

"Just get out of here," she said aloud, driving from muscle memory, thinking nothing. At the main gate she stopped simply because there was a sign, a barrier over the road and two guards barring her way, not because she understood what she was doing.

"Open the trunk," one of the men said, causing a flurry of conceptual panic. The car was a rental. Was there a button to open the trunk from the inside? She didn't know and got out to open it with the electronic key.

"You didn't need to get out," the guard said. "You coulda just hit your remote from inside. Hot out here."

"Yes," Danni said, getting back in and fastening her seatbelt. "Hot." The words felt gritty in her throat, against her teeth.

The second guard had been on the ground, shining a flashlight under the car. He stood and brushed dust from navy blue pants with wide red stripes down the legs. "You're good, go on," he said, and the barrier rose like the second hand of a clock, deliberate and relentless.

She drove slowly, mentally naming landmarks. The convenience store where once people bought picnic supplies for a park now empty and silent. On the left a post office with a sign saying, "Angola, LA, 70712," as if there were a town called Angola. But there was no town. There were thousands of people, but no town.

On the edge of the road ahead three turkey vultures tore at a carcass, a rabbit or possum, maybe something else. The vultures rose lazily as Danni passed, hideous things hanging from their jaws, their pink, featherless heads stupid and obscene. The birds were a poetry of death, mindless and necessary.

"He's going to die," she pronounced aloud. The words seemed impossible, but in her rear-view mirror she saw the vultures, again methodically biting and tearing. The image, grisly but natural, might have been an Audubon print. It did not appall her. Nevertheless, something like a storm was rising inside her, and when she reached the kudzu-covered shack beside the "Solitude" sign, she turned onto the dirt road and stopped.

The sob began in her gut and filled her body, tearing across her jaw. He was alive, a good man, he had committed no crime. He couldn't die, it wasn't right. Yet she understood that he would.

A man named Hoyt Planchard would kill him. Planchard had ordered others to harass Timer with puerile cruelties until the old man died. A sordid, shameful murder. Planchard had orchestrated the slaughter of Bastet, a depravity thwarted by the magical intervention of a carved cat. Danni didn't question that implausible rescue; it happened. But she also understood that such events were capricious, unreliable. They occurred in response to laws outside human awareness, emerging and vanishing like will o' the wisps. There would be no magical rescue for Antoine. Hoyt Planchard would orchestrate his death.

Danni wept, pushing her head softly against the steering wheel. Through her tears the world beyond the car was a blur of green – swarming jade, flickers pale as asparagus, shadows moving in shades of moss. For a while she existed in the colors, which seemed to curl and sway like a choir. Trees, long grass, kudzu – all were for a time a silent chorus of green, reprising a sorrow she realized was laced with anger.

Antoine would perish at the hands of a sadist, as did thousands, millions throughout time. Prisoners, slaves, women and children, the sick, weak, disabled, animals, the earth itself – all were fair game for the cruel sport of those who had power. It was wrong, it was *evil*, but it was a fact of life.

The green choir before her moved silently in the wind, but Danni no longer watched. Instead, she looked at her hands clenching the steering wheel, the opposable thumbs that set humans apart from all other animals. The hands, the thumbs, the brain capable of speech and abstract thought. Anyone in possession of these had choices, could alter "facts of life," could fight! In the swarming green, she determined to do just that. And it wouldn't hurt that as an adept she might have an extra edge.

When she got back to the B&B Vicki was checking in guests, an elegantly dressed older couple. Danni watched as the woman, her white hair gleaming in the sun, took her husband's arm as they smiled in delight at the ducks and made their way over gravel paths to the cottage on the other side of the pond. The man placed his hand over his wife's in an affectionate gesture that made Danni smile. They seemed to be nice people, like Wendy and Ron, like Antoine. They didn't deserve to be tortured and killed. Neither did he. She stood beside her car, watching the couple walk away.

"Danni," Vicki called, walking toward her, "how did it go… hey, you look funny, like you're about to blow something up. What happened up there?"

Danni shrugged. "Nothing, just… I really hate rotten people."

Vicki nodded sympathetically. "It's that guy, Antoine, isn't it? Did something happened to him?"

Danni considered trying to explain the murky, almost occult world of prisons with their barbaric and impregnable codes of behavior. Vicki wouldn't understand, would believe that a call to the warden could derail Antoine's death. Any rational person would assume as much.

"Yeah, I won't be... seeing him again," she said, unable to control the shudder that moved through her body at the words.

"Oh honey," Vicki said, wrapping Danni in a hug, "it's hard, isn't it. But you'll be okay. After a bit. Right now, how about a stiff drink? I've got most of a two hundred dollar bottle of hundred and forty proof George Stagg bourbon a guest left in one of the cottages. Been saving it for a special occasion, which I'd say this is."

Danni followed the older woman to a kitchen with bright blue cabinets, and accepted two inches of bourbon, neat, in a juice glass. The alcohol burned her throat, but left a pleasant aftertaste of smoky molasses and dark chocolate. It also relaxed, slightly, the knot of rage and despair in her chest. She was ready to fight Hoyt Planchard and every other predator in the world, but she didn't know how to begin.

"Thanks, Vicki," she said. "I think I'll go lie down for a while."

"Best thing," Vicki agreed.

In her cottage Danni kicked off her shoes and curled on the bed, pulling one of Vicki's colorful quilts up to her shoulders. Warmed by the bourbon, her hands and feet still felt cold, as if she'd been standing in an icy stream. The unicorn stood in a stream before the spears tore his flesh, she remembered, detoxifying with his horn water poisoned by snake venom, so that animals could drink. In the Middle Ages people believed that snakes released their venom into streams every night, and that the horn of a unicorn touching the water would purify it. As a child she'd wanted the animals to drink the water made safe by the unicorn. But the ugly men with spears killed the unicorn and broke her five-year-old heart. Drifting into sleep, she knew what she had to do.

The sun was low when she awoke hours later to Grimaud's voice.

"I beg your forgiveness," he said from the doorway. "I had no idea you were…ill."

She saw his nostrils flare, a look of pain, then contempt, crossing his face.

"I'm not ill," she said, pushing aside the quilt and standing. She wanted a shower, clean clothes, something to eat.

"Yes, you are ill," Grimaud pronounced, his deep voice harsh. "You have made a commitment to this man. You want to save him. Did you think I would not know?"

Danni stared at him. "Do you think I *care* what you know?" she said. "And you don't understand, which is not surprising since you're *dead*! Go away. Leave me alone. I need to work."

She felt light-headed, still half-asleep, and pressed her hands against the disheveled bed behind her to steady herself.

"The prisoner, Antoine," Grimaud said bitterly. "To him you pledge your fealty?"

"Oh please," she said, shaking her head, "take your corny vocabulary and go back wherever you came from. I don't have any more time for your games!"

"Games?" His eyes were wide and nearly black, something green and murderous smoldering deep in the pupils. With both huge hands he grasped her arms above the elbows and held her rigid, inches from his body. "Don't you know that I can kill you in an instant?" he whispered. "I can do what I want, you little fool!"

Danni met his gaze. "No you can't," she told him. "You can't kill me because you're forbidden to harm an adept, and you can't have what you want because I do not choose to give it! So either violate your rules and kill me or leave. There's something I have to do, now!"

His grip tightened, pushing her arms against her sides with such force that she saw her ribs and breastbone arching unnaturally outward against her blouse.

"Know that you murder not only me," she exhaled through pain, barely breathing.

Grimaud loosened his grip. "What do you mean?" he demanded.·

Danni drew desperate breaths, then felt the muscles of her legs dissolve. Grimaud caught her as she fell and held her against his chest. His heart was like a muffled gong.

"Antoine will die soon unless I help him," she said into the sound. "He will be killed."

"And this is the work you must do? Save this man from his fate?"

"It's not his fate, there is no 'fate,'" she told Grimaud. "There are only evil men. One of them will kill Antoine unless I can..."

"You long to save him," Grimaud interrupted, distaste evident in his voice. "Have I not told you that such human attachments can never suffice the needs of an adept? Why do you waste yourself on such a man?"

In the question she heard something like jealousy, yet refined over centuries to emotional rarity. Stéphane Grimaud was *antique*, she realized, a sort of heirloom but still strangely human. He needed her, and her commitment to a mortal man hurt and offended him. The understanding changed nothing.

"He needs help and I have offered it, so if you're going to murder me, do it," she said, arching her neck to meet his eyes. "Otherwise, leave me alone."

He sighed and released her. "Why do you not heed the things I tell you?" he asked.

Danni crossed her arms over her chest, her hands kneading her triceps. The vampire was irritating but irrelevant in the face of what might be happening to Antoine, might already have happened. She wondered if she'd know, somehow sense the moment of a friend's death. Surely an adept would have that ability.

"I don't *heed* you because you're useless!" she said. "You can't help me."

His look was thoughtful. "What is it that you need?" he asked. "I've assisted your research and will help you find the man who committed the crime for which this Antoine…"

"It's too late," Danni said. "He'll be dead before any of that can happen."

"Tell me," Grimaud said, drawing her to sit at the table. "Why is this man doomed to die?"

Danni explained Hoyt Planchard, Timer's sad death and the rescue of Bastet from an assailant by a carved cat like the one now watching from a Victorian writing desk beneath the window. She wasn't surprised when the wooden cat moved to stand on all fours, its tail raised in greeting. At Grimaud's nod of acknowledgement it resumed its original, motionless position.

"Planchard will order Antoine's death," she told him. "He has slaves or something, men who do what he tells them to do."

Grimaud took a seat across from her, nodding. "Men always organize themselves in this way," he acknowledged. "But why doesn't Antoine merely kill the man named Planchard? He appears to have no other choice."

"He has made a choice," Danni said. "He will not kill."

"Ah," Grimaud said, seeming to look deeply into the table for a time, then at Danni. His eyes were hooded but she sensed intention beneath the thick lids. "And if I can save him?"

The air felt suddenly heavy, palpable.

"How?" she whispered. "By killing Hoyt Planchard?"

"Perhaps," he answered. "Although I would prefer a solution of more refinement. Killing him would unnecessarily endanger others, who might bear the blame. And it would arouse a dangerous awareness of my presence. Leave the disposal of Planchard to me. The question is rather what you would give to save Antoine's life."

She understood then, saw the transaction he offered as if it were penned on soft vellum and placed on the table between them.

"The stories written in your blood in exchange for his life," Grimaud pronounced, watching her.

"I know what you want," she said, years of intellectual training locking into place a set of guidelines essential in any situation, crucial in this one. The terms must be defined. "What I don't know is what you mean. What is his 'life'? The word has countless meanings beyond mere viability. Before I agree I have to know what it means to you, who are dead."

"Brava," he said, pulling his lips tight across teeth that seemed to stretch and recede in his gums. "You expect deception, a trick of words."

"Of course."

"Do you not trust me?"

"No."

In the silence that followed Danni felt a pulse, like the quiet steps of an animal in darkness. Outside the sky fell in layers of lavender and grey as a single green tree frog began its chant. She merely breathed, waiting for his answer.

"I can deflect the murder of this man," he said. "But only you can save his life. That life is suspended now in a cage. There has been no time in which such an existence, with its diminished access to all but the most impoverished experience, would meet the requirements of 'life.' You must free him, solve the crime. It will require that you allow the full expression of your abilities as an adept, and immediately."

"Why immediately?" she asked.

He turned from her to regard the sky, deep in thought. "Mortals, in their brief existence, do not imagine the labyrinthine nature of the world. An event may only happen at a confluence of factors immeasurably fleeting. For this man, that moment is now. Yet a failure of any thread in his story will obliterate the moment; one possible future will dissolve to be replaced by others. Do you understand?"

Danni bowed her head in acknowledgement. She'd always known. Every moment was a chance to create a story or allow it to vanish. She would do whatever necessary to free the creation of Antoine's story, his life.

"If you prevent his murder *and* help me use these skills as an adept that I don't begin to understand, I will give you what you want," she said with finality, clenching her fists to hide her shaking hands.

The frog chorus was joined by an antiphon of cicadas, their call and response like an ancient psalm unheard for centuries.

"I have work, then," Grimaud said, rising. "When I return you must be ready. We will go to this place where a man was killed and you will employ your gift in disclosing a truth long buried."

Danni touched her throat. "Yes," she said. "I'll be ready."

CHAPTER TWENTY-TWO

Antoine heard the rasp of metal as a guard secured the dormitory for the night. The familiar sound assumed a dimension he'd never noticed, the simple fall of tumbler pins both crisp and musical. The lock, the cement floor, the coarse weave of his sheets all suggested centuries of human activity from which he would soon be absent. He wondered what small contribution he might have made if he had lived. If he hadn't been outside the Palace Café when John Thierry was killed, if six-year-old Hoyt Planchard had stepped on a cottonmouth while fishing in a swamp, if Annabeth had gone to Baylor instead of Northwestern and they'd never met. The stories making up his life seemed so random, so fraught with patterns that flared and extinguished as he watched.

"Toothpaste," a voice muttered.

One of the inmate counsels had just passed Antoine's bunk on his way to the TV room. He didn't appear to have noticed the man with whom he'd worked for years, but there was no one else nearby. Antoine understood the warning and carried his toiletries to the communal bathroom as he would carry a towel full of scorpions.

At a rust-stained sink he turned on the water, removed the cap on his tube of toothpaste and squeezed a string of brown into the drain. The hot water carried a scent of excrement to his face as behind him snickers erupted.

"You got some bad hal-i-to-sis, Monk. You get confused over where to use your tongue?"

Antoine turned to see Perry Bordelon leaning against the wall. Behind him at the door stood Hoyt Planchard.

"Evenin', Monk," Planchard mocked, his fleshy nose casting a thick shadow across his mouth.

Antoine regarded the author of his death with distant curiosity. The man had the look of a ruined boxer, his dark eyes downturned and sullen with failure. Yet Planchard was too spineless ever to have stepped into a ring, too weak for

even that primitive expression of strength. His ruin came
from inside, from some moment when he fled the demand of
adulthood and chose to remain a child forever. A
handsome, secretly diseased child who delighted in pulling
the wings from moths and watching the dismembered body
writhe. Hoyt Planchard was a malignancy.

Antoine took a step forward, every muscle tense with
the need to rid the world of at least one horror. It would not
be difficult. Glancing overhead, he saw a possible weapon
in the exposed water pipes. One was loose, corrosion
visible at the connections. He could reach it from one of the
sinks. It would break off in his hands and then...

Planchard followed Antoine's gaze, saw the sweating,
rusted pipe, and lurched backward. His fear had a sour
odor like spoiled custard, and for a moment Antoine thought
he would have to kill the man or be sick from his mere
proximity. But as he flung a leg up onto the sink in
preparation for a leap to the pipe, he stopped. He had been
a decent man before John Thierry's death consigned him to
prison. Even then he'd used his trained mind to help right
wrongs done to other men. In the park he'd remembered
the man that he was, complete and unbroken. He would be
that man now. He would not lose himself to savagery.

"Get him!" Planchard yelled, his voice screeching from
fear, and five men emerged from behind him to join Perry
Bordelon in soundlessly pounding and kicking Antoine until
blood streamed from his mouth to the drain in the floor. In
the TV room a blaring commercial announced a special on
Chic-Fil-A Nuggets as he lost consciousness.

It was dark when he awoke in his bunk, the scent of
dried blood like a tight mask on his face. He moved gently,
trying feet, legs, arms and trunk. Nothing was broken; he
had only spreading bruises and a ringing headache. It
wasn't over.

Forcing both swollen eyes open, he saw sleeping men
and a strange blue light that seemed to flit above him as if

studying his face. He assumed the flickering thing was a result of his injuries, broken blood vessels pushing against nerves in his brain. He moaned and closed his eyes, falling into a wounded sleep.

Hoyt Planchard woke to a slight pressure on his wrist. It felt like somebody was taking his pulse, and he jerked awake to an alabaster face in which crimson lips curled to bare something white. Teeth, sharp and shining in moonlight drifting through the louvered windows. He wanted to scream but only a faint rasp escaped his throat.

"Do you know what I am?" the creature whispered, its grip on Planchard's wrist now a painful vise. "Answer!"

Planchard wept in terror, nearly swooning as the pain ripped through his arm. "Vvv...pi...," he tried to pronounce, but the word was a cartoon, a Halloween caricature, a joke. The thing leaning over him was real, its eyes swirling coils of amber, paralyzing and dead.

"Yessss," the creature murmured, leaning close as if to kiss. "Will you have me? Will you choose the gift I can give you?"

Planchard understood what the vampire offered, and saw himself in the world, free to indulge his every desire. An expensive car, fast and sleek. Silk shirts, Italian shoes, a beautiful woman on her knees at his crotch, a knife in her throat when he was through with her. The images moved in the air before him, then faded.

"Forever," the creature whispered, his lips caressing the stubble at Planchard's neck. "Everything here will age and die, this place, these people, all will vanish, but you will not. I can make you... immortal."

Blind with need, Planchard arched his neck against the pressing mouth. "Yes," he pronounced without sound, "I want..."

But the vampire pulled away, suddenly remote and thoughtful. "You must give me something in return," he said, "to seal our agreement."

Planchard could barely breathe, so intense was his eagerness. "What? What can I give you?"

"I ask only that you delay the death of the man named Antoine Dupre until the end of the public event, the revival. You may kill him then, but only then. In three days you may kill him in the presence of many, a celebration of your mortal power. And then I can give you power beyond your imagining. I can make you a vampire!"

Planchard saw himself triumphant in the sawdust of the rodeo stadium, Monk Dupre lifeless at his feet. The stadium lights revealed a titan, a superstar, a gleaming god rising above the crowd on leathery black wings that swept the night sky. He could torture and kill whatever he chose; he was free to be exactly what he had always been, but now nothing could constrain him.

"Yes!" he tried to shout, but the sound was only a scratch on the humid darkness.

The vampire began to sing, his dark eyes unblinking and close as his breath bathed the other man's face. *Ez ahaztu*, he crooned. "Do not forget." And then there was nothing but a dancing blue light that fled, insectlike, through a tear in the screen over one of the louvered windows.

Hoyt Planchard stroked himself violently beneath the sheet, imagining the screams of the woman who turned him in as he sliced wide the bodies of her children. Release came when he forced open her mouth and laid two small, quivering hearts on her tongue.

*

Danni woke from a jittery half-sleep as the numbers on the digital bedside clock slid to 3:00 a.m. She wasn't surprised to see Grimaud standing beside her in shadows, his attitude businesslike.

"Give me the official information regarding Antoine's trial," he said. "I will go now and retrieve it. You must drive to this place, Opelousas, and I will meet you there. The distance is   sixty-three miles, a difficult journey that will exhaust me, but it must be done. I've printed a map for you from the Internet. But what is most important..."

"You printed a map from the Internet," Danni repeated. "Only weeks ago you didn't know how to type..."

"The Internet rivals even vampiric knowledge in its scope and may be the subject of our discourse later," he replied. "At the moment we must devote our attention to the task at hand. We have only three days. *You* must function now as the adept that you are, allowing every impression access to your mind. I can uncover the path carved by events surrounding the death of John Thierry, but only you can perceive what may inhabit that path."

"How do I do that?" Danni asked, dragging herself out of bed to stand before the dresser.

Grimaud moved into the kitchen. "I don't know," he said from the dark, "but I assume the process to involve a shutting out of the quotidian while cultivating a sensitivity to what may lie hidden behind it."

"The person who really killed John Thierry is hidden behind it," she said while pulling on a skirt and knit top she thought a savvy female FBI agent might wear. She was in a play again, except this one was real. And possibly pointless. Antoine might already be dead.

"Stéphane," she whispered to the form by the kitchen door, "you said you would save him. Have you?"

"He lives," Grimaud said. "The creature called Planchard will not kill him yet. But time is running out for the saving of his life. A window in the nature of things is open for a single pulse, and then closes. That you have come here and met him at the moment in which his life hangs in balance, that at the same time I have awakened and needed your help, that a wooden cat was roused to life for the sake of a mortal cat – all are a confluence that even now moves on, dissipates. We must act within this window of time, quickly. When it closes, all my knowledge, all your skill, can do nothing. Events will proceed as they would have if you, and indeed I, had never been here. This is a universal truth most mortals cannot accept, but you must."

"I do," she told him. "What you're telling me I've always known."

"Because you are an adept."

"I guess," she said, sufficiently awake now to focus on details. "I assume you have some magical way of getting to Opelousas while I drive through backwoods Louisiana at three o'clock in the morning?"

"The effort will be taxing, but yes."

"Great. So how will I find you?"

"I will be at the courthouse," he said. "Park near there and I will come to you."

She frowned. "The courthouse will be closed," she said.

"Indeed," he answered, smiling. "Now give me the necessary information."

"Antoine's trial was in August, ten years ago," she recited the information she'd memorized when Antoine gave it to her. "The docket number is V-20096. With that number you can get the case record, which will include a trial transcript that costs about seventy-five dollars, except there won't be anybody there to get it for you."

"I have studied the Louisiana court system online in preparation for this, and will find the documents," he said dismissively. "Let us not waste any more time."

She watched as he dissolved in a globe of blue light and vanished into the moist darkness beyond her cottage. Scrawling a quick note for Vicki, she grabbed her bag and Grimaud's Mapquest printout. Bastet followed her to her car, purring so plaintively the sound might have been speech. She understood.

"I'll try," she told the cat. "I promise you, I'll do the best I can."

The roads were sparsely populated and blanketed with a pale fog in which sounds and images seemed to quiver, then fade.

"Focus!" she told herself. "You're an adept, a witch. You *have* to be!" It was hard to drive, to perform the countless engagements with reality required by piloting a car, while consciously stripping her mind of its connection to the road, the landscape, a tractor left in a field. Stopping beside a muddy creek she closed her eyes and merely listened to the hissing mist.

People were singing, a rough choir of few voices, but fervent. Danni captured the tune and rode it into a moment she knew had flown long before she was born. The music was simple, a sort of hymn or anthem, each verse followed by a chorus. The voices were faint, their accents peculiar, but with intense concentration she caught a few lines. "War to the hilt, theirs be the guilt, who fetter the free man, to ransom the slave."

The people were singing around a campfire at the edge of the little creek beneath trees that were no longer there. A family maybe, an old man in high, buttoned shoes, a little girl with red hair Danni then saw as a young woman dying in a primitive hospital as a man in a bloodstained jacket said, "Childbed fever."

But then the young woman was a little girl again, and the group sang clearly, "God save the South, God save the South, Her altars and firesides, God save the South."

Danni inhaled deeply and opened her eyes. There was nothing before her but a muddy creek moving toward a cement bridge that looked as if it had been constructed as a WPA project in the 1930's. Only a grackle was singing somewhere near the creek, its noisy tweets and clucks devoid of human interest.

So this was the capacity Grimaud had named "adept." Danni checked herself for side effects and felt a little tired, but then she hadn't had much sleep. Maybe the gnawing discomfort in her stomach? Except it felt familiar.

"You're just hungry!" she told herself. It wasn't the price of seeing long-dead Southerners singing around a fire, it was the price of eating nothing for twenty-four hours. But she'd done it. She'd pushed aside the clutter of the real world and seen what lay beneath. In this case what she'd seen was a moment that had no bearing on Antoine's life, but at least she'd practiced.

Driving on, she scanned the roadside for anything that looked like an open restaurant. It was 3:30 in the morning and still dark, the road lit only by occasional mercury vapor yard lights illuminating empty feed lots. But she saw a faded road sign advertising "Penny's Diner, Livonia, 15 miles, Open 24 Hours." Ignoring the speed limit, she was there in twelve minutes.

The diner, a rectangle of shiny chrome with red and blue trim, sat incongruously in the parking lot of a motel. A couple of parked big rigs, their engines idling, announced the transport of goods to Walmart and from a lumber company in Covington. Danni heard chain saws and the screams of slaughtered trees as she parked beside the lumber truck, then deliberately silenced the sound by concentrating on food. Truckers gravitated to the good stuff.

Inside, she slid into a vinyl booth and grabbed a big laminated menu from behind a sugar dispenser. The first item, "Onechal's Hearty Breakfast," involving two of everything plus grits, would do. Except for the grits. An attractive African American woman who seemed half asleep came to take her order.

"First time I've had to work graveyard in ten years," she told Danni. "Two of my night staff got the flu and I am SO careful about that. What would you like?"

The odd name on the menu was compelling, a beckoning corridor. More adept stuff. Danni seized the opportunity to practice while safely not driving.

"I'll have this one," she said. "Onechal's. What an unusual name!"

"It's my name," the woman said. "For my great-great-grandmother's sister Onechal. We don't really know where it came from, but she was Choctaw so maybe it's a Choctaw name."

Danni stared into the name on the menu. If she could follow it maybe she could do the same in Opelousas. Maybe she could find John Thierry's killer. Closing her eyes, she relinquished her awareness of the brightly-lit diner and found herself standing ankle-deep in water, although her feet didn't feel wet. The scene was like a mirage, shifting and unreal yet oddly genuine.

There were rows of plants in the water, and people nearby. A muscular black man seemed to direct a group of others, black and bronze-skinned men and women, in tending the plants. Danni thought she was seeing a rice paddy. The scene looked like a video someone in her high school World Citizenship class had shown while reciting statistics about global food resources, except the video had been about China.

"Are you all right?"

Danni opened her eyes to see the woman named Onechal offering her a cup of coffee.

"It looked like you fell asleep," the woman said. "Better have some coffee."

"Yes, thank you," Danni replied. "Um, is rice grown in Louisiana?"

Onechal sat in the booth across from Danni. "Since the 1600's," she said. "I know because my sister's a high school history teacher, bores us all to death telling the story every Thanksgiving! French settlers brought slaves from Africa and they all would have starved to death if the Africans didn't already know how to cultivate rice. The French government didn't have enough money and troops to colonize the New World, so the French gave up and went home but they left their slaves here, which I'll bet was fine with them! They sort of merged with the Choctaw Indians, intermarried and kept growing rice. I guess it was pretty nice for a while."

"Then what happened?"

"The French came back," Onechal said with distaste. "And the Spanish and the British. They enslaved the Africans, the Choctaw, anybody they could get their hands on. Why are you asking about rice at four a.m.?"

Danni shrugged. "I don't know. Something about your name..."

The other woman stood to get Danni's plate from the cook. "Like I said, my great-great aunt was Choctaw," she said. "You must have been thinking about history because of my name."

Danni smiled in agreement, wondering how she was supposed to use her skill as an adept to find a killer when she had no control over the images that emerged in her mind. She'd meant to follow the name "Onechal" and instead had wound up in a 17th century rice paddy that made no sense until it was explained to her. What would happen in Opelousas when she tried to see John Thierry's death ten years in the past and instead saw the local tryouts for "American Idol"?

She dug into her sausage and pancakes, hiding the grits under a huge sprig of parsley. The sky was shifting from inky black to a color like wet slate in which she saw absolutely nothing.

CHAPTER TWENTY-THREE

Danni had no trouble parking on the street beside the Art Deco courthouse in Opelousas. There were no other cars, and an early morning haze dripped from the leaves of oaks shading the cracked sidewalk. A sign saying, "St. Landry Parish District Court," roused a dim curiosity about who "St. Landry" might have been. Closing her eyes, she tried to follow the name back in time but saw nothing. "Landry" didn't sound like a saint. Maybe there was nothing to follow, the name so eroded by time that its story was lost. Or maybe she'd exhausted her capacities as an adept at the diner. Did it work that way? Could you waste the skill on frivolous pursuits and then have to wait for it to recharge?

Grimaud believed that the revival at Angola, only three days away, was crucial, and Danni sensed that he was right. The revival was scheduled for one o'clock on Saturday afternoon. In less than seventy-two hours the window in time that had opened on the story of a vampire, a prisoner and a history professor, would close. There would be no story. She had to find John Thierry's killer *now*. Screwing her eyes tightly shut, she took deep breaths and tried to clear her mind until something heavy jarred the car.

It was Grimaud sliding into the passenger's seat, a thick sheaf of papers clutched in one fist. "I copied the trial transcript," he said conversationally. "Even had time to make myself a birth certificate. What are you doing?"

"I was trying to follow that name," she told him, pointing to the sign. "I couldn't, and I was afraid I'd worn out my skill just when I need it most! And why do you need a birth certificate?"

Grimaud sighed. "I think there was a bishop in Paris named Landericus, but that was before my time. It is of no importance, and a birth certificate is necessary to the procurement of documents proving my existence."

"Before *your* time?" Danni interrupted, laughing. "I didn't know the Cro-Magnons had bishops."

He smiled thoughtfully. "It is natural that mortals have a distorted understanding of time," he said. "Your lives are so brief; not one is more than the faintest spark. Millions of years passed before a single word was recorded, and thousands more since ... but I digress. Our concern is one event only a decade in the past. Look." He pointed to a dim neon sign on a light standard in front of a corner building across from the courthouse. "Palace Café – Steaks, Seafood."

As Danni watched, the neon sign flickered to life, followed by a light deep inside the restaurant. "That's it," she gasped. "That's where it happened. And somebody's in there."

Grimaud shrugged. "The cook. Patrons will arrive soon for breakfast. I suggest that a more concise representation of the event 'happens' in these pages," he said, handing her the stack of paper. "I will seek a place to rest now and return to you when you have need of me."

"You're leaving?" she said. "How am I supposed to...?"

"You will know," he told her as he unfolded his bulk from the car, grimacing as hazy sunlight filtered through the trees. "The journey has exhausted me. See the names, Danni, see the story, ask for threads that are missing. When I can be of use I will come."

With that he was gone, his absence an instructive weight, like the echo of an order in the steamy air. Danni felt the weight solidify in her mind, become intent. There was no space for insecurity. She knew how to research and possessed at least a beginner's skill as an adept. Antoine's life hung in the balance of both. Already sweating, she took the trial transcript to a grassy spot beneath an oak and sat down to read.

The document revealed that five other people were in the Palace Café when a court clerk named John Thierry and a stranger from Chicago named Antoine Dupre, argued. Jacques Boutte, the cook, was in the kitchen. *Jacques.*

Danni underlined the name and dog-eared the page. A dying prisoner had tried to tell Antoine something about "Jacques," but death had silenced the man before Antoine arrived.

The transcript went on to document the fact that Gaston Savoie, a local sausage maker, came through the front door on that day ten years in the past, and greeted the waitress, Marie Melancon, and an elderly couple named Fontenot. These five people, the only witnesses to events surrounding John Thierry's death, had testified at Antoine's trial.

Danni carefully read the statements of each. The waitress, Marie Melancon, heard the stranger, Dupre, threaten Thierry, telling him to step outside. Melancon broke down during her testimony, requiring a brief recess, which Danni thought odd. Why would the woman become so distraught during questioning in which she was accused of nothing? She didn't claim to have seen the murder, only to have heard Antoine urge Thierry to step outside, presumably for a fight. Danni couldn't imagine the gentle, studious Antoine in the role of macho thug, but reminded herself that ten years had passed since the day John Thierry died. She knew so little about Antoine Dupre. Too little.

A whipworm of doubt hatched in her mind, its infinitesimal movement spreading rivulets of unease. If Marie Melancon was telling the truth, then Danni Telfer might be on a fool's errand, chasing shadows for the sake of a man who had beaten another man to death between two buildings only yards from where she now sat. For a moment she allowed the possibility. Antoine had been only twenty-six and broken by grief. He was obsessed with the need to complete the work Annabeth had loved, and John Thierry thwarted that need. The pointless barrier would have been intolerable. But even when young and emotionally overwhelmed, was Antoine Dupre capable of rage so violent that it resulted in murder?

Danni silenced the reality surrounding her and cleared her mind. Pressing her hands to her eyes, she felt the core of the man in her mind. There was sadness, wry laughter and a decency so deep it glowed. Antoine had killed no one. Marie Melancon, perhaps accustomed to belligerent male customers, might have imagined Antoine's remarks. And she might have lied under oath. But why?

The elderly Fontenots, Alma and Gilbert, both testified that Antoine had spoken to Thierry in the restaurant, asking Thierry to allow him access to some court records. Thierry had refused, both men had paid their bills and both had left the restaurant, Thierry leaving first. The Fontenots did not hear Antoine threaten Thierry and did not see the murder.

In cross examination the district attorney pointed out that Gilbert Fontenot suffered from impaired hearing, wore aids in both ears and might not have heard Antoine's threat. Alma Fontenot reminded the district attorney that he was blind as a bat without his glasses and had been since she taught him in first grade, and nobody was questioning his ability to see what was in front of his face. Danni grinned and made a note to find Alma.

The cook, Jacques Boutte, said that he paid no attention to anything but the orders Marie handed him but did hear Antoine Dupre threatening somebody because Dupre was yelling. Boutte was also busy filling out an order for Savoie. A tour bus of Civil War buffs would arrive at six that evening, requiring additional Boudin sausage. Boutte stated that he knew nothing of Thierry's death until Alma Fontenot yelled at him to call the police. Boutte said Alma had to yell because Marie wouldn't stop screaming.

Gaston Savoie said that he'd come to deliver sausages and see if Boutte would need any extra for the dinner crowd, and heard "angry words" from Antoine Dupre, directed at John Thierry. He couldn't quote Dupre because at the moment he was in a conversation with Marie Melancon, but he was certain that Dupre was "all agitated, like a gator when you throw marshmallows in the water." Danni considered the image and shook her head.

The town was stirring, people driving into parking lots, ducking into the now-open Palace Café for coffee and walking languidly toward offices. Early risers, who could afford a leisurely approach to the day. Danni had never been one of them and wondered if the extra minutes of freedom were worth the effort. Probably not.

She was uncomfortable on the ground and suspected that everyone on the street was aware that a strange woman reading a ream of paper was getting grass stains on her skirt. Standing, she smiled efficiently at the transcript, stashed it in the car and made her way to the café. If anyone asked, she'd say she was in town from New York to research a book. Her accent, or lack thereof, would be convincing. Especially if she asked why anyone would throw marshmallows at alligators.

The interior of the café was still muggy from the night, its air conditioner struggling audibly to diminish bacon-scented moisture. Danni sat deliberately at the counter in order to watch the cook, a bald man in a white jacket and a hairnet over his sparse goatee. Danni wondered if this could be Jacques Boutte.

"I'll just have coffee, please," she told the waitress, a heavy-set teenager with a narrow streak of magenta in thick, jet black hair. Her smile was friendly.

"Your cook looks so much like my high school algebra teacher," Danni said, returning the smile. "His last name isn't Adams, is it? I mean, they could be brothers!"

"That's Sonny Tassin and his mama's name was Crook, if you can believe," the girl answered. "'Fraid there's no Adamses on *that* family tree, but you have not lived until you've had Sonny's crawfish gumbo. We don't serve it 'til lunch, but y'all can come back then."

"Umm, sounds wonderful," Danni replied, wondering how to ask if the waitress knew anything about Jacques Boutte or Marie Melancon or the rest of the witnesses. There seemed to be no way to ask without revealing her purpose. The traditional route was safer.

Returning to her car, Danni grabbed her laptop and found a seat in the lobby of the courthouse where there was sure to be wi-fi. The *Opelousas Daily World* was only archived online from 2004, but that was sufficient. First she checked the obituaries, name by name, learning that both Alma and Gilbert Fontenot had died within months of each other three years after the trial. Marie Melancon, Gaston Savoie and Jacques Boutte were not listed among the Opelousas dead, which might mean they were still alive. She did find "Gaston Savoie Jr.," who had died five years after the trial at the age of four.

A phone book search yielded seventeen Melancons and Danni rummaged through her bag for her cell phone.

The first Melancon, Ambrose J., was awakened by Danni's call and unwilling to chat, although eloquent in his command of colorful epithets. Pondering exactly how one might manage "a rabid possum up your ass," she dialed the next three. Catherine, who ran a day care center, was too busy to talk, and neither Edgar nor Homer and Dottie were home. The fourth call, to Larry P., was helpful.

"Marie Melancon?" he asked in the booming voice of an auctioneer. "That's my cousin Rosie Melancon's niece, came to stay with Rosie for a while a few years back, then she left."

There was no Rosie in the phone directory, but then maybe Melancon was her maiden name.

"Could you tell me how I might reach Rosie?" Danni asked.

Larry P. laughed, a warm, conversational laugh that reminded her of her Ron. "If I could tell you that I'd be a rich s.o.b., excuse the language. You could try, though. She's buried between both her husbands up there in Bellevue Memorial Park. You let me know if she talks, okay?"

Danni smiled. "Well, is there anyone else who would know how to find Marie? It's really important."

"She win some money or what?" Larry asked.

"No, but I just... have to find her. She..."

"She's *gone*," Larry interrupted jovially. "You're not gonna find her. Been gone for years. My cousin Rosie, she took that girl into her home, but... say, what's this all about? Why you tryin' to find Marie?"

Danni considered launching the tale of a book being written, or an article, something brisk and interesting and distant. For some reason the fabrication stopped in her throat, a harmless lie, but still... Larry P. Melancon had done nothing to deserve a lie. "It's about the murder of John Thierry," she said.

"Ah," was his only response.

"Marie was a witness at the trial," Danni went on.

"I know she was; whole town knows she was," Melancon replied. "But who are *you*? What's your interest in all this?

Danni sighed. "Mr. Melancon, would you let me buy you a cup of coffee? My name is Danni Telfer and it's a long story."

"Larry Paul," he told her, "but my friends call me L.P. Palace Café in fifteen minutes?"

"Thank you," she said.

The morning was an accumulation of heat that seemed to infect every sense. It lay in wait outside the courthouse and washed through her like a sickness the moment she stepped through the door. It tasted somehow *planetary*, as if fallen on Louisiana from outer space, humming softly in her ears and shimmering against every sunlit surface. Only mid-morning and already she was exhausted. The heat was an enemy she couldn't fight, and she wondered if it more than any other factor would derail her intent to save Antoine. She felt like an insect, cooking in steam.

"Not used to our weather, are you Miz Danni?" L.P. Melancon commented after exiting a cream-colored Mercedes he'd parked in a loading zone across from the Palace Café. "Let's get you a cold drink and you can tell me what brings you down here lookin' for a woman vanished off the face of the earth five years ago."

Danni allowed herself to be escorted into the café she'd left earlier, and allowed Melancon to order an extra-large iced tea and a scoop of praline ice cream for her. He was at least six feet tall with tufts of snowy hair sprouting like a low-slung halo above his ears, and he wore McGregor plaid suspenders over a starched oxford cloth dress shirt. Santa's cousin, Danni thought as he handed her a business card that said "Melancon Commercial Realty."

"I'm retired, but I keep my hand in, manage a lot of farm property around here," he explained. "So now tell me about you."

The iced tea, strong and thick with sugar syrup, spread swiftly along her neurons like a calming breeze. No wonder Southerners drank it at all times. It was an elixir, a life-saver. "I'm a professor of American history researching ante-bellum quilts in Saint Francisville," she began. "Do you think Antoine Dupre killed John Thierry?"

His snowy eyebrows arched over a bemused smile. "I never thought that young fella did it," he replied, "but the evidence said he did."

Danni looked up from her ice cream. "What evidence?"

"Somebody smashed Thierry over the head with a piece of pipe," Melancon said, looking through the plate glass restaurant windows to the sidewalk. "Right in that passageway out there. The Palace only had the one big window back then; these here were put in later. Nobody in here saw them go back there because there was a wall in the way. So the pipe was right there next to Thierry's head and Dupre standing over him. But the thing was, there wasn't any fingerprints on the pipe. Thierry's blood and hair and brains, but no fingerprints."

"You said evidence," Danni prompted.

"Dupre had these little white cotton gloves in his pants pocket," Melancon said. "Looked like he planned it, put on those gloves so there'd be no prints on the weapon. I mean, why else would a man carry little flimsy cotton gloves on him?"

Danni felt her eyes widen in disbelief. "He was researching archival material!" she nearly shouted. "He'd been running all over down here trying to finish a project, reading old records. You have to wear those gloves when touching old paper because the oil in our hands is damaging."

Melancon shrugged. "His lawyer said the same thing, but I sure as shootin' don't know anything about little white gloves and I doubt anybody else did either. Dupre never said anything, just sat there with his head down. Jury thought he was crazy. We all did. And you still haven't told me why you're down here askin' questions."

Danni remembered Antoine's description of his grief over his wife's death. He'd been dead as well, he said. He hadn't understood or cared what happened to him. Such a man would appear "crazy" to people who didn't know him, didn't know his story.

"His wife died," she told Melancon. "Cancer. He was trying to finish her dissertation. And I really did come here to write about cotton, about fabric and design in the South before the Civil War, except it turned out that there *wasn't* any, and then I went to the craft show at Angola during the rodeo, and…"

L.P. Melancon scowled and wrapped a large hand over hers across the table. "Angola's not a place for the likes of you. You stay away from that place," he warned. "It's a hell hole full of killers, rapers, really bad guys - nothing you need to know about."

"I already know about it," she answered. "And I know Antoine Dupre. I'm trying to help him. What happened to Marie Melancon? What do you mean when you say she vanished?"

"It was an ugly thing all around," he said, not meeting her eyes. "Best forgotten."

"A man is going to spend his life in prison for a crime he didn't commit!" she urged. "*That's* ugly. Marie testified against him in court, so she knows something. Where is she?"

Melancon tore a paper napkin in half, then folded the pieces and tucked them beneath his coffee cup. "I told you. Gone. She took off one day five years ago and hasn't been seen since. Savoie had money, made a lot with those sausages, hired a pricey private detective over in Baton Rouge to find her. That was before the little boy died. She should have come back for that little boy, but she didn't. She left that baby with a drunken fool who couldn't take care of a dog if you paid him. What kind of mother..."

"Savoie?" Danni interrupted. "Gaston Savoie? He's another witness, he testified at the trial. What does he have to do with Marie?"

"He's her husband, or was," Melancon said. "They had a little boy, Gaston Jr. The boy died. He fell on the edge of a shovel, bled to death right there in the yard while Savoie watched the Disney channel with a bottle of hundred-proof. Neighbors said it was Savoie's Bluetick hound howlin' that got their attention. One of 'em called 911 but it was too late. Marie Melancon oughtta hang for leavin' that child. She ever shows her face around here, likely somebody'll kill her. She didn't even show for the funeral! Hate to say it since she's kin, but a woman like that? She's better off dead."

Danni pulled a notebook from her bag and scribbled notes. "Were Marie and Gaston married when Thierry was killed?" she asked.

"No, that was right after. Bun in the oven, y'know? My cousin Rosie said Savoie was crazy about the girl, always sendin' her flowers and hangin' around on the street, waitin' for her. I guess it was a couple weeks after Thierry died that they got married. I remember Rosie threw a combination wedding and baby shower for Marie, had me write a check. All the good that did."

"What about Gaston? Where is he?"

Melancon gestured for the bill. "Look, there's nothing here that can help Dupre," he told her. "I don't know how you got involved with all this, but it's over and nobody can tell you anything they didn't tell at the time. Savoie, the poor s.o.b., he can't even tell you his name."

"What do you mean?" Danni asked.

"I mean Gaston Savoie never saw a bottle he didn't love," Melancon said, glowering. "Used to buy Black Velvet by the case, said it gave his sausages a flavor on the grill, but for every bottle went into sausages, ten went into Gaston."

"You mean he's an alcoholic," Danni said.

"I mean there's nothin' left of him. The boy died, the sausage business went to hell and Savoie just kept drinkin'. Go see for yourself if you want. They got him up at the state hospital in Pineville. Brain damage. Gaston Savoie can't tell you anything, Miz Danni. His brother goes to see him once a month and says it's so bad they have to keep him packed in pillows because of the seizures, and all he does is scream. Whole family prays he'll die. You find Marie, you tell her we all hope she dies along with him."

Danni stared into the melting ice at the bottom of her glass and pushed away the   story of Marie Melancon, Gaston Savoie and their dead child. She wasn't there to see anything but a truth that could free Antoine.

"What about Jacques Boutte?" she asked. "Is he still alive?"

"Last I heard," Melancon said dismissively. "Think he opened a hamburger joint over by the high school. Good luck, Miz Danni. You're gonna need it."

He was gone before Danni realized he'd paid the bill. She tucked his business card into her wallet and made a note to email him a thank you. In the ladies' room she splashed cold water on her face and arms before heading into the heat. The face looking back from the chipped mirror wasn't the girl who'd stepped from a plane into Louisiana six weeks ago, but a grown woman. Danni wondered what the woman was going to do next.

CHAPTER TWENTY-FOUR

Antoine had dragged himself painfully from his bunk, dressed and made it to the law library before he realized that his right eye was swollen shut, several teeth were loose and beneath a map of blood-filled bruises on his abdomen and left side was a sharp pain probably indicating at least one broken rib. On his desk was the usual stick-out breakfast in its Styrofoam tray, but also four half-pint cartons of chocolate milk, a plastic bag full of ice and a long bandage made of torn t-shirts tied together.

None of the inmate counsels looked up, remaining silent and frozen until Antoine acknowledged the gifts with a deep nod of his head. Unbuttoning his shirt, he wrapped his chest in the makeshift bandage, then held the ice to his eye. The chocolate milk provided a surge of energy for which he was grateful. He needed to draft a job description for the man who would soon take his place, a document outlining every tedious step in the long legal process necessary if even one of the six thousand men caged in a swamp were to have a chance at freedom.

He thought about them, some long-reformed after crimes committed in youth, but destined to live and die without hope. And the few like Lamar Sellers, innocent but too impaired to understand legal procedures and too poor to pay for competent defense, lost in a system that might as well be on Mars. He was glad he'd helped some, that he'd done that much with a ruined life that was about to end, unless Danni...

Hope leaped unbidden in his bandaged chest, oblivious to reason. He hadn't killed John Thierry, he shouldn't be in this hell, but he was. Maybe his freedom would materialize as senselessly. Maybe Danni would stumble onto something, a bit of evidence proving his innocence before Hoyt Planchard ended his life. It was impossible, but so was the fact that he'd been convicted for a crime he didn't commit. It could happen, couldn't it?

With shallow, painful breaths he sliced the hope in his chest to pale ribbons that dissolved in reality. Danni could accomplish nothing; her efforts might allow her the comfort of heroic effort, and that would be enough.

He spent the morning pounding computer keys, defining a job he was afraid could not be filled by anyone but himself. By noon he'd fallen asleep at his desk, exhausted by pain.

One of the inmate counsels stood at his carrel and pulled off his regulation blue shirt, then walked softly to drape it over Antoine's shoulders. The four others working in the law library did the same. A security officer on rounds merely nodded when he saw five bare-chested men and the slumped form at the desk, swathed in blue. Ten minutes later the guard returned, flinging five t-shirts on one of the library tables. No one spoke, and the men left for lunch with downcast eyes.

*

Danni scanned patches of shade beneath the courthouse trees for Grimaud, but saw only squirrels. The day was half over and so far she'd accomplished nothing useful. Marie Melancon seemed the one most likely to have information that might save Antoine, since her testimony was suspect, but she'd vanished years ago. Danni took the trial transcript back into the courthouse and found a seat in the lobby behind a silk ficus. With her eyes closed and her palm pressing the page on which Marie described Antoine challenging John Thierry to "step outside," she tried to follow a trail in her mind, find the woman.

Images arose - a bus station that reeked of hot plastic and popcorn, a mirrored bedroom where a man yelled in Spanish, a dark-haired toddler with pierced ears playing on a rumpled carpet of artificial grass beside a doublewide trailer. For a second the little girl seemed to see Danni, her eyes widening in fear. Danni shook her head to stop the kaleidoscoping images. She was sure the toddler had seen her, but how was that possible? Was the child real, and what did she have to do with Marie Melancon?

Danni cursed her ignorance of a gift she had no idea how to use. Grimaud said it ran in families and was surprised that her family hadn't taught her the rules. What rules? How did you control it, constrain the awareness to a particular goal? How did you avoid frightening children? Or was it all just illusion created in her mind?

No unusual relative had popped in to visit, taken young Danni for an ice cream at Dairy Queen and mentioned the existence of strange powers passed to her by generations of adept ancestors. If there had been such relatives, surely one would have turned up at her high school graduation, ready to provide instruction when she was old enough to understand. But the only relatives at her graduation had been her adopted parents.

Danni stared into the fake ficus, trying not to imagine a near future in which she would leave Louisiana and everything would be as if she'd never stepped off that plane in Baton Rouge. Antoine would die, Grimaud would vanish and she would shelter the story in her heart until finally it became no more than a half-remembered dream.

She might be an adept, she *was* an adept, as apparently were unknown relatives. But they hadn't come, hadn't taught her, probably didn't even know she existed. Her use of the gift was clumsy, pointless. She couldn't use it to save Antoine, and felt a wave of despair.

In the courthouse lobby a clock ticked, a messenger delivered a manila envelope, two women in business suits conferred near the elevators. Danni watched from a remove, an invisible observer of fragments, stories in process. She had no part in any of them and had failed the story in which she did.

The clock was annoying, the determined movement of strangers an irritant. When a large woman in a motorized wheelchair began arguing with a guard about her right to carry a loaded pistol into a hearing on recreational land use, Danni felt herself swimming upward through the maelstrom of stories that swarm everywhere, always. As her head broke the surface, she smiled.

"What was I thinking?" she whispered to the ficus. "That I could call some unknown relative to email me the *Adept User's Guide*, enabling me to dash out and find the bad guy before dinner?"

"May I help you with something?" asked a security guard with an ominous smile, no doubt drawn by the trouble likely to arise from people who talk to decorative plants in public places.

"Um, thanks, I was just rehearsing a speech," Danni answered while fumbling through the transcript. "Do you know if this lawyer..." she pointed to the name... " is still in Opelousas?"

"Call the Bar Association," she was told as the guard wandered away.

Danni did, and learned that Antoine's court-appointed attorney, someone named Bobby Vidrine, was not listed as a member of the St. Landry Parish Bar Association. Nor was there a listing for Bobby Vidrine in the Opelousas phone directory, but Googling the name plus "Opelousas" turned up "Vidrine Pipe, Plumbing and Fence" in Carencro, a town twenty minutes south. And there was Bobby in the white pages. Bingo.

Danni dialed the home number, which was answered by a child who happily offered the fact that his daddy was at work.

"At Vidrine Pipe, Plumbing and Fence?" she asked.

"Well sure," the child said. "We sell fences to cows."

"That's wonderful," Danni answered. "Thank you so much."

Bobby himself was not so forthcoming.

"Look, I'm busy, I can't help you," he told Danni after she explained the reason for her call. "Dupre... I dunno, did he kill Thierry? I had to defend a guy who stared at the floor, didn't have any friends or connections, acted crazy. He didn't *care*."

The voice was strained. Antoine's trial was apparently a stressful memory for Bobby Vidrine.

"It must have been tough for you," she said. "A tough case..."

"Hell, I was just outta law school at S.U., barely passed the bar and got a job with the public defender's office," Vidrine said angrily. "Dupre was my *first* case, and I don't mind tellin' you, my last."

"What do you mean?"

"I mean I've got a good head for business, and knowing the law sets me above most around here, so it all worked out. But I don't ever want to stand in a courtroom again tryin' to keep somebody outta prison. Or in. I can sell you some irrigation pipe, design you an award-winning goat corral, but I can't tell you who killed John Thierry."

"But you must have an idea," Danni pressed. "Marie Melancon's testimony is questionable and her behavior was strange. Why did she break down during questioning?"

"She was pregnant, you know how women get," Vidrine explained. "Married Gaston Savoie a couple of weeks after Thierry died and had a baby five months later. Marie, she was the emotional type, just couldn't handle herself on the stand."

"I understand she left town a few years later and nobody knows where she is."

"I heard that," Vidrine said.

"And Savoie's in the state hospital. What about Jacques Boutte?"

"What about him? He was the cook. I think he's still around. Look, Miz Telfer, I really can't help you, but good luck. I hope you find what you're lookin' for, but I doubt you will."

"Wait," Danni said. "What about the white gloves? You did explain why he had the gloves?"

"I did, even got an archivist from LSU to come and testify about skin oil messing up old documents and all that, but it didn't help. Dupre was a stranger, acting crazy, that's what the jury saw."

Danni took a breath. "Did the fact that they also saw a *biracial* stranger acting crazy have any bearing on the verdict?"

Vidrine was silent for several seconds, then sighed. "I can tell you're not from around here," he said, "but it's not like you think. We have our ways, sure, but there were three blacks on that jury and any one of them could have hung it. They didn't. Dupre didn't go down because of race; he went down because nothing about him made any sense. He *scared* the jury, and that's the truth of it."

"I appreciate your talking to me," Danni said. "I really do."

The guard was openly watching her, so she quickly found the listing for Jacques Boutte and jotted it down. She made much of glancing at her watch, arranging papers and dramatically snapping her laptop shut. Then she strode to the door as if she had somewhere to go.

Nearly one o'clock and the heat was life-threatening, but she tried to ignore it as she stood on the steps and dialed Boutte's number on her cell. An answering machine reminded her that Boutte Burger proudly fed the Opelousas Tigers after every home game, and invited messages for Jacques, Patsy, Tim or Mickey. L.P. Melancon had said that Boutte had a hamburger joint near the high school. That must be "Boutte Burger." Hoping she could still get wi-fi, she leaned against the building near the door and propped her laptop on a bent knee. It worked and she swam through stifling air toward her car while reciting the address. The car was a blast furnace, but she keyed the address into the GPS before the air-conditioner made a dent in the heat. Finding Jacques Boutte was her last hope.

Boutte Burger was the flagship business in a strip mall abutting the high school parking lot. Flanked by two hair salons, a convenience store, a tattoo parlor, a Christian thrift boutique, a long-closed pet store with yellowing shredded newspaper still in the windows and an Army recruiting office, the restaurant fairly shined in comparison.

Danni sat in the car pondering her next move. Antoine had said that a dying prisoner meant to tell him something about "Jacques" but was gone before Antoine reached his side. If only she could remember the prisoner's name, maybe mentioning it to Boutte would lead to something. *Eugene.* Antoine had said the man's name was Eugene, but she couldn't remember the last name. Maybe Antoine hadn't said the last name. She'd go with Eugene.

The restaurant was clean and attractive with red vinyl booths and stools at a long aluminum counter. At the back an old-fashioned jukebox flashed rainbow colors on a white-tiled floor. Clearly a kid's hangout, Boutte Burger also catered to the grownup dinner crowd, as evidenced by a blackboard menu featuring exotic Cajun dishes served after 6:00. The only customers were an elderly couple eating ice cream at the counter. Danni took a seat in a booth and nodded to the waitress, whose pink uniform had "Patsy" embroidered over the pocket. Maybe Jacques' wife?

"I'd like an iced tea, but I've really come to see Jacques," she said. "Is he in?"

"In the kitchen flippin' burgers," the woman said. "Kids are out of school at 2:00 today and the place'll be a zoo. I'm Patsy, his wife. Maybe I can help you."

Danni smiled. "A friend of mine at Angola knew Eugene," she said.

Patsy Boutte's eyes narrowed as she scanned Danni from head to foot. "Eugene LeBlanc?" she asked. "He was

Jacques' uncle, died up there not too long ago. How do you know Eugene?"

"I didn't know him; a friend did," Danni said, grasping for what to say next. "He asked me to speak to..."

"You from Angola, social worker or something?" Patsy interrupted. "Stuff of Gene's we need to pick up?"

"No," Danni answered, her throat tight with panic. "It's about something Eugene said right before he died."

"From what I hear he never said much when he was alive," Patsy noted with distaste. "Let me get you that iced tea and I'll yell at Jacques to come on out here. Hope this isn't some kinda bad news."

"I don't know," Danni answered, thinking it might be. Especially if Jacques Boutte was the one who killed John Thierry ten years ago. And if he did, she was about to confront a murderer. As if on cue, the elderly couple finished their ice cream and left, creating a wake of silence in which Danni could hear the rapid pounding of her own heart.

"How can I help you?" a man called as he pushed open the kitchen door behind the counter, drying his hands on a red paper napkin. "Gene was my uncle. Hear you got a message or something."

The man was lanky, with close-cropped dark hair, a moustache and warm brown eyes. He didn't look like a murderer as he slid into the booth across from Danni, an observation she realized was ridiculous. Of the hundred men she'd seen in the prison visiting room, not one looked like a murderer. Yet at least a third of them were.

"In the moments before his death, your uncle asked to see another prisoner," she began, tucking her hands beneath her legs to keep them from shaking. "Eugene had a message about 'Jacques'."

"About me?" he asked. "What other prisoner? Must be a couple hundred guys named Jacques between here and Baton Rouge. What's this about?"

Patsy placed a glass of iced tea on a cocktail napkin in front of Danni.

"It's about Antoine Dupre," she said.

Both Bouttes seemed to freeze in place for only a second, but Danni felt their alarm like a gong in the quiet restaurant. They didn't exchange glances or show the slightest sign that the name Antoine Dupre meant anything to them, but the missed beat left an echo.

"I'll go on back and finish the prep," Patsy announced. "You two can chat."

"I don't understand," Jacques said, clasping his hands on the table and leaning forward. "My uncle didn't know Dupre."

"Yes he did," Danni said, now holding the iced tea glass with both hands. "Antoine volunteered in the infirmary. He talked to your uncle, read him articles from fishing magazines. For at least a year. And when Eugene was dying, he asked to see Antoine. He wanted to tell him something important about 'Jacques', but he was dead when Antoine got there."

The eyes across the table were so focused on her face that Danni squinted, but not before seeing the faint relaxation of tiny muscles behind his lashes and over his nose. Jacques Boutte was *relieved*.

"So you came here to tell me this?" he asked, smiling.

"I came here to ask you who killed John Thierry," Danni said over her raucous heartbeat. "Because either you killed him or you know who did. I think that's what Eugene was trying to tell Antoine."

Boutte leaned back, his eyes no longer warm. "My uncle was a dying old man who could have said anything," he said. "I haven't killed anybody and who are you anyway? You don't *look* crazy, but you coming here like this? That's crazy. I think you'd better leave."

"Please," she said, "it's a matter of life and death. You were there when it happened; you know something; you can save Antoine's life!"

He stood, shaking his head. "Do I have to call the police?"

"No," Danni answered, defeated, "I'll go."

*

Antoine was still asleep, his head resting on a completed job description he meant to instruct one of the inmate counsels to copy in the warden's office, when Perry Bordelon appeared in the door of the law library. He didn't step inside, but stood like a swollen shadow, backlit by the late afternoon sun. Antoine felt his presence and looked up.

"Hoyt says you better enjoy tomorrow, Monk," Bordelon whispered. "'Cause it's your last day. You gonna die on Saturday at the revival."

Antoine went back to sleep, seeing no point in mentioning that he was already dead.

CHAPTER TWENTY-FIVE

Danni strode toward her car in the parking lot, aware that the Bouttes were undoubtedly watching. She'd blown it, muffed it completely, been too nervous and inexperienced to do anything but blurt out a stupid accusation that would only put them on guard. They knew something; that was obvious the moment she pronounced Antoine's name. If only she'd thought it through, approached them with a credible story, something oblique and non-threatening. Instead, she'd walked in, sat down and accused Jacques Boutte of murder. And that error would cost Antoine his life.

In the car she felt a wave of anguish taking form inside her mind. The feeling rose, massive and mindless, a swelling expanse of failure in which she would drown. For a moment she almost welcomed it, that capitulation to a sobbing emotional release in which she would be absolved of responsibility. But it seemed inauthentic, wrong, beneath her.

"No," she spoke aloud. And the feeling froze. She could see it in her mind, a dark painting of a wave rolling upward, its surface smooth just before the point at which it would break and crash in a rubble of foam.

Good. The feeling could stay that way, frozen. At the moment she didn't need it. She needed to think. And where was Grimaud? He'd said he'd turn up when he could be of use, and this was definitely that moment. She'd run out of leads, Jacques and Patsy Boutte weren't about to tell her whatever they knew and she had no idea what to do next.   A jangling bell drew her attention to the nearby high school from which teenagers erupted in animated clumps. Many were running toward her, an alarming sensation until she realized they were running toward Jacques Boutte's hamburgers. Kids, hamburgers, a juke box – all curiously *normal* – as opposed to an unsolved murder, a missing vampire and a New York history professor/bumbling adept running around a Southern town trying to find a killer who did not want to be found.

Danni drove out of the parking lot with a sense of nostalgia. She'd once been sort of normal, hadn't she? Before Louisiana. Before a prisoner who carved cats and a vampire who'd been buried since the Civil War. *A vampire.*

Pulling the car to the curb in a residential area, she stared at yellow brick tract houses beneath overgrown oak trees and considered the word. It was a myth, an ancient story born of primitive human fear and ignorance, now nothing more than a diversion for bored children. Had she imagined Grimaud, created a vampire out of a stranger who happened to be in the vicinity? The movie blossomed in her mind. Fragile young woman, cruelly jilted by her handsome, older seducer, flees to atmospheric middle-of-nowhere and, driven mad by heartbreak, lives in a delusional world where she has magical powers and a vampire suitor. Bergman might have done the movie, she thought, but he was dead. The contemporary American version would be a farce. And she wasn't fragile.

"Uh, excuse me, y'all all right?" asked a face leaning into the passenger's side window. It was a blonde woman in a tank top, her right arm extended to jiggle a stroller in which a blonde baby placidly chewed on the top snap of its onesie.

Danni rolled the window down.

"I'm fine," she said. "Just thinking about vampires."

When the blonde woman backed away, quickly pulling a cell phone from the pocket of her shorts, Danni put the car in gear and left. So much for normalcy.

Whatever Grimaud was, he wasn't present. She was on her own at 2:00 p.m. in a strange, suffocatingly hot town where she'd just exhausted her last hope. Or had she? There was one witness left.

L.P. Melancon said Gaston Savoie was so brain-damaged he couldn't remember his own name, but maybe an adept could sense bits of the man's ruined memory. The idea was both frightening and repulsive, an intrusion into a space made sacred by its own confusion. Conjuring images of the past felt acceptable, but the living were entitled to uncrossable boundaries. Especially those so damaged that they could no longer protect themselves with the layers of shifting stories that comprise reality. It was wrong, she wouldn't do it, wouldn't even try. She'd go back to St. Francisville and prepare for the call that would come from Angola. The call that would tell her that she had failed and Antoine Dupre was dead.

But as she typed "St. Francisville" into the GPS and a disembodied female voice said, "Turn right on East Prudhomme Lane," her hands on the wheel didn't turn right. It probably wouldn't work anyway; she wasn't sure Grimaud's definition of her as an "adept" was anything more than a sort of dream. But if she didn't try, and Antoine died, she would have to live with the fact that she stopped short of a final step that might have made a difference. It occurred to her that ethical behavior, sanctimonious and safe, may at times share a bed with cowardice.

"When possible, make a U-turn and then turn right...," the GPS told her. Danni pushed "Clear" and then typed the place where L.P. Melancon said Gaston Savoie lay banked in pillows – "State Hospital, Pineville, LA."

*

Antoine woke blanketed by fabric in which he recognized the scents of the men with whom he'd worked for years. Marlboro smoke, Big Red chewing gum, starch from the laundry. For a moment he swam in the warmth; it was familiar, a kind of home, and gave him strength. Then he stood and carefully laid each shirt across his desk.

"Appreciated," he told the men quietly working in the library as he walked toward the open door.

The pain in his chest and abdomen was acute, and he had to lie down. Only one more task – his will – and he could write it lying in bed. Not that he had anything of value to leave behind, but he wanted his cats, all his carved Bastets, to go to the inmate counsels. They could sell them at the rodeos and maybe the money could be used to fund the costly work necessary for even one prisoner to have a chance at freedom. And he wanted his blue shirt to be laid in Danni's hands like a flag.

He stumbled and fell against the door frame. The guard on the Walk had been there all day, through two shifts. He approached Antoine brusquely, thumbs tucked over his belt.

"You gonna make it, Monk?" he asked.

"Just need to lie down," Antoine answered.

"You know I have to take you to the infirmary if you can't keep workin'. Can't let you in the dorm."

"If I go to the infirmary they'll keep me in there," Antoine said. "Won't let me out in time for the revival."

The guard lit a cigarette and stared at the sky. "What I hear, you don't wanna be at that revival. Don't I hear that right?"

"You do," Antoine said, "except the part about what I want. I will be there. Right now I just need to lie down."

"This once, Monk," the guard said, studying his lit cigarette as if it were about to speak. "You get some rest."

Antoine nodded. "Tell your wife she married a good man," he said.

"I'll do that," the guard answered, quickly pressing something against Antoine's palm. "It'll help," he said, then roughly pushed Antoine ahead on the Walk.

The dorm surged with silence as Antoine sat on his bunk and studied the object in his hand – a white lozenge with "Vicodin" stamped on one side. He swallowed it without compunction, wrote the directions for disposal of his belongings on a sheet of paper he stuffed in a shirt pocket, and lay down. The drug brought a cloudy comfort that reminded him of chalk dust, and in minutes he was asleep.

*

Danni drove the sixty-eight miles on I-49 from Opelousas to the Alexandria suburb called Pineville in an hour, focusing on sporadic announcements from the GPS regarding exits she should not take. She couldn't imagine where the exits might go, since there was nothing but farmland extending beyond the reach of her vision. When a large black snake crawled from the shoulder to cross the road in front of her car, she slammed on the brakes to avoid hitting it, grateful for the distraction. But when a sign saying, "Exit 85A Pineville," appeared ahead, she marshaled her thoughts to razor sharpness. There could be no more mistakes.

The hospital on four hundred acres at the edge of town was practically lost in an expanse of scrub grass and longleaf pines. White pillars at the entrance reflected a stab at Southern ambience, but beyond that the sprawling brick building could have been one of identical thousands built all over the U.S. between 1930 and 1960.

"Stroll around the grounds until you feel at home," Danni sang a line from "Mrs. Robinson." Simon and Garfunkel again. The song kept her grounded as she parked and walked past a small, faded billboard announcing the future construction of a new hospital on the site. The present hospital seemed to reflect its own uncertain existence; it felt transitional, half-forgotten, resigned. At a large desk in the lobby a woman in hot pink scrubs was reading what appeared to be a textbook on hairdressing.

"I'm here to see Gaston Savoie," Danni said slowly, trying to approximate a drawl without overdoing it. "His brother couldn't come and I'm from the church. We try to help, y'know?"

"Y'all from their church?" the woman repeated.

"St. Landry's," Danni improvised, pulling the only saint she could think of from thin air.

"Well, he's right up that hall, room 107, but he ain't gonna say nothin', won't even know you there."

"I understand," Danni answered, flattening the long I to "ah." "They just want him checked on. Won't take me long to check."

"Go on, then," the woman said and turned back to a diagram of a shingle cut.

Danni found the room immediately and fought to control her response to the man on the bed. Shock, then pity. Frail, bruised white arms moved restlessly against padded Velcro restraint cuffs attached to the metal bedframe, and a low keening escaped the slack, drooling mouth. His teeth were broken, his eyes closed by fluttering purple lids.

A young man in jeans and another pink scrub shirt sat in a plastic chair beside the bed, playing a game on a cell phone.

"They just give him his meds," the boy said without looking up. "He calm but somebody have to stay with him, see he don't choke or nothin'. I'll jus' step outside, leave you with him, but holler if he choke or start seizin'".

Danni nodded, then closed everything in her mind but a single corridor stretching toward what remained of Gaston Savoie. The corridor was quickly infested with a rush of pain. She felt it in her gut and struggled not to double over, clutching her stomach, her heart. And the terrible keening was a song;

Les maringouins ont tout mangé ma belle, Gaston Savoie was singing. *Ils n'ont laissé que gros orteils.* Danni grabbed a pen from her bag and tried to scribble the French words on the palm of her hand. The song had once been happy but now it dripped from the corridor walls like stained, melting snow, a dirge. For a moment she saw a little boy in a sagging diaper playing with a speckled white hound whose ears were black. Then the same child, older, dressed in a white shirt and red bow tie, lying in a coffin.

Danni felt herself hit the boundary of her ability as an adept. She couldn't absorb any more, had no defense against the smeared chaos of the man's mind. It burned with a weakness she recognized as the gift of alcohol, blithe in a single, sparkling glass, but masking a poisonous subtext. Gaston Savoie had drowned in it, leaving only a tattered song to fill the space where he had been.

Backing toward the door, she curbed the impulse to run. There was nothing there, no track she could follow to the moment ten years in the past when a court clerk named John Thierry was beaten to death with a piece of pipe. And Gaston Savoie had been her last chance. The frozen painting of a dark, swollen wave began to move, then was suddenly lit by a flickering blue light behind her. She felt a familiar presence.

Grimaud. His dark eyes broadcast respect.

"You have done well," he said. "You have shown courage and deserve my help." He turned toward the form on the bed. "What do you see?" he asked.

Danni squared her shoulders, stopped the threatening wave. "Pain, self-pity, pointlessness" she said. "Glimpses of a little boy, probably the child who died, and a song." She showed Grimaud the words scrawled on her palm.

"'Mosquitoes have eaten my darling,'" he read. "'They only left the big toes.'"

"That's horrible!" Danni said, now hearing nothing but a guttural howl from the bed.

"It's an old Cajun song," Grimaud explained without interest. "The rest is worse. The man uses the toes to cork his half-empty whiskey bottles. The song's very old, a classic. But we must go, Danni. You must tell me what you've learned."

She turned toward Gaston Savoie a last time and saw him suspended, trapped and miserable in a body whose systems were close to complete failure, and wished an end for him. "It will come soon," she whispered and turned to go.

But Grimaud had moved to lean over the bed, his dark hair gleaming against the white pillows, his face buried in Gaston Savoie's neck. In a moment he stood, blood leaving a red thread between his lips. The sound from the bed was now a dull whine, weak, fading.

"Oh God, you didn't…!" Danni whispered, one hand, unbidden, leaping to cover her throat.

"No," Grimaud answered, licking his lips. "I merely hastened his release. He will die within the hour. Is that not what you wanted?"

Danni met his eyes, finding the answer like a gold ring in an icy stream. "Yes," she said.

The boy waiting in the hall frowned in puzzlement as Danni left with Grimaud, but said nothing. The woman at the lobby desk merely glanced up and said, "Bye now." The place seemed insubstantial, as if it were not moored, not entirely there. Danni had the sense that were she to return the next day, she would be unable to find it.

"I've done everything I can," she told Grimaud, "and I…"

"You must eat," he said, observing her closely. "The work of an adept exhausts the chemistry of the mind. Fish is said to replenish it, blueberries, lentils, I'm afraid I don't remember more."

"Fish," Danni repeated and typed "Fish restaurant Pineville" into the GPS. There was only one.

"I'll drive," Grimaud said. "Don't worry, I've studied the skill and the GPS will provide instruction. You are weakened. Tell me what you've learned."

Danni reprised everything L.P. Melancon had said about the witness, Marie Melancon. She explained what Antoine's public defender attorney, Bobby Vidrine, had said about the trial, and closed with Jacques and Patsy Boutte.

"They know something," she told Grimaud. "They know what really happened."

At the restaurant Danni forced herself to eat two fried catfish filets washed down with the sweet tea to which she suspected she was becoming addicted. Grimaud read the trial transcript while she ate, drawing a diagram on the back of a paper placemat.

"Boutte, the cook, was in the kitchen," he said without looking up. "It is unlikely that he would come out into the restaurant, but would simply hand plates to Marie Melancon, the waitress. Yet Savoie said he had come to deliver sausages and to ask Boutte if more sausages were needed for a tour bus expected at six o'clock."

"Right," Danni said.

"Wouldn't Savoie have to go into the kitchen to make his delivery and take the order for additional sausages if they were needed?"

"I suppose, yes," Danni replied, suddenly more attentive. "Savoie and Boutte would both have been in the kitchen." Her mind created the scene. "Unloading sausages from a box to a refrigerator!"

"What of it?" Grimaud asked.

Her eyes were wide, her breath rapid. "Health standards for groceries and restaurants demand that anyone handling raw meat wear plastic gloves," she explained. "It's to prevent contamination from the meat carried to other foods and utensils by the hands. Either Savoie or the cook, Boutte, would have been wearing plastic gloves that leave no fingerprints!"

Grimaud smiled. "From the kitchen there is a back door to an alley from which trash is collected," he went on, drawing arrows on his diagram. "This alley intersects with the narrow passage between the Palace Café and the adjacent building, where John Thierry was killed."

"So either one of them could have gone out the back door, still wearing plastic gloves, picked up that pipe and called to John Thierry," Danni said. "But why?"

She picked a stalk of parsley from her plate and stared at it, then at Grimaud. "If it were Savoie, wouldn't you know? I mean, you just..."

"I consumed his story," Grimaud interrupted, his voice deepening and assuming a chantlike cadence. "A Celtic tribe long-settled in the *Massif de Bauges*, now the French Alps near Italy, they spoke a language based on trees until Romans came. Indeed his name, Savoie, and the French region that bears it, is derived from a Latin word meaning 'fir trees.' The blood of Gaston Savoie, now dilute, nonetheless bears the memory of a god called Grannus and three milk-white female spirits who still appear..."

"Stéphane!" Danni said, pulling herself with effort from the hypnotic flow of his words. "We don't care about ancient history! What does Savoie know about the death of John Thierry?"

His shoulders jerked slightly, as if he'd tripped even though he was seated. After a silence of several seconds he resumed the chant, which might have been a ship's log or church record. Names, dates. "Vallaincourt Savoie died in St. Albert, Arcadie, in 1658," he said, staring through Danni. "The bitter cold, the long voyage, he was so weak. It was a horse. He was kicked by a horse in the snow."

She didn't know how to stop him, to cancel the litany of ages he contained and make him focus on one story in the present.

"Gaston Savoie," she pronounced with as much gravity as she could manage. "Only this man, now."

Grimaud shook his head, grimaced. "The man has no story," he said. "His life was wasted, leaving nothing but the ancient markers, which are strong and do not fade. This man alone has no significance. It is as if he never was."

Danni closed her eyes in defeat, then opened them again.

"Jacques and Patsy Boutte," she said. "They know. Jacques may have done it. Can't you threaten them, materialize as a bat in a cape, scare them into talking?"

Grimaud's tight smile showed teeth. "Do not mock me," he said. "You diminish yourself in so doing, and risk incurring my contempt. As an adept you know better."

"I'm sorry," Danni said, fighting the tidal wave of despair she felt like a fatal weight suspended above her. "It's just... I'm out of options. There are no more options, no more possibilities. I'm desperate."

Grimaud leaned back, flexed his shoulders. "There is your answer," he said. "In desperation, mortals abandon reason and, like you, become reckless, dangerous, cruel. One of the two men in the Palace Café kitchen was sufficiently desperate to kill another man. You must determine which man was the killer. I will do the rest."

As they left, Danni idly inspected a shelf of coffee mugs, baseball caps and t-shirts bearing the restaurant's logo, a catfish smiling inside a bun. "Boutte didn't feel desperate to me," she said, eyeing the catfish. It looked like Jacques Boutte. "He and his wife seemed okay together; they have kids; his restaurant is successful. Savoie, yes. I felt nothing in him *but* desperation. But if Savoie did it, why did Boutte lie? And Marie Melancon. Both Boutte and Melancon lied to protect Gaston Savoie. They condemned Antoine! But why?"

"There will be a reason," Grimaud said when they reached the car, pointing to the trial transcript on the back seat. "It will be hidden in that document but discernible through the information you now have. I will drive back to St. Francisville while you join the threads of a story that has been hidden for a decade."

"And then what?" Danni said.

Grimaud gazed at clouds darkening the Southeastern sky. "Then I will do as I have promised," he said. "As will you."

Danni didn't reply, but joined him in regarding the sky. A storm was massing. She wondered if the bite of a vampire was like lightning, and shuddered.

CHAPTER TWENTY-SIX

"We need to find Marie Melancon," Danni said as Grimaud focused on driving.

"Then find her," he said.

"I can't," she answered. "And don't leave the bright lights on unless there's nothing in front of you in either lane, no matter how far away. Bright lights blind people."

"Light is the scourge of history," he agreed. "A vampire must avoid its acidity that eats away the past, but mortals revel in it."

"Not while they're driving, they don't," Danni insisted. "Pull that lever on the left of the steering column toward you. That's how you shift the intensity of the headlights."

He did so and smiled with satisfaction. "Now find Marie Melancon," he said. "Read her testimony in the transcript. Perhaps her words will make a path."

Danni turned on the visor light over the passenger's seat and fumbled through the ream of paper until she found the right pages and pressed her hand to the words. Marie Bernadette Melancon had calmly stated her name, said that she lived with her aunt and worked as a waitress at the Palace Café, then begun to sob when asked to describe events surrounding the death of John Thierry. The judge allowed her several minutes to calm herself, after which she named the other people who were present. She explained that Gaston Savoie was frequently at the restaurant because he made the sausages used in several dishes. On the day John Thierry died, Savoie was present to deliver sausages and check on the restaurant's need for more.

"Did you personally know all those present except the defendant, Antoine Dupre?" the district attorney asked. "That is, did you personally know Messrs. Savoie and Boutte, Mr. and Mrs. Fontenot and Mr. Thierry?"

The question caused another eruption of sobbing during which Marie said only, "Yes, yes I knew them, I knew him!"

Danni stopped reading and stared into the darkening farmland outside the car. What had the woman meant by adding, "I knew <u>him</u>"? Thierry's name had been the last mentioned. Did Marie mean that she knew him in particular? Or merely that she was upset at the fact of his death?

After a recess Marie returned to the stand, still trembling and prone to tears. When the District attorney asked her to recount the exchange between Antoine Dupre and John Thierry, she said something so quietly that the judge asked her to repeat it.

"Him," she wept, pointing at Antoine, "that man, he told John to step outside. They'd been arguing, something about records that man wanted to see at the courthouse and John told him no."

John. Marie Melancourt had known the man well enough to use his first name, even in a court setting where all parties were as a matter of form referenced by their surnames.

"And then what happened?" she was asked, eliciting an emotional outburst of such intensity that the judge released her, allowing the district attorney's request that her deposition taken earlier be allowed in lieu of further testimony. Bobby Vidrine had objected and been overruled.

The deposition was read, in which she stated that she heard a sound outside and went to see what it was. In the narrow passageway between the Palace Café and the adjoining building she saw John Thierry on the ground, bleeding profusely, and Antoine Dupre standing over him. She saw a length of pipe on the ground and recognized it as similar to pipe recently installed in the restaurant kitchen. She didn't remember whether or not Antoine Dupre was wearing gloves at that point, but said that his hands "looked white."

Danni searched the transcript for the testimony of the other witnesses. Jacques Boutte had identified the length of pipe as debris left over from the replacement of the trap beneath the kitchen's floor sink earlier in the week. The plumbing debris was left in an open box in the alley behind the restaurant for pickup by a salvager. Boutte also remembered hearing Dupre threaten Thierry, but under cross examination by Bobby Vidrine admitted that the kitchen was noisy and insulated from the restaurant's seating area except for the swinging doors, which were closed, and the pass-through where he placed the plated food. He stated that he and Savoie both ran through the restaurant's back door to the alley and then the passageway when Marie screamed. They saw Thierry on the ground and Dupre standing over him.

Alma and Gilbert Fontenot were certain that Dupre had not threatened Thierry, and remembered only that the two men left the restaurant at nearly the same time, Thierry leaving first. In subsequent moments they heard no sound outside, but did see Marie Melancon go to the door and step out. Then they heard her screams and rushed outside to see Dupre standing over Thierry. They saw no gloves on his hands.

Gaston Savoie's testimony was identical to Boutte's. With the exception of the Fontenots, every witness pointed to Antoine Dupre as the killer.

In his closing argument, the district attorney told the jury that Antoine Dupre was unwholesomely obsessed with moldering old documents he imagined to be hidden in the Opelousas courthouse. When denied access to records in the custody of St. Landry Parish by a duly appointed official, John Thierry, Dupre became deranged, attacked and killed Thierry.

Bobby Vidrine countered with the facts that Antoine Dupre had no prior criminal history but did have legitimate research interests in certain parish records, and appeared to have been merely in the wrong place at the wrong time.

The jury deliberated for less than two hours, finding Antoine Dupre guilty of murder.

Danni leaned against her seat belt to press her head against the stack of paper in her lap. The answer was somewhere in those pages; it had to be.

"Where is she?" Grimaud asked.

Danni looked up. "Who? Marie? I don't know; there's no way to know. When I tried before all I saw was a dark-haired little girl with pierced ears playing on a fake grass carpet outside a double-wide trailer. I didn't see Marie."

"Try," he urged.

"Why? What can you do if I find her?"

Far ahead a thread of lightening splintered the eastern sky.

"I can talk to her," Grimaud said, rolling down the window and sniffing the moist night air. "If she's close by."

Danni turned to regard him. "Just how far can you go, when you turn into that blue light?"

"Not far," he answered. "As I've explained, such movement drains me and is therefore dangerous. A vampire will only employ that gift when necessary. For great distances I must travel as mortals do. But if Marie Melancon is close, I can go to her. You must search."

Danni closed her eyes, touched the page of Marie's testimony, drawing her mind to narrow on a single image – a woman sobbing on the witness stand in a courtroom. The woman was really a girl, she realized. Marie had been nineteen ten years ago, torn between a ripening sexuality and a child's need to be taken care of. The panicky sobs were a little girl's, a mix of terror and infantile entitlement. Yet the panicked, sobbing child on the witness stand was a pregnant woman.

There followed an impression Danni knew only too well. A man's eager caresses, Marie's headlong, welcoming passion. It reminded her of herself, that giddy sacrifice of personal boundaries driven by childish entitlement – "I *deserve* this because I *want* it!" The memory was unpleasant but she couldn't turn away. The memory lit a path to Marie Melancon.

Then there was another man whose body Marie merely tolerated in a queasy exchange Danni hadn't experienced but recognized. It was like her friend in high school who allowed the groping of a local laundromat owner in exchange for a job paying twice the minimum wage. Every evening Danni's friend cleaned lint traps, bagged forgotten clothes, mopped floors and endured ten minutes of heavy-handed fondling, but nothing more, from the sixty-year-old owner who left his wife washing dinner dishes while he went to close the store. Danni admired her friend's hard-eyed approach to life, but didn't share it. And neither, she saw, had Marie Melancon, who was no opportunistic realist. Marie was simply a child.

There followed a dark, featureless time Danni couldn't see, then money hidden in a coffee can and buried. A baby crying, a man's drunken shouts. Then the same bus station again, smelling of plastic and popcorn. Another bus station at night in a city, danger in sneering eyes. Then a final bus station, this one full of flashing color and an uncomfortable confusion of small mechanical sounds. Slot machines. It was a bus station with slot machines like a casino.

Danni opened her eyes, feeling the intense effort the attempt had cost. But unless she'd made it up, she'd followed a trail left by Marie Melancon when she fled her husband and abandoned her young son to fall on a shovel and die. Marie, Danni concluded, had never grown up.

"Marie was silly, immature, didn't want responsibility" Danni told Grimaud, who shook his head.

"Her essential nature is not our concern," he said. "Our concern is her *location.*"

Danni tried to force open the door to the avenue of bus stations through which Marie had fled, but the facility with which she worked had grown weak. The door was there, but it remained closed.

"I can't," she said. "It isn't working. But there were three bus stations. The last one had slot machines and a sign saying, "Welcome to Las Vegas!" I think that's where she stopped. Maybe she's still there, someplace where there are slot machines everywhere – in airports, grocery stores, bus stations. She's in Las Vegas!"

Grimaud nodded. "Nevada was made a state after I lay buried, but while the Civil War still raged," he said. "Statehood was rushed to secure additional electoral votes for Abraham Lincoln. If Marie is there, I cannot reach her in time. What is a 'slot machine'?"

"Gambling," Danni replied. "You put money in a slot, push a button and if you get matching symbols you win. I don't really know how they work, but Nevada is the only state in which they're not controlled by the government. They're everywhere there. How do you know when Nevada was made a state?"

"I read," he said. "There was an encyclopedia at the library in St. Francisville."

"But you skipped 'slot machines'?"

"My interest was in recent history, not in games of chance," he said. "I am sorry that you failed to find Marie. There seems to be no other avenue to saving your paramour. A shame." His smile was unpleasant.

Danni bristled. "I didn't 'fail to find her'; she's in Las Vegas," she insisted. "Maybe the little girl I saw before is her daughter and the man yelling in Spanish is the father. Maybe she ran away to Nevada and started a new life. That you can't turn into a bat and fly there is not *my* failure, and Antoine isn't my 'paramour.' Stop being vile and *think*."

He stared at the approaching storm, then turned on the CD player. Danni had forgotten the old song she'd burned while researching the quilt at the state library, but its sweetness again touched her.

"You're weeping," Grimaud said. "Why?"

"The song... everything," she answered, groping in her bag for a tissue. "I'm driving into a storm in Louisiana with a corpse who's been dead for centuries, and an innocent man is going to die and that song is so sad..."

"*La Belle Louisianaise Valse,*" he said and then hummed the music in a soft baritone.

"It is a waltz," he said thoughtfully. "To this song I once danced with a beautiful woman at a wedding ball held at The Willows. Her name was Alais, and the light in her eyes was like the moon on leaves. In them I saw myself as she saw me – noble and gracious. I am not a monster, Danni. Why do you not see?"

"What happened?" Danni asked, confused by his wistful story. "Did you...?"

He sighed. "Did I kill her, bring her to my side for eternity with the only gift I could offer?" His hands on the steering wheel were locked and white with feeling. "She was adept; she knew me for a vampire but saw me entire. I wanted to be with her, see myself in her eyes forever, yes. I offered; she refused, and the waltz ended. She will have been dead for over a century now, Danni, only her bones remaining, brittle and forgotten in a grave long lost. She is gone, but I am not. I'm sorry... the music..."

"You loved her, "Danni said, turning to look at him. "You loved a woman named Alais; you held her in a waltz; you asked her to become a vampire so she could be with you and she refused. Why are you telling me this? She was an adept, like me. You don't mean you want me to..."

"No," he said as a scent of rain swept through the open window. "I only want... a faint reflection. I want the taste of your story, one taste. The connection to you would be enough, a first, slender link in the chain I must forge now, the new existence I must create. Do you understand?"

Danni rolled her window down and let the rain-scented air bathe her face. She felt the weight of his need, felt herself yearning to meet it. The feeling was curiously warm, deep and silent, ancient as the stone she sensed far beneath the black ribbon of highway. Against its solidity she saw herself a wispy, transparent thing, an iridescent bubble on a sunny breeze. But a bubble aware and committed to its nature.

"I do admire you, maybe even love you in a way," she told Grimaud. "I am adept; I see you: You're... *luminous* or something, strange and brilliant and even kind sometimes when you're not being incomprehensible or vicious. But what you ask of me – what I *think* you ask - I choose not to give. I don't have the strength, don't even know who I am or what I want to do. I must *be* a story before that story can be given to anyone. Do *you* understand?"

"I do," he said somberly. "But even so, you have promised the gift of your blood in exchange for his life, or what will remain of his life if you fail to free him."

"Yes," she said, fear making her shiver in the warm rush of air. She had stretched her awkward talent as an adept as far as she could, and still had failed to uncover the story that would save Antoine's real life, the life he could have in freedom. What would happen to her if Grimaud merely kept Hoyt Planchard from killing Antoine but nothing else changed? Would she keep her promise, allow the bite of those eager, waiting teeth? And what would Grimaud do if she didn't?

"There's still time," she told him.

"You have exhausted your skill as an adept," he said. "What more can you do?"

Danni straightened her shoulders against the seat as the first drop of rain imploded on the windshield dust, leaving a tiny, clean crater. "I can think," she told him. "If not as an adept, then as an ordinary person."

"When the truth hides, seek the probable," Grimaud offered. "Descartes. How do I turn on the blades that sweep across the window?"

"Windshield wipers," she replied. "Push the lever on the right. Did you really know Descartes?"

"Yes. Do you know who killed John Thierry?"

"Yes," she said. "Almost. Let me think."

The rain fell in sheets then, wind buffeting the car like a cat with a toy. Danni used the accompanying sense of isolation to focus on a woman named Marie who heard a sound no one else heard. The restaurant walls were brick, the front door closed, an air-conditioner running. Marie Melancon could not have heard the soft crunch of metal on skull or the thud of John Thierry's body falling to the ground. She must have run outside for another reason, one she chose to hide with a lie.

She was the first to see the event occurring in the darkened passageway, several seconds, perhaps a minute elapsing before her screams brought the Fontenots, Boutte and Savoie to the scene, according to their testimonies. The couple exited through the door to the street, the cook and sausage maker through a back door to an alley. Marie, arriving shortly after Thierry, then Antoine, left the restaurant, could have seen the attack but the others could not. If so, she chose to protect the killer and condemn the life of a stranger. But why?

The frantic thumping of the windshield wipers brought Danni back to the moment. They continued to shave water from glass, but the hum of the car's engine was still.

"We're not moving," she said.

"Unaccustomed to the control of an automobile under optimal circumstances," Grimaud answered from the dark interior of the car, "I elected to preserve your life by stopping to wait out the storm." He pointed into the rain. "What is a 'caterpillar'?" he asked.

Danni rolled down her steamed window enough to see that they were stopped in the parking lot of a farm equipment dealer. A row of tractors gleamed green in flashes of lightening beside two yellow backhoes.

"Caterpillar is a company that makes earth-moving equipment," she said, brushing rain from her sleeve. "And you were smart to stop, although you need to turn off the lights and wipers. They'll run the battery down. I think Marie saw who killed Thierry. I think she lied in court but I don't know why."

Grimaud merely nodded. "It was such a Caterpillar that removed the earth from atop my grave," he said happily. "An impressive advance in building equipment!"

Shaking her head, Danni was about to suggest that he collect the entire set of Tonka toy trucks and earth-moving equipment to decorate his future home, when she heard the chime of her cell phone in her bag on the floor. The sound was jarring in the rain-swept dark. It could only be news about Antoine, she thought. Vicki calling with a message.

"Hello," she whispered as Grimaud watched, interested.

The answering voice was not Vicki's. It was a man's, and she gasped.

"I... I've missed you," her department chair said as if months had not passed since their parting. "A letter came to the department office regarding a journal article you're to publish, about a 'vampire quilt' of all things! Rather unprofessional, wouldn't you say? But the letter contained your current address. There's a symposium at Loyola this weekend. I'm a speaker. That is, I'll be in New Orleans and I could drive... I'd like to see you, Danni."

His voice, distorted by the storm, was scratchy and hollow, a mechanical facsimile. Yet she remembered a time when that voice had thrilled her, that fake British accent. How she had wanted to help him, rescue him like the unicorn. She'd been little more than a silly girl, but that voice had once drawn her to him as another man's had drawn another silly girl named Marie.

"I'm afraid not," she said, nodding wide-eyed at Grimaud. "But thanks for calling. You've been more helpful than you'll ever know!"

"Who was that?" Grimaud asked as she pushed the button that darkened her phone and closed a chapter in her life. "It seems he has made you happy."

"Oh, he has," she agreed.

"In what way?" Grimaud urged.

"He's told me who killed John Thierry," she answered.

CHAPTER TWENTY-SEVEN

Antoine awoke from a druggy sleep and glanced at the clock on the dormitory wall. Ten o'clock. He'd slept since falling across his bunk early in the afternoon and felt refreshed. The bruises still throbbed and his eye was still puffy, but if he moved carefully the sharp pain in his side was manageable.

A few of the men who shared the dorm lay on their bunks reading or writing letters, but most were in the TV room watching the news or playing cards. He could hear a commercial announcing a sale on Halloween candy at Piggly Wiggly, somebody yelling, "Reese's Peanut Butter Cups! Yeah, man, best thing when you're stoned, 'specially if they're frozen."

"PayDay," somebody else replied. "PayDay's better for munchies, y'know?"

The voices were those of ordinary guys, Antoine thought. Their world, even before prison, was juvenile, formed by media and popular culture rather than education and considered decisions. But that was what ordinary guys did, and he wondered at what point each man now bantering in a locked pen had stepped from "ordinary" into "criminal." And what each would give to go back in time to that point and *not* take the step. Some of them, like Bordelon and Planchard, would change only those details that had resulted in their getting caught. But others would welcome a chance to reverse that first move on a path that would only lead to this dismal cage.

God knew *he* would go back if he could. The slightest alteration in his behavior ten years in the past would change everything! If he'd just ordered dessert that day at the Palace Café, maybe the aroma of warm pecan pie would have diminished his frustration enough to keep him in his seat. He wouldn't have been anywhere near John Thierry's body. Nobody would have accused him of murder. He wouldn't be in a Louisiana prison. And Hoyt Planchard wouldn't be planning his death within forty-eight hours.

But he hadn't ordered dessert, or gone to the men's room, or sat reading the paper for the extra minutes necessary to alter his own future. He'd gone outside, hoping to change John Thierry's mind with no idea whatsoever of how to do it. By then John Thierry was dead. And you couldn't go back.

His body was sweaty from sleeping in his clothes all afternoon, and he took a towel from the locker at the foot of his bunk, then headed for the showers. From the adjoining TV room Hoyt Planchard smiled in Antoine's direction, his eyes alive with an emotion Antoine could only identify as greed. Planchard apparently longed to hurt and kill in the way that most men longed for wealth and power. Antoine wondered what confluence of factors had produced the sadistic freak who would take his life, not that it mattered.

Planchard would orchestrate the event, but one of his drugged-up goons would dutifully wield the homemade "shiv" and bask in a fleeting notoriety that would last only as long as it took security officers to throw him in lock-down, where he might or might not eventually see that he'd been a fool. Either way, that man was expendable, merely collateral damage in Hoyt Planchard's private war. Planchard himself would preen and gloat and wait for the next opportunity to torture and kill.

Beneath a cascade of warm water in the shower Antoine glanced again at the pipes overhead. Yes, he could still rip one down where corrosion weakened the metal at the T joints. And yes, he could storm naked and dripping into the TV room and bury that pipe in Planchard's skull. That Planchard's death would mirror John Thierry's gave the fantasy an elegant, ironic touch that made him smile. What a shame that the price of that irony – the sacrifice of himself – was too high.

*

Danni and Grimaud, having returned to her cottage after the long drive, were not watching the news. Instead, she was scooping Savory Salmon Feast into a dish for Bastet as Grimaud struggled to open a bottle of wine.

"Corkscrew," she pronounced after putting the cat's dish on the floor. "Let me show you how it works."

"Your facility in identifying the perpetrator of the crime was most impressive," he said, watching the corkscrew demonstration closely. "But without proof your ideas are of no merit in securing Antoine's freedom."

"I know," she said as he then twisted the chrome coil into cork, successfully releasing a scent of black currants and oak into the air. "But there's one more day. I'll contact the district attorney in St. Landry Parish, alert the press, do *something!*"

Memories roused by a voice from her past had been the catalyst, the moment in which her adept forays into Marie Melancon's past became a map. After that, John Thierry's death made sense.

"Marie was involved with both men, Thierry and the sausage maker, Savoie," she'd told Grimaud as they drove through Louisiana dark. "I think she was in love with Thierry, but Savoie was wealthy, at least by small-town standards, and according to L.P. Melancon he was crazy about her, showered her with gifts and was always hanging around her aunt's house, waiting for her to come home."

"What makes you think she favored Thierry?" Grimaud asked.

"I... saw it," she answered. "I saw her with two different men, one she wanted and one she barely tolerated. But then she was pregnant and needed someone to support her and the baby. She may not have known which man was the father, but she wanted Thierry. I'm guessing he wasn't enthusiastic about assuming responsibility, particularly if he knew the child might not be his, but Savoie's. Four months had gone by and she was desperate. Who knows what was whispered between them when Thierry came into the Palace Café that day, but when Savoie showed up at the same time, Marie knew there would be trouble."

"Even the gods fell prey to such lusts," Grimaud said thoughtfully. "They plague us all."

"True," Danni said, biting her lip at the memory of her own pointless affairs. "And the gods were not averse to murdering their rivals," she completed the thought. "Which is what happened at the Palace Café. Savoie wanted Marie; Marie wanted Thierry; Thierry apparently wanted out. We'll never know what drove Savoie over the edge. Maybe he heard Marie begging Thierry to marry her. Maybe Thierry said something unpleasant in response. Maybe it was just the way she looked at him. But the result was that moment when Gaston Savoie exited through the kitchen, still wearing the plastic gloves he'd worn to handle sausages, as John Thierry left through the front door. Savoie grabbed a piece of pipe from a box outside the door and must have called to Thierry, who entered the dark passageway beside the café. He never came out."

"Maybe Savoie didn't mean to kill Thierry," she went on. "He probably didn't. But something happened. Thierry insulted him, moved the wrong way to deflect the blow, who knows? But that pipe caused a hemorrhage in John Thierry's brain and killed him."

"And Marie?" Grimaud had asked as they slowed behind a scabrous pickup truck with no tailgate. A lifeless deer lay on the truck bed, an arrow through its neck.

Danni shuddered, then continued after the pickup turned off onto a gravel road. "Marie ran outside because she saw Savoie go through the kitchen door right after Thierry went through the front door," she told Grimaud. "She *knew* Savoie was angry and going to do something to Thierry. But it had already happened in the minutes it took her to muster the courage to go outside. What she saw was John Thierry in a pool of blood on the ground with Antoine standing over him, and she screamed. But she knew. She knew Savoie was the one who held that pipe."

Grimaud had nodded appreciatively as Danni dissected Marie Melancon's behavior for the rest of the drive to St. Francisville. Now he merely pointed out the obvious.

"Marie married Savoie for the financial security he could provide, then gave birth to a child," he recited. "Less than five years later she fled, abandoning a drunken husband and a young child who later died accidentally. Her motivations, however reprehensible, are clear. But they do not explain the role of the cook, Jacques Boutte, who at the very least would have seen Savoie exit the kitchen door and seize the pipe from the box outside. Indeed, he may have witnessed the attack. Why did Boutte lie to protect Savoie?"

Danni was nursing a glass of wine at the table, Bastet in her lap.

"If Jacques Boutte would only tell what he knows, tell the truth..."

"He will not," Grimaud interrupted, standing. "Indeed, unless either Marie or Jacques admits to perjury, which in a trial involving life imprisonment such as this one, carries a fine of up to one hundred thousand dollars or imprisonment up to forty years, or both, everything you have done is irrelevant. And even if one of them did tell the truth, witnesses commonly recant testimony and are ignored by the courts. That you know the truth is a tribute to your skill, but it cannot free Antoine. And his time is running out."

"How do you know all these legal details?" she asked. "And where are you going? We have to keep working!"

He shrugged. "As I told you, I investigated the Louisiana court system in order to understand this situation prior to going to Opelousas. It is clear, is it not, that if Antoine Dupre did not commit the crime, then either Boutte or Savoie did, both of them and Marie lying in court, which constitutes perjury. It was only sensible to ascertain what the penalties for perjury would be, should you successfully reconstruct the crime. To your credit, you have done so. But surely you see that neither remaining witness, Melancon nor Boutte, would risk forty years in prison in order to free the man they willingly condemned only a decade in the past, even if anyone listened to them. And no one would."

He stretched, the muscles in his shoulders making a landscape of rolling hills beneath his shirt. "And I am leaving because I am tired and require nourishment," he said. "There is no more work to do, Danni." His look was both somber and exultant. "I will not see you again until Saturday, at a ridiculous event hailed as an exorcism of a vampire. Remember your promise."

He turned his back and moved toward the door as Danni watched, anger pulling her to her feet.

"What, no dramatic exit as a blue light bulb?" she yelled after him. "Great. Go chomp aortas someplace, guzzle bloody stories until you stink like a slaughterhouse!"

There was no response and Danni sat again, burying her face in Bastet's gray fur and sobbing. She was so tired, she'd done everything she could, and it was all for nothing. Grimaud had seemed to help, but hadn't he really just been playing a game, some ancient, manipulative vampire game meant only to exhaust her so that when his moment came she would have nothing left with which to fight? If not, why would he leave her now, when she didn't know what to do next, when Antoine's life hung by a thread?

Bastet jumped from her lap and stood on the Victorian desk beside the carved cat she'd bought at a prison rodeo that now seemed unreal. Surely none of it could have happened, was some kind of crazy dream. Dwight Tilly, bizarre in a Roman chariot, Timer who would be dead only days later, she and Antoine in a forgotten park where ghosts sang *You Are My Sunshine*. And a centuries-old vampire determined to drink the stories hidden in her blood.

The two cats, living and wooden, regarded her intently. They made a painting, a duality she recognized. Yang and

Yin, Comedy and Tragedy, the two hemispheres of the human brain. The cats were a mystery in plain sight, a diagram of the nature of things. Including the nature of Danni Telfer.

Grimaud, she admitted, had made her aware that she was adept, a "mortal" possessed of an ability to see beyond the quotidian. That was the world of the wooden cat, impenetrable to most but visible, at least in fragments, to her. The carved cat nodded to her and gently licked a paw, then resumed its frozen pose.

But she was also a creature of the real world, and perfectly capable of action in it. She had promised to do her best, and her best didn't involve quitting, succumbing to that wave of despair suspended just outside her mind. The live cat meowed purposefully and leapt to the floor, prowling back and forth as if measuring the braided carpet.

"You're right, Bastet," she said, and pulled her wallet from her bag. Jacques Boutte, a successful restaurant owner and family man, wasn't going to talk. Whatever his reasons for lying at Antoine's trial, he was established, had a deeply rooted presence in the world. Under no circumstances would he sacrifice that presence for the sake of the stranger he'd condemned a decade in the past.

But the troubled girl who had loved one man, married another and then run away from her own child? Marie Melancon would never have those roots, that solid presence, anywhere. She would always be fragile and unfinished, a child who under pressure might break and tell the truth. And no matter what Grimaud said, the truth would make a difference. Somehow.

Danni opened her laptop and typed "Baton Rouge to Las Vegas" into Google. There was a flight at 6:30 the following morning and she booked it, charging over seven hundred dollars to her credit card without a thought. She had to find Marie. Nothing else mattered.

*

Antoine lay on his bunk and thought of his life. He planned to think all night while the others slept. In the dark he would imagine the thousand lives that might have been his if any single event in the past had been different. The elderly, facing death, probably had different thoughts. Regrets, maybe. But he had no regrets, and found the realization comforting. His life would end too soon, but he had done the best with it that he could. In his mind he saw Angola Road curving away toward the world, and nodded his farewell.

CHAPTER TWENTY-EIGHT

Danni told herself she'd get some sleep, but first she needed to search the Internet for people named Melancon in Nevada. The White Pages listed forty-nine Melancons, but no Marie. She didn't think Marie would list her phone under "Savoie," but searched anyway. There were twenty-four, but again, no Marie.

L.P. had said that Gaston hired an expensive private detective to find Marie, and that the detective had failed. Danni wondered how she was going to find a woman so vanished that even a professional investigator couldn't find her. But the detective, she reminded herself, lacked a singular skill that she possessed. The detective wasn't an adept.

It crossed her mind that with her academic career tanked, she might hang out a shingle as a private investigator. An adept would be a natural at that work! The idea was crazy and she struggled to corral her thoughts, be rational. But the single-minded track she had set for herself wasn't rational; *she* wasn't rational. That world had faded to shadow beside the need to save Antoine. What remained was an adept's world where strange ideas drifted up from parts of herself she'd forgotten were there. Grimaud could help her make sense of it, except Grimaud was gone and she was on her own.

"Focus, Danni!" she said aloud, resulting in four perked ears, two wooden and two covered in gray fur. She closed her eyes and tried to make a path through the night sky to a doublewide trailer where she'd seen a little dark-haired girl playing. At first she saw only stars, but after what felt like hours, a long cement-block fence emerged from the dark. Tumbleweeds blew against the fence, then ricocheted across a road lit by streetlights, yet as uninhabited as the moon. Beyond the fence were rows of mobile homes, their aluminum roofs hazily reflecting moonlight. Only the tumbleweeds moved and there was no sound except a wind that seemed lost. The image lasted only seconds and then dissolved.

Danni opened her eyes to an exhaustion so deep she wasn't sure she could stand. The trailer park looked like every trailer park she'd ever seen. The rows of identical, rectangular shapes surrounded by six-foot privacy fencing, were generic. Except for the tumbleweeds, they could be anywhere.

She'd wanted to stay up all night gathering information, but a spiraling emptiness behind her eyes warned that without rest she would fail utterly. Staggering to her bedroom, she pulled off her clothes, threw them on the floor and only managed to set two alarms and drag a t-shirt over her head before she collapsed under one of Vicki's quilts and fell asleep to the sound of purring.

Hours later the purring was accompanied by a paw batting at her hair. The yellow eyes were insistent, the alarms five minutes from ringing.

"Thanks for getting me up," Danni said, kissing the small gray head. "You know I'm still trying. I won't stop trying, Bastet. Not as long as there's a chance!"

On the drive to Baton Rouge she scoured her memory for shreds of information about trailers and found none. She'd never been in a trailer or even close to one, although her friend in Binghamton had an aunt, a retired teacher, who bought a modular home in a senior community. Danni had visited once with her friend and remembered the woman's home as indistinguishable from any other house. But a doublewide trailer would be entirely different, wouldn't it? A metal box set on a concrete slab amid rows of identical boxes. And the only thing she knew about the one she had to find was that it boasted a small yard of artificial grass. Thousands might fit that description.

On the dark highway she found a rational pattern in driving and clung to it. But the pattern, the one shared with all functional people, was critical. "This is crazy," it said.

"You can't do this; it's nothing but pointless melodrama; it's impossible! Turn around, go back, cancel your flights. Face reality."

"This *is* reality," she said aloud, her hands firm on the wheel. "Mine."

At the airport she got a cup of coffee and a beignet, oblivious to the rain of powdered sugar falling from the pastry to her navy blue skirt. Opening her tablet on the table beside her coffee, she typed "Las Vegas mobile home parks" into Google and gasped. There were seventy-seven! It would take at least a week to visit every one of them. She had a single day, really half a day since she had to change planes in Houston and wouldn't get into Las Vegas until eleven. It didn't matter; nothing mattered but that she keep going.

The flight to Houston was only half full, the passengers either sleeping or working on laptops. Danni looked around, fighting panic. She couldn't do any research for hours since neither flight had wi-fi. What did people do without the Internet? Through her buzzing panic the answer drifted like a falling feather. For millennia people had simply gleaned information from other people! They had *asked.*

When the flight attendant approached with the drinks trolley, Danni looked up brightly. "My mother is recovering from lung surgery and the doctor says she needs to be someplace dry for a few months," she said. "I'm going to Vegas to find, you know, a mobile home to rent? Do you know anything about mobile home communities there?"

In true Southern fashion, the attendant did not fail to engage. "Never heard that before, but I guess it makes sense since it's so damp in the South. Now, my brother-in-law, he likes to go to Vegas for the gambling even though we've got casinos right at home in Baton Rouge. We kinda suspect he goes there for more than the gambling, if you know what I mean."

Danni smiled knowledgeably. "So I guess he'd stay in a hotel," she said. "Not a trailer."

"No trailer," the woman answered. "Sorry I can't help. Would you like coffee, tea, tomato or cranberry juice?"

"Nothing, thanks," Danni answered, wondering if she should just walk up and down the aisle asking random passengers about Las Vegas trailers. But these passengers weren't going to Las Vegas, they were going to Houston. The next flight would be full of people with some connection to Las Vegas. Surely one among them would know something about local trailer real estate.

At the Houston airport she remembered Grimaud's advice about food. Adepts needed to eat lentils, fish and something else she'd forgotten. She grabbed a fish sandwich at McDonald's and then wandered among the passengers waiting for her flight. A large woman in sparkly tights and a pink velvet tunic looked promising.

"I apologize for bothering you," Danni began after taking a seat beside the woman, "but you look like you might know your way around Vegas."

"Oh I sure do, honey," the woman answered. "Me and my husband go all the time. You going for the shows? Right away you need to know this: you can get discount tickets at these little booths in all the hotels. Here, let me give you a map. It shows where all the booths are!"

"Well, thank you," Danni replied, "but I'm really going to look for a place for my mother. She's just has surgery and..."

"Oh, I've heard about that," the woman interrupted. "People going to the desert for the air. Lung, was it? Now Ted's Aunt Gloria, Ted's my hubby over there in the boots, she stays in a *gorgeous* retirement community every year for the winter, and I know folks like your momma go there, too. For their health and all."

She gestured to a red-faced man in cowboy boots and an Astros baseball cap. "Ted, come on over here," she said. "Tell this lady about Gloria's place. It's for her momma."

As the man approached, smiling broadly, Danni felt queasy about lying to these perfectly nice strangers. They were so open and endearing, and she was a lying, manipulative con artist. Still, there was no other way.

"Fantastic place Gloria goes to," the man began. "Two pools, miniature golf course, gym and club house with activities all day long! Gloria, she does the bridge tournaments, water aerobics, took a landscape painting class last year. Everybody in the family got one of her paintings for Christmas."

"It sounds wonderful, but, um, isn't it expensive?" Danni hedged, realizing that a fictional post-operative mother suggested a need for retirement communities. Marie Melancon at twenty-nine wouldn't qualify, and Danni had seen a little girl playing beside the trailer. "See, mom takes care of my sister's little girl, too," she said. "I mean, she'd have to be in a place where you can have children."

The woman in pink nodded. "Happens so much," she said sadly. "Drugs?"

"What?" Danni said.

"Your sister. She get into drugs and couldn't take care of the baby?"

"Um yeah," Danni answered, feeling the sudden weight of a drug-addicted sister and a toddler niece *she* ought to be caring for instead of this post-surgical mother who obviously needed some down time. The story was fiction, but still brought a flush of shame to her face.

"We all do the best we can," the woman said, patting Danni on the shoulder. "Ted, you know of any place in Vegas that would do? You know, not too expensive but nice and clean for the baby."

"It's only for a few months," Danni went on. "I was thinking maybe a doublewide trailer in a nice park."

"Prob'ly lots of those," Ted offered. "I just don't know any."

A man sitting behind them swung massive shoulders to face Danni. "I'm sorry, but I couldn't help overhearing your conversation," he said. "My brother owns three mobile home parks in Las Vegas and I know a little about the business. Perhaps I can help you."

Danni experienced a wave of gratitude for the intensely social nature of human primates, especially American human primates whose cultural training included an often misguided need to offer helpful opinions. In this case it was not misguided. "Thank you," she said to all three, then moved to join the man with the brother who owned mobile home parks.

He stood politely as she approached, then gestured to the seat beside his. Bulky and curiously ugly, he nonetheless wore knife-creased gray dress pants and a black cashmere sport coat with brass buttons, his patchy hair neatly cropped above gold-framed glasses. Ex-military, Danni thought, rejecting a sense that she'd seen him somewhere long ago. He was wealthy. The black Burberry attaché case at his feet had been expensive.

"You'll need to do your homework in selecting a place for your mother and the child," the man said. "There must be a hundred mobile home parks in Las Vegas and not all are well managed."

"I found seventy-seven online," Danni told him, still haunted by his familiarity. "At least thirty of them were restricted to seniors, no children allowed, or too expensive. I don't know how to check out the rest. I don't have much time…"

The rumpled head nodded. "Since there's a child, your first concern is safety," he said. "Registered sex offenders have difficulty with housing and often wind up in these places, so be sure that the management does background checks on *every* tenant. They all say they do these checks, but the only way you'll know for sure is if they insist on doing background on your mother."

"Sex offenders?" Danni said, grimacing.

"Yes. Also make sure that the park evicts any tenant who is visited by police, even once. After that you need to see the rules for property maintenance. Grass must be mowed biweekly, no more than two vehicles visible and these must be licensed and drivable. No clotheslines, antennas or external hanging banners other than the American flag, which must be retired at dusk if not illuminated. You want a property that is safe and well maintained. Any you see that observe these rules will be best. Here, I've jotted the addresses of the three owned by my brother."

"Thank you so much," Danni said, accepting a business card with three addresses neatly inscribed on the back. There hadn't been any American flags in her glimpses of Marie Melancon's trailer, which probably meant Marie didn't live on any of the brother's properties. "You've been so helpful."

When her flight was called Danni hurried to find her seat, wishing everybody would board immediately and they'd take off early. Every minute counted. The ex-military guy, she noticed, was ensconced in first class and didn't notice her when she walked past his seat. Hunched into an expansive first-class seat, he looked vaguely like the troll under the bridge in *Three Billy Goats Gruff.* Well, at least had provided a rough outline she could follow. Background checks and flags.

She watched clouds and wondered what Antoine was doing. He didn't know where she was, might try to call her at the B&B. Would he think she'd given up, that she'd abandoned him? They hadn't talked about the revival; he wouldn't know for sure that she'd be there. But she would, even if she failed to find Marie. She would go just to see him one last time across a rodeo ground full of people who wanted to exorcise a vampire. But the vampire was already gone.

As the plane began its descent, she noticed a black cashmere arm reaching across the other two seats in her row. It was the guy with the brother, standing in the aisle.

"I happened to find this in my briefcase," he said. "It's a map produced by the Las Vegas American Mobile Property Owner's Association, indicating all mobile home parks whose owners are members and maintain the high standards set by the organization. I suggest you restrict your search to these."

Danni took the map, highlighted with ten or fifteen red dots. "Thank you," she said. "But why does it say 'American' mobile property owners? Nevada is *in* the U.S., so what else could they be?"

"Foreign interests," he said as he turned back toward first class. "The Association admits only *American* property owners. Most have served in the armed forces and prefer tenants who are American. Your mother should be among her own kind."

"Ah," Danni said, smiling. Her fictitious mother might fit right in, but Marie Melancon and a dark-haired toddler with pierced ears might not. Because dark-haired little girls with pierced ears might be foreign and unlikely to fly illuminated American flags.

In the airport she rented a car and then looked for a place to sit down and formulate a plan before heading into the white glare beyond the airport doors. There was no place to sit except on one of the many stools facing slot machines. She chose a bank of older machines in a corner. They still had the old-fashioned levers and spinning cylinders embossed with sevens, lemons, cherries, grapes and the word, "bar." A blond man in false eyelashes and lip liner nursed a drink at a quarter machine called "Louisiana Louie." It featured a smiling crab in sunglasses holding a saxophone in one claw. Or maybe it was supposed to be a crawfish. The man smiled at Danni and waved sparkling purple two-inch fingernails.

"Buy you a drink?" he asked.

"Um, no thanks," she answered, taking a seat at an identical machine. "I just thought, you know, the crab might be good luck."

"Crab means you're on a crooked path," he said. "And you're not going to win if you don't play."

"I know that," she said, snapping open her tablet and pulling up the page with a map pinpointing all seventy-seven mobile home parks. "Everybody knows that." She copied the map on a separate screen and quickly eliminated those she'd already determined were restricted to seniors or too expensive. Then she eliminated those on the map the man in black cashmere had given her.

"No, everybody doesn't know that," he said, regarding her closely. "I, on the other hand, know what you are."

Danni bristled with discomfort, then returned his gaze. Did he mean he knew she was an adept? Was *he*? Did adepts have some way of identifying each other? Or was he some other creature she ought to recognize, like a vampire? His eyes, pale blue and full of mischief, held no swarm of history.

"I'm busy," she said.

He shrugged. "I'm not. I can help you. For a price."

She raised an eyebrow.

"Guess my name," he said.

She shook her head. "That's the price? Guessing your name?"

"Yaaa," he answered, drawing out the vowel. "Three guesses."

It was too easy. "Rumplestiltskin," she said.

He shook his head. "Wrong language. You've got two guesses left."

Danni didn't question her participation in the game. It felt strangely ordinary, even fun. And she remembered her favorite childhood book; it had the same fairy tales in different languages. She knew the names, and the man had said "ya." *Ja.* He would be German, Dutch, Swedish or Norwegian. The German *Rumplestilzchen* sounded the same, so that wasn't it.

Repelsteeltje, she said, trying the Dutch.

"Nay," he said. "One more!"

Nej. So he was either Swedish or Norwegian. Of course, the blond hair and blue eyes. Danni cursed herself for failing to factor that in, and now she had only one guess.

Rumleskaft, she said, choosing the Norwegian name simply because her book hadn't included a Swedish version.

"Scandinavian and close enough," he said, laughing as he stood, snapped his fingers and began to dance. "You should catch my act at Piranha," he said. "On my way to L.A. for the weekend, but I'll be back for the Sunday matinee. You've *got* to see my flapper dress! Beads everywhere and ostrich feathers on the bosom!"

He'd finished his drink and was dancing away, whistling *The Charleston* and crossing his arms over his knees in the classic step.

"Hey, you were supposed to help me!" Danni yelled after him.

"I did," he answered and vanished into the crowd.

The encounter darted back and forth in her mind like a silvery fish. What had just happened? The man was so strange, and yet curiously familiar. The game had felt like a test, and she'd passed. But what was he except a drag queen who apparently did a show as a flapper? Grimaud would know. Maybe the guy was an elf or a brownie, one of the elementals who, according to Grimaud, sometimes aid humans. Maybe adept humans. Or else he was just a weird guy, high on something and having pointless fun in an airport before catching his plane.

She glanced at her watch. Eleven-thirty. Her return flight left at six. Allowing time to return the rental car and get through security, she only had a little over five hours to find Marie. And even after eliminating thirty-five possibilities, forty-two remained. She couldn't possibly visit forty-two mobile home parks in five hours, but maybe she'd find Marie in the second, or the twenty-fourth, or the thirtieth if she got that far. She had to try.

Scanning the map, she decided to move north from the airport, then circle back. As she folded the map, a street name caught her attention. It sparkled on the page.

"Oh my God!" she said aloud, then glanced in the direction the strange man had gone. Above the crowd she heard a brief jangling of bells, silvery and fresh against the mechanical dinging of slot machines. The sound quickly faded. And running across the breadth of Las Vegas was a street near which there were only five mobile home parks – a street named Charleston!

CHAPTER TWENTY-NINE

At noon Antoine sat at his desk in the law library, polishing its surface with a soft rag. His thoughts were diffuse, dreamlike. Would something of him remain in the desk where he'd worked for years? Surely his DNA must permeate the surface, the drawer pulls. Did he *want* something of himself to remain there when he was gone? Nobody wanted to be in prison, and yet the man he had been – Monk Dupre, Head Inmate Counsel – belonged there among the law books. He had been a good man, had used his mind to help those abandoned by the world outside. He thought it would be okay if years in the future somebody laid a hand on his desk and felt like getting to work, knuckling down to build a road for some guy who'd gotten lost long ago. With the flat of his own hand he sealed the idea, his ghost, into the wood.

He'd thought about Danni during the night, imagining a labyrinth of scenarios in which he might repay her efforts to save him. He imagined himself in Egypt, saw her eyes reflected in a deity named Bastet.

But the morning light shattered his thoughts, pressing reality against his mind like a dull knife. Egypt was his dream, but he would never see it. He hoped Danni was gone, that she wouldn't come to the revival only twenty-four hours away. He didn't want her to see his death. He wanted her to carry his memory into the life she would make for herself.

He decided to spend the rest of the day thinking about Egypt, the life he'd planned when he was young. Ancient names rose in his mind, cities now buried in sand, a culture so complex and beautiful he'd longed to devote his life to exploring it. He would go there now. The wooden cat beneath his outstretched hand moved against his palm.

*

Danni guided a red Ford Fiesta through Las Vegas streets on which no one walked. No dogs loped along the baking sidewalks, no cats stretched on lawns of gravel dyed blue, green, occasionally pink. The intense, parched heat was like a presence, invisibly absorbing every molecule of moisture. The only plants were cactuses and spindly, pea-green trees with no leaves. And yet it was a city.

The streets were crowded with vehicles, there were sprawling subdivisions, strip malls and of course the famous tourist belt of gleaming hotels and casinos. Her eyes were drawn to a profusion of billboards promoting entertainment, dining, and games of chance. It was like an elaborate carnival midway, unaccountably grown to towering proportions in the middle of terrain inhospitable to all but the most ancient reptiles.

She would find Marie Melancon, she told herself. She would learn the secret kept for a decade by three people whose lies sent Antoine to prison. And then she would never, ever, set foot in any climate where the temperature climbed above ninety degrees. Maybe eighty.

The little car's air-conditioner rattled and wheezed as she found the first of the five mobile home parks on the street called Charleston. It was called "Desert Moss Oasis" and the wall separating it from the street was lime green stucco, not the cement blocks she'd seen in her vision. But the green stucco might just be the façade, the side and rear walls unfinished. She had no idea from what direction she'd seen Marie's trailer. If it was Marie's trailer and not a dream.

She'd framed a new story after leaving the airport, jettisoning the druggy sister and surgery-weakened mother to the junkyard of outworn fiction. Assuming property managers might ask for identification before revealing the names of residents, she glanced at the only identification she had – a New York driver's license. Obviously, she couldn't say she was from Louisiana.

"My name is Danielle Telfer and I represent Eastern Search Resolutions," she practiced before exiting the car.

"We work with attorneys, locating beneficiaries in significant insurance and death benefits claims."

It was sufficiently vague to buy her time for the next line – "I'm looking for a beneficiary named Marie Melancon Savoie." She'd have to wing any questions arising after that.

Desert Moss Oasis boasted an attractive office framed by palm trees. Danni moved briskly along a walk bordered in artificial grass, noticing that even though a palm tree-shaped thermometer beside the office door read 102, she wasn't sweating. It took several seconds for her to realize that she *was* sweating, had to be, but the arid environment devoured moisture like a massive sponge. A human body would be reduced to parchment in a matter of hours.

"Marie, why in God's name did you come *here*?" she whispered as she opened the office door. The air inside was so cold that her eyes watered.

"How may I help you?" asked a tanned young woman in a pale green business suit, seated at a rattan desk.

Danni made her pitch, causing no apparent reaction in the tanned face.

"You'll need to speak with our manager, Mr. Flores," the young woman said. "He's at lunch but should be back in an hour. Would you like to wait?"

There was no time to wait.

"Thank you, I'll come back later," Danni said.

Outside again, she felt the moisture in her eyes evaporate as she took note of row upon row of doublewide trailers fanning away from the office and a central pool pavilion behind it. Every single one had a small yard of artificial grass.

The second park was called "Palo Verde Desert Estates" and Danni drove around the entire complex before approaching the office. The cement block fence was there, facing a street at the back. A single tumbleweed rested in the bare dirt at the base of the fence. Maybe this was it!

Palo Verde's manager was in, but deep in conversation with a man whose shirt bore a patch saying, "Desert Computer Repair."

"Sorry," the manager said as Danni wondered why every business in a desert felt compelled to remind customers that they were in a desert. "I'm Harold Brady, the manager. Were you interested in long or short-term rental?'

Danni recited her lines again, resulting in his shaking his head.

"Happy to help you but the computer's down," he said. "What makes you think this woman is here?"

"It's her last known address," Danni answered. "A doublewide mobile home at this address. Our information indicates that she may be living with a child, a little girl."

"I've got ninety-five sites, singles, doublewides and modulars mixed," he said as the phone rang. "Couples, families, seniors. You can look around if you like, ask around. Because my damn system isn't going to be up any time soon. I can't find her until tomorrow, if she's here."

"Thank you, I'll do that," Danni said as he grabbed the phone and the computer repairman laconically pulled a box of orange Tic-Tacs from his shirt pocket.

The place felt right, and there *was* the tumbleweed, but she'd later regret spending an hour and a half knocking on plastic doors behind which people offered her Gatorade and salty potato chips, but were sure there was no twenty-nine-year-old woman named Marie in their park.

"Try Desert Meadow Springs," a woman who made earrings out of colored phone wire suggested. "It's just up the street and there's lots of kids there. Nice big playground. And here, these are for you. Match your eyes."

Danni accepted a pair of Kelly green earrings in spirals that fell to her shoulders.

"They're lovely," she said, thinking robots would probably love them. Then she headed for Desert Meadow

Springs. It was nearly two and despite several glasses of Gatorade she felt drained and fragile. She was tired; the heat was killing her; and she was no closer to finding Marie. The mobile homes nowhere near a meadow or a spring lay shimmering beneath an American flag the size of a king-sized bed sheet waving from a two-story pole.

"You look like you been rode hard and put up wet," a woman with curly silver hair in a crisp white cowboy shirt with pearl snaps observed as Danni approached the desk in the park office. "And those earrings look like the inside of a bomb. What can I do for you?"

Danni was halfway through the pitch when the woman shook her head, grinning.

"Honey, this is Las Vegas," she said. "Every scam since the dawn of time gets played here every day and you don't even make it to the training bra level, so don't waste my time. What are you doing? Skip trace? Runaway wife? Witness who ducked out on a mob trial? Or maybe you're working *for* the mob?"

Danni slumped in a white canvas director's chair and considered her options. There weren't any.

"I have three hours to find a woman named Marie Melancon," she said.

"And if you don't?"

"A man in a Louisiana prison will die."

The other woman shrugged. "Hardly a headline. Now, if you said a man in the *White House* will die, a few people might listen. Go home and practice on the locals before you try your game in Vegas, okay? Because you are *so* out of your league here!"

Danni considered the remark. It was true. She was out of her league here and out of her league at a prison. As an adept she was pretty sure she didn't even have a league. She was a historian; she had written an article about a quilt. That was it. She stood to leave.

"Want some advice?" the other woman said. "Don't, that is *do not* waste your life trying to rescue men. This town's full of fifty-year-old showgirls just now figuring that out."

Danni felt the vertebrae in her spine lock, pulling her shoulders back.

"I made a promise," she said evenly. "And I'll keep it. This is about me, not him."

As she turned to go the woman said, "Wait a minute," and came around the desk, extending her right hand. "Master Gunnery Sergeant Liz Galasso, USMC Retired. And your name is...?"

"Danni Telfer. I'm a history professor," Danni said, now understanding the presence of the gigantic flag. "So I guess you're a member of the American Mobile Home Association thing?"

"That bunch of right-wing wackos? Wouldn't go near 'em in full body armor," Liz Galasso said. "This Marine's a democrat, Telfer. Now, show me some identification and tell me about this woman you have to find."

Danni sat in the director's chair again, the aging Marine straight-backed in a matching chair. "Here's my driver's license," she said, then told the whole story, leaving out Grimaud and her clumsy identity as an adept. There were apparently magical creatures like the blond guy at the airport and maybe even the troll on the plane, who might appear, offer help and then vanish. And there were regular, good people like Liz who might help but to whom it would be unwise to mention vampires.

When Danni concluded the tale of her research, the prison rodeo, Antoine and his trial and murder conviction, Liz Galasso nodded. "If this Marie has a kid and lives in any of the nearby parks, she'll have come around here. I run the most child-friendly park in the city - separate toddler playground, safety monitor eight to eight, scout troops for the older kids. Moms drive miles just to hang out here and

I've got a waiting list for sites a mile long. You sit tight and let me ask around."

Danni thumbed through a magazine called *Vegas Seven* that listed local events by days. A lecture on the Nevada Bomb Test Site looked interesting, but given her recent experience, a gallery showing titled "Art of the Dark Side" held greater appeal. Especially since the poster for the show featured a Dracula character in a hot pink tux and cape.

After ten minutes she'd read the whole magazine and began to pace. Liz wanted to help, but maybe this would be another dead end and Danni couldn't just sit around waiting. Eight minutes later she was about to leave when Liz came through a rear door, leading a young woman and a boy of about three.

"Tell her," Liz instructed the young woman, scooping the toddler to sit on her lap.

"Well, there's a girl, Bernie's her name, not Marie. She lives over in Desert Moss, right up the street. I know it's site 43 because some of us went over there once to help tint her hair. 'Sparkling Amber,' that was the color. It can't be the girl you're trying to find, since her name's not Marie, but she comes here a lot with her boyfriend's little girl, Angelita. I guess the mother ran off or something. Bernie, well, we figure she comes here because the rest of us keep an eye on the kid. She mostly has her earbuds in, listens to music and reads magazines. Anyway, she talks Southern, you know how they do with 'y'all' and that? And Angelita, she has this coal black hair and pierced ears. Looks like her daddy. I think he's Mexican or something, name's Jesus, if you can believe!"

Liz stood to hand the toddler back to his mother. "Thanks, you've been a help," she told the woman, who exited the way they'd come in. To Danni she said, "So?"

Danni remembered a trial transcript in which Marie stated her full name – Marie *Bernadette* Melancon. "It's her middle name," she told Liz, eyes wide. "She's using her middle name! I've got to go there, right now."

"Going with you," the older woman said, taking a pistol from the desk and tucking it into a weathered shoulder bag.

Danni stared. "What's that?" she said.

"That is a Ruger .357 Magnum," Liz answered. "Let's go."

"I mean why take a gun?" Danni said.

"Oh, I don't know," Liz sighed. "Maybe because you're about to confront an unstable person living under an assumed name who's fleeing felony charges for perjury? And that doesn't factor in the boyfriend, who may have issues of his own. How have you survived as long as you have? I'll drive. A familiar car with Nevada plates won't attract attention." She gestured Danni's red Ford in the parking lot beyond the office. "Yours has California plates."

Danni hadn't noticed. "Okay," she said.

Liz waved at the receptionist as they drove into Desert Moss Oasis. A tanned hand merely waved back, and then they were there. A doublewide trailer beside which a tiny, dark-haired girl played with brightly colored plastic blocks on a patch of artificial grass. A sunburnt woman in tight red cropped pants and a yellow tank top sat on the trailer's cement steps. Beneath tangerine-colored hair her big eyes regarded her guests with little interest.

"Bernie," Liz said as she and Danni climbed from her car and approached, "somebody here to see you."

Danni tried not to frame the moment as a quest, completed. Because this was only the beginning, and she couldn't make a single mistake.

"I need your help," she told Marie Melancon. "Gaston Savoie is dead and..."

"Shhh!" the woman suddenly warned, glancing in fear toward the trailer's open door and standing quickly to move away. "Don't say that again! You can't tell him!"

"Tell whom?" Danni asked as a dark-haired man appeared in the door.

"What is it?" he asked. "There a problem?"

"No, hon, it's just Liz from over to the playground, y'know? They're gonna repaint the little swings tomorrow, so we shouldn't go over 'til they dry."

"Oh," he said and vanished inside.

"Don't tell him my husband's dead," Marie Melancon whispered, shaking. "He'll want to get married right away. You can do that here, get married really fast. He wants to go back and live someplace in Mexico where his mother is. I *can't* ..."

Liz Galasso had moved to lean against her car, leaving Danni a space with Marie.

"You want to get away," Danni said, an unaccustomed hardness settling across her mind. She felt like a python with a mouse. "You want to leave."

"Oh God, do I!" Marie agreed, running her fingers through her hair. "I told him I couldn't marry him because, you know, of Gaston, but now..."

Like the Rumplestiltskin game, it felt too easy. Danni searched for possible glitches, disasters, and while they were there, she saw no other way to proceed.

"How much would you need to get out of town tonight?" she asked.

The hazel eyes grew bright. "Hell, a thousand I guess," Marie answered. A thousand would last me 'til I can get someplace, land a job. I was makin' good money with tips, waitress at Rao's. That's Ceasar's Palace. I can go to Reno; plenty of waitress jobs there. He won't come after me. What do you want for a thousand that I've got?"

"I want to know why Jacques Boutte lied at the trial of Antoine Dupre," Danni said, carefully excluding Marie from any accusation. The response was immediate.

"That was between Jacques and Gaston," the woman said as if the information were of no consequence. "See,

Jacques needed money to pay a lawyer. His uncle... but wait a minute. I'm not sayin' any more until..."

"Of course," Danni agreed. "I can get the money at a bank right now."

Liz Galasso, close enough to hear, moved closer.

"Not a good idea in Vegas," she said. "Why don't we just go to my place, get the cash."

Danni scrambled to understand what was going on. "You mean you...?

Liz shot a look that clearly meant "Shut up" as Marie called through the trailer door. "I'm going over to Meadow Springs for a sec, sign Angel up for baby yoga. It's free. Be right back."

"Okay," the man said and came outside to watch his daughter.

In the car Marie chattered happily about her plans, which involved catching the next bus out of Las Vegas, no matter where it was going.

"I'll just double back to Reno," she said. "Maybe work one of those cruise ships later."

"Sounds good," Danni said. She understood that Marie was permanently immature, self-centered and silly, but her actual presence made Danni want to slap her.

At the Desert Meadow Springs office, Liz opened a safe and counted fifty twenty dollar bills, handing half of them to Marie, then standing at the door. Danni pulled her cell phone from her bag and told Marie she needed to make a video of her statement.

"No problem," was the response. "Nobody's gonna come after me. It was so long ago. I mean, who cares now?"

"Just say your name and the date and then tell me what those arrangements were, between your husband and Jacques Boutte," Danni said. "When we're done, you'll get the rest of the money and walk out of here."

Marie smiled. "Okay, Jacques had this uncle up there in Angola. You know, the prison? He needed money to pay a lawyer, try to get the old man out. Cajuns, they're real tight about family, so Jacques thought he had to help this uncle. It was Gaston that killed John, hit him with a pipe." She looked pensively at the floor. "John loved me so Gaston killed him."

The story was a child's, its arrogance pathetic. Danni withheld all reaction as Marie described blackmail, perjury and the ruin of Antoine's life. Jacques Boutte, Marie explained, threatened to testify that Gaston Savoie had killed John Thierry unless Savoie paid for his silence. The stranger standing in the alley over Thierry's body just made it easy. Everybody thought he did it anyway, so they just went along. The sausage maker had plenty of money and paid Boutte thousands during the years that Marie stayed around.

"Gaston was rich, but he'd get drunk all the time and be disgusting," she told Danni, cocking her head at the cell phone as if expecting its approval. "I couldn't stand it any more and I left. I guess he kept paying Jacques until he died, but I really wouldn't know."

She seemed to have forgotten that she left her son behind, or that she even had a son. Danni bit the inside of her mouth and didn't mention the child's death.

"You got enough?" Liz asked from the door.

"I do," Danni answered, and watched Marie Melancon pocket the rest of the money and walk determinedly into a baking street.

After writing Liz Galasso a check and offering profuse thanks, she drove to the airport, turned in the car and called Vicki from her cell near the security gates.

"Please go to Grimaud's cottage and tell him Savoie killed John Thierry, Boutte was blackmailing Savoie all those years, and I've got Marie Melancon's testimony on video," she told Vicki's answering machine.   "I'll email him the video."

It was over. With the help of at least one elemental and a Marine she'd uncovered the last piece of a story that never should have happened. And yet she sensed that it wasn't really over at all.

CHAPTER THIRTY

Grimaud studied Danni's email and the attached video of Marie Melancon, then paced restlessly about the cottage. He'd fed deeply during the previous night, relishing the smorgasbord of stories available at Angola. Just a taste from each of twenty men, their blood choirs of history. In one he watched a Roman sentry teach a Gaulish cook to mix crushed mustard seeds with grape juice to glaze a roast boar, and in another he saw the sweltering hold of a ship in which dark-skinned people sang genealogies in complex, layered voices. The stories filled him, bringing a sense that his time of renewal was over.

He was ready to create a role for himself in this new world.

A century and a half in the past he had left New Orleans bound for St. Louis, and found the idea of continuing his journey attractive. Painted steamboats no longer churned the Mississippi, but he would purchase an automobile and drive beside the great river, absorbing the intervening years. There would be other vampires in St. Louis; river cities with their impermeable mysteries drew the undead. And, he knew, there would be vampire hunters as well, drawn by the same mystery but frightened of it. He was ready, and looked forward to the journey.

He'd settled arrangements with Vicki Stewart and ordered the delivery of eighteen mature acanthus plants to arrive the following week. He hoped she would understand the gift as a celebration of the taste and artistry of her inn.

About the adept, Danni, he was ambivalent. She had been his tutor, a clever and amiable companion as he struggled to survive in a world that had long passed him by. He admired her spirit, and had concluded that a suitable parting gift would be the annulment of their agreement. He would release her from their bond, simply leave her, and the man Dupre, to their fates. The tales written in her blood would not sing in his throat, and Antoine Dupre would die at the whim of a beast. He had planned to leave that night. Until Danni's message arrived.

Pacing, he thought of what she had done. The impossible! Her skills as an adept, clumsy as a child's, were exhausted. Yet with no more than mortal intelligence, and apparently a bit of help from a troll, a puckish elemental and a shrewd old Marine, she'd tracked down the truth. She was amazing, and his longing for connection to her returned with dizzying force. He wanted to stretch into his new life with her stories inside him. She was strong, she was his friend and she was worthy of history. It had to be!

Turning to his computer, he read for hours, printed a document and folded himself to a sphere of light the color of sapphire.

*

Louisiana's governor stood with his wife in the hall of the mansion and said good-bye to the last guests at a small dinner party in celebration of something he'd already forgotten. An expanded river recreation area in Calcasieu Parish? There had been a lot of talk about fishing.

"I'm going upstairs," his wife said, smiling as a servant ushered out the last departure. "If you so much as mention the word 'bass' when you come up, I will kill you."

"Copy that," he said, laughing. Then he wandered into the drawing room, turning off lights in elaborate crystal lamps as the staff cleared the dining room. He didn't have to turn off lights; he just liked doing it.

"Governor," a baritone voice politely intoned behind him. The speaker was a pale, muscular man in an expensive suit, gold flashing at the cuffs of a blinding white shirt. The man had not been at the dinner party. "As a performer of exorcisms you are no stranger to the world of shadows," the man said. "I believe you know what I am. And we have business."

The governor nodded, swallowing his fear. It had been decades since the reckless curiosity of an intelligent boy had led him to explore the ancient rituals of magic, but he hadn't forgotten. The creature before him was almost certainly one of the undead, probably the vampire said to be roaming the grounds of the state prison. But what was he doing here?

On an end table the man placed a legal document and a computer disc. In his hand was a thick envelope. The governor nodded thoughtfully and studied the items, but said nothing.

"Here is one hundred thousand dollars, the maximum fine for perjury in a capital or life imprisonment case in Louisiana," the stranger went on. "I chose the amount solely on its ironic merit, its symbolic elegance, but of course the uses to which you may put such a sum will be more practical. Proof of a wrongful conviction in your state ten years in the past is on the DVD, should you require it as evidence that two living citizens, one who still lives in your state, committed perjury and condemned an innocent man. Will you sign?"

"Is that actually a question?" the governor asked.

"Not really," the stranger answered, then held out a diamond-banded gold pen.

"This is a Visconti!" the governor observed as he signed.

"You may keep the pen," the stranger said, folding the document into a pocket of his jacket and vanishing in a flash of indigo light.

CHAPTER THIRTY-ONE

The following morning Danni awoke in her bed at the B&B to the rhythmic pushing of paws against her back. It was already ten-thirty, and she remembered that Sarah Reeves would be there at eleven for lunch before they left with Vicki for the revival. The idea of lunch with friends felt eerily *vintage*, a reenactment of some quaint social ritual from an earlier time. She didn't have time for lunch. She had to find Grimaud.

Dressing quickly in shorts and a tee shirt, she fed Bastet and then ran barefoot to the cottage called the Tree House. He hadn't been there the night before when she returned at two in the morning, but surely he would be sleeping now. The cat had followed and circled her feet, meowing in a minor key as she pounded on the door.

"Stéphane, wake up!" she yelled. There was no answer and the cottage exuded that slightly shocked sense typical of a space suddenly vacated. A single leaf falling to settle on the upper deck reprised the feeling.

"He checked out yesterday while you were gone," Vicki called from the edge of the duck pond where she was tossing chopped lettuce from a mixing bowl. "Asked me to tell you good-bye."

Good-bye? Danni felt the word in her chest. It was cold, empty. Grimaud had said that the confluence of events that might save Antoine would occur now, or would never happen. She knew it was true, felt the statement as a single unchanging verity, a First Cause. That was the nature of everything. Now… or never.

She had done her part, had extended both her adept and mortal capabilities to their extremes. She had found Marie; she had proof of Antoine's innocence. And she was prepared to offer Grimaud the gift he craved, in exchange for Antoine's life. The thought of those teeth and suckling lips brought a paralysis of terror, but she had given her promise to the vampire as well as to the man. Everything depended upon her honoring both. And yet Grimaud was gone. What would happen now, without him?

She approached Vicki, who was dressed in black silk pants and a matching top scattered with ebony beads.

"One o'clock in the afternoon's not exactly the cocktail hour, but I figured black's pretty much *de rigueur* for exorcising a vampire," she told Danni, grinning. "You'd better get ready. Sarah called and said she's on her way, and I've got a quiche warming. We want to get there in time to get good seats. I hear it's sold out and traffic on Angola Road's going to be a nightmare."

"Did he say where he was going?" Danni asked.

"Who?" Vicki said.

"Grimaud."

The older woman shook her head. "No. Guests don't usually tell me where they're going. They just leave. He paid in full with a nice tip for the maid and left the cottage in immaculate condition. Good guest. Why do you ask?"

"Uhhh, I just wasn't expecting..."

"Oh, there's Sarah!" Vicki interrupted, waving toward the parking area. "Hurry up and get dressed while I open the wine."

Danni dashed back to her cottage, trying to find footing in two different worlds. In one she was having lunch with friends prior to a show, and in the other a story, begun when a backhoe dug up a Civil War-era vampire and she stepped from a plane in a Louisiana town, was ending. She didn't know how to accommodate both. Sarah and Vicki would think she was crazy if she told them something portentous was nearing its close, but how could she sit chatting over quiche and wine when she didn't know what would happen to Antoine now that Grimaud had vanished?

He had given his word, but had he, as she had considered in weak moments, decided to turn away? To break a promise and choose convenience instead? She understood how easily that choice could be made. But as she stood dressing before a mirror, she saw a woman who understood the price of such a choice. The price was immeasurable.

She took the russet dress from her closet and traced its neckline with her hand. She'd worn the dress on the day she and Antoine recited poetry in a park full of ghosts. The day had been a commitment made both to the man and to herself. She had found her strength and used it. No matter what happened, she had that.

Pulling the dress on, she fastened Grimaud's silver-frothed copper torque about her neck. With it she would carry the vampire's spirit into the conclusion of a tale he had abandoned before its end.

"White or red?" Vicki asked as Danni joined her friends at a pretty table in the shade of an oak. The older woman gestured to two bottles of wine, one green and sweating, the other bronze and dusty with age.

"Red," Danni whispered.

*

Antoine had closed the law library at noon, leaving the carved cat on his desk. No one would move it, ever. When the desk collapsed from age, someone would say, "That was Monk's cat. It stays." Someone else would put the carving on a new desk, or on a shelf. By then maybe nobody would remember who "Monk" was, but there would be stories. He heard them, heard his name in an echo from the future, and then closed the door.

Every prisoner who'd finagled permission was heading for the revival, anticipating a good show. Visits were cancelled, but families who could afford the trip would be in the audience and could wave and smile at their imprisoned loved ones. And everyone was looking forward to the gospel choir. With a full orchestra the place was going to rock!

Antoine stood in line waiting to be bussed with the men from Ash One to the rodeo grounds. Perry Bordelon was more jumpy than usual, but Hoyt Planchard was oddly calm.

"Enjoy your last hour alive," he whispered to Antoine, squaring his shoulders and stretching in the sunlight. He exuded an arrogance so vast that Antoine assumed he was high on something. Yet he didn't seem drugged. He seemed eager, exultant.

It didn't matter. Antoine was far away inside his mind, standing beside a cat-headed Egyptian statue holding the musical *sistrum* in one hand and in the other an *aegis*, a golden collar embossed with the head of a lion. Bastet, also called Bast, the protector of the sun. He would stand beside her until the end. His only wish was that Danni would remember him as an honorable man, and cherish the connection they'd shared.

*

The orchestra was playing a medley of upbeat hymns as Danni found seats in the rodeo bleachers, each marked by a white plastic cross outlined in sparkling, battery-operated lights turned on by a tiny switch. The rodeo stadium, 7,500 seats surrounding a huge sawdust arena, was filled to capacity. Sarah had dashed away to get refreshments and Vicki was laughing and snapping photos with friends from her garden club who all sported plastic vampire teeth sold at the ticket booth.

Danni surveyed the stage decked with white banners and sparkling crosses. The seats and stage were covered and lost in shadow, highlighting the effect of video projections on two giant screens flanking the stage. Images of praying hands, rosaries and flower-bedecked Bibles flashed and vanished only to be replaced by church steeples at sunset and rows of crosses at Arlington cemetery. An image of Christ arm-wrestling with a horned red devil brought enthusiastic shouts from the crowd.

The gospel choir in shimmering blue robes with silver stoles stood swaying on a set of risers at center stage. Folding chairs filled most of the sawdust floor where less than two months ago Danni had watched Dwight Tilly parade in a Roman chariot flanked by winged horsewomen.

The center seats appeared to be occupied by department of corrections dignitaries and prison security officers. Far across from her and flanked by guards, rows of prisoners in identical blue shirts watched the crowd, some waving at friends or relatives. She saw Antoine before he saw her.

"I found Marie!" she shouted, standing to wave her arms. Of course he couldn't hear, hadn't even seen her in the mass of people. He merely stared into space, a mantle of calm seeming to rest on his shoulders.

"Who's Marie again?" Vicki asked.

Danni sat again and provided a brief synopsis of her search and its significance to Antoine's future. "Like I said last night, I've got her statement on video," she told Vicki. "They lied at Antoine's trial, Marie and Jacques Boutte. I've got video of her telling the truth! It proves Antoine is innocent; we can get his conviction overturned and..."

"Sounds like you did some impressive work," Vicki said, "but don't get your hopes up. He'll need a lawyer, a new trial. Take years if it happens at all. Hey, here comes Tilly. The show's starting!"

"What do you mean, 'if it happens at all'?" Danni asked as Sarah Reeves hurried to her seat burdened with popcorn and drinks for all of them. Vicki failed to answer in the shuffling of popcorn, and a spotlight flared to illuminate Dwight Tilly onstage in a white suit and string tie worthy of Colonel Saunders.

"We all know what the Lord has to say," he pronounced to the suddenly rapt crowd. "And he says right there in the King James Bible, 'No soul among you shall eat blood.' Now that can mean a lot of bad things, so I'll leave it to you to decide what we're drivin' out with the sword of righteousness here today. But believe me, when we're done there won't be nothin' unholy left in Angola!"

The crowd cheered, popcorn spilled and against a background of hummed chords Tilly introduced a gaunt man Danni thought might have stepped from an Albert Eisenstaedt photo documenting the Dust Bowl.

"Reverend Guidry will give the invocation," Tilly announced, and dramatically bowed his head.

Danni didn't listen to Guidry and barely noticed when the choir and orchestra broke into stirring versions of *Onward, Christian Soldiers* and the *Battle Hymn of the Republic.* The audience, including Vicki and Sarah Reeves, knew all the verses and sang along with gusto as video images of American soldiers praying, holding bibles and shooting rifles flashed on the screens. Danni watched Antoine intently, willing him to see her.

Somebody gave a sermon about the lurking presence of evil and the choir sang *Swing Low, Sweet Chariot* a call-and-response style that brought Sarah Reeves to tears.

"That's the old way; that's how it should be done," she told Danni. "Neecie would know it this way, don't you think?"

Danni thought of the slave named Neecie who stitched a quilt documenting the attempt by her husband to kill a vampire. A vampire who had promised to save Antoine's life, and then vanished. Across the sawdust floor she watched as a dark-haired prisoner sitting immediately behind Antoine avidly searched the crowd for something. His long face and meaty nose were etched by light and shadow, a portrait by Doré, one of the damned souls in Dante's *Inferno.* She experienced a familiar awareness, a way of seeing just beyond the known. Although she'd never seen him, she knew the man sitting behind Antoine was Hoyt Planchard.

There was another sermon, Dwight Tilly recited something about "the infernal hunt" she remembered emailing to Antoine, and the choir launched into a spectacular rendition of *We'll Understand It Better By and By* that brought the audience to its feet, clapping and shouting. In the pandemonium she noticed one man who had taken a seat several rows below hers in the bleachers. His back was to her, just brown gabardine shoulders beneath grizzled gray hair. She didn't know why he'd captured her attention until he turned for a moment, nodding at her with curious solemnity. She recognized him, the yellow shirt printed in tiny palm trees! It was the old man who'd sat beside her on the plane when she first arrived in Baton Rouge. The one who'd said, "History a big problem sometime, when it don't stay buried." She nodded in return. He'd been right. He'd known.

The mood changed as a soloist with a bass voice like buckwheat honey sang *Wayfaring Stranger*, the choir and orchestra gradually building to a wistful conclusion as overhead a little plane drew crosses of white smoke in the air. At the song's end, the music moved seamlessly into the soundtrack from *The Exorcist*, the choir creating a low chant behind the famous tubular bells.

"We have a job!" Dwight Tilly bellowed from the stage as clouds of colored smoke rose at his feet and the spotlight bounced off his white suit like sunlight on water. Videos of fires, collapsing buildings and people sobbing over coffins were punctuated by flashes of demons, gargoyles and bats. "Evil has come, it always does," Tilly shouted. "It's the disquieting stranger in our midst, the shadow on the wall when nobody's there, the thing that comes to suck the life out of us and leave us empty."

There were shouts of amen and people crying as they waved their hands in the air. "But we have a *power*," Tilly boomed, "to defeat that stranger and cast him out. I ask you to join me in casting the unholy from our midst!"

He held aloft one of the white crosses and the crowd, apparently having anticipated this, instantly raised their own.

"We cast you out!" Tilly called, and the orchestra segued into a minor piece Danni didn't recognize as the crowd picked up the chant.

"That's the theme music from *The Texas Chainsaw Massacre*," Sarah Reeves told Danni, laughing and waving her plastic cross.

Behind Antoine the man she was sure was Hoyt Planchard looked about with increasing desperation.

Something was wrong, it was all happening too fast, the revival was at its feverish climax and she sensed a door in time swinging shut as Planchard sneered and suddenly changed seats with a smaller man. A little man with bulging muscles, bad teeth and raw scars deforming a face in which one eye was missing. Scars left by the claws of a wooden cat, Danni knew. The grotesque creature was Perry Bordelon, and Hoyt Planchard had told him to kill Antoine!

"No!" she screamed, leaping to her feet, but her voice was lost in the deafening chant of the crowd. Bordelon bent to retrieve something from the floor and Antoine's eyes met hers across the haze and thundering crowd.

"Look out!" she cried, trying to point to Bordelon's hand, something metallic, moving toward Antoine's neck.

She wasn't watching but heard the crowd gasp at something happening onstage. Planchard also saw and smiled suddenly, his face exultant. With one hand he pushed Perry Bordelon's wrist aside. Then he stood and held out his arms toward the stage. Danni turned in time to see a vampire fold dark-veined wings beneath a black velvet cape amid clouds of dry ice smoke. The creature's skin was like alabaster and its sharp canine incisors dripped red.

Danni knew the vampire. It was Grimaud!

"Oh my God, this is fantastic!" Vicki said. "I wonder how they did it."

"Special effects," Sarah answered. "I'll bet they got a crew in from one of those production companies in New Orleans. Look at those teeth!"

The choir, at first disoriented, apparently assumed this was part of the show and began a low chant. Danni merely stared, her gaze locked on the face of Stéphane Grimaud. He returned her look and bowed to her from the waist. Then he handed Dwight Tilly a document rolled in a tube and tied with trailing red ribbon. The warden, at first open-mouthed in surprise, quickly resumed his role, staring with righteous authority at the creature before him.

The crowd, delighted, resumed its chant. "We cast you out!" they roared, thrusting twinkling plastic crosses in the air. Tilly untied the red ribbon and read the document, a look of amazement animating his face. Then he moved toward the bleachers where a sea of blue shirts waved white crosses. The vampire leaped from the stage to the sawdust floor, arousing screams and overturned chairs as those in the first row fled, only to stand yards away, thrilled and laughing.

Danni saw Hoyt Planchard break away from a guard and jump to the sawdust, then kneel before the vampire, his eyes streaming with joy. He ripped open his shirt and bared his neck, imploring the bite of gleaming teeth. The vampire's red lips receded in a grimace and he leaned toward the kneeling man, sharp teeth gleaming. The eyes of every prisoner were watching, transfixed, as the crowd screamed "No! We cast you out! Save the prisoner! Save the prisoner!" And then the vampire stood, unfurled immense rodent wings, and vanished in a flash of blinding azure.

The exhilarated crowd applauded for fifteen minutes, but Danni stood silent, watching as Dwight Tilly moved toward her across the sawdust floor. Antoine walked beside the warden as if in a trance. The crowd dispersed quickly, chatting about the show as the two men reached Danni, standing amid bleachers strewn with abandoned crosses.

"I do not know how it happened or who sent that guy in the vampire suit, but your buddy here is free, or will be in a few days," Dwight Tilly told Danni, rattling a piece of paper in his hand, red ribbons trailing from it. "Pardon from the governor. Monk said you had to know right now, but it'll be the middle of next week before he walks out the door. Lotta paperwork involved when a man goes free, y'know. Think you can be at the main gate on Wednesday morning, take him on outta here?"

Danni couldn't begin to react. What had just happened? Grimaud was there, the vampire show was his, but why had the governor pardoned Antoine? Her knees were weak with relief and happiness, but nothing made any sense. "I'll be there," she told the warden, then turned to Antoine, who appeared to be in shock.

"How did you...?" he began, then merely stared at her.

"Marie Melancon," she answered, scrambling for a simple explanation. "She told the truth. Gaston Savoie killed John Thierry. You're free, Antoine!"

"I'm free," he repeated, dazed.

Tilly explained legalities that Danni didn't understand, Antoine nodding wide-eyed but already distant. The minutia of imprisonment fell from him like bits of broken shell.

"The governor!" he said. "Danni, how...?"

She couldn't answer, but knew Grimaud had done whatever had been done. And knew the meaning of white roses, a silence protecting the bond between adept and vampire. She would never reveal Grimaud's role in the play now ending. She would never speak of Grimaud at all.

"It was Marie; she told the truth, said Jacques Boutte blackmailed Gaston Savoie for years. Boutte needed the money to pay a lawyer to get his uncle out of prison. But then Savoie drank himself into ruin, and..."

"Eugene LeBlanc," Antoine interrupted. "He knew, he knew all of this. He knew who killed John Thierry. That's what he was trying to tell me the night he died."

Tilly cleared his throat. "Interesting story, but I gotta get you back, Monk," he said. "Guess there'll be some celebratin' in Ash One! Planchard won't be there, by the way. Told security to put him in a cell for a while 'til I figure out what to do with him. After that scene he pulled, getting' on his knees with the vampire? I don't know what in hell that was about, including where the damn vampire came from or went to, but Hoyt sure set himself up for a fall!"

Danni watched as Antoine joined the other prisoners exiting the rodeo stadium, high fives and slaps on the back erupting as he told them the news. The stage lights had been extinguished and afternoon shadows stretched across the sawdust where a few prisoners methodically folded and stacked empty chairs. She climbed down to the ground slowly, turning to follow the few stragglers far ahead. Vicki and Sarah would be waiting in the parking lot, but Danni's steps were slow. From the striped shadows beneath the bleachers she saw a blue light, and turned. She had known he would come.

"Danni," Grimaud said so softly she felt more than heard the sound. He was wearing the sage-scented sportcoat with which he'd covered her as she lay sleeping beside Vicki's pool, but the modern garment did little to disguise the man. In bands of shadow cast by the bleachers he seemed to wear strips of a hundred costumes – a leather jerkin, armor, a Shakespearian doublet, a ruffle of lace at the sleeve of a red velvet jacket. But his eyes were unchanged, his fists were clenched and the aura around him thrummed with longing so intense that the air recoiled from it.

"How did you manage the bat wings?" she asked, trying to lighten a moment so portentous she felt the weight of it crushing her lungs. She was barely breathing.

"A mere illusion," he answered, the gold in his eyes burning. His need for her moved in the space between them, muscular and silent as a panther. She felt it and didn't turn away.

"You did your part and I will do mine," she said, and with one hand pulled the bronze torque from her neck. He had said this would be the sign, the moment when she would offer the stories in her blood. She held his gift at her side in a trembling hand and raised her face, exposing her neck. The pounding of her heart filled her body, her fingers and feet and spine, as she watched his teeth stretch against his lower lip. Then he leaned over her.

For a span of time too minute to measure or name, she became a wind of music so sweet that her bones wept for joy inside it. But as suddenly, she stood in sawdust under wooden bleachers in a wash of late afternoon sun. What had happened? She touched her throat, frightened and lost, as he stood back from her.

"I cannot," he said, his voice hoarse with feeling. "Not now, not unless the gift is willingly given. The stories I long for, you offer merely as payment for a debt. But in that you have earned the respect of a vampire, Danni. Few may claim that honor. I hope we will meet again."

A haze of blue light vanished from the shadow where he stood, and she heard the distant laughter of people outside. In her neck beneath her left ear she felt the crimson rush of stories in an artery that was like a road. On the skin above that road a nearly imperceptible stinging sensation, like the low charge from twin electrodes, throbbed and faded. She touched the space and felt no wounds. His teeth had barely grazed her skin.

On the ride back to Vicki's place Danni took mental snapshots of the road as her friends barraged her with questions. There was the convenience store where visitors once purchased supplies for picnics in a park now abandoned and silent. There was the road to The Willows, a ruin where a vampire toasted the Confederacy and danced with a woman named Alais, who wisely declined his invitation to immortality. And there the kudzu-covered shack beside which Danni had wept only long enough to make the decision that would shape the rest of her life.

*

The ensuing days were busy. She completed the first draft of the vampire quilt article and emailed her college friend in Binghamton to say she'd be there on Wednesday night.

"Perfect timing, the leaves are gorgeous, plan to stay as long as you want," her friend wrote back. "Gretchen and I – did I tell you I adopted a dachshund who thinks she's a drill sergeant? Totally runs this place! – will pick you up at the airport and don't worry, your car's fine. See ya soon!"

Leaves, dachshund, car. The words established layers of some future reality in which it was autumn, there was a dog and there was a car she'd driven in another life. The dog part required attention.

In another of many emails to Antoine in which plans for his departure from Angola were discussed, she wrote, "We haven't talked about Bastet. Vicki's happy for her to stay here, and I'm going to be living with a dachshund until I figure out my next move, which isn't exactly optimal for a cat, so what do you think?"

The answer came an hour later in an email from the warden's secretary. "Monk will take the cat with him," it said.

Danni smiled. Antoine would return to Chicago where a few friends and Annabeth's family were eager to welcome him. They would try to help with the difficult readjustment faced by every prisoner released to freedom after years in which every decision is imposed, not made. But Bastet would be the best help, grounding him in the past while accompanying him into the future.

About her own future she was completely unclear. Finish the article, publish it and then what? Wandering out to memorize the duck pond, the ancient oaks hung with Spanish moss, scene after scene of an experience she thought she'd never forget, she realized it was already fading. Or she was. Her mind was elsewhere, looking forward to the New York autumn she'd always loved, wondering what sort of work she could do if she didn't teach. And beneath the practical concerns was a new determination to discover her origins. A vampire had told her more than she'd ever known, even though the knowledge hadn't led to her family. She was an adept, a witch, born to a lineage of people who possessed unusual gifts. A historian could research witches, couldn't she? The idea, taking root, made her grin.

*

Wednesday morning came with a torrent of feeling she could barely control. Sarah Reeves arrived early with beautiful sandwiches she'd made for both Antoine and

Danni, pointing out the dearth of edible food on planes. Vicki gave her a little quilted pillow on which an embroidered figure held a stick beneath a yellow cross, and another lay on its back, a bit of red thread dripping from its mouth.

"So you won't forget," Vicki said, hugging her.

Amid tears and hugs and promises to keep in touch, Danni said good-bye. She walked a last time to her car at the edge of broad-leafed grass in which an armadillo had scared a young woman who was now somebody else.

The Angola road was still draped in early morning mist as she drove, obscuring tin-roofed houses and bobcat tracks beside shallow green creeks. When the guard tower across from Angola's darkened reception center appeared above a sheaf of haze, Danni turned into the parking lot and killed the engine. The silence was weighted with stories she pushed away, thousands of long-forgotten stories swarming from behind razor wire and barred doors. For a moment she was dizzy and reached into the back seat to pet Bastet through the wire bars of her carry-on cage.

"He'll be here soon," she said, "and you can ride in his lap all the way to Baton Rouge."

Both cat and woman looked up then, as the wooden barrier at the main gate rose through fading mist and a van drove to stop beside Danni's car. The passenger-side door opened and Antoine jumped to the ground wearing tennis shoes, a pair of brown dress pants that were too big and a maroon shirt bearing an embroidered Chic-Fil-A badge that said, "Jerry." In one hand he held a carved cat and in the other a cheap nylon duffle bag.

Danni hurried to hug him, them urged him to get in the car.

"Someone's dying to see you," she said as soon as the doors were closed, and opened Bastet's cage. The purring reunion brought tears to her eyes as the prison van drove back through the gate and the barrier again fell.

Antoine looked up from gray fur nuzzled against his chest and stared at the gun tower and razor wire for minutes, then said, "I'm ready."

The haze was burning off as Danni drove in silence, not wanting to intrude on his first experience of freedom. It was he who broke the silence.

"Think there's time to stop somewhere for a better outfit?" he asked, grinning. "It's going to be awkward enough, getting off that plane in Chicago and greeted by people who haven't seen me in ten years. They're really going to be confused if my shirt says 'Jerry'."

Danni laughed, the poignant moment now past, and the hour drive into Baton Rouge was filled with their usual banter. When she parked in a shopping center he handed Bastet to her.

"This won't take long," he told her.

"Wait," she said. "I mean, I thought I'd use my credit card..."

"It's covered," he told her. "There are some great people in Louisiana, Danni. Last night I was informed that a local philanthropist provided five thousand dollars to help me out, get me on the road back to life. I've got it, in cash. I can pay for my own clothes."

"You're carrying five thousand dollars in cash?" she said. "That's crazy! What if somebody tries to rob you?"

His grin was devilish. "Who's going to mess with a convicted murderer fresh from ten years in America's most infamous prison? I'll be right back."

Twenty minutes later he bounded into the car, stylishly attired in a checked maroon shirt, sharply creased gray pants, black leather belt and black buckle loafers. "I left Jerry's shirt and those clown pants in the dressing room," he said. "Kept my sneakers, though. Good for running beside the lake."

"You're gorgeous," Danni said, smiling. "But I still can't believe there's somebody who just gives freed prisoners so much money! Did you get the name?"

"Hard to forget," he told her. "Guy named Daguerre. Must be the most benevolent rich coonass in Louisiana!"

Danni pretended to punch directions to the airport into the GPS to mask her reaction. A "guy named Daguerre" had also sent her two dozen white roses. Antoine would never know that a vampire had underwritten this first step in his return to life.

At the airport she again made sure he had her email address and cell phone number as they laughed and waited for Bastet to use the litter box Vicki had created in an old wash pan she slipped into the back seat floor of Danni's car.

"Poor thing can't make it all the way to Chicago without a bathroom break," she'd told Danni. "Just throw the pan away when you drop off the car."

As she watched Antoine and a gray cat vanish into the terminal, Danni hoped she might learn to be as gracious as Vicki and Sarah and the army of Southern women who preserved every essential illusion. Being an adept should help.

An hour later the rental car was successfully returned and she stopped outside the terminal with her wheeled duffle to breathe the moist air a last time. The cypress cat she'd purchased at a prison rodeo had already been mailed to Binghamton, but she didn't think she'd be telling her college friend the story behind the sculpture. She didn't think she'd be telling anybody.

The story was hers. And Stéphane Grimaud's. As the automatic terminal doors opened, she felt a pulse in the tattoo on her shoulder and wondered if she'd ever see him again.

"Grimaud," she whispered before heading into the cool interior air, "I won't forget."

ACKNOWLEDGMENTS

As ever, thanks to writers Ann Elwood, Oliva Espin, Lynda Felder, Mary Lou Locke, Carolyn Marsden, Janice Steinberg, Sheryl Tempchin and Anne Marie Welsh for all those critiques!

Additional thanks are owed writer Linda LaBranche for detailed locale editing and to individuals with knowledge of the Louisiana State Penitentiary at Angola who prefer to remain anonymous, and to Dan Podgorny for a crucial beta read.

This book would not have been written but for the hospitality provided by Anne Butler at Butler Greenwood Plantation Bed and Breakfast over the seventeen years in which I made my way to Louisiana and a prison buried in a swamp.

And special thanks to Michèle Magnin for her multifaceted support and spectacular skill at line-editing.

ABOUT THE AUTHOR

Abigail Padgett is the award-winning author of the Bo Bradley mysteries – *Child of Silence, Strawgirl, Turtle Baby, Moonbird Bow, The Dollmaker's Daughters* – the Blue McCarron mysteries – *Blue, The Last Blue Plate Special – Bone Blind* and paranormal mysteries – *The Paper Doll Museum* and *An Unremembered Grave.*

Made in the USA
Charleston, SC
25 January 2015